Daughter of Deception

Savage Heirs

Ruby Vincent

Published by Ruby Vincent, 2022.

Prologue

*M*ackenzie

The trunk opened up, allowing air in the fetid, moldy space. I coughed and agony racked my jaw. Don didn't care an ounce about Luca's order not to hit my face.

They pulled me out of the trunk. I squinted at my surroundings.

Luca told them to get me ready to leave, but we weren't at an airstrip or dock. It looked like an old bed-and-breakfast. By the skyline and driving time, I knew we hadn't left Cinco far behind. We were thirty minutes out.

Thirty minutes. That's how long my daughter's been in the hands of a sociopath's drug-addled mistress. I have to get out of here. I have to get to Laurel!

They practically carried me up the steps. Inside, the lights flicked on and I got a proper look at them. Both dark-haired, tattooed, and sporting guns shoved through their waistbands, but Don boasted a scar above his right eye, and when Louie sneered at me, two rows of cracked, brown rotting teeth turned my stomach.

"You deal with her," Louie said. "I'll start on the rest."

My feet skimmed the floral carpet. I was certain then that the place used to be a charming inn—complete with cream wallpaper, pastoral paintings, and doilies over the lanterns. I knew this because it was still there, albeit cracked, peeling, and covered in dust.

Don tossed me inside a small sitting room. "Take off your clothes," he ordered, closing us in. "Or I'll do it for you and..." He buried his nose in my hair, inhaling me. "Take my time."

His hands pawed my wrists, then the cuffs sprang open. I spun, elbow slicing up and smashing across his jaw. Grunting, he rocked to the side and that was the distraction I needed. I snatched the gun from his belt loop.

Ripping out my gag, I croaked, "Tell me where my daughter is."

Don straightened slowly, gazing down the barrel. He said nothing.

"Tell me where she is!"

He moved and I shot back—his swipe going wide. We circled till my back faced the door. Don sized me up and down and laughed.

"You're going to give me the keys and tell me where Laurel is, or I'll—"

"You'll what?" His guttural, wheezy laugh grated on my ears. "Shoot me? You can't even aim that thing. You're shaking like a leaf."

"Could you torture him to find the bomber that almost killed Tricky?"

Roaring pressed on my eardrums. Sweat collected on the small of my back. I was shaking. Shaking, throbbing, twitching, and panting so hard, I couldn't suck in a full breath before it was out. All I could hear—louder than his laughter—was my baby crying.

"Can you break bones to maintain fear?"

"This is your last chance—"

"Save it, bitch." Don cracked his knuckles. "A delicate, round-eyed little princess like you isn't going to shoot me."

"Can you do what it takes to be the monster that monsters are afraid of?"

"Put that down before you make me—"

A gunshot tore through the room.

"Ahh!" Howling, Don crashed against an armchair, clutching his ruined knee. I fired again, ripping through the other one.

Don flushed pale as paper, eyes rolling up in his skull. He bellowed—tears, snot, and blood gushing free.

I cried along with him. Panting, twitching, and sore body throbbing, but... not shaking. My hands were steady leveling the gun between his eyes.

"Tell me where Laurel is," I rasped, "or so help me, I will kill you."

"Wait! Wait, you d-don't have to do this!"

"You have three seconds."

"It's not me you want!"

"Three."

He tossed his head, sobbing. "I don't— I don't know! Luca didn't tell any of us where he really lives."

"Two."

"I swear I don't know!"

"One."

A hard hit struck my temple. I tipped, gun sliding out of my hand. Louie shoved me the rest of the way down.

"What is with this bitch?" He wrestled the cuffs back on. "Hey, man, you okay?"

"What the fuck does it look like?! Get me a doctor!"

Black crept into my vision.

"We'll lock this one up—chains, cuffs, restraints, cage. She won't see sunlight till Europe."

Darkness swallowed me whole.

I woke sometime later, though I couldn't tell the difference. Walls pressed in on me—pushing on my knees, touching my toes, pressing on my head's sore spot.

A box.

I was bound, gagged, and trapped in a box... and it was moving.

SUNNY

"Vito."

The crooked-teeth scum grinned at me. "Good to see you, Sunny. You're looking good, man. Amazing what a little trip off a bridge does for your complexion."

I slid off him to Adams. He relaxed on the wall, foot propped on it, and arms folded. "Where are Mackenzie and Laurel?"

"Don't worry about them," he said, waving the question away. "I'll take good care of them. You should worry about yourself right now. You're not going to walk out of here."

"Twelve armed men against one guy? Everyone standing in a neat little row—just in case one of you cowers on the floor to suck your thumb, the other guy will step in." I laughed. "You two really are piss-your-pants afraid of me."

"Look around. Does anyone look afraid?" Luca moved in front of me. "I know you didn't come alone. Liam? Ba—?"

"Now!" I hit the floor, covering my head and ears. Bane and Liam tossed the flash-bangs inside, exploding light and sound, triggering gun blasts and shouts from the stupid fools who thought twelve men were enough to take us.

Liam, Bane, and River rushed into the room—snatching guns while Adams's men were too disoriented to point them the right way up. They weren't alone.

Ryker, Makai, Athena, and Athena's team rushed in behind them. Ryker would always and forever be the only call I needed to make when shit was going down.

Makai and Ryker descended on Vito, ripping the gun out of his hand. Ryker kicked him across the face. He hit the floor and had to be lifted on his feet. Luca didn't try running or reaching for his weapon. The two guns Bane had leveled on his eyes kept him still against that wall, arms up. Moving down the row, Liam helped Athena's girls restrain the groaning men on the floor, securing their wrists with zip ties.

I stood up amid the clearing smoke, bearing down on Luca and Vito. "Well, that was the shortest ambush in criminal history. Not a surprise since that's the one thing I hear you excel at, Adams—finishing too quickly." Muscles ticced in his jaw. "Which one of you geniuses planned this? Where are you holding Mackenzie and her baby?"

Luca tossed his head back, laughing. "I wish you could see yourself, Sole. Chest puffed and strutting around, damned proud of yourself for curling up on the floor while your big brothers and stronger friends saved you. Your only contribution to ending the shortest ambush in history is a jizz crack. But we can always count on you for that," he said, grinning away. "Sole 'Sunny' Bellisario. The jokester. The *clown*. Taking over territory his daddies gave him, and running it like the weak little bitch he is—giving out second chances and refusing to kill unless you absolutely have to."

I grasped Bane's shoulder, silently moving him to the side.

"You had me in that factory, and you just let me go." He shook his head in mock disappointment. "Set me free to snatch up your little girlfriend and stash her away where I get to have my fun with her again... again... and again."

An emotion sludged through my veins—thick, cloying, and familiar.

"Mackenzie's already made me money. That pretty little white baby of hers will sell for a great price. Then Mackenzie will sell over and over until I toss that slut in the trash like a used condom. What are you going to do about it, Sunny? Aw, let me guess." He snapped his fingers. "Crack another joke, flounce around acting the fool, then get someone else here to do what you can't stomach and force the information out of me. Admit it. You're so predictable."

"I mean, the thought that—that we could be afraid of you," he wheezed. Adams howled till his eyes watered. Vito and his subdued men joined in. "*No one* is afraid of you! All of North Quay laughs behind your back. So, go ahead, clown. Put on another show for us, then excuse yourself so the big kids can talk."

I nodded along, lips pushed out. "Wow, Adams," I began, chuckling. "You've given me a lot to think about. There may even be some truth to what you say. I am the guy cracking jokes, chasing a good time, and waking up in the morning with a daily affirmation on my tongue. I can see how I may have gotten a certain reputation."

"As a pathetic fool who still has his momma's milk on his upper lip," he helpfully clarified.

"You see, here's the thing." I erased the distance between us step by step. "Reputations are tricky. Easily manipulated, shattered with a word, repaired with a single act. Anyone can be just about anything in the eyes of those who see only what you allow them to see. But if there's one thing I learned from my parents"—my smile, my laugh, my *sunny* personality leeched away—"it's the benefits of wearing a mask."

"You—"

My hand whipped out, burying my blade in his torso. Adams's eyes bugged, and the laughing stopped. He grasped the knife.

"I wouldn't do that," I sang. "I just severed something very important. Pull that knife out and you'll bleed to death in exactly seven seconds. Keep it in and you have time to stumble your way to a hospital. Maybe they save you, or maybe they won't. But those odds beat seven seconds."

Luca choked, jaw working. I patted his shoulder. "What everyone gets wrong is that I don't refuse to kill because I can't stomach it. I hold off because I tend to get carried away. But what can I say? Crazy's genetic. My father is proud to know that of all the Savage Princes"—I tugged a gun off Bane and shot Vito through the thigh—"I'm the worst one."

"Ahhh!" Vito collapsed, clutching his thigh.

I shrugged. "Ah, what the hell?" I shot three more guys—their screams echoing in the empty shipyard.

"Here's how it goes," I shouted over their noise. "Whoever tells me in the next ten seconds where Mackenzie and Laurel are, gets to live. For the rest of you, your prize is bleeding out on the floor to the last sound you'll ever hear—this clown laughing."

"The boss's house!"

"The hotel!"

The hired hands shouted me down, clawing over each other for their lives.

"You can't let me die," Vito half sobbed. "I know... things. I can help you!"

I advanced on him. "What exactly do you know? And be quick. If that bleeding isn't stopped, you're dead in five minutes."

"This wasn't about Blaine," he rushed out. "That was just to get you here. We—"

A hand gripped my shoulder. "W-wait." Luca ripped my sleeve, hanging on to keep himself up. "Help me. She's at... 152 Bayview Way. I swear." Blood dribbled down his cheek. "Help me... please."

Smiling, I said, "Of course." I ripped the blade out of his chest. The pure shock on his face was as good as sex.

Luca slid onto the floor. "You... said..."

"You hurt my girls." I kicked him away. "Should've known I was lying, dumbass."

He flopped flat out on his back, light dimming in his blackened soul, and whispered one final word.

"Demone."

"River, Bane," I said. "152 Bayview Way. I'm right behind you."

They didn't waste another second tearing out the door. I knelt in front of Vito, my knife tip dripping Luca's blood on his pants. Pain washed him out, soaking his face and chest with sweat. "I believe you were in the middle of bargaining for your life by explaining why anyone would do something so stupid as to come after my girls."

"I have information too," shouted Athena's captive. The three goons were begging and carrying on, but I focused on Vito. He'd been at the heart of this since Genny's warehouse blew up six months before. I was very interested in what he had to say.

Vito licked his lips. "It... wasn't just me," he rasped. "All of us—me, Grant, Adams, and Snyder planned to get you four here to end you once and for all. We work for—"

"Bane," Liam said. "Why are you still here?"

I turned as my brother and River filed into the room, ready to fling the same question, until I saw their hands up. Shooting to my feet, I backed against the wall where the door concealed me from the person coming inside—their shotgun leading the way and pressed to my brother's head.

"Oh, dear." A deep, nasally voice filled the room, clear over the bellows of dying men. "It looks like we've come just in time."

The side of his bald head appeared past the wood.

"Snyder, look out," Vito cried.

Too late. I reared, knife set to fly straight and true to its path. As I released it, my muscles seized—spasms rolling down my arm and jerking my fingers. My knife buried in the door, missing him by centimeters.

Snyder spun and fired. I threw myself to the floor, showered in wood paneling.

"Ryker! Makai!" Even as I shouted—as my people raised their guns—they poured through the door, a never-ending stream of armed, shaved men. We were overwhelmed in seconds.

"On your knees," Snyder ordered. Five men jumped me, one of them, Lochlan Grant, wrestled me down at his feet. River, Bane, and Liam were lined up next to me, while Ryker and my people stood with their hands in the air, no less than three guns aimed at each of them.

"Brother Walker, Brother Blake, Brother Hawkins, and Brother Ramos." Snyder nodded at four of his men. Traveling down, I landed on the walking boot encasing his left foot. Kenzie said she heard him scream when she drove away. Apparently, it wasn't out of frustration. "Get our injured brothers medical attention and bury Brother Adams somewhere dignified. He gave his life for our cause."

I bore a hole in Grant's head—wishing against all the riches in my vault that I carved that man up for parts when I had the chance.

Snyder swept a smile around the room, his gaze leaving frost where it landed. "Let us not waste time, gentlemen. Finally, after all of our work and effort, we take our first victory."

They cheered. Grant bellowing loudest of all.

"Aim," Snyder said.

They cocked their guns, his pressed to my forehead.

"Fi—"

"Stop," I bellowed. "Who the fuck are you people? What do you want?"

"Isn't it obvious?" Grant sneered. "Kill them!"

"Hold on." Snyder held up a hand. "It is a fair question and the final request of a marked man. I will grant it.

"We, Sole Bellisario, are the Brotherhood. A group of men bound in one purpose: to rid Cinco City of the Merchant plague. For years, you've corrupted and controlled our home—creating a kingdom with you on high and the people your serfs. It is our mandate— No, it is our right, to kill you, and all who help you maintain your subjugation. Your question is answered," he announced.

"Brothers, on my mark, aim—"

No, I would not die here while Mackenzie and Laurel were out there waiting for us. I promised her I'd be there.

I latched on to my last chance. "Grant put you up to this," I said quickly. "Whatever he's paying you people, I'll triple it. Let us go and—"

Snyder's high, gasping laugh stood my neck hairs on end. "Brother Grant? He is no more in charge here than you are, Sole. You cannot corrupt our purpose with bribes or empty promises. The one we serve has a higher vision for this city—one where we are finally free. It is our honor to hand down your executions, knowing we further that goal."

Liam said, "Who do you—?"

"Enough," Snyder barked. "Brothers, aim!

"Fire!"

Gunfire rang in the empty, starless night.

Chapter One

Snyder rocked on his feet, eyes growing as big as mine. We stared at each other and something passed between us—an understanding that would link us in life and death.

Hatred.

Snyder staggered forward, his gun clattering to the floor. I twisted away as he dropped, lips curling at the body. With the hole blown through his chest, the fuck was fit to fall over my head and let me wear him like a necklace. Two other shaved brothers fell on top of him.

Grant and the others swung around, aiming their weapons at the door. Bugsy let loose, blowing Grant off his feet. A wave of tatted biker chicks flooded the room.

"Sunny, up!"

Bane hauled me up and threw me at a shaved guy who was shouting at Ryker not to move. Normally, throwing your kid brother at an assassin would lose you the Sibling of the Year award, but Bane believed in using any and all weapons at his disposal... and I was his best one.

I crashed into him, using the distraction to snatch the gun from his loose grip. I shot through his neck mid-plea.

"Ryker! Makai!"

They were way ahead of me, snatching up their fallen weapons to join the fight. We spun as Missy shot the last man.

Bugsy swept the carnage, shaking her head. "Candace, call FGH."

"Bugsy, your timing is incredible," I said as I knelt beside Snyder, patting him down. His phone disappeared in my pocket.

She snorted. "It isn't actually. Sienna ran to Eve immediately after you left, and she called in the real guns. You're lucky we got here in time. Cardinals riding in to save your asses again." Bugsy snapped her fingers for Candace's phone. "Yeah, FGH? They're still breathing but it looks like your girl and her kid aren't here."

I yanked Snyder's semiautomatic out from under him, nodding at Bane, Liam, and my guys who were picking all the bodies clean. We needed everything on them, including the weapons.

"Still want us to deliver your message?" Bugsy asked. "Okay. Candace. Missy."

I stood up. Bugsy, Candace, and Missy punched me and my brothers dead in the face. "What the fuck!" I barked, head snapping back.

Bugsy shrugged with a smirk. "That's from FGH." She put the call on speaker.

"—lucky that's all you get!" Our sister's dulcet tones filled the office. "Don't know where you fuckers get off doing this without telling me. At least Mini Blaine has some sense."

"Thank Loki for that," I breezed. "You're a peach, sis. Thanks for sending the rescue crew. Now if you don't mind, my girls are waiting for me." I hit *end*.

"152 Bayview Way." My other side, Demone, stepped into my skin like a new driver taking the wheel. "We're bringing them back. Anyone gets in your way, you kill them, then hunt down their mothers, brothers, former babysitters, and their accountants! Send the message through all of North America that Mackenzie and Laurel Blaine are off-limits!"

Liam flicked blood from his weeping lip. "You're getting soft, little brother. We're not stopping at their accountants." Liam glared at Snyder with pure hate.

"The whole city burns for this."

MACKENZIE

I peeled my eyes open, wincing in the gloom. My whole body, from my roots to my toenails, ached.

Pushing up, a dizzy spell hit me—dropping me flat on my back. I bounced on a firm, springy surface, fighting to remember what happened.

Weight pressed in on my skull, forcing my thoughts apart as they struggled to come together.

"Wha...?" I croaked, then grimaced at the thick film coating my mouth.

What's going on? Where am I? Where's—

Laurel!

I bolted up and tumbled off the mattress. Nausea bowled me over and I vomited on the concrete—heaving and retching until there was nothing left but bile.

I breathed slowly, forehead pressed to the cool concrete, as my mind began to clear. Whatever was wrong with me, I think I just purged it from my system.

Forcing up on shaky knees, my vision adjusted in the dark.

I was in a small room with a window high above, out of reach of my fingertips. An opaque window covering stopped me from seeing out, but let in just enough light from a streetlamp, I assumed. I could make out a glowing circle but nothing else about where I was.

Turning back, I made out the room.

A bare mattress lay on the concrete floor beside a bucket and bottle of water. I wished there was more to mention because I wished there was more in the room. But there was nothing.

Four walls, a mattress, a bucket, and bottle were all my captors saw fit to give me. Tears welled imagining what kind of conditions my baby was holed up in with Luca's crack whore.

I have to get out of here!

I lurched toward the door and fell flat on my front—an unbreakable force wrenching my leg out from under me. Twisting around, my dulled senses noted the weight around my ankle for the first time. I was chained to the wall.

"...back in business..."

My head snapped up. Voices echoed from the other side of the door, heralding heavy footsteps.

"...boss gets here..."

"Hello?" I called. "Hello! Let me out of here! Let me out!" The scream ripped out with all the pain, frustration, and helplessness that built in me—ripping through my soul harder than the bullets I put in another human being. "Let me out!"

The door banged open.

Tattoos, muscles, and a shaved head blew in fast, backing me up a step as he bore down. I stopped and held my ground, rising to the height of his oddly bent nose.

He grinned, flashing rows of crooked brown teeth. "Ah. Our newest treat. Aren't you tasty?"

Ripples of disgust went up my spine. "For your own sake," I rasped, "let me go."

"For my own sake?" A deep chuckle rolled out of his chest. "And what will you do if I don't?"

"It's not me." I gave him a grin to match. "It's what's coming for you."

If anything, his smile widened. "I'd worry about yourself if I were you. We're back in business, and in a few hours, your first client arrives. Fix yourself up." He threw me at the water and bucket. "And remember, biters lose their teeth." He flicked to the puddle of vomit. "Clean that up!"

Despair gripped me, springing tears to my eyes. How would Sunny find me? I didn't know where I was or how long I'd been here. Gnawing hunger promised it'd been several hours since Luca captured me and kidnapped my baby.

Several hours.

Sunny, Liam, Bane. Where are you?

SUNNY

Bane and I climbed the steps of an abandoned bed-and-breakfast. Sienna followed on our heels.

She arrived as we cleared out of the shipping yard and refused to go back to the compound. She gave us one hour to bring her sister and niece home safely. Our time was up. She wasn't going anywhere.

Fanning out around us, Liam, Ryker, my guys, and the Cardinals crept around the building—armed and converging on every door and window. No one would escape.

I frowned, closing over the doorknob. "It's quiet."

Bane nodded, raising his blade higher. "Too quiet. Open, then hold. It may be a trap."

I agreed. We sprung the last trap and almost died in it. Saved only because the cavalry rode in on motorcycles.

Snyder had us. Him, Adams, Vito, and Grant. All of them working together to take the Merchants down, and in one move, they nearly wiped out the Savage Princes. This threat was more formidable than we knew.

And that pissed me the hell off.

I kicked the door, banging it off the inside wall. A darkened hallway greeted us.

We waited, holding for someone to shout, run out, point their guns at our skulls.

Nothing.

There wasn't a sound from the depths of the inn.

"I'll go in first—"

"We," Bane corrected.

"We'll go in first," I amended. "Sienna, don't move until we say it's clear."

She bobbed her head, face pale but determined. I had a lot of good things to say about the Blaine women. High on the list: they are strong.

Bane and I crept inside, weapons up and ready to fly. We stepped soundlessly on the floral carpet, taking in the cream wallpaper and dusty lamps.

"Using a hotel as cover for your sex slave ring," Bane said. "Where have we heard that before?"

I grimaced. "We wiped out the Kings, but not their influence."

"Did we wipe out the Kings?" Bane plastered himself against the wall, feeling around the corner for a light switch. It flicked on, illuminating an empty hallway. "Someone is behind what happened tonight and it wasn't Grant or Snyder. We lost the chance to find out who with the bullet through the last *brother*, but a former King or their vengeful heir fits the profile."

"I don't know, man." We split in the hall, reaching for opposite doors. "I've been wrong about everything so far. I've got to think. Put together the little Snyder revealed before his chest blew open."

Cracking the door, I fell on more hideous carpet, a twin bed, dresser, and lamp. There was nothing and no one else inside.

"Once I have my girls back, we find this bitch." I raised my voice. "Sienna, we're clear."

She blew in, heading straight for the stairs and bounding up.

"Wait!" My shout signaled everyone to pour in.

Racing after her, I stopped her throwing open a door and went in first.

My caution wasn't necessary. There was no one in that room or in any of the others.

Laurel and Mackenzie weren't here.

"Fuck!"

MACKENZIE

I ripped a strip off my shirt, wrapping it around the jagged plastic. Those fools looked at the bucket and saw a degrading toilet. That day they'd find out with one stomp, it became a weapon.

I crouched against the wall, as close to the door as the chains allowed me. The door would swing toward me, concealing me for a few precious seconds.

"...going on..." someone called.

"Take care of it!"

Jerking, I held the plastic tighter. Whoever that was sounded from the other side of my door.

Come on, I thought. *Come back in here to taunt me with that key ring hanging off your hip. I got away once, I'll do it again. Nothing will stop me from getting to Laurel.*

"Where's Marko?" someone shouted. "Get the—"

Bang!

I jerked, hitting my shoulder against the wall. Something heavy hit the floor. The thud resounded through my bones and kicked off chaos.

Shouts, thundering footsteps, and *thud, thud, thud* covered my panting breaths.

"Ahh!" I scrambled back as a bullet pierced the plaster, striking inches from my feet. Climbing over the mattress, I pressed my back to the wall.

Horrible visions went through my head of rival gangs, vengeful johns, or police raids. Cops would detain and question me. They'd hold me back, wasting precious seconds while Laurel needed me. The other two groups... would do even worse.

Nothing and no one will stop me. I raised my sole protection as silence rang, broken only by creaking, approaching footfalls. *I'm coming, baby girl.*

"Kenzie?"

The plastic slipped through my grip.

"Kenzie, are you here? Kenzie!"

"Sunny?" The rasp croaked out of my throat, barely above a whisper. It couldn't be him. He couldn't really be here. After wishing, praying, and hoping he'd come for me, his voice had to be a cruel joke. "Sunny, is that you?"

"Kenzie, I'm here." The doorknob rattled. "I'm here, baby. Are you okay?"

Relief weakened my knees, dropping me on the threadbare mattress. *He came for me.* Tears leaked down my cheeks, revealing the soundless sobs that squeezed my chest. *He promised, and he came.*

"Kenzie? What's wrong?" The knob rattled furiously. "Shit— Get this open!"

"I've got it." That voice could only be Ryker.

"Kenzie, talk to me."

"She... She t-took her," I cried. "My baby. She took her, Sunny." My head fell to my knees as the dam broke. The agony, the fear, the helplessness, and my failure claimed me, dragging me further than I've ever fallen. Laurel's screams as she carried her away echoed in my ears. "She's g-got Laurel. We have to get her back."

"Someone took Laurel? Mrs. Bellisario"—the door swung open—"you know Super Stepdad would never let that happen."

Laurel beamed at me from Sunny's arms, waving her chubby fist. "Da."

"Laurel?" Shaking, I clambered to my feet. "Laurel!" I ran to her and the chains held on to their prize.

"Whoa." Ryker caught and stood me up. He bent to set me loose. "Makai, help me with these."

I barely heard him, straining for my daughter. Sunny handed her to me, wrapping his arms around us both. I sobbed and wailed and kissed Laurel all over, unable to stop even as she squirmed and tried to tuck her head in the hollow of my throat. I just kissed all over her curls, relief almost dropping me on the floor again. I would've fallen, but Sunny held me up—strong, perfect, there for me.

"I'm so sorry, baby. I love you." My nose buried in her sweet-smelling waves. "I love you so much."

"Let's go home," Sunny whispered.

Makai and Ryker freed me, then fell in step, flanking the three of us on both sides as Sunny led me out. I held Laurel tighter, covering her eyes. Sunny had the presence of mind to have the bodies cleared away before he brought my baby inside, but the large smears of blood leading to closed doors told of where they went.

The dirty hole of a room they put me in was a clue this wasn't a nice place, and still stepping into the hallway made me shudder. The once polished hardwood was splintered and rotting. Fist-sized holes dotted the peeling plaster under the flickering bulbs.

I jumped back as a door opened. Broad shoulders, blond locks, and piercing eyes came out, a sturdy pillar for the thin, shaking girl clinging to him. "You're safe now," Liam said. "We're getting you out of here."

Liam saw me and the smile shattering his stoic mask banished the chill from my bones. "Mackenzie." Cupping the back of my head, Liam kissed my lips, smothering my gasp. "Are you okay?" His fingers stiffened. "Did they hurt you?"

"They didn't get a chance." I pressed my forehead to his, eyes fluttering shut. "Thank you."

"Don't thank me," Liam said, voice hard. "None of this should've happened, Mackenzie. This is our fault."

"Don't say that."

Liam nodded at his brother. "Take them back to the house. We'll be right behind you."

"On our way."

"Wait, Liam," I called over my shoulder. "Come with us."

"Right behind you," he promised.

We came out onto a landing. This place seemed to be another hotel, though it was abandoned and left to rot long ago. As we descended, other captive women streamed past us, fleeing toward freedom, fresh air, and safety.

I stopped breathing wondering how many women were *girlfriends* of Luca, believing they found the love of their life, when actually they tangled in the web of a monster.

We climbed off the last step and rounded the corner. My breath truly did stop.

Lined up along the wall, crouched on their knees and hands above their heads, were Luca's men. I knew they were Luca's men because the people leveling their guns between their eyes were Athena, Olive, Bugsy, Candace, Liam's people, and Bane.

Bane met my eyes and smiled—saying nothing and not needing to. Then he cocked his gun, pressing it to the temple of the man who threatened to break my teeth for biting.

Sunny took my hand, kissing my knuckles. Looking at me, he said, "Finish up here."

The click of cocked guns filled the room.

"No, please!"

"Wait."

"Let us go."

My eyes widened realizing what was about to happen.

They were disarmed. They were on their knees, defenseless and begging, and Sunny looked me in the eyes as he ordered their execution.

My lips parted, but nothing came out as he calmly continued to the door, holding me close.

Cool air blew through the alley, ripping through me. Laurel let out a soft sigh as she snuggled against my chest, drifting off to sleep in familiar, comfortable arms. My baby would have peaceful dreams, never knowing what took place here tonight. But me...

I looked behind, my head moving on its own power. A single dingy window granted me a view as the hotel set alight with muzzle flashes.

"I understand that some men become monsters to fight them," I said only days ago. *"But I also know Sunny, Liam, Bane, and Genny. They do what they have to do, but they're open to other ways. They'll listen to me. I'll convince Sunny this doesn't have to end in blood."*

"I'd love to sit in on that talk, if you don't mind," River replied. *"It'll be deeply satisfying to witness the moment you find out who Sole Bellisario truly is."*

I turned to Sunny to find him looking at me, handsome face expression-less. *This is the true Sole and—*

"I love you," I whispered. A car door, then Sienna screamed my name, running to me. "I love you, Sunny."

"Well, that's good." He kissed me slow and deep. "Because I love you too."

I half sobbed, resting my head on his shoulder. "Let's go home."

"As soon as the pilot is ready, baby. I'll have you safe in my bed where you belong."

"The pilot? What?" I stopped to throw myself at my sister, hugging her as tight as Laurel allowed.

"Thank goodness you're safe."

"I am now," I said. "But where are we?"

"You can see for yourself." We came out at the top of the street. Sunny pointed in the distance, drawing my sight over the buildings. Holding her torch high was the Statue of Liberty.

Chapter Two

Sunny and I held hands across the sheets, murmuring softly to each other in the dark.

The clock read three in the morning. We should've been passed out asleep after the most harrowing days of our lives, but the only two people in this bed sleeping peacefully were Laurel between us, and Sienna snuggled in a tight ball against my back. She refused to let me out of her reach, and I wasn't fighting her.

"How did you find us?" I asked softly.

"Adams gave us the name of an abandoned inn." Sunny stroked my temple—gentle and soothing. "Cleared out, but we could tell people had been there."

"I was there, but Laurel wasn't with me." I kissed her smooth cheek. "I questioned one of the men who took me." Gunshots and screams rang in my ears. "He said none of them knew where Luca lived. How did you find her?"

"Adams didn't bother to tell him, but one of his guys knew. They were all shouting addresses at me. When we couldn't find you at the inn, River, Bane, Liam, and I split up and searched the other places. River ended up at another abandoned building like the one we found you in tonight. It was bad, Kenzie. Women chained to the wall. Men brought into their rooms to do what they wanted with them."

I squeezed my eyes shut, stomach heaving at what I narrowly escaped.

"Are they okay? Did you rescue them?"

Sunny nodded. "It killed him, but River couldn't walk away after stumbling into that. Expecting those women to spend another night in hell waiting for rescue was too much." Sunny caressed my cheek, gazing into my eyes. "Otherwise, he would've been there for you tonight. He needed me to tell you that."

I shook my head roughly. "River doesn't owe an apology or explanation. He did the right thing. I wouldn't have wanted him to abandon those women to fly to New York after me." I peered over his shoulder out the window, where the towering Empire State Building insisted I was hours from home. "You all were coming for me. Someone had to be there for them. Another night in hell is too long."

"So is one night in hell." Sunny rested his hand over Laurel. "Bane and Liam busted into the stash houses—money, drugs, and new identities that would get Adams out of Cinco. I was the one who ended up on the steps of a Waterford townhouse.

"It wasn't what I expected. Flower garden, three stories, call box, and an Aston Martin parked out front. Luca saved the roach hole for his captives, and the swanky dive for himself."

"And there's a dark, filthy hole waiting in hell for him." I kissed my daughter again, unable to stop though I might wake her. "Was Laurel at the townhouse?"

"She was," Sunny confirmed. "The place was nice on the outside, but inside..."

I tensed. "Tell me, Sunny."

"Disgusting." The word dragged out of him. "Trash, beer bottles, and drugs everywhere. Among the garbage was a woman passed out with a needle in her arm."

"Oh my goodness." I heaved. "Laurel was around all of that."

"No, actually." He winced. "Seems because she didn't have a crib, Luca's girlfriend decided to put Laurel in the tub and lock her in the bathroom. I knew I had the right place because I heard her crying when I came in."

I couldn't speak. Couldn't think. Horror sent me to a dim, silent place.

"Hey," he whispered. Sunny tipped my chin. "She's safe, baby. I got her before that monster could do worse. Laurel is safe, unharmed, and with you. No one will ever touch her again."

That she was unharmed, I knew. After Sunny rescued me, I refused to go anywhere except a twenty-four-hour clinic. I made two separate doctors check her over twice. There was nothing wrong with Laurel other than being sleepy. As for his last statement—that no one would ever touch her again.

My fist curled beneath the sheets. *I will make sure of that.*

"How did you find out I was in New York?" I asked when speech came back to me.

"I sobered her up. Getting your head dunked in a tub full of ice wakes you up fast. After laying out her options and explaining what would happen if I didn't get you back, she spat in my face." Sunny swiped his cheek as if wiping off the memory. "She was more forthcoming when I told her Luca was dead and her protection gone."

"Wait, what?" I hissed. "Luca's dead?"

Nodding slowly, silver pools held my gaze. "He was also less than forthcoming. I got him to open up, but the poor little rapist pimp didn't make it," he said. "I don't want to lie to you. If it bothers you that I—"

"No," I sliced, gunshots roaring through my mind. "You rescued me and my daughter, Sunny. You don't have to explain or apologize either."

"Okay." Sunny tugged me closer, burrowing Laurel between us. His lips were gentle drops of rain on my eyelids. "In the end, she told us you and the other women would be in New York for a week while they waited for the corrupt piece of crap who'd sneak you into a shipping container and send you all off to Europe."

"I don't know what I would've done if you guys weren't there for us tonight. Laurel and I... we owe you everything."

"You owe us nothing, Kenzie. I'd crawl across glass for you and Laurel just to make you smile. There's no end to what I'll do to keep you both safe."

"Oh, Sunny." A smile I never thought I'd see again stretched my lips. "My makeover hasn't turned me into the Harley Quinn clone that'll laugh at your maiming, but it's still pretty sweet you'd do that for me."

"If we're going to stay up late talking, then let's talk about something that'll keep this on your face," he said, tracing my smile. "We're going home tomorrow. Genny's waiting to hug the crap out of you. Or beat the crap out of you for worrying her. Can't tell with her."

I laughed softly. "I'll stay out of reach while she decides."

Sweeping the grand room, I got a better look at it than when I staggered inside exhausted and running on fumes. A massive king-size bed claimed the middle of the room. Around us was a big-screen television, sunken sitting area, wet bar, and the massive closet I walked into thinking it was a bathroom. The actual bathroom was the size of my old apartment.

"What is this place?"

"When I was five, Mom got on this kick about us all seeing the world outside of Cinco City. That's how I crossed those places off my map," Sunny said. "They never felt completely safe with us in school, so pulling us out and homeschooling on the road didn't make my parents blink.

"This is the place my folks bought the seven months we lived in New York while my mom trained under chefs, and Papa Sinjin taught me to trail a target and lose a tail."

In more than one way I was reminded of the different lives we lived. Another penthouse outfitted with all the luxuries, just sitting here empty waiting for a random day one of the Merchants would stop by. A private jet on the tarmac to whisk them to my side. Parents that were there for him every step of the way. I had a feeling it wasn't just resentment toward the Merchants that burned inside the criminal underground. It was also envy.

"I'd like to meet your dad one day."

"You will. My parents are already asking to meet you."

I raised my head. "They are? They know about me?"

"Course they do. I've told them everything about you from your saving me to your coming acceptance of my proposal. Tricky spilled about her new best friends when she went to stay with them. Fuller beat me to the phone the day we got Laurel back." He winked. "They know more about you than you know about them."

My eyes went round. "Um, please do something about that before I meet them."

"I will. You're one of us now."

Smiling, I hid my face in the pillow. That made me happier than I'd ever put into words. Being there with him made me happier than I could say. The only thing that would make it better was Liam, Bane, and River beside us—the men who risked everything to save me.

For twenty-three years, I could only say that about one person, and she was imprisoned for it. Now I'd have four men willing to do anything to protect me and my daughter.

I gazed at Laurel, watching her tiny chest rise and fall.

Because once again, I'm the victim that needs saving.

LAUREL BOUNCED ON MY lap during the plane ride, giggling at the funny faces Sienna made at her. I smoothed back her curls, reclining on the lounger seat with a glass of chilled apple cider by my side. I couldn't help but think of the other women chained in those buildings. Did they have a life like this waiting for them? Or would they end up like I was a few months ago? Free from Luca, but still in the gutter.

"I have to find River when we get back," I spoke up. "Make sure those women get the help, money, clothes—whatever they need to get back on their feet."

"One thing at a time, sis." She squeezed my hand. "First, you need to catch your breath. Then you can save the world."

I cracked a smile. "Not the world, just our tiny corner of it."

"Ba! Ba ga ba ba ba!"

Sienna bobbed her head seriously. "That's what I'm trying to tell her, baby. You try."

"Oh? Is my infant telling me I need to take a breath too?" I asked, amused.

"She's saying she'll recover from this. She won't even remember it happened." Her hand was still holding mine. "Right now, you need to focus on recovering."

I clenched my teeth, gazing out the window. "I'm fine, Sienna. I'm recovered. It's not like *Luca*"—I spat the name—"hasn't done this to me before. The only thing different this time is he'll never hurt me again."

"This isn't like last time," she whispered. "Our Laurel wasn't ripped away from you last time."

"Sienna." I pressed my lips tight, stopping their tremble. "Please, stop."

"I'm not trying to push you. All I'm saying is don't think you have to be strong and put on a face like everything's fine. Break down if you need to. Cry, scream, or break something. Whatever helps you get through this, I'm here for you."

I swiped a stray tear off my cheek, offering her a half-grin. "If I didn't know better, I'd think you're the big sister."

She shrugged. "Big sister or little sister. The point is that we've got each other's backs. That's what sister means."

"Especially the way we do it."

Sunny left his seat and crossed the aisle to us. He kissed my cheek bending down. "We're thirty minutes away. Do you want us to go straight back to the Fairfield or make a stop?"

"Make a stop?"

"I heard you say you wanted to see River."

"Oh," I said, brow smoothing out. "I do, but later this evening. I want to get Laurel home and settled. About security and the guards—"

"Every new hire was fired. We're back with the crew that's been with us for ten years and more. Nothing like this will ever happen again."

I cupped his cheek, wishing I could smooth out his brow. The agony he felt at hiring the man who betrayed us was etched on his face. "I was actually thinking no more bodyguards. I'm sorry, Sunny, but I'll never feel fully comfortable with a stranger at my back. Not after this."

"I understand. We can think of something else. But we have to think of something." Laurel reached for him, so he picked her up as naturally as me and Sienna. "We didn't get into it all last night, and we won't get into it now." He glanced at my baby. "But the threat against us is more serious than we thought. They know more about us than we know about them. Like the fact that if they kidnapped you and Laurel, we'd run headfirst into their trap. It's not a stretch to believe they may try what nearly worked the first time."

My stomach flipped, shotgunning bile in my throat.

I cried along with him. Panting, twitching, and sore body throbbing, but... not shaking. My hands were steady leveling the gun between his eyes.

"Tell me where Laurel is," I rasped, "or so help me, I will kill you."

"You're right," I said louder than I meant to. I shoved the vision down far. "We'll think of an alternative *after* we have that conversation."

"Yes, ma'am." Sunny bounced Laurel. "Let's go find the snacks, Mini Blaine."

"Wait." I tried to get up and the seat belt dropped me on my butt. My chest tightened watching him carry her off. "Sunny, hold on—"

A figure stepped in my line of sight. Liam curled his fingers around my outstretched hand, stilling me.

"Sienna, would you mind giving me a moment with Mackenzie?"

"Sure. I'll grab a cup of tea. Some for everyone?" she offered.

"No, thank you."

"No," I echoed as Liam claimed her seat.

"Liam, what's wrong?" I twisted, watching Laurel. She babbled to Sunny at high speed while the three of them kicked back at the snack cart. Behind them, I peeked the ink spiderwebbing Bane's foot, hanging over the chair he was sleeping in.

"You don't have to wait for us to get home to have that conversation. Actually, I'd prefer we have it now. You need to know what we're facing."

That made me look at him. "What are we facing? Is this all about the guy who's been sabotaging and setting traps for you? The bald man."

"He's dead."

"What?" I cried.

Liam aimed a raised brow over my shoulder. "You really don't know what's gone on in the last twenty-four hours. Luca Adams was working with the bald man we now know was called Snyder. Him, Vito, Grant, and two other men I remember by face, but not by name."

"Wait, Vito? Vito was there too? With Luca and the man who tried to kill Sunny?" Saying it out loud didn't help it make sense. "What's going on?"

"That is what we asked. From the little Snyder shared before his death, those three were a part of an organization called the Brotherhood. As far as I can tell, their sole purpose is the end of the Merchants and our reign over Cinco."

"The Brotherhood?" I repeated. "I've never heard of that gang. Sunny told me about all of them when he prepped me to run the Sons of Saint."

"Sunny didn't include that one because none of us have heard of it. A call to Genny confirmed she doesn't know that name either. And that is what concerns me most of all."

I nodded, knowing where this was going. "How could an entire organization devoted to your demise spring up out of nowhere?"

"They can't, Mackenzie. At least, they shouldn't." He tossed his head, helping himself to my drink. One sip and a grimace told him it wasn't alcohol. Liam settled for carding his fingers through his untamable waves instead.

"A big part of what I do is collect information. We easily run every gang in four boroughs because I know what they're doing at all times.

"I know the head of the Tongs is setting a meeting with the head of the Jin family before the runner delivers the message. It's been decades and, excluding the day that man got close enough to snatch Bane and a *present* for me got into Lizzie's hands, we've plugged the holes in our security. Years and not a single serious threat.

"Then all of a sudden, Gen's warehouse is blown up. A bomb's put in my car. Sunny is almost killed. One of our men betrays us, and we're lured into two death traps. All acts apparently committed by a group of men no one has ever heard of. Their name isn't whispered in bar back rooms or floating through the dark web. If they were, I'd know." Liam leaned in, clouding my head with his cedar cologne. "They're prepared for everything, Kenzie. Even escaping my notice."

I drew closer, dropping my voice. "How bad is it, Liam? What are we dealing with here?"

Yes, we. I long ago gave up any idea that their fight wasn't mine. I'm with the Merchants till the end. They've more than proven they feel the same about me.

"A group that is smart, well-funded, and wider reaching than we believed. That loudmouth Vito is from Harlow and that fool Grant was based in Rockchapel. They're recruiting our enemies across boroughs."

"But you said this Snyder guy is dead. He tried to kill Sunny, then led you all into the warehouse. Surely he's the mastermind and now he's gone."

Liam was shaking his head before I finished. "We can't assume anything. We've been doing that for weeks and it's gotten us nowhere. At this point we accept two things: there is an organization called the Brotherhood operating in Cinco, and they want the Merchants dead. Everything else is speculation."

"If that's true, where do we start?"

"Vito got away," Liam replied. "He and the men who carried him out are the only ones to survive that night. First thing we do is find and question him."

"This must be what he was hinting at the night I made a deal with him. He warned that he was a real threat to the Merchants and the Cardinals. Genny said he was the type to taunt and throw it in her face if he had a secret like this to use against her. Seems Vito can keep a secret better than we thought."

"Vito had a damn good reason to keep his mouth shut," Liam said. "They were relying on our cluelessness to pick us off one by one. Sunny drugged and dropped off a bridge. Me killed by car bomb. Genny taken out by drive-by shooting, and who knows what they planned for Bane. Our deaths would've driven him out of the woods. Once he was out in the open, they'd strike."

A shudder climbed my spine. "It's a good plan. A terrifying, evil, but smart plan. It's even worse that it almost worked. I take back my question, you don't have to tell me what we're dealing with here. Those bastards were willing to sell me to Luca and put my daughter in danger. They're monsters."

"We assume nothing and rethink everything from this point. Sunny's back in charge of the Sons of Saint, so for now I believe it's best you stay close to the compound." Liam turned away, jaw ticcing. "I can say to you that we'll do everything to protect you and Laurel, but we've failed in that once."

"Liam, don't say that." I found myself squeezing his knee. "You had no reason to believe Coates was rotting, duplicitous garbage that would sell his soul for a buck. I know you ran the same background checks on him that you did on me. Some things you can't see coming."

"I don't accept that," he said, "not when it comes to you."

I quieted, cheeks staining red. How was I supposed to reply when he said things like that—especially with things so up in the air between us?

"I don't want you to feel trapped or restricted, but at least until we know more about the Brotherhood, will you keep to the compound?"

Sighing, I replied, "That's an easy promise for me to make right now. All I'm thinking about is keeping Laurel safe and with me. When I can close my eyes and not picture that woman walking off with my kid, then I may be up for taking my chances with a crazed band of killers." I shook my head, forehead screwing up. "I just don't understand. Why now?

"Vito's nursed a hatred for the Merchants since he was young. Grant's wanted payback for months. Luca would've wanted to protect his disgusting business since the first time Sunny threatened him. I could see those three banding together and hatching something up, but from what you said, they weren't in charge."

"They weren't," Liam confirmed. "It was obvious the one they obeyed was Snyder. They raised and lower their guns on his orders."

"But none of you have seen or dealt with Snyder before," I said, working this out. "It's hard to believe a stranger woke up one day and gathered all your enemies to kick off a war. That has to be proof Snyder was also taking orders from someone else. The person bankrolling this entire thing who hates the Merchants enough to want you all gone, no matter how many innocents are taken down too. Still," I whispered. "Why now?"

"I'm not following."

"What made now the perfect time to strike?" I spoke up. "And *how* did they know it was? I keep coming back to that, Liam. The night Snyder picked Sunny up at Laser. Coates wasn't working for you then, so it's not like he tipped him off. Ryker swears none of their people are dirty and the club owner is clean too. The night they make their first real move just happens to be the same night Sunny is ripe for drugging and kidnapping?

"I'd say it was perfect timing if I didn't know that was impossible. They had to have it planned out in advance. But again impossible, because how did they know Sunny would be there when he didn't know he would be there until a last-minute impulse decision popped into his head?

"And you!" I cried, shooting up in my seat. "The night we went to La Belle's. That was another last-minute plan. We decided to go only hours before, and yet, there was already a bomb and a corrupt parking attendant waiting for you."

Liam stilled. "You're right. Dammit, you're right, Mackenzie. I eat there often, but I never call ahead and I didn't do it that night either. They keep a table open for me. For us to just happen to arrive on the night Calvin was ready to put a bomb in my car. It doesn't make sense."

"That doesn't make sense and neither does Banana Tree," I continued. "They knew that we were watching, and I still don't understand how. River may have a rocky relationship with you guys, but I know he wouldn't put me or Sienna in danger. If River didn't tip them off, how did Grant and Snyder know he was watching or that Sunny would get a peek at the time and location for his trap?

"I'm asking why now because somehow they knew the timing was perfect. Sunny would be on his own, you would show up to the restaurant on the right night, River would spot the meeting, and Genny would walk out of a safe house no one knows just as the shooter pulls up to the curb. Shit, Liam, if I didn't know better, I'd say the Brotherhood has a psychic on their side too."

Propping his elbow on the armrest, he rubbed the bridge of his nose. "That's beginning not to sound so farfetched. I certainly can't think of another explanation for how they've managed to strike at the right time, every time. It's only chance that we've survived these encounters. One or all of us may not be so lucky the next time."

My heart thumped an extra beat, throat squeezing. "Don't say that so calmly. Nothing is going to happen to any of you, because I may not believe in any of those fakes out there, but I do believe in my sister. She says we're strongest as long as we stick together, and so far, that's true. We can figure this out together too, Liam. If you're absolutely sure we don't have another traitor in the compound—"

"I'm certain," he sliced in. "Besides, a traitor in the compound wouldn't explain how Snyder got to Sunny the first time. No one in the Fairfield knew where he was going that night."

I nodded, accepting this. "If we're ruling out traitor, then there has to be another explanation for how the Brotherhood has managed to stay one step ahead." I snapped my fingers. "Thatcher once said that deliveryman is a favored role for an assassin. Anything that gets you into a building without questioning. What if someone masqueraded as a deliveryman, electrician, or plumber to get a bug in?"

Liam shook his head. "We sweep for bugs, Blaine. I'm telling you, every hole is plugged."

I glanced at my baby, who was trying to fit Sunny's head in her mouth. "Obviously it's not. You said we have to rethink everything, so let's say somewhere there's a leak. If it's not the staff, what's the next option?"

Liam sat back, considering.

"And remember they could've been planning this for years," I added. "Sienna believes this stretches back to your father, St. John. Maybe they set off the dominoes back before you had all your measures in place."

"It's possible," he said, almost to himself. "Definitely possible."

I didn't push him. Instead, I used the break in conversation to get Laurel and cradle her in my arms in prep for her nap. My muscles unwound as she chattered up at me.

"It's not a bug," Liam said, snapping my head up. "Those don't have an eternal battery life. The longest a professional one lasts is six weeks. Before you ask, the only strangers that have been in the compound that could've planted it within the last six weeks are you and Sienna. Since you didn't know Sunny before his attack, we can safely exclude you."

"I like to think that's not the only reason." The corner of his mouth tugged up. "What about a delivery? I know they're all screened, but could something have gotten through?"

"Thatcher is thorough."

"Any other ideas?" I asked. "You know your home and security better than me. You know its potential weaknesses."

"I do, and if you had asked me before this went down, I would've said the only threat to security was Elizabeth figuring out the code and letting every and anyone onto our floor. But even that wasn't a concern because someone dangerous would never make it through the front door.

"If I accept that our security is *leaking*, I still can't think of a hole that explains everything that's happened."

"What do you mean?"

Liam held up a finger. "First, there's the restaurant. I announced in Sunny's place that we were going. This could've been picked up by a bug that somehow made it into his apartment within the last six weeks. But that wouldn't explain how they knew Sole would be at Laser, since he hardly announced that in the living room before sneaking out. One method explained for my attack, but discredited for another.

"But all right, let's go back to Sunny's attack. He didn't have his security, but he did have his phone. Maybe that was bugged or infected with a tracking app. Maybe mine was too. That's how they knew where we were. Again, it doesn't explain Grant and Snyder lying in wait for River to find them, call you, and *then* for you to call Sunny and send him running.

"Speaking of the setup at the café, I have considered that Coates was on staff by then. It's possible he caught on to our searching for Grant in

Rockchapel. He could've told him and Snyder to be ready. Then when he drove you to Banana Tree, he warned the con was on."

He held out his hands. "Even if there's an explanation that covers all of those incidents, we're leaving out Genny. We don't know the location of her safe house, so neither guard, bug, nor tracker could've picked it up from us."

I had to give him something, Liam did look at it from every angle... except one.

"Liam, it's hard to accept this, but maybe you have to consider there isn't one explanation that covers it all... because all are possible. If the *Brotherhood* has been planning this for months going on years, they could've used that time to turn a valet and a bodyguard. They could've snuck bugs in past your security once, twice, or enough times that a six-week end date didn't stop them getting what they needed. Then, on a random day you don't remember, they lifted your phones, installed spyware, then tucked it back in your pocket."

"Mackenzie, what you're suggesting isn't a leak, it's a flood. That would mean our security has failed in every way. I may as well fire Thatcher and his team, and take my chances."

I sank in my seat, rocking Laurel. The last few days would be forgotten for her in every way, which included getting her back into her schedule. That meant it was naptime, though she had a look in her big beautiful eyes that said she wasn't sleeping anytime soon or missing out on her plane ride in the private jet.

"All we're doing is guessing anyway," I said. "We don't know how they're following you guys around the city, only that they are. What we do know is this enemy has to be well-funded and connected, right?"

"Correct."

"We know they're smart because they managed to hide all this time, building an organization of murderers in secret. We know they're patient. For as much as they obviously hate the Merchants, they didn't make a move until they were certain they could take you all out—which tells us something," I mused. "They also don't care if you know *why* you're suffering or who's behind it. They only care that you do. I'm assuming most of the enemies you deal with aren't like that."

Liam inclined his head. "Also correct. Most people after revenge want you to know why. More than that, they need to look in your eyes while you scream. They have to be the one tossing you over the bridge or pulling the trigger. It's more than ego. It's compulsion," Liam admitted. "Once I find the bastard who almost killed my daughter, I will not outsource his death. He will suffer long and hard under my hand."

I covered Laurel's ears. She didn't have a clue what we were talking about, but I couldn't help it.

"Seems to me all of that adds up to a specific type of person," I said. "Cold, efficient, calculating, intelligent, rich. Does that help us narrow the list of people this could be? For example, Vito is involved, but I can say without doubt he's not in charge."

Liam snorted. "That is for certain. The person you describe does paint a singular picture. If I didn't know better, I'd say you were speaking about me."

"You're not cold," I said so quickly there wasn't a chance to stop. "Anyone who sees you with Lizzie would slap themselves for thinking it. My point was that we can narrow down the suspects with that picture."

"Yes, but..." His gaze drifted over my shoulder. "Maybe not for us. The more I think about it, the more what you said bothers me. If this person hates us so much, why were they willing to let Snyder do all the dirty work? If they're that cold and removed, can it be termed as revenge?" His eyes glazed, brow wrinkling. "It doesn't make sense unless... Your sister truly is psychic."

"What? Sienna?"

He nodded, rising out of his seat. "I do not know what we did without you both, Mackenzie. Your sister had it right from the start. You have it right. Why weren't we listening?"

"We had it right? Listening to what?"

"Why whoever is behind this doesn't care who kills us or how we die," he said. "It's not about us at all."

"Not about you?" I repeated. "Seems like it is to me."

"Sole. Bane," Liam called. "Sienna."

My sister blinked at him from over her mug of tea.

"Sienna, you were right. These attacks aren't about the Cardinals, the Sons of Saint, or any of us. The leader of the Brotherhood doesn't give a shit about us. They want us dead to get to the real people they hate—our parents. Our deaths destabilize the empire *they* built. It drives *them* out into the open.

"We can't think of an enemy behind this because it's not an enemy we made. It's one that's been waiting, recruiting, and lying in wait for years, and they have no need to come out and face us because it's not us they want."

"Shit," Sunny swore.

Bane emerged from the back, face grave. "That can't be the only explanation."

I bounced between the brothers. It was Sienna who voiced my confusion.

"What's wrong?" she asked. "You must've suspected before that this could be an enemy your parents made."

"We suspected that back when it was two guys," Sunny said. "The assassin and the guy who hired him. That's a manageable situation, bestie. But an entire organization headed up by a fucker we've never even met is not manageable. We can't use ourselves as bait to drive them into the open, because we're not the catch. We can't assume they sent their best people after us, or that if we pick up Vito, he'll have information worth extracting."

"Wait." I got up and joined the huddle. "Why can't we assume that?"

"Because if they're gearing up for the main fight with our parents, they won't send their army after us," Bane replied, "and they didn't. They sent one assassin after Sunny, Liam, and Genny. That showdown at the shipping yard only happened because Snyder finally realized we weren't to be underestimated. We're not the endgame, Mackenzie. Our deaths are merely the tools used to torture our folks, and tools don't get your attention or resources."

"I still don't understand why you three look so grave. Okay, we're dealing with an organization instead of one man, but you knew that for the last two days and you weren't as bothered as you are now."

Liam grasped my shoulders. "Cold, efficient, calculating, intelligent, rich. Despite your high and flattering opinion of me, this person... is me. And if it's me behind this, there's nothing Sole could do to force me to reveal myself, and then give him a chance to warn our parents about who's after him.

"He can search for as long as he wants. He can kill all the faceless assassins I send after him. He can walk past me on the street and receive no more than a passing glance. A cold, efficient, *patient* killer doesn't get tripped up by the collateral damage. If we can't force him to face us, we have to find him with nothing to go on."

"Well, now that we know this is bigger than Snyder and bigger than the four of you, it's as simple as asking your parents who they believe could be behind it," I told him. "They'll narrow the suspect pool for us."

Sunny slumped in a seat. "I wish it was that simple, sugar butt, but I'm not exaggerating when I say they have about a thousand enemies."

"You have to be," Sienna cried.

"No," Bane echoed. "It's not just the gangs they crushed under their boots or forced to work for us. It's the ledger. Mom revealed every secret in that book, Kenzie. Every bribe, every murder, every cover-up, every atrocity. Acts that people killed for or obeyed the ledger owner to keep quiet. All of that dumped on the internet to be trending worldwide news for months.

"The bomb that set off in Cinco is what left it too weak to fight back when our parents took over. Villains were exposed, and then killed by the families of their victims. Businesses ended in ruin when the CEOs drained accounts and fled to a non-extradition country. Fortunes lost. Parents imprisoned for life. Reputations destroyed."

"You see, love?" Sunny said. "This could be anyone, or their kids. From the governor to the lowest gangbanger, they all have a reason to hate my parents. Do you see now that while I believe in your sister's gifts, I'd have liked her to be wrong about this one?"

I thought of the little I knew about the ledger and the kind of names that were in that book. I thought of how much they'd hate the person who exposed them. Then how much their disgraced, penniless, and humiliated wives, husbands, and children would hate the Merchants too.

Hundreds, if not a thousand enemies. Now to find one cold, ruthless killer in the midst of that all with no guarantee you or your parents have ever met them face to face.

"Yes," I rasped. "That is... unmanageable."

Chapter Three

B*ang!*

"*Tell me where Laurel is,*" I rasped, "*or so help me, I will kill you.*"

"*Wait! Wait, you d-don't have to do this!*"

"Kenzie?"

"*You have three seconds.*"

"Kenzie."

I jerked, glancing up to Genny's cocked brow. She rolled into my room, two beers riding shotgun on her chair.

"Thanks, but none for me."

"No one offered you any. These are both for me." Genny locked her wheels beside my bed and heaved herself on. I looked on in amusement as she propped on my pillows.

"Please, come in. Make yourself comfortable."

Genny winked. "Already did."

She wore another Genny-patented outfit. Black see-through mesh top, hot-pink bra, and a pair of shorts she shouldn't have bothered with because they were doing nothing to cover her behind.

"How are you? Is your leg on the mend?"

"You're asking how I am after what you've been through."

I glanced away, jaw clenching.

"Ahh. You're asking how I am *because* you don't want to talk about what you went through."

And her brothers say I'm insightful. Seems to me Genny can see through the bullshit too.

"Hey, I get it. I flipped and sent every Cardinal in the city after that fuck when I found out he took the toe-nibbler. Can't imagine what you went

35

through, trapped in a hole and not knowing if she was safe. I wouldn't have the words to talk about it so soon either."

I swallowed hard, falling on my toe-nibbler. Laurel was fast asleep in her crib, which was now in my bedroom. We got into Cinco that afternoon and the first thing I did was move it in here for her nap. For months we slept apart. Spending the next several or more months sleeping together made sense to me.

"Then let's not talk about it," I rasped. "Have you talked to the guys? Did they tell you they're officially on board with Sienna's vision?"

"You mean Sienna's common-sense deduction?" she corrected. "Yeah, they told me about that. Doesn't change a thing."

"It might change something. If what this guy really wants is a showdown with your parents, or with St. John like Sienna says, then their returning to the city might bring him out into the open."

"Oh, yeah?" She grinned wide. "They are in their sixties. You suggesting we ask a couple of seniors to trot out as bait for a maniac who sanctions the death of six-year-olds? Seniors who happen to be my loving mommy and daddies? Damn, girl, you're vicious." She put a bottle in my hand and clinked it. "Whatever it takes to get the bastard who messed with your baby."

"No," I cried. "I didn't mean— That's not what I was saying!"

Genny cracked up. "Sounded like that's what you were saying."

"Wow, Genny, I would never suggest using your own parents as bait. I'm saying *you're* the bait. If he wants your deaths to drag your parents out of the Hamptons beach house, take away the option. They're already here safe in the Fairfield. Now he needs another plan that doesn't involve sending a hundred faceless assassins after you."

She shook her head, blonde hair practically floating around her. "He would move on to another plan, babe, but not a good one. We're thinking like my older brother here. If it was Liam and all of his targets holed up in one building that I couldn't get into, I'd force them out by declaring open season on their gangs. The Cardinals, the Scourges, the Sons of Saint, and every uptight suit that bows down to Liam. He'd slaughter them one after the other, knowing we couldn't hole up in here, kicking back in the hot tub while our people die. We'd come out and our parents would too. He'd get what he was after either way."

Genny rubbed her arm. "I've survived every attempt to kill me and I'll survive the ones coming. But I won't sign my girls' death warrants. I've lost three of them already. I won't lose any more."

Slumping over, I dropped my head on my knees. "You're right. That's a stupid idea. I should've thought of that."

"Don't beat yourself up." Genny thumped my back. "You haven't learned how to think like a sociopathic killer. That's not a bad thing, Feisty."

"So what do we do now?"

"Same thing we were doing before all this started: run our city. He'll send faceless assassins after us, and we'll kill them. He'll try to sabotage us and we'll stop him. This guy isn't doing anything that countless others haven't tried before. The Merchants will never lose."

I turned on her. "Does this mean after you're healed, you're skipping back to Harlow to act like it's business as usual?"

"It is business as usual," she stressed, "and I'm in charge of it, not Bugsy. Looking out for my crew includes not leaving them to run my borough while I take a vacation."

"This isn't a vacation. You were shot and run over," I drew out.

She flapped her good hand, waving that away. "Whatever you call it, I'm going back to Harlow tomorrow."

"No."

Genny cocked her head, looking at me like I slipped into another language. "What was that?"

"I said no. You're not leaving. All we know about this guy is we don't know anything about him— Scratch that. We know he's recruiting hit men and everyone else in the city who wants the Merchants dead. You're not going. It's too dangerous."

Don't get me wrong, Liam and Genny already looked alike, but when Genevieve had that smirk on her lips, she was his twin. "How do you plan to stop me?"

"I'll pop your tires."

Genny barked a laugh. "Touché."

"I'm serious, Genny. Since the bullet didn't convince you, I'll say it. You're not made of steel."

"Ugh, you sound like Fuller. I may not be made of steel, but I'm also not a three-year-old. Your baby is over there," she said, pointing to Laurel. "She's not lying in this bed with you. Give your orders to someone else."

Irritation heated my skin. Oh yes, Liam and Genny were twins no matter what their years apart said. "Those aren't orders, you deeply vexing woman. It's called concern. It's been a very hard *decade*. I couldn't stand it if something happened to you."

"Huh." Genny eyed me over her beer. "So you're falling for me too. Knocking my brothers down one by one, and you decided to add FGH to the conquest list."

I flung myself on the sheets. "I give up."

"So easily?" Damned if she wasn't enjoying herself. "Gonna have to work harder than that if you want me."

"I thought the threesome was already booked."

We laughed. Genny sobered first.

"Seriously, I'll be fine. I've got a new place and I've increased security around Barbarella's. No one is getting that close again."

"How do you know this new place is any safer? You don't know how they found your last one."

She raised her shoulders. "I was tailed by someone good. I'll be more vigilant from here on."

"Where is it?"

Winking, she tapped her nose. "Nice try."

"That wasn't a test. Tell me where you'll be, so next time we can send the rescue crew to you instead of you crashing into it."

"Rescue crew, my ass. Anyone comes busting in like I'm some damsel in distress will get their asses kicked too."

"Genevieve!"

"Whoops. Now you are starting to sound like Fuller." Genny rolled off the bed onto her seat. "I'm gone, but come up tonight with some of Shonda's cooking and we'll hang out. Last night before I leave, bring up more booze too. Hendrix doesn't want me drinking while I'm on pain meds."

"Ah, okay. So I won't be bringing booze."

She rolled her eyes like I was being difficult. "You can still come, but don't forget the food. If Shonda makes her green chile ribs, take the whole pan while she's not looking."

Thankfully, Shonda didn't make her green chile ribs, so I didn't have to face the consequences of running off with her cooking. I brought up three plates of roasted pork sandwiches, my sister, and my baby. The four of us stretched out on the couch watching movies while Laurel climbed on us, and I took my shot during the lulls to convince Genny to stay. Even backed up by Sienna, we couldn't get through that stubborn wall of badass confidence.

"How about this?" Genny broke in. "I will consider it. Genuinely consider it... for a beer."

My eyes narrowed to slits. "That's evil."

She grinned wider than a kookaburra. "Isn't it, though? I'm so naughty. So what's it going to be, Feisty? If I leave and something happens to me, you'll regret that you didn't do everything you could to stop me."

"Sienna, what does the future say about me killing her myself?"

They were both laughing at me. "It's looking likely."

Huffing, I handed Laurel off to Sienna and went to get the manipulative menace a nonalcoholic beer. I didn't care if I had to go to the corner store.

I rushed out and collided into a hard chest.

"Oops—"

"Sorry—"

"I didn't—"

"Are you okay?"

Bane and I untangled ourselves from each other.

"Sorry," I said.

"Don't have to apologize." Bane straightened, stretching his tight white tee across his pecs. It hurt how handsome he was. An easy smile hung on his lips, sticking even as awkward silence came in, threatening to kill us.

He gestured. "I'm just here to see Genny. She wants to outfit her crew with some new, upgraded firepower."

"She wants me to circumvent doctor's orders and get her drunk."

Bane chuckled. "Sounds like her. All right, see you."

He made to sidestep me, but I moved with him. "Bane, what's going on? You've been weird since we left New York."

Pushing out his lips, he shook his head. "I haven't been weird. Why would you say that?"

"Because we haven't talked. We didn't talk this morning at the house while we ate and got ready to leave. We barely spoke on the plane, and when we got home, you just said 'get some rest' and went up to your place. Now you're shaking me off after barely a conversation."

"I'm not shaking you off, Kenzie. Just going inside to talk to my sister." He reached behind me for the knob. "Unless you want to talk about last night. I can stop by Sunny's in the morning—"

"—and we can talk about this: I'm not a victim."

"What?" he said, hand falling off the knob.

"I'm not a victim, Bane, even though your words have been playing non-stop in my head, trying to convince me otherwise."

"My words? Hold on, I never called you a victim."

"Didn't you?" My eyes stung, squeezing out tears as strangled as my throat. "Can you break bones to maintain fear? Can you demand half the contents in a man's safe while he's on his knees begging and pleading that he needs the money for his family? Can you do what it takes to be the monster that monsters are afraid of? Can you love a man that does?

"You flung those questions at me, thinking you had me figured out. You're the one who punches first, and I'm the one cowering before the monsters, hoping someone saves me."

"Whoa, hey." Bane cupped my cheek. "That's not what I meant."

"Then what did you mean, Bane? What else am I supposed to think after you morph into this quiet, polite stranger who doesn't have three full sentences for me after the worst night of my life? I know what you're thinking. I'm opposite of what you've trained and sacrificed to be.

"You've done everything to make sure you're no one's victim. That your death or capture can't be used against your family. Then here comes some tragic homeless girl whose abduction almost got you, River, and your brothers killed. I'm everything you hate."

"Kenzie, enough!" He made me lift swimming orbs to his—wide and imploring. "I never said any of that. I don't think it either. None of that shit is true."

"It's not?" I pushed his hand away. "Because I understand why you refuse to be my boyfriend, but maybe you can explain to me why lately, you're not acting like a friend either."

With that, I walked off, leaving him calling after me. I made it all the way to my room before the dam broke.

THE NEXT MORNING, SUNNY alternated between rubbing cream on my ankle and rubbing my feet. The skin chafed where the chains bit into me.

The two of us—three of us were in his room. Sunny and I shared breakfast in bed while Laurel entertained herself on the play mat. Gunshots ran in my ears as I ate Shonda's French toast and vanilla smoothie.

"Gorgeous, you're uncharacteristically quiet. What's on your mind?"

I came to, fixing my expression. "Uncharacteristically? What's that supposed to mean?"

"It means the last time we sat in silence this long, you were fighting your attraction for me and biting your lips, so you didn't use them to make things interesting." He sat up straight. "Unless of course, that's what's happening now..."

I laughed, tension easing. No matter what happened, I could always rely on my Sunny to be... sunny.

"I was thinking about what we're facing. Sienna is so sure we'll be okay as long as we stick together, but it's hard to feel secure when the Brotherhood could be anyone or anywhere."

"We've faced worse and mowed those 'insert profanity here' down. This time won't be any different." He resumed rubbing my arches, making me purr. "Though I am wondering what the radius is on Sienna's vision of togetherness, because Genny took off."

"She did? Already? How did she get out of here so fast with a busted leg and hurt shoulder?"

He shrugged. "Probably had her crew carry her out on a golden litter. The scariest bunch of Amazons you'll ever meet, but when Genny snaps her fingers, they fall in quick."

"That would make me feel better if she planned on telling us or the Amazons the location of her new place. What if they ambush her again and she doesn't get away? Why is she so stubborn?"

"'Cause she's pissed, baby. The Brotherhood got this close." He held his fingers up. "This close to showing that despite inheriting all the good and the *better* traits of our unstoppable mother, she can be sent running with her tail between her legs. Genny hates weakness—others' and her own."

Something about that lodged a lodestone in my stomach. I understood that better than I wanted to. "There has to be another way," I whispered. "A way to overcome weakness that isn't reckless."

"Maybe, but I think there will always be some involved. It takes a little recklessness, a little wild, a little rage to run into a fight you can't hope to win if it means saving someone you love. Being disciplined, calculating, or practical isn't what makes you strong. It's picking up your crutches, going outside, and showing them all they can't make you afraid."

I stroked his early morning stubbly jaw, loving him so much in that moment my chest ached. "You might be onto something, Sole Bellisario."

Twisting, he kissed the palm of my hand. "You said yesterday you wanted to see River."

"Yeah. I tried calling but he didn't answer."

"He's still with my people, helping those women. A lot don't have families to go back to, and we can do better than leaving them in a women's shelter and walking off."

Bringing him to me, I kissed him slow and deep, tasting the vanilla on his tongue. "Mmhhm. I'm definitely in love with you."

"Better be," he teased. "I've been secretly planning our wedding since we met."

"Not so secret." I pecked his nose. "Tell me where River is. I'll get dressed and go help as soon as I'm done."

"You okay to leave Laurel? You've been keeping her pretty close."

"I'm not leaving her," I said too loud. "She's coming with me."

"Okay, no problem." He was as calm as I should be. "You don't want guards, so I'll come with. Ryker should already be there too."

"You don't mind being in the same room as River? I was getting the vibe off you guys that you were mortal enemies."

"Mortal enemies?" Sunny rested his head on my lap. "Such a title goes to men like Luca Adams, and as you've seen, they don't live long once they make it to that list. River and I aren't enemies or friends. Now we'll never be enemies because he helped me save you."

I smiled, running my hands through his hair. "Will you tell me now what happened between you two?"

"You should ask Delaney."

"Ugh, Sunny, come on."

"It's not like that," he said. "I'm telling you to ask him because it's his story to tell. I've got some goodwill for the guy at the moment. Least I can do is let him explain things to you himself."

I settled back on the pillows. "Okay, that's fair. But you should know all this mystery is piquing my curiosity. I'm building up the story more and more every day. At this point we've reached a tale worthy of Shakespeare."

His smile tinged enigmatic. "Shakespeare couldn't write this story."

LIAM

I leaned back in my chair, scanning the security screens. The benefits of operating the majority of my business through nightclubs was also its disadvantage. Too much noise, movement, and bodies to overhear a sensitive conversation, pick out a particular shipment among the crates of beer bottles, or separate who worked for me amid the regulars looking to get laid.

All of that also made it near to impossible to scope out on my three months of security footage who could be working with the Brotherhood.

They've been following and watching us—that wasn't in question. The natural assumption was at some point, their men have entered my clubs, getting a sense of my resources, backup, and exits.

I leaned in, squinting at a green flash on the screen. Three weeks' worth of footage, and so far, I've spotted the man in the green coat four times. It said enough about my progress that one ill-dressed guy slumped on the bar was the closest I had to a suspect.

A knock sounded at the door. "Boss."

"Come," I called.

Blake walked in, leading two of my men behind him. I wasn't one for the right hands, beers with my crew, an inner circle of my bestest friends like Sole was. My men were hired for their skill, efficiency, and ability to do what they were told without question. The day they failed in one or more of those areas, they were removed and replaced.

Blake Dagon handled a majority of tasks for me and stepped in to run the business when I was otherwise indisposed—almost always for Elizabeth-related reasons. For this reason, he was termed my lieutenant. Otherwise there was no hierarchy or stations to move up within my organization.

Why pretend as though one man was higher up than another, or that man had some kind of power with the promotion? The only power was mine.

Blake, Henry, and Roman lined up before my desk. All three of similar heights, but that's where their similarities ended. Blake had a full head of thick, coarse hair and a multitude of tattoos detailing his time in the service.

Henry was shaved on top, but growing a thick, full black beard. He opted to show no affiliation of any kind. He refused to wear name brands because the worst thing you could do is announce your favorites to the world. All an assassin has to do is lie in wait outside your local Ralph Lauren. A tad paranoid but that's the kind of man you have oversee security.

Then there was Roman. Pale-green eyes, thin lips, streaks of red in his brown hair to match the red oxfords on his feet. He had many tattoos but their meaning was only understood by him. A bunny pulling itself out of a hat, a cartoon ray gun, and a line of characters going down his arm that did not translate into any language.

Roman wound his head like he was drawing circles with his nose, popping his gum while he hummed to himself. More than once I've been asked why I employed a man like Roman. Didn't he belong with the *misfit toys* that made up the Sons of Saint?

The comments of the shortsighted did not penetrate. Despite his many quirks, Roman Pappas was the best retriever this city had ever seen. I gave him the fuzzy description from a four-year-old and Roman found the man who gave Elizabeth a basket of poisoned fruit and told her to say it came from her teacher. The man was begging at my feet four days later.

"You've never let me down, Roman." I turned away from the screens. "Tell me that's not about to change."

Roman paused mid-circle, speaking with his head cocked at an odd angle. "I tracked Vito as far as the Westside clinic, boss. They patched up his leg, then moved him to a safe house for the night. It's cleared out now. The whole apartment stripped and bleached."

"And?" I prompted. Roman knew better than to walk in here with useless information like that.

"And from there they took him to Harlow thinking his girlfriend would play nursemaid. She slammed the door in his face. *The tiny-dick shithead's been sleeping with my sister,*" he cried, adopting a high-pitched tone. "*I hope he's dead. If he's not, find and kill him for me.*" Roman jerked his head like he was shaking her voice out of his ear.

Henry took a step to the left. He was naturally wary of someone with the ability to remember everything he heard and saw. He claimed Roman was the equivalent of a wire and the only safe way to let him leave the crew was a bullet through his uniquely wired brain. Like I said, my organization wasn't made of bros.

"After that, the Brotherhood guys took him to the sister," Roman continued.

I reached for my desk drawer and the gun inside. "Is he there now?"

A shake of Roman's head clenched my jaw. "He was there as of yesterday morning. Minute he could hobble, he put himself in a cab... headed for Rockchapel."

I punched the desk and screamed, "Fuck!" but only in my head.

Outwardly, I steepled my fingers and channeled my hatred for the man working with Laurel and Mackenzie's kidnappers into its apex—a technique my father taught me for controlling emotion. Anger and hatred were someone's control over you. Strategy, reason, and revenge were my control over them.

And my relief when she came down those stairs—dirty, bleeding, and dripping tears on Laurel's resting head—that was the end of both.

No one had control over me or I over them. What I had was a mandate that would drive my time on earth: to put every member of the Brotherhood through torture the likes of which would sicken generations to come.

"This Rockchapel business is becoming inconvenient," I said simply. "It's common knowledge among my enemies that all they need to do to escape my punishment is drive thirty miles east. They, and Vito, will quickly discover that is incorrect. Find him in Rockchapel, Roman. Now."

He bowed deeply—a mocking act from anyone else, but Roman bowed to everyone he respected. "Yes, boss."

"Does this mean new terms were negotiated with the Rat King?" Blake asked.

"No, but he will give us a pass for this. I have no doubt he has his own people looking. We share a common goal in this instance. He'd never turn down the assistance of Cinco's best retriever."

Roman beamed wide and unsettling. "You flatter me."

I waved him off. "Go."

Roman left, leaving Blake and Henry behind. "What have you found out about the Brotherhood and the man who called himself Snyder? Was he just a hired gun or someone important in the organization?"

Henry stepped forward. "From what he said to you, I suspect the latter. He said it was their right and their purpose to end the Merchants. Those are the words of a zealot, and considering he had every intention of killing you, he'd have gained nothing by putting on a show. There is a group of men dedicated to breaking the Merchants' hold on the city, and this Snyder was the one tasked with carrying out your death. A fact that points to his reputation because whoever is in charge, thought one man was enough."

"A reputation that fearsome is talked about. Why have I never heard of a Snyder?"

"An alias for certain, but there's something else." He nodded at Blake. "We know why neither you nor the family recognize him. An examination of the body revealed he's had facial reconstruction, and a damn good job too. The scars are so faint, you had to be inches away to spot them."

"Plastic surgery," I breathed, mind racing. "Of course. Our first thought was we didn't know him because he's a hire from out of town. But someone who isn't from the city and a zealot *freeing* the city from our reign doesn't add up to the same person. He was a known player in this city, and he changed his face to hide the fact.

"Henry," I barked. "I want a list of every hit man in this city going back thirty years. Put the ones that suddenly vanished off the map on top."

"Already on it."

"Boss, how can we be sure this guy is the lieutenant and not the mastermind?" Blake asked. "Bernardi probably took off to Rockchapel because he heard the boss was dead, and there was no one to protect him."

"We can't be certain of anything. I do know this much, the kind of money, patience, and planning that it takes to achieve their supposed purpose is massive. There's killing all of us and then all of you. Draining our accounts, ending our allies, and protecting the throne so someone worse doesn't take it and put them back where they started. To get this close requires a fearsome intelligence that Snyder did not have."

"Didn't he?"

I shook my head. "Choosing a warehouse with so many exits, then a shipping yard office with none proves it. If it was me, I would've led us into that warehouse and blocked all the exits. If it was me, I wouldn't have walked into a room with no windows, making it impossible for me to notice the biker gang surrounding the place. Not to mention he didn't bother to check if there were witnesses before he dumped Sunny off the overpass.

"He was a strong opponent, but cocky. Stupid. The person truly behind this is neither of those things. They can't be. A cocky, stupid brute wouldn't have gotten so close to getting everything they wanted."

My men nodded, faces chipped from granite. I could see them working through my logic, and coming to the same conclusion.

"We're doing everything we can to find the Brotherhood and discover how they've gotten past our defenses," Henry said. "We've tapped every rat in the city. We'll know something by the end of the week."

I shook my head, rising to my feet. "No, don't bother wasting the coin. From this point, we assume everyone is dirty, especially our informants. If they were doing their job, I would've heard about the Brotherhood before they had a gun to my head."

"If they have money to hire the best plastic surgeons, they've got money to pay off snitches. Not just to keep us in the dark," Blake said slowly, "but to spread the word too. How else have they been recruiting?"

"I'll pull a few in," Henry agreed. "Lean on them till something useful comes out."

"I like what I'm hearing, gentlemen. You have three days."

They inclined their heads and swept out, leaving me to my steepled fingers and Father's words in my ear.

I couldn't be with Mackenzie. That was still true.

She was too young for me. That was true too.

Focused icy rage wasn't that of a boyfriend avenging his girl. It was that of a man protecting a person under his charge.

Convince yourself you're not reacting out of love, son. Convince yourself you've never felt love.

Because its control is unbreakable.

MACKENZIE

Minestrone splashed in the bowl, breaking my attention from River. "Here you are."

A blonde woman with a thin blanket wrapped around her shoulders mumbled thanks, put the bowl on her tray, and continued down the food line. My eyes found their way back to River.

He sat at the edge of the lunch table, deep in conversation with a girl about my age. Maybe I kept staring at him because I hoped the prickling on his neck would prompt the guy to pull me in for a deep conversation. Not to say he was ignoring me.

When we arrived, River threw his arms around me—holding me tight and close for a solid five minutes. Neither of us saw the need to pull away, though when we did, River gave Laurel the same attention—praising her and saying how happy he was she was safe. My daughter was smitten with him in three seconds flat, and when he was that wonderful, it was impossible for me not to feel the same.

But there's so much we need to talk about. Like where the heck we're standing right now.

I glanced around, marveling at the shelter. When Sunny, Laurel, Sienna, and I took off that morning, I wasn't expecting him to turn right instead of left for North Quay or Rockchapel. He drove farther and farther into Leighbridge, pulling up to the curb in front of New Bridges Shelter.

In the two hours I'd been here, I searched for an employee, administrator, manager—someone in charge. But from what I was seeing, that person was River.

River asked me to hop on the serving line with Marty and Nathan. He was the one telling his people and Sunny's where this went or where to find that. All questions and requests were going through him.

If I had to come to the conclusion that he was running this place, I had to wonder how. New Bridges was nothing like the homeless shelters Sienna and I used to frequent. The serving tools I was using were spotless stainless steel. The appliances were bought within the last five years—bought, not donated.

Long lunch tables filled the middle of the cafeteria and surrounding them were couches, beanbags, and a jukebox that made the room feel like a hangout. Polished floors gleamed. The paint was still fresh and unchipped. And a peek inside one of the rooms showed six single beds each with a trunk, bedside table, and lamp. The last shelter I stayed in packed twelve bunk beds in a room half the size, and there were no extras. Even if you didn't have a home, Leighbridge proved it was the place to live.

"Looks like you have questions, mama," Nathan said. He sidled up next to me with a tray of rolls.

"So many questions. Is the crew running this place?"

Nathan held his hands out proudly. "Running this location and living in the other two. You're not the only one who traded up."

"Apparently. This shelter is amazing. I'm almost afraid to ask how you got your hands on it."

"No bribes, blackmail, or tricks." River appeared in front of us, smiling that smile. "I promise."

I couldn't stop myself smiling back. "Guess I have to trust you, then."

He jerked his head toward the exit. "Got a minute?"

"Sure?"

I handed my ladle off to Nathan. River met me at the entrance of the kitchen, holding out his hand. I wove my fingers through easily, following him out into the courtyard. It was no less nice out there than it was inside.

A small vegetable garden sat across from a flower garden, boasting reds, greens, yellows, and purples of the growing beauties both meant to feed our souls and our stomachs. Between was a cozy painted bench. We sat, looking out over the playground. There were no kids playing on it, but it wasn't empty. A figure sat on top of the slide, gazing at the Cinco skyline.

"I'm sorry I wasn't there."

"Don't apologize, River. You put aside your feelings for the Merchants and risked your life to save me and Laurel. The last thing you need to say is sorry."

River didn't speak for a long time. "I'm never what you need when you need me."

"What? River." I grasped his chin, turning him to me. "Why would you say that?"

"Because it's true." There was an odd note in his voice. Flat. Resigned. "When that trash Adams forced you onto the street, you joined our crew. But you couldn't follow someone like me or condone the things I do, so you were forced to leave us too."

My jaw worked. "No, I— It's not that simple—"

"It was Sunny who got you off the streets, protected you, helped you get Laurel back. And it was me who led you out of safety and made you vulnerable to Coates's attack."

"That's not true," I cried. "If I wasn't going out to meet you, I would've been heading out to Brocade, or swinging by the baby store, or a hundred other things. The guy was my driver and bodyguard, I was vulnerable from the day that monster took the bribe. You can't blame yourself for that."

"You don't trust me," he said, piercing my soul. "I can blame myself for that."

I swallowed hard, fighting the urge to drop my gaze or hide the emotions swirling within. "I trust you to be there for me when I need you. I couldn't say that about anyone other than Sienna for twenty years. That matters, River. It's the only thing that matters now. The rest will come... when you trust me."

His jaw clenched beneath my fingers as I voiced the true issue at the heart of our relationship. River lied, evaded, or danced around the truth of his past because he didn't trust me yet. Maybe that should've hurt me, but it didn't. The past is a dark, winding path haunted by your demons. No one wants to take you inside if all you're destined to do is abandon them in the maze with one more regret.

River claimed my hand, dropping kisses on my fingertips. "Even though I'm not all the way there, I trust you more than I do anyone else. I hope that's what matters now too."

"It is," I whispered. "But one thing... promise you won't lie to me anymore. If you don't want to talk about something or you can't tell me, then say that and I'll respect it. Just please don't lie." Laurel's screams rang in my head, echoing over the orders of a man I once thought I loved, barking to rip her away from me. "You can't fathom how sick to death I am of men lying to me."

He cracked a mirthless grin. "I can guess, and I can promise. No more lies, Kenzie. I can give you that much."

Sighing, I felt something tight and painful inside me finally begin to loosen. "I like this. You and me being real with each other. Let's keep it up: how did you get your hands on this place and *two* other locations?"

"Oooh." He pulled a face. "Promise you won't get mad?"

I laughed. "Nothing good starts off with that question, but yes, I promise."

"I did make a deal with Makai and Athena. They gave me something valuable to the former owner of these shelters in exchange for letting the Sons of Saint into Rockchapel."

My expression gave nothing away as I processed this. "You let them into the one borough they can't go, and they did the same for you."

"That's the gist. I am sorry I lied when you caught us, but I knew Sunny wasn't dead and you would've told him what we did. This deal was too important to risk." He shook his head. "That's not an excuse. It's just the reason I did what I did."

"Okay," I began. "I can understand. I'm not happy you lied, but you're not wrong. I would've told Sunny. It's hard to fault you when I look around this place. This is a much better shelter than a dirty quayside warehouse." I bumped his shoulder. "Even when you're being an asshole to me, you're being a savior to someone else."

"Savior." River rolled it around on his tongue. "The Vagrant Savior or the Drifter Savior. Why don't they call me that on the streets?"

"'Cause your big head couldn't take it."

We laughed, breaking the tension.

"So the guy trades you for all of this," I said. "Wow. Are you all set for money? Donations? Inspectors?"

"Everything's on the up-and-up. These are private shelters, so no government money comes our way, but I have a friend that'll help me organize biannual charity donation events." He motioned to the city. "In this borough, the checks are large."

"You have a friend who's going to help you throw those super-exclusive events where everyone pays ten thousand dollars a plate for two morsels and then bids on their future third yacht."

"Yep."

"Damn. I was doing this homeless thing all wrong."

River cracked up. "I've given out a lot of favors, knowing the perfect day would come to collect."

"Does it bother you the things you have to do in exchange? I'm making no judgments since I don't know the full story, but you've fought to keep the Merchants out of Rockchapel all this time. Can you and Sunny, or you and Liam, handle sharing boroughs without friction?"

River stretched his legs out and draped his arm around me. "This would've happened anyway. At least I got something good for my people before we were forced to work together."

"What do you mean? Why are you forced together?"

"Grant figured out he could escape the Merchants' notice by hiding out in Rockchapel. I'd bet my looks those other Brotherhood bastards got the same idea in their head. My crew can't track them all down by ourselves. The Merchants know better than me the enemies they made. Therefore, until the Brotherhood is put down, the Rat King and the Merchants are allies."

"But, River, this isn't your fight. The Brotherhood are after the Merchants, not you." I motioned around. "Plus, you have all of this to look after now. These shelters could help a lot of people."

River's eyes hardened to chips of granite. "Kenzie, I walked in on the fate those bastards chose for you. Chained to the wall like an animal. Raped over and over again without end. This isn't *your* fight and still they handed you over to Luca just to get to the Merchants.

"All these women. You. Laurel." His voice cracked. "That the Brotherhood recruited Digger instead of putting him down like a rabid dog is why I won't stop until every one of them is gone from my city. They will never hurt you again."

My lips trembled, painted with tears. I started to say something—what I didn't know.

Turning away, I drew my legs up to my chest, hugging them as it all emptied out. River didn't push. His hand was warm comfort on the back of my head until I finally lifted it, wiping my cheeks on my sleeve.

"I should get back to Laurel. It's almost time for her lunch."

"Okay. I've got some papers to sort through, but don't take off. I'm close to the Fairfield now. I'll walk you two back."

Smiling, I kissed his cheek. "That's sweet, but we took the car and Sunny will just drive beside us the whole time."

"Shouting catcalls like he's not already your boyfriend."

I almost giggled. "That is so him. We'd just end up drawing attention."

River was gentle drying my eyes. "I hope we can still see each other. Not just me and you, but you, Sienna, and the entire crew. We had the most fun when the Blaine sisters were running with us."

"Of course we'll still see each other. We're going to see a lot of each other," I said, bumping his shoulder and not pulling back. "Why wouldn't we?"

He flashed me a wry look. "The Fairfield is a fortified paradise. It's easy to shut yourself in there and ignore the world while the serfs do your bidding, keeping the money flowing."

"You speak like you know from experience."

River flicked over my shoulder. "I lived in the Fairfield once."

"You did? Wait, when? Were you one of the family's staff?"

"Not staff, Kenzie. Family."

My lips parted and nothing came out.

Sighing, River scrubbed his face. "I'll say this, I promise the whole story will come later, but not today. Sunny is technically my nephew. His mother and I are half-siblings."

Eyes bugging, a billion questions crowded my tongue and I strained to hold them in. Nephew?! Half-siblings?! The Merchants have been warring with their own family? Why?

River relaxed when he saw I wasn't going to ask the questions written all over my face. "Look, I told you that so you know I understand. From the palace in the sky to the streets, you can bet I had second thoughts when I left that place. The Brotherhood is an unknown that's already put you through so much. I understand if you want to stay safe inside with Laurel and only come out with Sunny, Liam, or Bane by your side."

He looked over my shoulder again and I turned to see Sunny in the window, giving away blankets in between glancing out at me. No, watching over me.

"All I'm saying is when you get to the point of feeling safe outside the Fairfield, that you leave them home and spend real time with me. I swear I'll protect you better than I did."

I blew out a long, deep breath. "I shouldn't be scared to go outside, let alone need to get to a point where I'm not. I shouldn't need protection, River. I'm as sick to death of being lied to as I am of always needing someone to rescue me."

"We're in a world of killers, abductors, traffickers, and revenge sworn in blood. It's almost a guarantee that someday, we'll all need a rescue." He gestured with his chin. "Even people who aren't in this world do."

I followed his line of sight to the woman on the slide. "What's her story?"

"Two years ago, she lost her job and moved into one of Digger's slum houses. The same story, he started off sweet, charming, and loving, and she fell hard. After manipulating her into sleeping with a few guys he claimed he owed money to, Adams drove her straight to that building.

"She believed they were going out on a romantic weekend away to put all that awfulness behind them, and instead, he walked her right into hell. She hasn't seen her son since."

Horror leadened my bones. "She has a son?"

He nodded, genuine pain on his face. "He's nine years old. Marie doesn't know what happened to him after that day. She begged Luca and the men holding them there to tell her, but they laughed in her face. After we got them out, we went back to the apartment of course, but Jake wasn't there and the neighbors didn't know anything was wrong. They were all told the two of them packed up and moved—nothing out of the ordinary."

"Oh my gosh," I breathed, clapping my hands over my mouth. "But we're going to find him. We have to find him!"

"We're trying, Kenzie. Digger taunted us in the short time before his deserved death. He said he planned to sell Laurel for a high price. Could be what he did to Jake... and the other three kids that are missing."

"I can't believe this." I was physically ill. "He has done this before. Sunny said Digger wouldn't have done it with me unless it worked more often than it didn't, but I didn't want to believe that demon made a habit of preying on desperate single moms. We have to find those children, River."

"I have every homeless person, in my crew and out, searching the city for them. If there's any time we work together, it's for missing kids."

"What about the police?"

"I took her to file a police report. It's been months though. The cop that took her statement didn't even fake optimism."

"That poor woman," I said, squeezing my chest. "Even when Charlie had Laurel, I knew she was safe and that one day I would get her back. What she's going through right now... I'd only wish that pain on the Brotherhood."

Taking my hands, River stood, helping me up. "You should talk to her. I've tried but all she wants to hear from me is that I've found Jake. There's nothing I can say to make her feel better, but it might help to talk to you. You're a mom. You understand."

A soft kiss on the lips, over as soon as it started, was my parting gift.

I watched her at the top of the slide. Taking a step, I stopped.

What could I say to this woman that would help? Tell her Adams stole my baby too? That I couldn't stop it or save her? Should she know that I had to be rescued from the hole he threw me in, and the one who saved my daughter after I promised we'd never be parted again, was Sole?

What did someone like me have to say to her other than sit tight, the ones who fight the monsters are out there risking themselves while the victims hide in the palace in the sky.

I shut the door softly behind me, returning to the kitchen and my ladle.

Chapter Four

I trudged into Sunny's apartment, carrying a snoozing Laurel. Sienna squeezed my elbow.

"I'll be in my room, meditating. If I keep the pathways open, I may receive a vision of where those kids are."

I offered her a smile. "Good idea. I'll bring your dinner in to you."

"Thanks, sis." She kissed my cheek, then Laurel's.

Inside Laurel's room, Ms. Fuller puttered around straightening up and putting away her toys.

"You don't have to do that. I'm planning to move it all into my bedroom anyway. I just came for Boots." I picked up the stuffed black cat with white feet. "Laurel will lie in her crib, talking away at him like they have secrets."

Fuller chuckled. "Precious baby. She's so sweet."

"That she is," I whispered, stroking her hair.

"Why don't you put her down for her nap and I'll get started moving these things into your bedroom?"

I loved Fuller for not asking why I was moving my baby out of the beautiful nursery the guys worked so hard on.

"By the way," she said, stopping me in the doorway. "Bane stopped by three times looking for you. He asked that you go up and talk to him."

Our conversation the day before came back to me. Every raw, shouted word.

"Good," I said. "Because I want to talk to him too."

I laid Laurel in her crib, then stopped by Sunny's room to give him a kiss and her baby monitor. Steeling myself, I rode the elevator to his floor—the sound of gunshots echoing in the metal cage.

Bane opened on the second knock. Every heart-stoppingly gorgeous inch of him filled the entrance. Nothing but a gray shirt, Caddell jacket, jeans, and he put models to shame.

"Kenzie, finally." He grasped my shoulders, pulling me in. "Listen to me, all that stuff you said, I never thought it for a second. You're one of the strongest people I know and—"

"But not strong enough," I sliced in. "I promised Laurel nothing would separate us, then came Coates and Luca."

"That wasn't your fault!"

"I know it wasn't." My voice shook. "But people keep doing this to me. Lying to me, deceiving me, fucking up my life, and hurting me. It was one thing when it was just me... but then that bitch locked my screaming baby in a bathroom.

"People aren't afraid of me," I hissed. "They look at me and see another doe-eyed, naïve victim, and that *is* my fault."

Bane took my face in his hands, eyes huge and pleading. "No, it's not."

"It is. I let Lyla, Damien, Charlie, Luca, and so many others get away with crushing me under their heels and smearing me across the sidewalk. What else do you call that but weak?! But no more, Bane. Not again."

I nodded to myself—more secure in my decision than I'd ever been.

"For my daughter. For my sister. For the man I love. I can be the monster that monsters are afraid of." I grasped his face in turn. "Bane, teach me to be a Merchant."

BANE

"Bane, teach me to be a Merchant."

I heard the sentence, but it was not penetrating. "Excuse me? Kenzie, what are you talking about?"

The wild, blazing fervor in those haunting eyes burned brighter. "That day in my room after Athena clocked me in the face, you said you could turn me into someone people wouldn't dare hit, challenge, or mess with. Someone like Genny. Like you."

I tossed my head. "I did say that but—"

"But what?" she cried. "You've been teaching Sienna to fight. Why not me?" Kenzie pulled away, marching up to my wall of weapons. "You all have these fierce reputations in Cinco—Demone, Bane, FGH, Rat King. People who don't even know you know to be afraid of you. None would take your daughter and hand her off to a crack addict while they lined up someone to *buy her*." Kenzie took one of my guns off the wall, propelling me across the room.

"But I shot him," Kenzie gritted. "I put two bullets in his knees, and I would've put one through his head."

"What?" My brows blew up my head. "Who?"

"I've never understood my mother more than I do now. I would've killed to protect Laurel." She aimed the weapon at my television. "I will kill to protect her. No one will touch her again. The Blaines are through being victims."

I promptly disarmed her and returned the gun where it belonged. She kept pacing like she didn't notice. "Kenzie, slow down. Who did you shoot?"

"A piece of sludge," she replied, lips twisting. "Human waste, but still human. A person. I would've killed him to save Laurel, so you can stop thinking of me like a doe-eyed, naïve victim too."

"Dammit, woman, I don't think that!"

She jabbed my chest. "I'm strong enough to learn what you have to teach me, so say you will. Say you'll turn me into a Merchant."

"Kenzie—"

"Say it!"

"Okay," I bellowed, so damn turned around I finally understood the confusion I dealt people when I bowled them under my rapid-fire speech. "I said I would and I will, but you need to take a breath and talk to me."

"I am talking to you, Bane. I'm telling you exactly how it's going to be from now on, because I'm tired of life happening to me." I received another jab to the chest. "If you don't want a relationship with me, that's your choice and I respect it. But we're done with this avoiding-me and keeping-me-at-arm's-length nonsense.

"You're into me, and I'm into you. So with your consent, we're going to casually screw each other until you either break your vow or make the biggest mistake of your life and end it with me."

Now I really wasn't understanding what she was saying. The words I was hearing could not be the ones actually coming out of her mouth.

"We're going to what?"

"Give in to all this ridiculous sexual tension." She threw out her hands, and grabbed the hilt of a knife. "It's that doe-eyed thing that makes you believe I can't handle a casual relationship without falling hopelessly in love and getting my heart broken.

"Believe it or not, I don't waste my time getting hung up on men who don't want me. But then of course"—she bunched my shirt and sliced it with one swipe—"you do."

"What the fuck?!" Reacting out of instinct, I seized Kenzie's wrist and twisted her around. The knife hit the carpet and she went after it, legs tangling. I tried to catch her and we both went down, tumbling onto the couch.

Kenzie moved fast and flipped me over, straddling me. How stupid was I teaching her that move?

"Casual," she said, bearing down on my shoulders. "No strings. No commitment. We can't be around each other and not have sex. We can't be apart without feeling like we lost a friend. So, this is the compromise."

"We can't do this—casual or otherwise! You're dating my younger brother."

This did not slow her down. On the contrary, her shirt was off and across the room in a blink. "Sole and I already discussed it. He's got no problem following in your parents' footsteps."

I broke free of her easily, snapping her arms to her side. My ability to overpower her wasn't the problem, it was my capacity. She was tossing me around like a sex toy because the element of shock gave her great advantage.

"Just because he's okay with a poly relationship, doesn't mean he's cool with the other guy being his brother."

If anything, her smirk widened.

"Except you and Liam were specifically brought up and Sole said he's fine with it. You could call him and ask, but that would dampen the mood."

My mind spun. "Sole said that?" *That's not right. He couldn't have.*

That guy wouldn't share his candy, toys, and sometimes even his mother growing up. Wasn't afraid to bite every hand that got close when Mom was carrying him. I'm supposed to believe he gave the green light for the woman he loves to sleep with his brother?

"But that doesn't—"

Kenzie broke free and tore apart my zipper. "Pants off."

"Fucking hell," I cried as my button bounced off the wall. "I believe you mentioned my consent!"

"Oh?" Kenzie climbed off me, backing away. "Naturally, this only happens if we both want it. Can't have you pulling the same crap on me that you did after we kissed, saying it was a mistake and you got carried away."

She brushed one strap off her shoulder, then the next. A strangled noise left my throat as her jeans flew at me.

"So now's the time, Bane." Draping herself on my sectional, a naked Kenzie picked up the fallen knife and trailed it between her breasts. "Go ahead... say no."

My cock strained traitorously through my ruined zipper. That was one compelling vote against no.

But this could not happen. Believing her word about my brother's agreement while she was in the middle of a breakdown wasn't the best move. She talked about what I would regret. What about what Kenzie would regret when this feverish mood lifted, and the law-abiding single mom from North Quay realized she didn't want to learn to kill without conscience, or casually screw her teacher?

This is a recipe for disaster in every way, and no matter what she thinks, she is my friend. I can't help her fall apart—

Licking the flat of the blade, Kenzie crooked her finger. I sprang off the cushions and launched at her.

We collided in a shower of sparks, moans, and clashing tongues. It was a good thing Mackenzie could make me a replacement, because she shredded my jacket—slicing it to bits by way of taking it off. I took the damn thing off her and flung it across the room over her giggling.

"Say it." Kenzie ripped my pants down to my ankles. "Say it."

Tangling in her hair, I tipped her head back, breath stopping at that impish grin. "What am I agreeing to now?"

"Say that we're casual and you will worship my body on demand, until you're finally ready to accept we belong together."

I chuckled. "Fuck no."

Grinning wider, she slid up my body, wrapping her arms around my shoulders. "That's alright for now. I'll have you saying all sorts of things before this is over."

Something deep and primal burned in my chest, lighting the fire eroding all sense of rationality. I had good reasons to avoid relationships, and Mackenzie freaking Blaine. One night talking with her and I wanted to throw everything I promised out the window. I couldn't fathom what would happen if we started sleeping together, except for exactly what she threatened: I'd give in.

So stop, fool.

My fingers skated down her chest, finding their prize and tweaking soft, addictive sounds through those parted lips. Her peaked pebbles were tasty, soft prizes on soft mounds. They fit perfectly in the palm of my hands.

Back away. Stop kissing her.

Our tongues tangled, bursting flavors of my mint toothpaste and the chocolate cake she clearly had for dessert. Mint chocolate—a combination as perfect and illicit as us, and a fucking taunt from Mercury, the god of merchants.

End it now. Alarm bells rang from our first meeting. If anyone can make me weak, it's Mackenzie.

My boxers pooled on the floor. Kenzie reached for me and I tipped her, making her squeal. The woman had been tossing me around like the doe-eyed, naïve one. If I was about to make the biggest fucking mistake of my life, I was enjoying every minute of it.

Spreading her flat on the couch, I ran my palms down her arched body—groaning deep in my soul. "Fuck, you're incredible."

"Yes."

"And very frisky when the clothes are off."

She winked. "Also yes."

"Are you sure about this?" I had to ask, so later, when I was kicking myself, I could remember I did. "You went through something traumatic. The kind of thing that change a person." I flicked one pebble with my tongue, then the other. "But when you come out on the other side, you may not like who you've become, or the fact you can't go back."

"Are we talking about you training me or you fucking me? I promise I'll still like myself in the morning."

Chuckling, I replied, "Training. Neither of us can stop the second part now."

I slowly lifted and parted her legs, hissing at the damp beads collected at her entrance. She was already wet for me, and the stupid, infatuated idiot I carried in my pants had a gift in return. Kenzie swiped the precum off my tip. Holding my gaze, she swallowed her finger. I nearly came on the spot.

"I'm sure," she said. "There's nothing noble about dying or getting injured because you were too weak to win."

"You shouldn't quote me." I licked a stripe past her seam and was gifted another breathy moan to add to my collection. "I say a lot of stupid shit."

"Not that," she said. "You were right, Bane. There's nothing noble about not being able to protect myself or my daughter. I saw my fate today on a playground. I have to be stronger... not just for me."

I kissed the soft skin between her leg and pussy. "I'm going to work you hard, Blaine."

"Ooh, I hope so," she breathed.

"Still talking about the first thing." I smirked at her. "Kind of." The other side received a nip. "I'll ask you to do things you swore on your old morals you'd never do. I'll break you. Take apart the old Mackenzie Blaine and remove everything that made her who she is. The new you will be harder, fiercer, and unrecognizable," I said.

"At times you'll beg for me to stop. You'll say you can't handle anymore, and ask for mercy I never learned to give."

"Goodness. Are we still talking about training?"

"No."

Snapping her to me, I feasted to my heart's content. Licking, nipping, tasting her sweetness—Kenzie opened herself to me completely. It'd been weeks since I'd been with anyone, and years since my first time. You shouldn't forget what sex is like that quickly, and still I was discovering everything brand new.

Her thighs—both firm and soft beneath my hands. The stubbly prickles of her shaved middle against my nose. The sweet scent of arousal. The sweet pain of her nails digging in my scalp.

I stopped.

"Bane!"

"That was my favorite jacket," I said mildly. "There should be some punishment for that."

"No, there shouldn't."

Flipping her over, I covered her body with mine—marveling at her warmth. The soft shell of her ear teased between my teeth. "Yes," I whispered. "There should."

I kissed behind her ear, then the nape of her neck. "Say sorry."

"No," she growled.

What did it say about me that her stubbornness made my cock twitch?

Nipping and kissing down her spine, Kenzie shuddered beneath me. "Say it. You don't come until you do."

"You don't come until I do."

My grin was wolfish. "I'll take that bet."

Reaching the end of my trail, I curled under her legs and descended again. Over and over, I brought her to the end of orgasm and then pulled out. Kenzie was cursing and begging me in equal measure.

"I fucking swear, Alexander," she gasped. "You could have a blow job coming or a blow to the head. You are gambling away the last of your luck— Uh, yes, baby. Right there."

"Right there?" I crooked my finger, picking up the pace as her clit tortured under my tongue. Her cries turned higher, about rattling the walls. I was glad the builders soundproofed the mess out of the Fairfield decades ago. If anyone busted in to help the woman in "distress" and interrupted us right now, I would lose my mind.

No one would save Kenzie from me.

"So close," I gruffed. "Say it."

She whimpered. Beads of sweat slicked her skin, making her shine under the spotlight fluorescents. "Bane, please."

"What's it going to be? You're so close I can taste it. Be a shame to stop now."

"Add evil to your list of character traits! Uhh," she half moaned, half whined. "Dammit, I'm sorry. I'm sorry, baby, please don't stop."

I pulled one finger out. "Sorry for what?"

Kenzie whapped me square on the left butt cheek, ripping a laugh out of me. This was the most fun, violent sex I ever had.

"I'm sorry your blow job is going to be all teeth."

"Close enough." Lifting us both up—me on my knees and Kenzie practically on her head—I took my finger out, and slipped my tongue in. Kenzie moaned loud and without abandon as I tongue-fucked her sweeter-than-mint-chocolate pussy. Suddenly, she went rigid.

Kenzie came, digging so hard in the couch she pierced the leather.

"Wow." She slid boneless out of my hold, turning on her back. "You're not afraid to torture a girl, but at least it's worth the wait."

I fished a condom from the remains of my pants. "First lesson: like promises, threats are meant to be kept."

"Mmm. I'll remember that." Kenzie grinned, curling around my neck as I settled her on my lap. "What's lesson number two?"

"All in due time." Gripping her hips, I slowly lowered her on my cock—eyes rolling up in my head as I was sheathed in her warm, tight hole. "I plan on being thorough. Making sure every lesson"—I thrust hard—"penetrates."

"Uh!" Pleasure and pain laced her cry. She leaned back—head hanging, gripping my shoulders. I started pumping and Kenzie met me dip for buck.

We set a fast, punishing pace. Kenzie bounced on my lap like she was putting out a fire. Her screams definitely made it seem like she was feeling the heat.

I buried my face in her heaving bosom, thanking Mercury for the day this woman emerged from the trees. "I'm so glad you weren't a stack of porn."

Kenzie's laugh was part sharp intake of breath. "Not sure what that means, but I am too."

My balls tightened, and my grip on her waist with it. "This is just sex. Hot, dirty, sweaty sex, but just sex." I didn't know if I was saying it to her, or me. "We can't be more, Kenzie.

"When the Brotherhood took you— When they hurt you, I changed too."

"Oh, Bane," she whispered—almost too low for me to hear. Raising my head, she crushed our lips together. Or maybe I did.

Kissing passionately, I exploded inside her—pouring my fears, pain, ecstasy, and everything I couldn't say into Kenzie.

I came down like a skydiver without a shoot, collapsing flat on my back—spent. Kenzie curled up on my chest, practically purring.

"You're not out of practice at all."

"I wasn't worried about my skills." I tucked her between me and the couch. Our damp foreheads pressed together, gazes locked. "Were you?"

"Nope," she said, pecking my nose. "I knew it would be perfect."

Sighing, I traced designs on her hip. "We should have ground rules."

"Don't the standard ones apply?"

"What are they?"

"We're not boyfriend and girlfriend, so we don't act like it. No carriage rides through Mercy Park. No candlelit dinners at Estelle where we gaze soulfully into each other's eyes. No late nights talking on the phone—"

"No," I broke in. "Not that. You can always talk to me, Kenzie. Anytime. About anything. I've behaved like a jackass since before New York, but no more. No matter what, you and I will always be friends."

She smiled so happily it punched a hole through my gut. This is why she was kryptonite to me. I have no defenses around Mackenzie Blaine.

"Okay, lots of talking," she amended. "But no drama. We're both adults. We can be mature about a casual relationship. Last, no... no monogamy."

I caught the hesitation, but didn't comment on it. "Those are pretty standard," I said, "but you left out the big one. No falling in love."

Kenzie traced my lips. "Don't think either one of us has control over that. A fact I'm counting on."

"Final rule," I said wryly. "Be less up front about your master plan to ensnare me for good."

She giggled. "I can do that. So what about training? When do we start? What kind of things will we do?"

Eagerness laced her tone, filling me with an emotion of a different type. Liam told me about the time he subtly offered to let her *interrogate* the valet that nearly got her and Tricky killed. She couldn't get out of his apartment fast enough. Now she's chasing the cold, merciless life we've been living without a pause.

I said I always wanted us to talk. Do it now before this goes further.

"What kind of things do you want to do?" I asked carefully. "How far are you willing to go?"

"As far as it takes."

"Is it revenge you want? You can't take your rage out on Luca now that he's dead, so the Brotherhood is the next best target."

Calmly, she shook her head, moving against me. "This isn't about rage or revenge. I realized something today. The Brotherhood used me to lure you guys into a trap, and it almost worked. They could be thinking all they have to do is try again and get it right next time, and where does that leave me, Bane?"

"Hiding away in the Fairfield forever? Only stepping foot outside with a Merchant escort? That's not a life for me, Sienna, or Laurel."

"It'd only be until we find and stop the Brotherhood," I protested.

"How long will that take? The only thing you guys can agree on is that the leader could be one of a thousand people. We don't have a way to narrow the list yet. Besides, I don't want to wait until you stop them, I want to help. Help find Vito. Help stop the attacks. Help River find those missing kids."

She didn't need to explain the last part. I knew what Luca did to those other children. The death Sunny gave him was too quick.

"What's that look, Bane?" Kenzie smoothed the line between my brows. "You said you would teach me. You said it before all of this started."

"I will teach you. I'd never deny anyone the right to protect themselves. More than anyone, I want you to feel safe."

She relaxed. "Okay, good. Then what's wrong?"

"Motivation is everything, Kenzie. What we're going to do will blow leagues past your limits."

"My limits never kept me safe. They never protected Laurel. It's time to leave them behind."

I nodded. "Then, we start tomorrow. We—"

The door banged open. "Yo, Bane," Sunny shouted. "Is Kenzie still here? Laurel... is..."

We sprang up, trying and failing to cover ourselves. I tipped off the couch seizing a pillow as Sunny stopped dead on the carpet.

"Sunny, I— I was just—"

"Fucking," he completed. "Or were you going to tell me you were helping Mommy scratch her back like the time I walked in on my parents?"

Kenzie's jaw froze hanging open.

Sole laughed, making my heart attack complete. "Easy, sweet lips. It's my fault for not knocking. I hadn't realized you guys progressed this far in the relationship."

"We haven't," I said quickly. "I mean, I'm sorry. I should've spoken to you before anything happened. Made sure you were cool."

He shrugged. "I'm cool. Just came up to say Laurel's up from her nap and Tricky's claiming her time." Sunny backed toward the door. "Liam's taking her down to the pool and she's asking if Laurel can come."

"Not without me," Kenzie confirmed. "I'll come down and get her ready in a minute. Thanks, Sunny." Part of me sensed she wasn't just thanking him for playing messenger.

"No prob—" He halted. "Wait, what's this? What the hell is this?"

"What?" I stuck my head over the couch. At Sunny's feet was a piece of my jacket's remains. "It's leather. What's the problem?"

"This is." Crouching, Sunny pinched the strip, turning it for us to see. "But this is not."

My eyes widened, then hardened. "Holy shit. What the fuck is that?"

"A microchip," Kenzie whispered. "Oh my gosh, it's a bug. It's a—"

Sunny put a finger to his lips, shaking his head sharply. "Get dressed and meet me downstairs. I have a fuck ugly feeling."

MACKENZIE

Fuck ugly wasn't the description for the feeling that gripped me an hour later as Sunny, Bane, Liam, Sienna, Fuller, Shonda, and I gathered around the pile. Fifty-four little chips, and beside them, the tattered remains of Sunny's wardrobe.

I flinched as he tore a seam through the last jacket. He pried off the hollow metal cap of the pocket's snap. Beneath it was another device.

"That settles it," Fuller said, cheeks pale. "Those *things* are only in the clothes we've ordered from Caddell House."

"Not all of them." There was a hard, flat edge in Sunny's voice. He knelt on the ground. "I ordered these pants last year in November for the Christmas party and they came with something extra. These I ordered three or four months before that and they're clean."

Shonda shuddered. "Are we sure they're not listening to us? Liam?"

"I'm certain," Liam replied. "They're GPS microchips—made to be so small, they can be sewn into clothes. I remember researching it when it was first announced. The idea was to use it to protect royalty, celebrities, or athletes. Anyone tries to kidnap and hold them for ransom, it won't work out so well. The Brotherhood decided to put them to another use."

Of course it was the Brotherhood. It couldn't be anyone else.

I dropped next to Sunny, picking up a metal snap. "It's genius," I was forced to say. "They're metal, so X-rays won't see through to what's inside. A detector would beep the metal and nothing else. Plus, they enclosed the cap so water doesn't get inside when it's washed. Genius, but so simple. That's the worst part—how simple it was."

Grave expressions surrounded me.

"This explains everything," Bane said. "Everyone in this damn building wears Caddell. We put the entire staff on the account. That's how Snyder knew Sunny left the compound that night without security."

"That's how he knew I was on my way to La Belle's," Liam said.

It hit me like a brick to the head. "And how he knew Sunny was nearby watching the exact moment Grant passed him the note. This explains how the Brotherhood discovered your routes and secret warehouses. There was never a rat in the Sons of Saint! Whenever you wore Caddell, they've known exactly where you are every minute of every day."

"Please stop, Kenzie," Shonda cried, clapping her hand over her mouth. "I think I'm going to be sick. I've never felt so violated."

"For that I'm sorry," Liam said. "We're the ones who encouraged you to wear these clothes."

Fuller squeezed his shoulder. "Come, now, Liam. You couldn't have known. The only ones at fault here are the skulking sewer rats who did this."

"But who did do this?" Sienna asked. "I've lived with my sister long enough to know the work on that clasp was done by a designer. If they sewed the clasp on, then they're the ones who put the chip in. Not some hulking Brotherhood brute."

I bobbed my head to each word. "Sienna's right. This wasn't contracted out. See the stitchwork around the clasp and to sew it in?" I showed Sunny and Liam. "Whoever did this is a Caddell designer. Do you know who designs your clothes? We can question them right now—find out how deep with the Brotherhood they are."

"We don't know who it is," Bane admitted. "We all have access to an online account. We put in what we want, then the clothes arrive at a separate location to be x-rayed, then brought here. There's no need to talk to the person on the other side."

"You can help more than us," Sunny said. "You worked in Caddell House. You were around while our orders were coming in. The Johnson account. Did you ever clock the one sewing on our buttons?"

"You were the Johnson account? I can't believe it. Talia said you guys were VIPs. Only the best of the best could even sneeze in proximity to your fabrics, let alone design something for you. In this case, the best of the best were the senior designers."

Bane stepped forward. "That's it. The Brotherhood's man is one of the senior designers."

"Not necessarily," I said. "The seniors designed these no question, but sewing buttons and snaps is grunt work—intern work. I sewed a million of these when I first started. It's the closest we get to putting our stamp on couture. But," I said as he started to reply. "If the client is important enough, they don't trust interns with their clothes and pass those off on the junior designers. That's about thirty people right there. By the way, this is only assuming the senior designer is passing the final touches off. Now we're up to fifty."

"Why would that be the case?" Liam asked. "It's a simple matter of walking in there and demanding to know who sewed those snaps on."

I looked at him head-on. "You do that and dozens of hands will go up. That's what I'm trying to say, but I'm not doing it well. Anyone in Caddell House can sew on a snap, even the lowest grunt. In the mornings, we used to come in and find half a dozen racks of clothes waiting for their final touches.

"We weren't assigned specific accounts. We picked at random," I confessed. "But more important than all of that, there's the fact your finished clothes sit in the Closet until they're ready to be shipped out. Someone could go in, unpick the snaps, and sew their compromised one when no one is around. If they're not a complete idiot, that's exactly what they're doing. If the chips are ever found, no one could point to them."

"Basically," Liam said, "it could be anyone in the building."

"Any designer in the building. At least we can rule out the sustainability officer or the customer relationship manager. Anyone who isn't a designer works on another floor in a separate department. They'd be noticed if they were hanging around the Closet or on the floor."

"How do you suggest we find this person, Mackenzie?" Fuller asked. "If they're covering their tracks so someone else is blamed in their place, we have to be sure."

I chewed my lips, picking through the shredded fabric. "This is good work, but it's not unique. We're all taught how to do this stitch. I'm sorry, but the only way we can know for sure we've got the right person is to catch them in the act."

"We can't," Bane said. "People who work in the building are eyed suspiciously for being on the wrong floor. What do we say when they ask why we're hanging around the Closet?"

Liam put up his hand. "We are several steps ahead of ourselves. The most important thing is that we know how they breached our security, and we know where to find the person responsible. Whether they're just another hired hand or one of the brothers, will be discovered under interrogation."

"Liam's right. That bitch can wait a second," Sole said. "All of you, right now need to go into your closets and rip off some snaps. Do it in the closet. They're tracking us and that's the only place these chips are supposed to be together."

"Okay," Shonda said. She took off to do as he ordered.

"Big bros," Sunny continued. "I pretty much confirmed it, but we have to be sure. Check all your clothes, not just the Caddells. And keep track of when you ordered what. We're up to November of last year. If that's when this started, we can exclude anyone who left before then." He kissed my shoulder.

My brows popped. "Oh, I have to be crossed off the suspect list?"

"You're not on it," Bane said. "If you did this, you wouldn't have sliced my jacket like a ham."

"That's not the only reason you know I'm not behind this," I said, outraged. "Jerks."

They laughed—short, sharp sounds that were over quickly.

"We have an issue," Liam said. "I'll check my clothes, but if all the trackers are removed, they'll know we're onto them, and their accomplice in Caddell vanishes into the wind."

"I know," Sunny replied. "That's why the sexy designer with the bee-stung lips on my left will sew them back in. We have to keep going like nothing happened. Finally, we're a step ahead of them."

"Are you?" Sienna asked. "You all still have your gangs to run. How can you go on like it's business as usual while the Brotherhood continues collecting the information that's made you vulnerable? Genny's girls were blown up in that—" Sienna's eyes bugged. "Oh no."

"Genny!"

We shot up, racing out of the closet. What the fuck was wrong with us! Why did we sit in there chattering away!

"Genny wears Caddell," I said, tripping over my feet beating Sunny to the door. "She doesn't know about the trackers. She thinks she's safe in her new place when she's leading them right to her door."

"Perfect sitting target far from the Fairfield," Liam growled. "Where is she? Does anyone know!"

"She didn't tell me," Sienna said.

"No." I shoved my shoes on, throwing myself out the door on Sunny and Bane's heels. "But I have her number! I'll text her. Warn her." My phone was already out and fingers flying across the screen.

"She's probably at Barbarella's. She's fine," Bane said, though he punched the elevator button hard enough to pop it out. "Come on!"

"Guys?" Shonda skidded into the hall. "Guys, wait!"

"Not now," Sunny barked. "Genny doesn't know she's walking around with a target in her jacket!"

"It's about Genny!" We froze half in the elevator and half out. "I think it is— I hope not but it could— You just need to see this!"

She ran back inside. Our group shared a look.

"I'll see what it is," I said, stepping off. "You guys go to Harlow."

I hit *send* on the text. "I just messaged her. She'll know what to do as soon as she sees this. It's alright."

"Okay." Bane, Sunny, and Liam said goodbye as the metal doors closed shut.

Sienna and I ran inside the penthouse calling for Shonda.

"In here," she shouted. "Look at this."

We burst into her room. Sole treated his employees as well as he treated his girlfriends. Shonda's room was decked out with everything she could want—four-poster bed, plush carpet, vintage guitar collection, and a television rivaling the size of the living room big screen.

The news played on loud, drawing us to her side.

"—shock here in Harlow." A stocky, tanned reporter stood on a street I didn't recognize. Behind her was a horror. "An explosion in Goldie's Tavern rocked the sleepy street this morning. Residents say the bar has been closed for years, but there is an attached apartment on the top floor."

"No," I whispered.

"It's too early to say if someone or someones were in the apartment at the time of the explosion."

Flames engulfed the tavern, sending acrid smoke billowing into the sky—a beacon for all to see. My feet moved on their own power, carrying me to the window. There in the distance... was that beacon.

"If someone was inside," the reporter went on, "all we can say is God have mercy on their soul."

I STARED AT MY PHONE, willing it to buzz, ring, do something!

Sunny took it from me and placed Laurel on my lap. The baby looked at me curiously like she sensed I was sad and wanted to know why. I held her close, murmuring comforting words I didn't feel.

"That's not Genny," Liam said. He, Bane, and Sole returned to the Fairfield at my call. Where else would they go? They drove all over Harlow and went to Barbarella's. There was no sign of her. Bugsy said they hadn't seen or heard from her in hours. The Cardinals fled the bar, picking up the search when the guys headed back. They were worried. How did I convince myself not to be?

"It's not her," Liam repeated, flipping through news channels. The bombing in Harlow played on every one.

Cameras focused on attractive, well-dressed reporters, but the scene behind them was all we cared about. Firefighters hosed the remains down while cops swarmed the street and maintained the barricade. That's why we weren't there. We had no chance of getting close, and also because we refused to believe there was a grim truth waiting for us if we did.

"They can't have rallied that fast," Liam said. "We killed their assassin bomber and a number of their men. Recovering and rigging Genny's new place that quickly isn't possible. Especially when she would've taken precautions against that very thing. It's not her."

I'd never seen him like this. Agitated. Rumpled. Talking fast. Pacing. His reassurances aren't for us. They're for him.

"We know you're right, man," Sunny said. "Our sister? Taken out like this? Nah. Genny's going out on the back of a flaming bike, blasting two shotguns as she soars off a cliff. Dying like this is beneath her. She'd never allow it."

Sighing, I buried my face in Laurel's curls, wishing she wasn't picking up on the energy in the room. "Why isn't she answering the phone?" I rasped. "Genny does her own thing, but she wouldn't mess around, knocking back beers and laughing, while we're blowing her up because we think she's gone."

I gazed at each in turn. I saw on their face they wanted to argue with me, but couldn't. They knew Genny wouldn't put us through this hell for fun. Something was stopping her from sending a reply.

"We have to go out there," I said. "We have to know for sure."

"We can't get near the place until they put out the fire and the cops clear out," Bane said. "But by then, they'll announce... if they've found a body."

A heavy silence blanketed the room.

"No," Sienna said, dragging my attention up. "She's not dead. She can't be. My visions have been murky since our lives entwined with yours, but I have to believe I would've seen if such a dark, violent death was waiting on Genny's horizon. There's a reason why she hasn't responded, and she'll tell us when she swaggers into the Fairfield, looking amazing even with a cast and sling. Understand?"

Bane, Liam, Sunny, and I just gave her blank looks.

"Genny is fine," Sienna repeated, "but we do need to find her and tell her about these trackers before she does lead the Brotherhood somewhere she's vulnerable. The same goes for you, guys." Sienna dropped on the couch, bringing Sunny with her. "You said the trackers had to be put back so the Brotherhood doesn't get suspicious. There has to be a part two of the plan. What is it?"

"Sienna..."

"Please," she pushed, squeezing his arm. "We all agree we can't do anything until Genny calls or the fire is put out. If we have to stew in this hell, at least let us plan their downfall while we do it."

Something sharp and acrid leached into my veins. "That sounds like a good way to spend our time," I hissed. "What will we do, Sunny? They can't know we found the trackers, but we also can't let them continue tracking you guys while we're going after them."

Sunny forced himself to look away from the screen. "They— They can't know we found the trackers before we find the person sewing them in. The sooner we do that, the sooner we're another step closer to taking down the Brotherhood. I have an idea but there's only one way to pull it off—"

"Sole, listen!" Liam barked. The television volume increased to deafening levels, drowning Sunny out. I carried Laurel a distance from the noise.

"—firefighter has confirmed from the aerial ladder. The second-floor apartment was occupied at the time of the bombing. There is a body inside."

SILENCE STOLE THE AIR—SMOTHERING sound, breath, and movement in the car. Sunny, Sienna, and I didn't speak. Didn't look at each other. Didn't breathe loud enough to let the other know we were alive.

Harlow was a beautiful place at night. Its secrets were blanketed under neon lights, laughing couples flitting from club to club, and the buzz of a sleepless city. It was all a multicolored blur as I laid my head against the window, watching my tears fall in our mirrored reflection.

"Why are we doing this?" My voice couldn't climb higher than a whisper. "How will it make any of us feel better to see where it happened in person?"

"It's not Genny." Sunny didn't speak in his usual bright, why-frown-when-a-grin-looks-so-much-better-on-me tone, but that optimism was there anyway. He would not believe Genny was gone—even as the cops wheeled out the body bag. "A look around will prove it. None of the charred crap in the wreckage will be hers. After we confirm it, we can move on to tracking down where she really is."

"Lying low in a place that doesn't have a stitch of Caddell around," Sienna said from the back. "The more I think about this, the angrier it makes me. Part of me wanted to believe it was an innocent person who was being threatened. Harmless fashion majors get high-end couture jobs, not gangsters. But it can't be that simple."

I raised my head, turning aching eyes on her. "What do you mean?"

"This has gone on for months. Months and months, guys. If this was an innocent person who didn't want to do this, they could've figured out a way to sew in a warning like they did those trackers."

Sunny and I shared a look. I didn't know what went through his mind, but that thought hadn't crossed mine.

"You're right." I sat up straight. "After the clothes are finished, they go from the Closet to the garment bags to the customer. A Brotherhood minion wouldn't have a chance to check the clothes before they go to you, Sunny. A little note sewn inside your pocket, and the innocent people they sold out would be warned. Either they had a pretty sweet deal and didn't care what happened to the *Johnsons,* or they know exactly who you are and want to take you out like the rest of their friends."

"Not a victim of the Brotherhood, but an actual brother working in Caddell House," Sunny said. "They couldn't fake their way in there. They'd have to be a real designer with talent that earned their job, correct?"

I nodded.

"So, what does a designer working their dream job with one of the top designers in the country have to be mad at the Merchants about? Snyder said they wanted to free the city, but it sounds like this guy is doing pretty well for himself."

"Revenge against your dad. Against your parents," Sienna said. "For a crime that can't be washed away by money, fame, or a career."

"That can't be the motivation for every brother in this gang," Sunny replied. "My folks haven't been that busy."

"True."

"Then it's greed," I said, tone flat. "The Brotherhood pays them handsomely to sew in some trackers and go on like nothing happened. If a few bombs blow up and people d-die, why should they care?"

Sunny laced his fingers through mine. Miraculously, he smiled. "She's not dead. My sister plans to be the one to bury us. She's told us so multiple times. Genny will take no pleasure in it, but evidently our balls will lead us from one stupid act to another until testosterone is the cause of our early demise. Getting taken out first because we figured this out before her?" He snorted. "She'd come back from the dead before that happened."

I tried for a smile in return. "I love that sunny outlook," I said simply.

We didn't speak for the rest of the ride. Again, I did not know what was going through their minds, but there was a single thought in mine. The person who gave the Brotherhood the means to track Genny down while she was alone and outnumbered, was no harmless innocent.

And Bane would teach me everything I needed to know to ensure they suffered twice as much as Genny.

I will be someone so feared, no one dare hurt the people I love again. I will be a Merchant.

Sunny pulled up to the curb, dragging me out of my thoughts. We climbed out as Liam parked. He and Bane fell in beside us, staring across the street at the burned-out wreckage that was the tavern.

Most of it was gone. What the explosion didn't incinerate or blow seven blocks away, was left to be consumed by the fire. We ducked under the police tape, shining flashlights on charred booth remains and splintered wood. Sunny said we were looking for proof Genny had never been here. Why did it feel like we were looking for something else?

Liam moved toward where the bar once stood—if all the broken glass was anything to go by. He frowned.

"Liam?" I called. "What is it?"

"The report that there was another bombing concerned us all, of course. The last few were distinctly Merchant-related, but now that we're here, none of this is right." His frown deepened gazing around. "Empty bar. Second-floor apartment. This is the home of a wannabe actress fresh from community college. It's not the home of a Merchant, or a home that rivals the Fairfield. How was she supposed to be safer here than the last safe house?"

"You've got a point, brother mine." Sunny stepped over a fallen beam. "I clock three buildings where a sniper could line their shot. Also, this place is too out of the way."

"Why is that a bad thing?" Sienna asked.

"I told you my sister prefers to be where the trouble is. Like Barbarella's and her last place. If anyone's going to cause some shit, they'd better be prepared to do it with witnesses filming them and sending their mugs viral. Unfortunately, the Brotherhood was happy to spray bullets into the crowd around her safe house, but that's the same crowd that gave her cover to get away."

"Out here in this back-alley abandoned building, the Brotherhood would surround this place and no one would be around to see or call for help," I finished. "Oh my gosh, Liam, it's true. This isn't an upgrade on the locked-down fortress Genny walked out of. She was reckless, but not this reckless. She wouldn't live here."

I laughed—a joyful, light sound. Sunny's optimism and Liam's logic—together they were powerful enough to make me believe anything, and I believed in them. Genny would not choose this place as safe house number three. She was alive.

"But someone did die here." I curled around Sunny's fingers. "Some poor soul blown up. Why? If this isn't about the Brotherhood and the Merchants, who else is out here setting bombs?" My flashlight scanned the remains. "This isn't the most common murder weapon."

Dusting off his hands, Liam headed for his car. "That's for the Cinco PD to determine. We need to find our sister."

"We should check with Mom and Dads," Bane offered. We turned away, stepping over the mess, clearing out. "It's a long shot, but maybe she took the roundabout way up there and left her phone behind. She knows we're being tracked even if she doesn't know how. She wouldn't risk leading them to our parents."

"Wait. What about your parents?" I cried. "Do they know about the trackers?"

"They don't wear Caddell anymore," Bane said. "High fashion tends to be more about style than comfort. I'm told by the time you hit your sixties, you favor the latter."

"Fair enough. At least we know they're safe— Wait." I stopped, finally noticing someone missing. Spinning around, I fell on Sienna standing amidst the debris. She didn't seem to notice us all walking away. "Sienna? Sienna, what are you doing?"

"Shh. Do you hear that?"

"Hear what?"

She shushed me again. Kneeling down, Sienna cocked her head, brows furrowing. She flapped an agitated hand, signaling us to come back.

"What's going on?" Liam asked.

"I hear something. Guys, get over here."

I approached Sienna, listening close. She knelt beside the beam, practically putting her ear against it.

"Listen."

"Si, what am I listening—"

"...out..."

Shooting forward, I stuck my face against the beam. "What was that?"

"What was what?" Bane asked. "I don't hear anything."

My flashlight was on with a click, sweeping over the floor. This part of the bar floor was covered with the charred remains of a rug. *Strange in and of itself. Why put a rug down in a bar room? It's destined to get gross and grimy from a thousand dirty boots.*

I peeled the rug up. My eyes bugged.

"Guys, we need to get this beam off. Now!"

They didn't ask me why. The guys fell by our side, planting their hands on the wood.

"Ready?" Sienna called. "One, two, three. Push."

We strained—digging our feet in, shoving on the obstacle. It held stubborn, not budging an inch.

"Harder," I groaned. "One, two, three. Push."

Bane put his shoulder into it. His muscles rippled beneath the tight gray tee gifted the privilege of hugging his body. A gift I only received recently, and that's because I took it. Recent events got in the way of us finishing our conversation after I demanded he turn me into the deadliest version of myself, then threw myself at him. But we would have that conversation soon.

The beam scraped across the floor inch... by inch... by inch—

The rug popped up. "—me out!"

Shoving it the rest of the way, Sienna scrambled to throw the rug off, revealing a trap metal door. I flung it open and gazed down into the incensed eyes of Genevieve Hunt.

"It's about fucking time! What the hell were you all doing? Waiting for an engraved invitation!"

Genny climbed out only to be tackled by me. I smothered her—for all of a second. She snaked out of my hold and rolled away. Impressive with her leg still in a boot.

"Fuck's sake, woman, I told you about the cuddling. You want that, your toy boy is over there." She straightened, and got an armful of Sienna. I threw my arms around them both over her protests.

"Glad to see you're not dead," Liam drawled. "Also glad to see why. This bar is the worst safe house imaginable, but apparently it comes with a secret."

"Course it does," Genny said, peeling us off. "This exposed piece of crap way out in the middle of nowhere? It'd have to have a secret for me to bother. Gangsters have always ruled Cinco. Back in the Prohibition days, this tavern was a dance club, but the underground room was where the real party happened.

"This place passed down through the family—each member smart enough to keep the basement off any city maps. The last guy remodeled and outfitted the place to withstand..." She gazed around the monument that stood for decades, now reduced to rubble.

"This," she finished. "The apartment upstairs was just a decoy. I've been sleeping down there. Good thing. They found me quicker than expected."

"They always knew where you were, Genny." Sunny motioned to her jeans. "GPS chips."

"What the—?"

"Trust me, you'll have time to let out that rant, but we've got to get out of here," Sunny said. "You got a change of clothes down there? Put on something that isn't Caddell. They'll find out you're not dead soon enough. Don't see why we should make it easy for them."

Genny didn't argue. She climbed down in her bootlegger bunker, leaving me on top to take my first real breath.

"There's one last question," Liam said. Something in his tone wiped away my smile. "If Genny was down there when the bomb went off. Who was upstairs? Whose body did they load in the back of a van?"

None of us had an answer for him.

Chapter Five

Sunny

Genny toweled off her hair, grimacing while doing it. Her shoulder still smarted but what a waste of time it would be to tell her to take it easy. Stretching out on my couch, she plopped her head on my girlfriend's lap.

"Putting trackers in our clothes for months," she repeated. "Whoever this guy is, they're a Liam type of cunning, and it pisses me off."

"This play was smart," I said, "but it's got nothing on what we're about to do next."

"What are we about to do?" Sienna asked. "I still say it's not safe for you guys to keep wearing those trackers, even if you don't want the Brotherhood to know you're onto them. They've graduated to drugging, murder, kidnapping, shooting, and bombing. They're not messing around anymore."

"That's what I started to say before." I left the kitchen, carrying a round of beers. Liam, Bane, Genny, and the underaged Sienna got one. My silver-tipped angel just let her head fall back on the couch, sighing through the strain etched in her perfect skin. "We only have to keep the charade going long enough to find their rat in Caddell House. If the trackers all go offline, they'll know we're onto them and run. Can't say how long it'll take to track down Vito. We're not losing another one of these brothers in the meantime."

"What's the plan?" Bane asked.

I dropped next to Kenzie, tucking her under my arm. She immediately rested her head on my shoulder, murmuring she loved me. I liked that—her loving me. I liked it quite a bit.

"Our dear uncle just came into a couple of homeless shelters. Being the generous altruistic people we are, and to celebrate our new truce, we decide to donate most of our old wardrobe to those in need."

Liam leaned forward in his seat, expression changing. "Yes. That's exactly what we do."

"We keep a couple of the tampered Caddells. Wear them around town while doing business as usual with our guards watching our backs. They'll have no reason to think we're dumping the trackers, because we didn't.

"Naturally, we'll need new wardrobes, so we put in a massive order." Now they were all leaning in. Kenzie turned her head up to me. Gen raised hers. They were rapt. "Jackets, pants, belts, dresses—everything and a lot of it. With all those clothes to tamper with, it'll give dozens of opportunities to catch the bastard in the act."

I swung to my favorite girl. "That's where you come in."

Kenzie blinked. "Me?"

"Yes, you, Candy Nipples."

Her cheeks flushed. "We talked about the nicknames we keep private," she hissed.

I popped a kiss on those pursed lips. "We need someone with a legitimate reason to be there, searching out the one who's doing this. Sienna said fate dropped me on your tent, and I believe it now more than ever.

"You're a designer, Kenzie. Get your job back and you can go everywhere this shit goes. When they make their move, you'll catch them, we'll pick them up, then we're a step closer to finding out who's leading the Brotherhood. We can stop this before it blows into an all-out war."

"Sunny, I love that plan, except there's one thing fundamentally wrong with it. I won't get my job back. They think I'm a fraud and a thief," she cried. "Talia bad-mouthed me to every fashion house in town. From Gucci to Green Mart. The hiring manager would sooner shoot me on sight than give me back my desk."

"Talia and that moronic shithead would stand in the way of you getting your job back, but they ran off to New York." I rubbed her arm. "Hollywell has taken over as creative director and he knows who the Johnsons really are. He's not stupid enough to argue when I tell him you're rehired."

"It's not just him." Kenzie pushed off the couch. "The Brotherhood knows I'm with you guys. What if they see right through this? A trap for the rat could easily become another trap for me. Bane and I haven't started training yet."

"Training?" Genny, Liam, and I said at the same time.

"Yes, training. He's going to teach me everything he knows so that the shipping yard and New York never happens again."

I turned raised brows on Bane. "I don't even know everything he knows." My brother beamed at me. "If training is what you're after, why didn't you say? Watching you knife-throw is a recurring fantasy of mine, Angel."

"No one is saying that fantasy won't come true," she said, returning to my side. "But I'm serious. You put in a massive order, then install me in Caddell House? If this shadow leader is so smart, won't he put those pieces together?"

"It's all in what you say," Liam threw in. "They won't expect something's up because every move we make will be within the realm of possible. We have a new enemy that evades us by going into Rockchapel. Makes sense we'd decide now is a good time to make an alliance with the Rat King. The Merchants are also working with Delaney to help Adams's victims. Why wouldn't we donate clothes to people who've lost everything?"

I nodded along. "Anyone who knows the story of your firing, should know you proclaimed your innocence far and wide. You've got yourself a boyfriend who can pull strings. Why not use him to take back everything unjustly stolen from you, and show up a few primp assholes while doing it."

"Because I would never use you."

"They don't know that," Bane said gently. "They don't know you, Kenzie. That's the point. You're not a banger, thief, con woman, or hit woman. You're a normal person who landed a rich boyfriend. They won't expect the next strike to come from someone they've labeled disposable."

She visibly stiffened. "Okay, you have a point. With my history at CH, most people would jump to me using my boyfriend's power to rub out the stains from my past. But even if they don't think my threat to them is real, their threat to me is. They attacked Genny at the first opportunity. Losing all those men less than a week ago didn't slow them down. Obviously, they're done with the subtle approach."

Kenzie looked to Bane. "I want to fight and protect all of you, but if there was ever a test of if I was ready to do it, it was when that monster took my baby. I wasn't strong enough to stop Luca, but I will be next time. After Bane trains me."

Frowning, I turned her back to me. "Kenzie, I want you to have all the self-defense training you want, but not because you think you have to protect me."

"Why wouldn't I think that?" She stroked my cheek. "Protecting me is all you think about."

I wanted to argue with her, but couldn't.

"Hey, I'm all for the Blaines becoming one of us," Genny said. "To be honest, I was going to train these two myself once my leg healed up. Next time these bastards try to kidnap her, we'll roll up to that crime scene and find out she already got the job done." Genny smacked Kenzie's thigh. "But she's not there yet. How about this? You guys work on getting her back in Caddell House, and I'll work out her security. There. We're done," she said before we got a word in. "Now onto other concerns. Who is the poor bastard who burned to death in my decoy bedroom?"

"Could it be the bomber?" Sienna spoke up. "Maybe it went off too early."

Bane, Liam, and I shook our heads. "If they were that close when it went off, there wouldn't be a body," Liam said. "They'd be nothing but mist."

Kenzie shivered. "What other explanation could there be? Did... Did one of your Cardinals drop in on you, not knowing you were downstairs?"

"None of my Cardinals knew I was there. Look, whoever was up there wasn't friend or family. Which leaves only one category."

"Foe," said Sienna.

"But what explanation is there?" Kenzie spoke up. "An enemy finds you and hides in wait on the same night the Brotherhood delivers their explosive package? That's too much of a coincidence. Plus, how did they find you? Is someone else keeping tabs on you another way?"

"All good questions," Genny said. "I hate that I can't answer any of them."

"You can answer this one." Liam got to his feet. "Will you move into the Fairfield until the threat is over? Sunny's plan to keep wearing the trackers doesn't work for you seeing as the Brotherhood has proven they're actively hunting you down."

Genny shrugged. "A bunch of bald, cowardly hiding-their-faces-but-not-the-shit-in-their-pants dudes don't scare me. I'd say bring it on if not for the fact that they've gone after my girls before. They could get tired of this cat-and-mouse game and roll into Barbarella's shooting.

"I will have to make adjustments while we hunt these guys down," she gritted. "Including trading in Prohibition bunkers for the one place in this town they're too chickenshit to attack." Genny cut Kenzie a look. "Happy now? You got your wish."

"I didn't say a thing."

She didn't have to. My Angel was smug as shit.

"But I won't hide out forever," Genny continued. "You've got till the end of the month to find the rat putting trackers in my jeans, or the Cardinals storm the place and beat every stitch bitch in there until the truth pops out."

"You can't do that," Kenzie cried.

"This is my city, Feisty." Genny rolled off the couch, managing to swagger off with one bum leg. "I can do whatever I want."

MACKENZIE

I finished dressing Laurel in a two-piece sunflower outfit that matched my sunflower dress. She tried her hardest to swipe and eat my phone as I snapped a hundred pictures of us. That done, we set off out of Sunny's place.

In the elevator, I buzzed in.

"Hello?" Tricky's sweet voice came through the speaker.

"Hey, it's Kenzie and Laurel. We—"

Tricky let us in without another word. I chuckled to Laurel. "How does she figure out the code, baby? Everyone says Liam is this formidable crime boss, but his six-year-old trips him up on the daily. You won't be nearly so crafty, will you? Promise Mommy."

"Da da da," she drew out.

I kissed her soft cheek. "You're already tormenting me with this 'mama' holdout, so I better buckle up for the ride."

The door swung mid-knock. Tricky threw her arms around my legs, smiling wide with all her missing teeth. She was still dressed in her pajamas, but from the looks of things, she started her day a while ago. The television was on, and her unicorn and juice box awaited her on the coffee table.

"Morning, sweetie. What are you up to?"

"I have to wake up Daddy, eat breakfast, then my tutor is coming."

"What are you learning today?" I took Laurel out of her carrier and lowered her down for her smooches. Tricky hugged and kissed my excitable girl. Despite what Liam told her more than once, Elizabeth decided Laurel was her new baby sister and she wouldn't hear a word otherwise.

"Ugh, I have French." She was the spitting image of Genny rolling her eyes. "I want to learn Italy like Uncle Sunny, but Daddy says I have to know French like my grandparents."

"I didn't know Sunny could speak Italian."

"Uncle Sunny knows *lots* of things," she cried, spinning around. "He said he's going to teach me everything he knows."

Bet Liam loves that. Hiding my smile, I set Laurel down and snagged a blanket off the couch. I laid it out, then loaded it up with toys. Laurel crawled over to the good stuff without me having to get her.

"I'm going to wake up Daddy." Tricky scurried away. A squeal pierced the air, followed by a loud groan and giggling.

I cooed at Laurel, hopping a little stuffed animal over to her.

"—many times." Liam came out with a six-year-old slung over his shoulder. "Daddy prefers not to wake up by cannonball to the stomach..."

Liam stopped dead, staring at me, and me staring back at him. The man wore nothing but a pair of black silk boxers. His plan to blindfold and torment me with imagined images of his body was coming apart at the seams.

Thick, powerful legs flowed out of those boxers, proving the man did not skip leg day. His smooth muscled chest rippled as he moved, and seeing his hair messy and lines on his face from the pillow, made me fall for him just a little harder.

"Good morning."

"How'd you get in here?" Liam blurted.

I winked at my co-conspirator. "How else?" I stood, crossing over to them. Liam flicked to the peekaboo hole I cut above my cleavage. "I thought the four of us could have breakfast together. Sunny and I are going to Caddell House later today, which makes now perfect to spend time together."

"I didn't intend— Fuller is coming up to watch Elizabeth when her tutor arrives. I have meetings all morning, Kenzie. I planned for a quick breakfast, then out the door."

I shrugged. "We'll have a quick breakfast together. I'll cook," I said, skipping to the kitchen. "How do stuffed avocados sound?"

"Yummy," Tricky said. "Can you make unicorn smoothies like Daddy too?"

"I can try." I started opening and closing cabinets, searching out the pots and pans.

"Lizzie, keep Laurel company."

I heard her little footsteps, then his presence bore over me, bringing scents of pine and licorice. How did he smell this good first thing in the morning?

"Mackenzie."

I shivered. "I love the way you say my name."

"Do I say it in some particular way?"

"Oh, yes."

A firm grip on my waist turned me around. "Mackenzie, now is not a good time. You should've mentioned it before. Made plans in advance."

"Sure, I'll make plans to see you in advance as long as you make plans to get over your hang-ups and commit to a relationship with me."

Liam's eyes narrowed to slits. "Deal. Now out of my kitchen."

Laughing, I kissed his scowling lips. "You think we haven't known each other long enough for me to have you figured out? Your plan is to keep just enough distance between us that your feelings fade and you come up for air. That's not going to happen."

"Is that so?"

"Yep," I popped. "In fact, I'm thinking we'll make breakfast for four a regular thing." Stepping close, I trailed a finger down his pec, enjoying hearing his breath hitch. "Along with midnight snacks for two."

"Hmm." Liam leaned in, lips brushing against mine, and it was my turn to stop breathing. I froze as his eyes pierced me. "I've played the seduction game much longer than you," Liam whispered. "Don't presume you can beat me at it."

The slightest pressure on my lips, then he was gone. I stumbled, blinking like I came out of a fog.

"Stuffed avocado sounds perfect," he said, strolling out of the kitchen. "Give me a minute to get dressed and I'll help."

"You can skip the 'get dressed' part."

Liam tossed a wink over his shoulder, and that ass. "Behave, Mackenzie."

My knees went weak. Seriously, I was going to ban him from using my full name out of the bedroom. *If we ever get in the bedroom.*

Getting my head out of the fantasies, I busied myself taking out ingredients while keeping one eye on Tricky and the baby. Elizabeth chattered at her nonstop and didn't seem to mind getting shrieks and babble in response.

"They're adorable together," I told Liam when he returned. Sadly, the man donned sweats and a tank. The messy hair was combed into submission. "I think I'll make matching outfits for the two of them."

"Only if you want Elizabeth to burst from happiness."

I laughed. "Take it from me, we can't resist a little sister."

"Don't know about that." Liam set on the coffee pot. I had a feeling he wasn't really awake until he had a cup in him. "I grew quite tired of mine when she started putting garden snakes in my bed."

"Oh my goodness. A young Genevieve Hunt. She must've been a handful."

"To put it mildly."

I clapped. "So I was thinking scrambled eggs, bacon, and cheese. Mix it all up and top it on half an avocado. Simple, but delicious. That's my specialty."

"Just tell me what to do. I'm in your capable hands." Liam turned to head for the fridge.

"You're not but"—I grabbed two palmfuls of his backside—"now you are."

Liam jerked, nearly spilling his coffee down his shirt. "Dammit, woman," he hissed. "What has gotten into you?"

Giggling, I tried to calm myself as the girls stared at us. "What can I say? I'm in a good mood today. My baby and I are safe. Digger's dead. Genny's back in the Fairfield. River is getting those women the help they need. We figured out why the Brotherhood always seemed to be two steps ahead, and today we're going to do something about it. On top of that, Bane starts training me tonight.

"I felt powerless for so long, Liam. The day you realize you're strong enough to face what's coming... it's a good one."

He cleared his throat, straightening. "I'm genuinely happy that you feel safe with my family. That's all I want for you—both of you. But grab my ass less."

"No promises."

I thought I peeked the ghost of a smile when he ducked his head in the fridge. "I'll do the scrambled eggs. You do the bacon."

We scrambled and fried in silence for a while—the good kind of silence. The kind a happy couple settles into on a lazy Saturday making breakfast for the family.

"Can I ask you something?"

I glanced up from the pan. "Anything."

"Why did you ask Bane to train you?"

"Oh, I..." I trailed off. I was expecting him to ask a lot of things ranging from caring to sexual, but this didn't make the list. "He offered to train me," I finally said. "A while ago, he said he could teach me to fight and protect what's mine. I don't know why I didn't take the offer seriously. Maybe if I had—"

"It wouldn't have hardened your head to the point you're impervious to blows," Liam sliced in. "Coates was a gutless coward who attacked you while your back was turned. If you're beating yourself up—thinking taking Bane up on that training would've prevented what happened to you and Laurel, you can stop now. It could've happened to any one of us."

Placing the bacon on a plate, I let what he said sink in. "That's true, I guess. I couldn't help some monster sneaking up on me while my back was turned. Still, it doesn't change how useless I was to stop that woman from taking Laurel, or to keep myself out of those chains. Sienna said we're strongest together, but not if I'm the weakest link."

I studied him out of the corner of my eye. "Why did you bring this up? None of you are saying it, but I've got a feeling you don't want Bane to train me. Tell me what you really think, Liam."

He didn't look up from the eggs. "What I think is those on the dark side of Cinco fall into this life for many reasons, but rarely by choice. For you, it will be a choice, Mackenzie. If you're doing this out of the fear I will fail to protect the two of you twice, I swear to you on every drop of blood I have and will spill, that fear is unnecessary. No one will ever hurt you again."

So many things to say in response, and they all stuck in my throat. Swallowing hard, I stood wishing he'd follow his dizzying promise with a touch, hug, kiss—anything.

Liam's only move was to lean over and grab the bacon. His lips brushed my forehead, pulling back.

Gathering myself, I put a smile on for the girls and brought them to the table. Liam was putting our plates down when Laurel stood on my legs, holding her hands up to him. My eyes widened at her. Laurel wasn't one for separation anxiety, but she only ever reached for me, Sienna, and recently, Sunny and Fuller.

Liam didn't skip a beat. He scooped her up and went into the kitchen to start on Lizzie's unicorn smoothie. Laurel rode his arms, watching the show and looking pleased with herself.

"We'll make this a thing," I said, melting as Laurel gave him kisses. "Breakfast together every other morning. At least a couple times a week. What do you think?"

"No."

My heart popped, letting out a wheezing screech as it deflated.

"Mornings are tough for me," Liam continued. "I work most nights and prefer to sleep in—with Elizabeth's permission." The six-year-old grinned around a mouthful of avocado. "How about dinner?"

I bit my lip to stop me cheesing too hard. "Dinner it is."

Her smoothie made, we sat down to eat. Liam held Laurel, feeding her avocado and laughing when she swiped some and smeared it on his face. Tricky and I talked about the outfits she wanted me to design her. Liam told me about the trips his parents used to take them on. I shared funny stories from college. It was, in a word, perfect.

Hours later, Sunny and I tore through the streets of Cinco, heading for the one place I thought I'd never see the inside of again.

"You really think they'll hire me back just because you tell them to?" My lips worried between my teeth, staining them with purple lipstick.

"I do." Sunny slid onto the very expressway he was thrown off of. "People rarely like the consequences of refusing me."

I studied him. "Do you hurt people who refuse you?" There was no judgment in the question. "Bane suggested as much when he was teaching me to play the part of mob boss. Is that the true and simple secret to instilling fear? Doling out pain for every no."

Wind blew through his raven locks, sweeping them clear from his achingly handsome smirk and glinting silver pools. *No. The truth is people don't refuse you because you're too damn beautiful to anger. Heaven forbid the sunlight is ever stolen from those eyes.*

"Bane gave you the crash course, gorgeous. Quick and dirty tips," he said. "It's not as simple as violence, Mackenzie. There are plenty of violent, abusive fucks knocking around everyone that looks at them cross-eyed, but they're damn well not respected, or even feared. They're just despised."

"That's true," I murmured, thinking of a few violent, abusive fucks that crossed my path.

"It's chess, Kenzie." Sunny's words floated to my ears. "You're not playing the game. You're playing the person. For some, a few threats will do. For others, a couple stacks of cash. Couple of the hard cores won't be put down for less than a beating so savage they want to crawl back into their mother's womb. But for the rest..." Sunny trailed off. The light dimmed behind his eyes. "Enemies like Snyder, Adams, and the leader of the Brotherhood, they'll never stop coming unless they're put down for good."

My grip tightened on the armrest. "Kill them."

"Depends on who you're dealing with, but charting their moves from the beginning is everything. To kill a man you could've easily persuaded with a bribe or threat just makes you a monster. But threatening a man who should've gotten a bullet in his head is how Luca Adams abducts and hurts my girls."

I laced my fingers through his. "Everyone's been saying this to me for days, but it's you who needs to hear it. This wasn't your fault, Sunny. I didn't see what Luca was until it was too late. Every time I thought I hit the bottom of his depravity, he proved to be even more vile and barbaric than decent people can comprehend."

I inclined my head. "But what you're saying makes a lot of sense. To have both fear and respect isn't about violence. I've met the people in your crew. They know not to cross you, but they also love you."

"Do they? The bastards forgot my birthday last year."

Chuckling, I elbowed, then kissed him for lightening the mood. "I'll need both to survive from here on. Fear and respect."

"You don't need those to survive this fight with the Brotherhood, Kenzie," he said angrily. "Because you've always had me."

Leaning lower, I nuzzle his cheek, peeking the five-story modern brick masterpiece rising on the horizon.

Caddell House.

"That's not the fight I'm talking about, baby."

SUNNY OPENED MY DOOR, offering his hand for mine. Lifting my chin, I stepped out wearing the crown jewel of the Kenzie Creations. A diamond-studded knee-length dress. The halter top wrapped around my neck, hiding my collarbone and leaving the scandal for the bare, exposed back. See-through diamond pumps graced my feet, click-clacking on the white-painted steps leading to the double doors.

I remember the days I was forcibly escorted through these doors. It was only shouting that I was pregnant that stopped the overzealous guards from throwing me down the steps. What it didn't stop them from doing was leaving twin bruises on my arms that didn't disappear for days.

"The only person you have to worry about inside that building is the rat sewing trackers in our clothes," Sunny said out of the corner of his mouth. "Everyone else is noise."

I knew exactly who he was calling noise. Lyla and her crew.

"They're more than just noise, Sunny. That woman went on a crusade to ruin my life and it worked. It'll be ten times as hard to find this guy while watching for the knife she'll plunge in my back."

"So kill her."

"Sunny!"

"Beat her up?"

"Sole!"

He shrugged. "Destroy her reputation, get her fired, and cost her everything?"

My glare ratcheted up a thousand.

"Running out of ideas here, baby. That woman needs both a taste of revenge and to stay out of your way this time around. Fear and respect, Kenzie. If you've got ideas for dealing with her, kick them in."

I sighed. Sunny could be extra, but he was always right. I swore I wouldn't sit back and take it while people fucked up my life. Lyla was going to test that resolve in a big way, so what did I plan to do about it?

"I'll think of something." I gestured to the oversized doorknobs. "Let's do this."

Stepping inside Caddell House was like entering a high fashion theme park. For a designer, this was the happiest place on earth.

Gorgeous models demurred at us from larger-than-life posters, rocking the most fabulous outfits talent designed. Gold-flecked marble spread out from under the welcome mat, leading to a grand reception desk with three stunning women and a man directing people where to go. Grand staircases the likes of which belonged in a palace led the way up the many floors, making me tilt my head back to the crystal chandeliers—those were new. They caught the light from huge floor-to-ceiling windows—those weren't new.

The lobby was all sunlight, beauty, and color. The design floors were no less fancy, but the only light pumping through those windowless rooms was artificial. So fierce was the competition between fashion houses in Cinco, Caddell did an entire remodel when a spy was caught on the opposite building, snapping photos of our creations.

Those days and my past in CH flooded my head as Sunny and I bypassed the calling receptionists, heading up the stairs for the creative director's office. The very room my daughter's father hid behind his fiancée, tight-lipped like the shameful coward he was while she effectively dumped me for him.

"Are you okay?"

I started, head jerking up. I hadn't realized I was tightening my grip on his arm until just then. "I'm fine," I rasped. "Bad memories."

"He's not here anymore." Sunny read my mind. "Both of them are gone. Damien Stone's deserved castration is postponed another day."

I cracked a smile. "I won't lie. Castration did cross my mind once or twice."

We weaved through the halls, coming up to another reception desk and the door it stood between—Vance Hollywell's office.

All five feet, seven inches of heels, makeup, and designer labels rose from her seat, surveying us with cold eyes. I wondered if I gave off that look when I was working here.

"Can I help you?"

"We're here to see Hollywell," Sunny replied. "We're the Johnsons."

She didn't move. "Do you have an appointment?"

"A standing one. Means I can walk in whenever I want, and consider taking my business elsewhere for every minute I'm kept waiting."

Lorna, as her nameplate read, lost the haughty lip twist. "Excuse me, Mr. Johnson. Director Hollywell is on a call with the New York office, but I'll let him know you're here."

Call with the New York office. Wonder if that means he's talking with Talia right now.

Lorna scurried to the door, sticking her head in. We were right on her heels.

"Sorry to interrupt, sir, but— Hey!"

Sunny pushed in—the firm hold on my hand tugging me behind him. I stepped around him as a breath-stoppingly handsome man shot out of his seat, angry words on the tip of his mouth.

I hadn't kept up with news of Caddell House after I was fired. At least I hadn't kept up with anything other than news of Talia and Damien. Obviously, she was replaced by a new creative director, but one look proved he wasn't an in-house hire. This guy didn't work here when I did, and I would've remembered the piercing blue, almost purple eyes. High cheekbones, hooked nose, strong chin, and a suit that clung to all the right places like Liam's always did. Whoever he had designing for the Johnson account was floating him a few suits too.

"What do you think you're—?" He stopped so suddenly you would've thought he was gagged. His face slackened, taking in my Sunny, and that grin. For generations to come, people will show a photo of that smirk and everyone will know it belongs to Sole Bellisario.

"Sunny," he rasped. His Adam's apple visibly bobbed. "What are you—? Is something—?" Hollywell flicked behind us. "Lorna, you can go."

"Vance? Vance, what's going on?"

I stiffened as Talia's voice filled the room. Forget Lorna, this woman knew how to do haughty.

"Forgive me, Talia. We'll have to reschedule our conference call." And just like that, Vance shut off the computer, hanging up on the great Talia Barker.

"Sunny." Vance tried to inject cheer in his voice as he came around the desk, arms out. "Wonderful to see you. I'm sorry I didn't know we had a meeting scheduled."

"We didn't."

"Sit, sit. Please." Vance held out a chair for me, taking my hand to help me down like I was royalty. I took a look around the place while he simpered to Sunny.

He made a lot of changes to this office—which was to be expected. Talia hung dozens of photos of herself from her model days. She loaded the room with vintage French furniture, and anything that could be pink, white, or purple—was.

With Hollywell taking over decorations, the photos of his predecessor were gone. As were the fancy, floofy furniture and the whimsical color palette. Instead, Hollywell opted for a simple, minimalist design with white leather chairs, glass desk, plush gray carpet, and photos of random models on the catwalk showing off Caddell designs. I liked what he did with the place much more than Talia—mostly because I'd like anyone more than Talia.

"Is there a problem?" Vance reclaimed his seat and attempted to look casual, reclining back and crossing his ankle over his leg. "I've assigned the very best to your account, Sunny. Every stitch of clothing made for you is given my final approval, and from what I understand, delivery is always prompt."

My ears quirked up. Hollywell gives the final approval before their clothes go out? Talia was hands-on, but she wasn't *that* much of a microman-ager. Why does Hollywell give the Merchants this special attention?

I mentally added him to my list of suspects.

"There is no problem, Hollywell. Actually, it's a testament to how well Caddell House dresses me that brings me here today." Sunny leaned back, crossing his ankles and resting a fist on top. He did effortlessly casual much better than Hollywell ever could. "Recent events have prompted me and my family to show our charitable side. We've given the majority of our old, last-season clothes to charity."

"Oh, I see." Hollywell sat up a little straighter, catching on immediately. I could practically see the dollar signs in his eyes. The Merchants got their clothes from Caddell at a steep discount, but that discount still added up to them spending more than the twin salaries of two working-class married professionals. Designing an entire wardrobe for the family and their staff would fill the Caddell coffers for years.

"We'll need new clothes," Sunny continued. "Me, Bane, Liam, Genny, and our staff. We're taking this opportunity for a new, fresh look. At least, I am. Liam will take the same boring, three-piece suits, but me"—Sunny threw out his hands—"think bold."

"We can absolutely do that, sir." Vance snatched up a pad, scribbling furiously. "It's funny that I was just thinking it's time for you to receive a fresh look for fall. You're really going to love what we're creating downstairs, Sunny. I'm sure of it."

Sunny snapped his fingers. "I'd also love a few of those features we discussed. Imperceptible pockets. Places to hide weapons. That sort of thing."

Hollywell's smile tightened around the edges. "Very funny, sir, but we also discussed that I cannot inform my employees to make hidden pockets for weapons."

I had to wonder about their relationship. Why did Hollywell know, and fear, the real people behind the Johnson account and no one else in Caddell House did?

Except for the sneaking traitor gift-wrapping them for the Brotherhood.

"Course not," said Sunny. "Why do you think I brought this lovely lady along?"

Hollywell took the first proper look at me since I stepped into the room. I attempted not to take it personally since Sunny was a dangerous crime boss. That was still hard to get my head around—the sexy, loving man who holds me while I sleep and blows raspberries on my giggling daughter's stomach is a dangerous crime boss.

"This young woman? I don't understand," Hollywell said, lowering his pad. "Who are you, miss?"

"My name is Mackenzie Blaine."

His face changed in a blink. "Hold on. Blaine? Blaine as in..." Vance pawed through his bottom drawer, pulling out a file. My eyes widened seeing my name across the top, and then my up close and personal employee photo. "This Mackenzie Blaine? The one who was fired not long ago for passing off others' designs as your own?"

I raised a finger. "The very same, but I'd like to point out I was framed and falsely accused."

His lips peeled back. "You would say that."

"Play nice, Vance," Sunny gruffed. "You're speaking to the new designer for the Johnsons."

"I beg your pardon!"

Sunny plowed on. "Of course you're not dumping all the work on her. She'll need assistants, junior designers, underlings—whatever you call them. They'll do whatever she says, but the one doing the actual designing, and putting my pockets in all the right places, is her."

"Sunny, please, slow down. Has Anastasia done an unsatisfactory job? Why must she be replaced?"

Anastasia must be the head designer on the account. Another name on the list.

"Is it because I refused to accommodate you on the imperceptible pockets?" Hollywell tried for a smile. "I might've been too hasty. Naturally, I can't tell my employees they're aiding in criminal activity but—"

"Whoa. Criminal activity?" Sunny got up, bearing down on him. "Who said anything about criminal activity, Vance? Those pockets are so that my family, staff, and friends can conceal legal, permitted weapons on them for self-defense. Why would you even say that word?" Sunny bent over his desk. "Are you recording this conversation? You wearing a wire, Hollywell?"

The man blanched so deeply he blended into his white desk chair. "No, sir," he croaked. "Never. I didn't mean— I don't know why I said that. You and your family are upstanding members of the community. You'd never engage in anything criminal."

He apologized five more times before Sunny sat down. It was wild seeing him in action. Only half an hour before I was asking how the Merchants controlled people with fear, and my demonstration came so soon. It was a subtle game of chess where the pieces on the board were your opponents. You had to know the right moves to navigate. Some people required a harsher touch, but others will cower without you laying a finger on them—fearing what you could do to them if you wanted.

But which approach will help me in the inevitable clash with Lyla Dawson? Assuming Vance really is so afraid of Sunny, he'll hire the woman with an entire file on her.

"As I was saying," Sunny went on. "Miss Anastasia has done fine work, but ever since Kenzie became a part of our little crew..." Sunny laced his fingers through mine, making it clear exactly what that meant. "Ever since then, she's designed the most incredible outfits for us with some scraps of silk and one sewing machine. We can't wait to see what she does with all of CH's resources at her fingertips."

Hollywell's color came back, staring at me. So did his glare. "I understand, sir, but I cannot hire her. She was fired for the worst crime a designer can commit. Hiring her back will permanently taint our reputation."

"Actually, it won't," I spoke up. "I already told you I was framed and fired for something I didn't do. What? You don't believe me."

Vance cut a look at Sunny. He didn't believe a damn word out of my mouth, but he wasn't stupid enough to say so. I decided to help him.

"Here's the truth, Mr. Hollywell. While I worked here, I began a relationship with Damien Stone, unaware he was engaged to Talia. When I became pregnant with his child, he saw his soon-to-be wife's bank accounts about to disappear out of reach, so he recruited Lyla Dawson to help him discredit me and ensure Talia never believed a single word that came out of my mouth."

Vance paled for an entirely different reason. I almost chuckled at his hanging mouth. "Lyla and Damien? Pregnant? You're lying!" he blurted.

"I am not." My reply was calm. "I've got the stretch marks and the nine-month-old to prove it."

"Doesn't mean the child is his." Vance burst out of his seat. "Damien is a friend of mine. He wouldn't cheat on Talia or abandon a child he fathered."

Sunny sliced in. "If you're really a friend of his, you know everything you just said is bullshit. He cheats on Talia every chance he gets. His favorite mistresses get an apartment on the Upper West Side. He's got three on the go currently. One of them is a Broadway star, Vivica Rostov. She's not half bad."

Hollywell slowly lowered in his seat, a thousand emotions battling on his face. Lies didn't usually have that much detail. "Even if what you're saying is true," Vance said to me. "Why would you tell me?"

"Why not?" I said. "Am I supposed to keep Damien's and Lyla's secrets? I see how that benefits them, but it does shit-all for me. The point is I did nothing I was accused of, and therefore, you have no conflict with hiring me."

I plucked the pad off his desk. "But let me help you along. I'll prove I deserve a spot here, not because Sunny orders it or because you should feel bad for me. Give me a concept, Hollywell. Gown, suit, swimwear—doesn't matter. Tell me what to design, and if it's not Caddell-worthy, we'll walk out now."

His eyes narrowed, flicking between me and Sunny. He likely didn't believe the last part. Sunny's orders were to be followed—test or not. But in this game of chess, I didn't need my boyfriend's intimidation on my side. There is one thing I've always been excellent at, and it's creating beautiful clothes that people of all types and styles want to wear.

"All right, Miss Blaine. One sketch. If it's up to my standards, you will have the job with conditions."

"What conditions?"

He flapped a hand. "Not worth listing until I've seen what you come up with."

"Careful," Sunny hissed. "Don't get too big for yourself, Hollywell."

Vance lost the superior look fast. "What I meant is, we'll get into all of that when there is an offer to be made. Now," he began. "Sketch me a wedding dress with a Queen Anne neckline." Vance placed a pencil in front of me. "Give me something I've never seen before."

A tall order. The wedding industry makes over sixty billion dollars a year, and there were tons of labels, from high fashion to bargain, cashing in with every classic to unique wedding dress design there was. White was left behind a long time ago and now they were in every color. Long trains gave way to short hems. Poofy gowns hung side by side with tight and fitted.

The challenge to give the creative director of a high fashion line something he's never seen before is nigh on impossible for the average designer.

Thankfully, I've never been average.

My pencil flew across the page, working fast but not fast enough for my whirling mind. I knew exactly what I'd draw before he finished saying "wedding dress."

The neckline materialized around a slender neck. The waist drew in, then flared out. I didn't know how serious Sunny was about wanting a new, bold look for the Merchant clan, but I'd been mentally sketching that wardrobe ever since he handed me a credit card and sent me off in the direction of Brocade. I'd always been the perfect person for this job at Caddell House. Now that it required me to find the person who helped the Brotherhood throw Sunny off a bridge, blow up Liam's car, terrify Elizabeth, and mow down Genny—I'd be the perfect person for that job too.

No matter what it took. No matter how many chess games I had to play. Snobs I had to impress. Demons I had to face. Or enemies I had to tame.

The world was done underestimating me.

I penciled in my last flourish, signed my name on the bottom, and dropped the pad on his desk. Vance studied it—his eyes giving away the thoughts he fought to keep off his face.

"Interesting."

I smirked. The design before him was a sheer trumpet gown with the requested Queen Anne neckline—that was for Hollywell. The lace butterflies weaving down the gown in an intricate pattern, growing in size and number as they flew down the darkening ombre train—that was all me.

For the minimalist man before me, the lines were clean and the flourishes were few. The gown was both simple and unique. Nothing he's ever seen before.

"I mean, there's room for improvement... but this is interesting."

I've worked under other creative directors and senior designers. This poor compliment was the equivalent of high praise. "I take it I have the job."

"With conditions," he finished. "You claim you were framed, but I assume you have no proof of this. And no, I do not take your child as proof."

"I do not have proof."

"Yet," Sunny cut in. "I'm working on tracking down their accomplice, Courtney Hicks. She doesn't have a job here to lose anymore, so she'll likely be forthcoming. If I can't find her, Miss Dawson can be encouraged to give a full confession."

"That is my first condition," Vance said quickly. "While you work here, you will not make trouble with my employees. Lyla Dawson has been a model employee in the year since I've taken the job. She may have done what you say, but as far as I'm concerned, it's in the past. You've got a position higher than the one you left, and you're handling our biggest account. All's well that ends well."

In other words, he wants me to let it go and park the drama at the front door.

"I can do that."

"Second, you work only on the Johnson account. I will assign you two junior designers and an intern. Final designs still go through me."

"Assign me the same designers who've been putting their time in for the Johnsons," I said. "They already have an idea of the sizes, cuts, and styles the family likes."

Vance inclined his head, accepting that easily. "You will work here under a probationary basis and receive no salary."

"Fuck that for a joke," Sunny snapped.

Silently, I touched his arm. "Why on earth should I work for free?"

"Your designs will not be featured in the magazine, on the website, in competitions, or during fashion week. As such, you'll be doing nothing to bring more business or attention to Caddell House. The only account you'll work on is the Johnsons', so you're essentially their employee."

"Incorrect. I did the math on the order they're putting in. Even with the discount, it's three times the revenue Caddell pulls in from their top accounts. I'm bringing in more than enough business. I get a salary."

"I will not—"

"She gets a salary," Sunny forced through gritted teeth. "Don't make me repeat myself."

Vance reddened. "She's paid the same as an intern and no more."

I shook my head. Here's an insight into my opponent: Vance Hollywell is a cheapskate. Funny how guys like that always find their courage when money is involved.

"I will accept that for now," I said to head Sunny off. "Once I start bringing in other accounts, I expect my salary to go up."

"You're not here to bring in more accounts. The Johnsons are to get your full attention."

My brow quirked. "Why is that, Mr. Hollywell? The truth is you don't *want* me to enter competitions, attend parties, or submit designs for the catalog because then Talia and Damien will find out you rehired me, isn't that right?"

The look on his face said it all. His mouth tried to tell a different story. "Not at all. I simply can't have you get distracted. Sunny and his family are valued clients, and whatever your relationship may be, I expect professionalism within these walls."

"You're full of shit." Sunny was as blunt as ever. "Don't be afraid of Talia and Damien, my friend. They'll get theirs soon enough."

I laughed because Sunny never said anything truer. Damien and Talia would get a taste of what they did to me and Laurel, and they'd get it soon. I was done letting people get away with hurting me.

"You truly don't need to worry about them," I said. "There's nothing they can do to you, especially if you make it clear Caddell House will lose the Johnson account if they make a fuss. Oops, don't make that face," I said when he blanched. "You can trust me, Mr. Hollywell. I'm not here to make your life difficult. I'm more than happy to clock in, do my job, and clock out. If any kind of drama kicks off with Talia, Damien, or Lyla, it won't be because I started it."

"Well, I'm pleased to hear that," he said slowly.

"I only ask one thing," I continued. "That you don't let them get in my way either. I know in many ways I'm still working my way up, and I have no problem with that. My talent will speak for itself like it always has." I got to my feet. "Now that's settled, I'd like to see my office and meet the designers who'll be working for me. I already know what the *Johnsons* want, so I'll start tomorrow."

"Very good."

Hollywell gave me an unneeded tour of the building, but I didn't mind it. A few things had changed in the days since I'd been gone, and even though he didn't introduce me to anyone, it was good that he didn't think he could hide me away in an office under a mountain of silk. Talia and Damien would inevitably find out that Mackenzie Blaine has returned to Caddell House. When that happened there would be fireworks.

Hollywell held open the door, ushering me onto the floor. Designers busied at their stations—some scribbling on a pad and others sticking pins through fabric on a mannequin. At my old station, there sat Lyla Dawson, fussing with the beads on a dress while barking orders at one of the women in her crew.

Naomi wasn't ignoring her on purpose. She was quite caught up... staring at me.

I smiled at her—the same smile growing wider as Lyla looked up at her, and then at me.

"Hello, everyone," I called, voice carrying through the silencing room. "I'm back."

Chapter Six

G*enny*

"You can't be serious, FGH."

Bugsy reclined on my couch, one leg slung over the back and the other on the floor. Candace spun beer caps off their bottles, using that leg as a target.

"Unfortunately, I'm deadly serious." I stretched out on my desk like I was sinking into my favorite beanbag chair, enveloped in the rightness of being where I was supposed to be: in my office, in my bar, in my borough. "My taste for the finer things almost led to my downfall." I knocked back a swig of beer and belched. "Trackers sewn into my clothes. That's how they found me in my safe houses twice. And it's how... they knew the right warehouse to bomb."

The three of us fell silent at the mention of Frenchie and our girls. The Cardinals lived a dangerous life and none of us expected to walk away from it unscathed, but in the years since I founded the gang, they were the only girls I lost.

For a good chunk of the Harlow population, joining a gang is the only way to secure protection. They certainly couldn't rely on the cops to protect them. Harlownites lived for decades under the fist of the Kings and the corrupt cops who lived in their pockets. The trust there was blown up and scattered into ashes. As a result, young women who wanted to ensure they could walk through the streets of their neighborhoods at night without a soul daring to touch them, joined behind power, and there was no power greater than a Merchants'.

I welcomed them all when I claimed this borough as mine. Every woman who couldn't stand falling in with the drugged-out junkies peddling coke on the corner. Those who refused to line up on the sidewalk, waiting for cars while their pimp watched from the shadows. All of them who needed the protection, but didn't need the future as a hollowed-out, soulless husk that awaited them if they fell in with traffickers, murderers, and kidnappers.

We were not a club of angels. My girls have broken almost every law on the books. Still, they knew if they joined with me, I'd never ask them to hurt innocent people, reduce themselves to my obedient bitches, or let a single person hurt them without getting it back tenfold.

The women of Harlow, in and out of the Cardinals, were under my protection.

And the fucking clothes I shoved on every day undid that in a few months. The whole time, the biggest threat to my girls has been me.

"The Brotherhood will pay for this," I hissed. "I can promise you that."

"Let us help, boss," Candace said. "You don't have to move out of Harlow. You said Vito is one of them. We'll pick up all his friends and wring them out until their secrets splatter the floor with their blood."

I barked a laugh. I was always particularly fond of Candace. She was barely higher than five feet, rocked size-zero outfits, and boasted the sweetest little cherub face with the button nose and full lips. None of that gelled with the violent, bloody declarations that spilled from those lips on a daily basis.

"That's the problem right there," I returned. "If Vito's friends are waiting around to be picked up, it's because they don't know anything. They'd have to be even stupider than I give them credit for to dangle out in the open while Vito is on the run."

Bugsy snatched a cap out of the air and threw it back at Candace. "Is it just me, Eve, or do you think they are that stupid?"

I mouth-shrugged. "Fair enough. Pick them up."

My phone buzzed across the desk. I half expected it to be one of my many brothers or the woman they were all so obviously in love with, texting to know where I was. I don't know why my mother insisted on giving me so many siblings.

I told her often she was lucky she didn't have any, to which she responded I'd burn the world down if anything happened to a single one of them, and I wasn't fooling anyone. I could move in on any city in the world and be running the place by the end of the week. According to her, I stayed in Cinco and contented myself with one borough because I loved my family.

I scoffed then as I did every time she said that. There was something deeply annoying about a mom who saw right through you. Anyone who wished their parents knew them better was an idiot.

Shaking myself out of my thoughts, I picked up my phone.

Bobby: Hey, you coming over tonight? I haven't had a taste of that pussy for ages. That cunt is begging for me to give it what it needs.

"What's up?" Bugsy asked.

"Bobby is texting for a hookup."

"Which Bobby?" said Candace.

"Damned if I know." I tossed my phone across the desk. I was booked in with Pedro that night anyway. Dear old Mom has one thing right: why settle for one guy when three, four, or more do the job just fine?

I blew out a gusty breath. "You're right, guys. Can't hurt to pick up Vito's boys and see what they know. At the very least, it'll give you all a chance to vent your frustrations."

"Our frustrations? What about you?" asked Candace. "What will you be doing?"

I absentmindedly stroked the new wound on my shoulder. "I have something else to take care of, and you can't help me with this," I said when they opened their mouths. "I have to do this without the Cardinals."

"You're doing a lot without us all of a sudden." I did not mistake the bitterness leaching into Bugsy's tone. "Didn't bother telling us where your safe houses were, so *we* could ride in and help you when shit went south. You're moving back into the Fairfield, and now you've got some secret mission that can only be carried out by you. Since when don't you trust us, FGH?"

"It's not about trust. We're dealing with a different kind of enemy this time around, ladies. Trackers in the buttons." I snorted. "It's genius in how simple it is. We've been running around searching for traitors and leaks for months, while the answer was literally right under our nose. To take down the Brotherhood, every move from here on has to be the right one. I can't afford mistakes, and I *don't* have time to argue about what I do. You either get that or you don't."

Silence smothered the room. It took a minute but, finally, they nodded—expressions hard.

"You can trust one thing," I continued, picking up my phone again to text Pedro to have his pants off by the time I got there. "Everything I do is for Harlow and my Cardinals.

"Everything."

MACKENZIE

"People always go for the guns or the knives in a fight. Fair enough, any banger that comes at you will too, but the most effective weapons you have are these." Bane cradled my fists, making them tingle strangely. "My father taught me that. You can't say the man is wrong since people have come at him with every weapon that exists over the years, and he's taken down every single one with his bare hands."

I swallowed through a tight throat, imagining being the cause with my hands around someone else's. *That's hard to imagine now, but when the day comes that I need to defend Laurel, Sienna, Sunny, or my Merchants, I won't hesitate.*

I repeated that a few more times until I believed it. I asked for this training. I wouldn't get nervous about it now.

"Do you fight with your bare hands?" I asked.

"I fight with every weapon at my disposal." Bane swept his wall of guns, knives, and antique daggers. "They're only so effective because I can win without them. Someone who relies on their gun panics when it's taken from them. It's that panic and hesitation that kills them. Understand?"

I nodded. Everything Bane was saying made perfect sense. It was putting his words into action that would be the hard part.

"Do you have a preference?" he asked.

Bane was delicious that early morning, wearing loose drawstring pants and nothing else. His chest was bare for me, revealing the faint collection of scars gracing his pecs, back, and side. For some reason, they didn't fill me with pity. All those scars told a story, and I'd spend the rest of my life hearing every tale that made Bane who he is. They couldn't all be as sad as the one that made him give up on love.

"A gun w-would be better, right?" I hoped he didn't notice my voice shake. "Stop attackers before they even get close."

"A gun is good as long as you have the aim to go with it. Ever fired one before?"

"Yes."

He cocked a brow. "You have?"

"Don't look so surprised. You don't know everything about me."

Bane laughed. The sound struck me with a hard and sudden urge to peel off the one article of clothing in our way, and ride him on the couch again. Part of me hoped that was his plan when he woke me at four in the morning for our first day of training. We had to get it in before I left for Caddell House.

"I'm allowed to be surprised," he said, grinning. "You look at my gun collection like they're a pile of writhing snakes. Why shouldn't I be shocked you picked one up?"

"I look at them like that because it makes me nervous to have so many weapons even in the same building as Laurel. But I have fired one before," I confessed. "You know the trouble I was having with that low-life pimp. Marty was worried about me, so he got me a gun. We spent a day in the woods with him teaching me how to aim. In the end, I decided to carry a knife instead. You can't get arrested for carrying an unregistered knife."

Bane swore. "I am stupid for being surprised. You faced danger long before you met the Merchants." He grasped my hands, kissing my knuckles. "Fuck, I hate what you've been through. I hate even more that you went through it alone."

I lowered my head, heart thumping a rapid beat. A tender touch and sweet words clashed with the no-strings-attached casual hookups we were trying to be. It was against the rules, but Bane was the kind of man to make his own.

"I wasn't alone," I said softly. "I had Sienna. She was right next to me, firing that gun too."

"Now you have me too." Our bodies drew together, hips knocking. His hands moved down my arms, stealing my breath with every inch that brought them closer to my breasts. "All this training, Kenzie, you won't need it. I won't let anyone hurt you again."

I flattened my palm over his heart. "I believe you. I shouldn't, considering all the men who've lied and fooled me in the past, but when you make promises to me, Bane. I believe them."

A faint smile crossed his lips. "But you don't believe I'll keep my promise to avoid love, kids, and commitment?"

"Hmm." I pulled a face. "I believe you'll try damn hard, but the difference with that promise is, I'll be working damn hard too to see you fail. The others you'll keep because I won't get in your way."

If I thought he'd be mad at that, Bane surprised me again by laughing out loud. "If there's an adversary I couldn't beat, it would have to be you."

My heart filled to burst, then it did when he let go—his serious mask slamming into place.

"Okay, you turned down a gun for a knife once, it's fine to do it again." My head spun at the subject change. "A blade is even better because you can hide it on you easily while you're in Caddell House. We don't know what this Brotherhood rat will do when you find them."

My mouth opened and closed forming a response. "Hopefully they won't attack me in a roomful of people."

"They won't, Kenzie. They'll wait until they got you trapped in a bathroom, empty office, or dark corner. People die in crowded buildings all the time. There isn't always safety in numbers."

I shivered. Genny was right. I wasn't thinking like a homicidal sociopath, but I had to learn quickly if I planned to hunt one down.

"All right, the knife," I said, steeling my resolve and shoving away my feelings. Bane was teaching me how to survive. We could have sexually charged moments after.

He took my hand, leading me down the wall and his collection. Knives of all types and makes hung before me. "Pick whichever one feels right in your hand. Though, if I can make a suggestion, go for one of the switchblades."

"Will you teach me to fight with it?" I picked up a switchblade with a blue and ivory handle, bouncing it on my palm. It weighed next to nothing. How could something so deadly feel like it was hardly there? "Or will Sunny be my teacher?"

Bane shrugged. "Don't get me wrong, Sunny could kill a man with anything on this wall. But his expertise is knife-throwing—a skill our dad has been teaching him since he was five. You don't have twenty years to learn."

"Good point."

"Another good point is it's not a good idea for you to be throwing your only weapon across the room."

I giggled, picturing all the ridiculous movies where people did just that. Flinging weapons all over the place while they screamed and ran about. "If I'm not throwing it, that means you'll be teaching me to fight up close and personal."

"That's exactly what it means." Bane winked. "Get ready, Blaine. I'm throwing you in the deep end."

It turned out throwing me in the deep end meant standing me in front of a life-sized practice dummy and having me repeatedly stab the areas he marked. One blow there would kill quickly. I winced with every strike. When he told me to aim for the throat, I dropped the thing, chest heaving as I hurled myself across the room.

Sienna described Bane's workout/training room well. It was filled with practice dummies, equipment, and a mat for Sienna to throw him around on—though I suspected he only let her do that to be kind and give her confidence.

Confidence. That's what you need, Blaine, and quick! Get a hold of yourself. The Merchants aren't an after-school baking club. Facing what they do every day was never going to be pretty.

"Do you need to stop?"

"Like I can say yes," I flung. "If I stop, you'll think I'm not ready. You all will. But I have to be ready. I walk into Caddell House in two hours. I don't have time to s-stop." My stomach heaved, threatening to spill the breakfast I didn't eat all over my shoes. Picturing stabbing a knife in a man's throat would do that to you.

"Not just any man, Kenzie." I hadn't realized I spoke out loud. "We're not talking about kind old fellas feeding ducks in the park, or smiling fathers playing with their kids. The only ones you'd ever use that knife on are the Lucas, Snyders, and Vitos of this city. And you'd only do it in self-defense." He trapped my gaze. "You can treat me to all the mind-blowing sex you want, but you'll never make me turn you into a cold-blooded killer."

I chuckled—surprised he made me do so. "I know that's not what we're doing here. I really do, Bane. It's just... stabbing even a practice dummy in the neck is cruel. If the movies have it right, they won't die right away. They'll bleed out gasping on their blood." Bile burned my throat. "I'm not interested in causing pain, Bane. I just want to know that if someone else attacks or kidnaps me, I can stop them."

He came up behind me. I stilled as he grasped my shoulders. "This is how you do that, Kenzie."

We didn't speak for a long spell.

"That's enough for one morning." Dropping his hands, he went to push the mangled dummy into the corner. "You have to get ready for work. Good luck today."

"Thank you," I said. "Will you visit me on my lunch break and screw me on my desk?"

Bane stumbled.

"I've got a swanky office with blackout curtains."

"What you've got is one more go at surprising me." Bane turned that grin on me. "Three is all you get."

I giggled, feeling like myself again. "I may try past that though."

"I will not screw you on your desk today. While everyone is out to lunch is the perfect time to look around and see if anyone is stashing expensive tracking software in their desk." Bane walked out, his smirk the last to leave the room. "But I will fuck you on your desk tomorrow."

It was the promise of that which kept the smile on my face as I showered, fed Laurel, then climbed in the car with Sunny. The guards were done following me around and protecting me, but Sunny was not.

"Nervous?" he asked.

We sped through the Cinco streets, my nails piercing Masie fine leather. Sunny's fingers were probing a very interesting spot between my legs.

"I'm not right now," I half moaned.

"Then my plan is working."

"Any time you want to finger-fuck the nerves out of me, please do." My head fell back on the cushion. Opening my legs, I sank in the seat, hoping to prevent all of Cinco from seeing my orgasm face. "Maybe I should be more nervous about the person in CH working for the Brotherhood, but the one who really raises my anxiety is—"

"Lyla Dawson."

"I'm not afraid of her. I just know how wickedly devious she is. If anyone can get inside the mind of a sociopathic killer, it's her— Oh." Heat rose between my breasts. Sunny truly was multitalented.

"A backhand is better than an open-palm slap," he dropped. "You get more power with a backhand swing, and knuckles across the face hurt like hell."

I gave him a crazy look.

"Advice, sweet treat, for when you smack the shit out of Dawson."

I snorted a laugh. "I've certainly thought about it enough times. Now, enough about her. My man is in the middle of making me soak this seat."

"His favorite pastime."

Sunny crooked his finger, arching my back off the leather. I had a shorter fuse than usual that morning. A little bit longer and I'd burst.

I moaned and clutched the armrest tighter. My foot pressed against the dashboard uncaring of anyone seeing me. Sunny pressed that spot and I exploded, coming hard, fast, and loud.

"Wow," I breathed, flopping on the seat. "Thank you, my love. Just what I needed on my first day." No sooner were the words out of my mouth than Sunny pulled up to the curb.

Taking a breath, I let it out slow. I may not be nervous, but I did know what was at stake. I had to find the person doing this, and it had to be fast. My guys were forced to wear those trackers to keep up the ruse. It terrified me that the people bombing, attacking, and ambushing them knew exactly where they were as they went around the city, pretending it was business as usual.

"You've got this, Kenzie." Sunny kissed me slow and sweet. "If there's anyone I trust with my life, it's the angel who already saved it."

I hummed, kissing him again. It was pretty damn wonderful being in love. The real kind of love, not the game of pretend it turned out I was playing with Damien and Luca. Sunny saw the truth of me and I saw it of him. If he knew I could do this, who was I to disagree with him?

Waving goodbye, I watched his car turn the corner before heading inside. I wore another Kenzie Creation that morning—a label I plastered all over my work like Gucci. The appreciative looks I got as I strolled past in my wedges, sequin tent dress, and handmade bomber jacket, turned my grin up high.

I belonged here no matter the reason I got the job. I earned my spot in Caddell House all those years ago, and it was still mine.

In the elevator, I hit the button for the fourth floor, steeling myself the whole way up. The day before, I met the designers who've been working for the Johnsons. Time to figure out if one of them was a duplicitous piece of garbage dressed in couture.

The door slid open on my new second home. The fourth floor wasn't nearly as busy as the third where the junior designers and interns clawed out space. Up here, the senior designers reigned.

I stepped out on plush red carpet, scanning the magazine covers that doubled as artwork in our world. So many of them featured models wearing designs by the very people behind the nameplated doors running down both sides of the waiting area. At the very end, written on a piece of tape while they ordered the real thing, was Mackenzie Blaine.

I made a beeline for my office. My juniors and interns should already be inside waiting for me to start the meeting.

"Good morning, everyone. I hope you..." Door swinging shut, I fell on the single person in my office—waiting for me.

"Lyla." At least, I think it was Lyla. The woman sitting at my desk had her lips twisted in such a snarl, it transformed a pretty face into something else entirely. "To what do I owe the pleasure?"

"Shut the fuck up, bitch."

"Whoops," I sang. "Careful, Lyla. Isn't your play the sweet, innocent act so you can keep on fooling people that you aren't dead inside? Don't go showing your true colors now."

"What did you say to Vance?!"

I cocked my head. "I said a lot of things to Vance. You'll have to be more specific."

Lyla threw a clock at my head. I easily ducked it, arching a brow at the smashed pieces. I may use that backhand sooner rather than later.

"Yesterday, I went to his office to inform him you're a lying, cheating thief and he said you told him *the truth*. He said he knows what I did and the only reason I still have a job is because he can't prove it and won't risk a wrongful termination suit!" Her eyes were straight bulging. "What the hell did you say?!"

"Exactly what he told you—the truth. I explained that you, Damien, and Courtney cooked up that bullshit to get me fired." I scoffed. "Obviously I told him. I wouldn't have gotten my job back otherwise. You didn't expect me to keep your dirty secrets like I owe you something, did you?"

I pushed my lips out. "Aww, you stupid fool."

"Watch your fucking mouth."

"Or you'll what?"

"I got rid of you once," she hissed, eyes slitted. "I can just as easily do it again."

Rolling my eyes, I crossed the room, flinging open the curtains. If she came for me, the people in the neighboring building would witness that she hit first, and I was justified in doing whatever came next. "Is that why you dismissed my staff and ambushed me? To deliver empty threats?"

"You don't have *staff*." She spat the word like it offended her. "You don't have an office. You don't have anything. What you have is another brainless idiot willing to give you whatever you want if it means you'll ride his dick. Once I find out the truth of whatever arrangement you have with Vance, you'll be out of here so fast, the sequins will fly off that tacky outfit."

I blinked lazily. "Yesterday was the first time I ever met the man. We don't have an arrangement. Not that knowing that will stop you from believing whatever deluded fantasies you cooked up in your head.

"I have a job to do, Lyla. Go waste someone else's time."

She didn't move an inch. "You think you're so clever. Bagged yourself a rich boyfriend, hauled your ass out of the gutter, and now you're here 'cause you think you're strong enough to face me this time."

"I didn't want to face you the first time," I cried. "Or the second. Or the third. Or the hundredth! You have had some creepy, twisted obsession with me since you first laid eyes on me, and I'm over it. I'm warning you, Dawson. I'm not taking your shit anymore. You come after me again, and you'll get it back three times as hard. That's a promise."

She snorted. "That threat would scare me if I didn't see you for exactly what you are and will always be: trash. You might think what I did to you was harsh, but all that happened was I put you in your rightful place. You'll end up back there again. Trust me." Standing up, she glided to the door, the lovely serene mask in place once again. "It's where you belong."

"Close my office door on the way out, boo." I blew her a kiss. "Oh, and send my staff in. We've got a lot of work to do for Caddell House's top clients. You know how it is— Oh wait, you don't."

Lyla rattled the building slamming the door shut behind her. With her gone, I pried the windows open, praying the smell of her Chanel perfume wafted out quickly. That was the smell of evil.

Sighing, I surveyed my new domain. I had both a desk and a workstation loaded down with everything I needed to get started—all brand new. In the corner, naked mannequins waited for me to cover them in beauty. And beneath my feet, more of that red carpet complemented the pink and gray wallpaper.

I dreamed of having my name on the door outside one of these offices for as long as I can remember. Lyla could threaten whatever she wanted, she would not take this from me.

"I'm a Merchant. No one takes what's mine."

Thirty minutes later, my team was assembled in my office. I studied them through my lashes while they tossed ideas at me.

First was Jace Carter. A junior designer with the taste to match. His jacket looked like a cross between a bomber and tweed, but for some reason, it worked. It probably helped that his strong, dimpled chin, long nose, and thick wavy hair fit everyone's idea of handsome. Jace couldn't look bad in anything he wore.

But are you the sneaking pig violating my family's safety?

Yes, at this point I considered Genny, Fuller, Lizzie, and everyone in the Fairfield family. Everyone except the Savage Princes who evoked heat in me that wasn't brotherly at all.

I slid to Zoe Middleton. *Or is it you?*

Zoe was so fabulous, I'd have believed it if she said she designed the clothes and modeled them. Not a strand of her blonde hair was out of place. Her makeup impeccable. Her outfit this season and expensive from the heels to the faux fur wrap. It was hard to imagine this gorgeous creature could work with a band of killers, but then, I've been fooled by a pretty face before.

As pretty as my intern, Rylee Brennan. Said intern sat up straight, beaming away as she wrote down everything we said. I knew from my time as an intern, we weren't invited to join meetings like this. She was twenty-four years old and eager for her shot.

Would she be this eager if she was sitting on a pile of blood money from the Brotherhood?

I shook the questions away for now. I'd only find out who it was when I caught the bastard in the act. Speculating was just that.

"—designing an entire wardrobe for Caddell's top client," Rylee gushed. "I've only fixed hems and snipped loose threads so far. Will you really look at my sketches, Miss Blaine?"

"It's Kenzie, Rylee, please. We're the same age." I smiled. "And I'll do more than look at them. If they're good, we'll make them."

I thought she'd faint.

"*If* they're good," Jace repeated for no good reason. Whether that pointed to a vindictive streak or a competitive one, it put him slightly higher on the list. "Only the best for the Johnsons, who have been perfectly happy with the styles we've come up with under Anastasia. I still don't understand why she was replaced."

That remark was definitely for me. "There's nothing scandalous about it. I've been making random clothes for the Johnsons as gifts for a while. I didn't know it was my audition for the job. When they decided to update their look, they put my name forth. It's not like she's been fired," I said. "She's just been given another account."

He sniffed, looking down his nose at me. Funny enough, I didn't take it as an insult. I had a feeling he acted this superior with his own mother. Jace couldn't help it. "Well, you must be good if they asked for you personally."

"So how will this work?" Zoe cut in. "We sketch designs and hand them in for your approval?"

I shook my head. "Even simpler than that. I know their preferences, and I assume you all do too from making their clothes for years. We divide up the family and create the clothes for the ones we're assigned. I will get final reject power, but otherwise, designing their wardrobe is up to you."

"Me too, Miss— Kenzie?" Rylee asked.

"You too," I said, earning shocked looks from Jace and Zoe. "But in your case, I approve your designs before you touch a thread."

I was nice but she was still an intern. The woman may be implanting trackers in those clothes, but they'd still be the best clothes to come out of Caddell House while I was in charge.

"Yes, absolutely," Rylee said. "Actually, I've got two pads worth of ideas I can show you."

"Love to see them."

Rylee was up and out the door before I could finish the sentence with "later."

"Are you two friends or something?" Jace morphed from shocked to shrewd. "Interns sew buttons. They don't design wardrobes for top clients."

"And she won't either if I don't love what she comes up with," I replied. "The Johnson I have in mind for her prefers simple, low-cut, and leather. Anything too frouncy stays in the closet. Anything that conceals her assets gets ripped up and fixed. With those guidelines to work with, Rylee will be fine. I'm more interested in what you, Jace, have planned for David Johnson."

The entire Merchant clan went by aliases under their account. David Johnson was Liam's. The irony is they don't go by their real names to discourage anyone from adding any *extras* in the package of clothes they ship out. Now we know how well that worked.

Jace grinned the Cheshire cat's smile. "I am bursting with ideas for David. He'll love what I have in mind for him."

"He's a single father running a business," I said. "He won't love anything too loud or ostentatious."

He and Zoe shared an amused glance. "Don't worry about me, love. I've handstitched almost everything in that mystery man's closet. I know his taste better than my boyfriend's."

"What about me?" Zoe asked. "I'm not interested in simple or business casual. Vance said the Johnsons were looking for a completely new look. I'm ready for a challenge, Kenzie. No more bringing other people's designs to life."

"You will have—"

"—she expecting you?" Rylee's voice floated under the door crack. "If you give me a minute, I'll let her know you're here."

"Not necessary."

My brows shot up my head.

"This isn't the queen's drawing room. You don't need to announce my presence." Genevieve Hunt did that all on her own, throwing the door open and striding in to the pleasure of my surprise. Surprise at seeing her, or at seeing her pink lace bra clear as day through her sheer see-through shirt. "Sup, Feisty. Damn, they gave us a nice office."

I shook myself and looked again. Genny was still there. "I'm sorry, did you say us?"

"Uh, yeah," she drew out. "I told you all you had to do was get the job, and I'd handle security." She stretched out on my desk like the runway pinup model she was. "Say hello to your security."

"GENNY, YOU CAN'T BE serious."

"I've never been more serious in my entire life."

Genny and I argued in the back of the cab heading home. Her motorcycle was out while she was wearing a boot, and I said no to Sunny's ride so we could fight it out some more.

"You can't just walk into a place like Caddell House and announce you're not going away!"

She laughed. "Can't I? Looks like I just did."

I pinched the bridge of my nose. The day went off course with Genny's arrival and went nowhere good after that. She was on my tail everywhere I went, sharing her unfiltered opinion about the clothes we passed, and the designers making them. On my lunch break, I tried to take Bane's suggestion of snooping while everyone was out, but Genny insisted on coming with me in case the person came back and caught me.

A sensible suggestion if not for her boot clomping so loudly on the floor, sneaking was impossible.

"Genny," I began. "I appreciate what you want to do. I feel a hundred times safer with you guarding my back than another faceless guard."

"Why do I sense a but coming on?"

"But I don't believe that's why you're doing this," I gritted. "You don't think I can find this guy fast enough, or maybe even at all. You're volunteering to babysit me, *not* protect me."

I expected a slick response, and didn't get one.

"You are perceptive," she said, turning from the window to face me. "That's why I know you can find him, Kenzie, but I don't know that it'll be quick enough. I need to be in my borough. I can't wait weeks or months. I gave you till the end of this month, and I meant it. Least I can do is help you meet the deadline."

I quieted. That was the most even, reasonable reply Genny had ever given me. "I don't know how to deal with you when you're like this."

"You don't know how to deal with me period."

"True."

"If you've got a better idea, let's hear it. Someone has to watch your back, and I need to be finding these guys. Sitting on my ass isn't an option."

I slouched against the cheap upholstery, sighing. "I don't have a better idea, but it doesn't mean this is a good one. It was one thing putting me in there. Won't the guy we're searching for get spooked now that you're hobbling through the halls? They won't make a move while you're around."

"What would you do if you found a machine that gives you twice as much money as you put in?"

"What?"

"Answer the question." Genny propped her bad leg on my lap like I was a footrest. "What would you do?"

"I'd... put money in it, obviously."

"You'd put every last cent you had in it, then you'd do it again and again until all the banks in the world ran dry."

I stared at her, waiting for the point. Genny chuckled at my expression.

"When you stumble on something that gives you everything you want, you don't just walk away. This little tracker-in-the-clothes idea was genius. Even I can admit it. For decades—*decades*—our enemies have tried to crack our security and take us out. One bastard in Caddell House finally gave the Brotherhood the key."

What she was saying burrowed in, convincing me with its truth. "They can't go back because they know nothing else is going to work. If you want wealth, you don't walk away from a machine that prints money. And if you want your enemies dead, you don't give up the only method that's gotten you close."

Genny flicked my nose. "Exactly. We'll get you thinking like a crime boss yet."

"It's still a big risk. With you hanging around CH, they'll be wary. Smarter."

"So will we." She nudged my shoulder. "You getting a vibe off that Jace guy? He was tossing me weird looks all morning, and he shouldn't know who I am."

"I get a fashion-snob vibe from him. Wearing the wrong shoes will turn you into their lifelong enemy. It'll be hard to separate his distaste from an actual hatred of the Merchants. That's why I was thinking the only way we'll know for sure is to catch them in the act. The how escapes me though."

"Hidden cameras?"

I shook my head. "CH is surprisingly light on the cameras. If they weren't, HR would've picked up on Lyla's constant harassment. That said, there are always people around day and night. We couldn't put in any cameras without being seen."

"This guy is sabotaging our clothes unseen. There has to be low-traffic spots where he does that in peace." She snapped her fingers. "Did you ever bring your work home with you?"

"Me? No way. If I was caught, I'd lose my job on the spot," I said. "CH is fanatical about preventing our designs from leaking out early."

"But..." she prompted.

I laughed. "But there were a few braver interns than I who snuck a few things home to work on. Missing Talia's deadlines also got you fired. Sometimes you've got no good options."

"You see where I'm going with this, right?"

"Anyone sneaking your clothes out of the building is who we're looking for. I'm with you, but could it really be that easy?"

Genny and I debated through the ride, going over every possible method our culprit could use. Every obvious method was hard to accept because you had to think they would've been caught much sooner. All the clever, devious methods made me feel the mounting pressure of the deadline.

I trudged into the elevator, wiped out and it had nothing to do with work. Everyone depended on me to figure this out. I knew I could, but would I do it on time with Lyla breathing down my neck?

That woman was planning something. I felt it in the dark pit of resentment I held for her. Lyla's hatred for me consumed her—that fact was written all over her face that morning. She would not leave me in peace, so I better be prepared for her opening strike.

The doors slid open, and I saw her.

Striding down the hall calm and casual, a strange woman headed for the only other door on Sunny's floor, with my baby snoozing on her chest. My heart shot into my throat, strangling my cry. "H-hey! Hey!" I screamed. "What are you doing with her?!"

I bolted out of the elevator. The stranger turned, blinking at me as my daughter jolted awake.

"Oh, no— Feisty, wait!" Genny called.

"Give her to me!"

Laurel burst into wails. The woman didn't fight me, handing over Laurel within seconds of me about to snatch her.

Shooting away, I put ten feet between us in a blink—cradling Laurel tight to my chest. "Who are you?" My voice was ten octaves too high. "Why did you have her?"

Inexplicably, the woman smiled at me. "I'm so sorry. You must be Mackenzie. This wasn't the greeting I had in mind."

"Who are you—?"

Genny moved as fast as the boot allowed her. Flying past me and my crying offspring, she threw her arms around the stranger. "Mom."

I put it down to the sobs in my ear that it took a full ten seconds for that word to penetrate. *Mom? Did she say Mom?*

"Hold on, you're Genny's..."

"Mother," Adeline Redgrave finished. "Yes, I am. Sorry again for frightening you."

Heat licked my cheeks. My goodness, I just shouted at my boyfriend's mother like she was a kidnapper.

"Sunny was busy with his fathers," Adeline continued, "and this little one was nodding off in her high chair. She fell asleep in my arms while I was looking for her crib. Got everything but in that nursery."

Of course there wasn't a crib in the nursery. I had it moved to my bedroom.

"I came out here to ask Fuller where to put her down, and naturally you didn't take too well to a stranger carting your kid off."

I laughed mirthlessly. "A perfectly reasonable explanation. I'm the one who is sorry. I went nuts, screaming and carrying on for no reason. I should've recognized you. You look just like Liam. Or Liam looks just like you."

They truly did look alike though Liam was blond and built, where this lovely older woman was redheaded and slim. From the shape of her brow, to the amused twist to her lips, and down to the same nose. Liam received the masculine frame from his father, but his everything else from his mother. A mother I was told was pushing sixty but could've been Angela Bassett for all the effect she let age have on her beauty.

"Liam does look like me, and it used to make him mad when people said it." She chuckled, dropping a kiss on Genny's head. "He claimed everyone was telling him he looked like a girl."

"Beat a few people up for it too," Genny mused.

"Ahh. The infamous Hunt temper. Even worse for how it smolders beneath a placid surface—building, building, building," Adeline said. "You don't know you did anything wrong until... they erupt."

"Wow, what a description," I said. *And why does it excite instead of scare me?*

I bounced Laurel, murmuring softly to soothe her. If it was possible for her to be cussing me out with her whines and shouts, I'd deserve it. I woke the poor kid up from a perfectly good nap for no reason. If I thought about it for half a second, I'd have realized Thatcher wouldn't let anyone in this building that we couldn't trust. "I'm sorry, baby girl. Want to go for a walk outside? You like the gardens."

"Ah!" I took that response to mean I better do something, or she was going to lose it.

"I'll walk her around," I said. "Hopefully, she'll fall asleep quickly and I'll be forgiven."

"I'll come with you," Adeline offered. Cupping Genny's face, she smooched her cheek. It struck me then that was the first time I witnessed someone be affectionate with the youngest Hunt and not be hurt for it. "You, my love, go upstairs and rest that leg. I'll be up soon with a case of Leffe Blonde—your favorite. Flew it in from Belgium yesterday."

"You're my favorite mom, did you know that?"

"It doesn't come free." Adeline hooked through my arm. "I'll trade you for everything you kids have been keeping from me. All of it."

Genny lost her smile quick. "Of course," she muttered under her breath.

The three of us were already walking off. I cast glances at Adeline in the elevator. I didn't know much about the Merchants when Sunny crash-landed into my life, but I knew quite a lot about them now.

I was standing in an enclosed space with the most dangerous woman in Cinco City.

"Five little monkeys."

I jerked. "What?"

"Five little monkeys," Adeline repeated. Her enigmatic smile said she knew what I was thinking, but how could she? "When my babies were fussy, I sang 'Five Little Monkeys' at the top of my lungs and it stunned them into silence. I have a horrid singing voice—even infants know it."

Snorting, I cracked up. A sudden vision of a dumbfounded baby Sunny, gaping at his wailing mother flashed across my mind. And with it, she suddenly went from legend... to human.

"I'll have to try that one day." Another day because my baby was settling, her angry cries reducing to soft sniffles. I buried my face in her curls, breaking under the fear that sent me racing down that hallway. *No one is ever going to take you from me, Laurel. Never again.*

The doors let us out on the lobby floor. To our right was the guard station and the room they held me and Sienna in when we first arrived. The left led to the swimming pool and Oasis. That wasn't my word. *Oasis* read on the sign beside the greenhouse.

Every part of the Fairfield screamed luxury, but to me the most beautiful corner of this complex was Oasis. Marigolds greeted us at the door, tickling my ankles as I walked past. Tucked within the greenery were little ponds bearing lotus flowers, and in one, the family of frogs that delighted Laurel the first time she saw them.

I paused beneath the apricot blossoms, pointing them out to her. Laurel rested her head on my shoulder, breaths evening out as she relaxed in her favorite place.

"How old is she?"

I felt Adeline's presence at my side. "She's almost ten months."

She hummed. "When I was your age, the thought of kids was so far off. Cinco was a dangerous place. Corrosive. Everything and everyone pure and innocent were stained by this city. You couldn't live here and escape that reality."

I blinked at her, not understanding what she was saying. Not knowing why she was saying it.

"It's hard to believe, but the things I did all those years ago were not for power. It was to give Cinco a new start—free it from the shadow the ledger cast over all five boroughs. I truly thought by the time I had my children, I had made the city safer for them, for you"—she stroked my daughter's fist—"for the innocent.

"I can't tell you how sorry I am to discover I was wrong."

My heart squeezed.

Adeline knew. About Luca. About Laurel's kidnapping. About the terrible reason the Merchants flew to New York.

"That wasn't your fault," I whispered.

"An enemy I created used you and your baby to get to my family. How could that not be my fault?" She motioned to a bench beneath the magnolia tree. "How are you? Both of you?"

"We're much better now." Together we sat. "Sunny rescued her within hours. She wasn't hurt and she'll never remember that woman touched her." I sighed. "As for me, I think I learned the lesson you did when you were my age. To survive in Cinco, you have to be strong."

"To survive in the underground, certainly," Adeline replied, "but I'll tell you what I told each of my children: this does not have to be your life if you don't want it."

I smiled softly. "I know that. I truly do. But I also know the easy life isn't guaranteed for any family. When I was young, my mother shot and killed my abusive father. She went to jail, and my sister and I went into foster care." The truth fell easily from my lips. It didn't occur to me Adeline wasn't someone I could talk to. "Fast-forward several years, one ex-boyfriend cost me my job and reputation. The other took my home and safety. I was living on the street, separated from my daughter and thinking about suicide long before I met a Merchant.

"Now I'm happy, loved, and, even though I can't say I'm completely safe, I'm surrounded by people who'll cross the country to save me. I didn't have any of that before." A thought stretched a smile on my lips. "When you find a machine that gives you free money, you don't walk away, you get every last cent out of that bitch."

Adeline's laugh rang like bells through the courtyard. "Well said. I see why my sons are so taken with you."

My ears quirked up. "Sons?"

"Oh yes," she replied, amused grin coming back. "They've all told me about you in great detail. Want to know how many women my three committed bachelors have told me about before you?" She pressed her finger to her thumb.

Zero.

I was proud of myself for not cheesing and giving away that I was a complete lovesick dope. "Whatever they said, I promise they exaggerated. By the way, Sunny also greatly exaggerated how far along we are in our wedding plans."

We cracked up, struggling to shush ourselves and not wake Laurel. "Now that you mention it, he is now exclusively referring to you as Mrs. Bellisario." She squeezed my hand. "Let's hear it from your lips. Tell me all about you, Mackenzie Blaine."

We stayed in the gardens for so long, Laurel had her full nap and woke in time to demand dinner. The whole time, I told her about me—not just the bad days, but the happy ones too. The best part, Adeline listened, understood, and opened up to me.

A weird feeling gripped me as we headed upstairs. It'd been so long since I had this—the warmth and attention of a mother. Adeline even kissed me on the temple the same way she did Genny when the elevator stopped on Sunny's floor. "Wonderful talking with you, Kenzie. And meeting you, Laurel.

"Now I must go against doctor's advice, and bribe my child with alcohol to get her to give up all the secrets she thinks she can keep from me."

I busted up as she was whisked away. That was Sunny's mother all right.

"HERA, SAVE ME," I BREATHED.

Warm breath ghosted my ear. "Should I be jealous?"

I jumped a foot in the air. Whirling around, I came face to face with that borrowed grin curling Liam's mouth. "Jealous of what?" I squeaked.

"Of the fact you keep staring at my fathers." He winked. "You can't have us all, Miss Blaine."

I seriously considered dumping the pot of lasagna soup over his head—forget that I was making it for everyone to celebrate our first night all together.

Sunny, Bane, Adeline, and Genny were upstairs in Genny's apartment, waiting for me to call and tell them dinner was ready. It was just us in Sunny's apartment. Us being me, Liam, Sienna, Adeline's husbands, Tricky, and Shonda.

"You're cute, Mr. Hunt, but my taste for older men doesn't extend that far."

"Hmm." He leaned over me reaching the glasses on the high shelf. Cologne scented the air, wafting from his exposed chest. At home and free, Liam let a few buttons hang loose, and it was doing terrible things to my internal temperature. "Just checking," he said.

"Why don't you help me finish this up instead? Pass me the noodles, please."

He turned to do as I asked and my gaze drifted back to Adeline's men against my will. I couldn't help it. We're fortunate to come across one silver fox out in the wild, but four in one room—there was nowhere else to fucking look! Even Sienna kept tossing glances at them.

Gray touched their temples. Wrinkles graced the corner of their eyes. A calmness slowed their movements as if they reached the point they had life figured out, and there was no reason to rush a minute of it. Down the row, Adeline's men were nature-defyingly handsome, but what really drew my eyes was Tricky chatting away with the man who had to be Sunny's father.

Sinjin.

His dark hair boasted blue and silver streaks. Yes, blue and silver. They weaved through his waves in the perfect mix of silver, ebony, and sapphire—the kind of bold look you wished you could pull off, but didn't have the balls to try. I got the feeling from the first instance he kissed my hand, said it was nice to meet me, then winked like we had a secret... that Sinjin had no trouble doing exactly what he wanted always.

Despite Adeline's guilt, it's Sinjin that kicked off this war. At least that's what Sienna's visions say. His children claim he's made too many mortal enemies to narrow it down to one, but I should talk to him. I can push aside the strange nervousness that raises my pulse when he's near.

I shivered. Liam's teasing was off. Sinjin didn't make me nervous because he was handsome. He set off something base and primal in me because I knew when I was in the presence of a predator.

That man is dangerous. A loving partner? Sure. A great father? I'm not denying it. But none of that changed the fact he was wicked through and through.

Sinjin suddenly glanced up from his conversation with Tricky, fixing on my wide eyes. Holding my gaze, he smiled slow—and winked. I was held in his power, feeling every thought, secret, truth, and lie plucked from my mind.

That was impossible nonsense and still I squeaked and spun away.

"Kenzie, careful!"

I crashed into Liam, knocking the strainer of pasta out of his hands. My foot slipped on a noodle and I was flying.

"Ahhh!"

"Kenzie!" Liam lunged to catch me and we both went down.

All one hundred and seventy pounds fell on me, knocking the wind clean out of my lungs. Maybe this was Sinjin's power: causing pain without laying a hand on you.

"Shit, Kenzie, are you okay?"

A high-pitched giggle broke into my gaze. "Oooh. Daddy said a bad word."

Fingers tangled in my hair, lifting my head to his shiny, concerned eyes. "Are you?"

Willing breath into my lungs, I tossed my head. "No."

"No? What's wrong? Did I hurt you? Where?"

Once again it surprised me that Liam managed to convince the world he was cold. The idea he hurt me accidentally wretched his voice.

"Hurts," I whispered. "I need..."

"Need what?"

"A kiss." Liam stilled. "I need a kiss. That'll make me feel better."

"You're ridiculous," he deadpanned.

I smothered a laugh—mostly because I did take a good fall and it hurt to think about laughing. "I'll have that kiss without sass, thank you very much." I tapped my mouth. "Right here. Now."

"I told you about playing this game with me."

"I told you now."

"Fine."

No sooner had the word penetrated my ears than his mouth was on mine. I gasped for an entirely different reason.

Soft, warm lips caressed me, stealing the gasp off my tongue and teasing it with his. There was an old anime movie where in exchange for his heart, a fire demon grants a man unimaginable power.

I finally understood that movie.

Liam claimed my heart. Reduced it to cinders on his palm, and left me with nothing but a faint memory of the person I was before, but what he gave me in exchange was so much better.

My whole body came alive in his arms. Things I didn't know I could feel. Places I never knew could burn. His tongue tangled with mine, chasing a moan past my lips, and suddenly I believed in it all. Psychics. Power. Fate. Demons.

Magic.

We broke apart—staring at each other. Our chests heaved like we ran ten miles.

"Looks like you don't need our help." Sinjin leaned against the kitchen counter, amusement written on his face. He saw the whole thing. Remembering he was sorta the reason it happened, stained my cheeks red.

"Uh, yes they do!" Shonda blew in. "You destroy my kitchen, dump pasta on my floor, and then make out on it? Out."

"Shonda, we didn't—"

"Out!"

We got out.

Liam and I stumbled into the living room. His lips parted, and I froze as his fingers glided down the back of my hand.

"Kenzie—"

"Daddy." Tricky tackled her father's legs and climbed his body like a tree monkey. "Play with me."

He shot me a wry look, somehow just as intimate as the kiss we shared. We were speaking our own silent language.

"Yes, boss," Liam said.

I let them go, knowing we would talk later when we were alone. Edging toward the kitchen, I called, "Shonda, at least let me clean up the mess."

The look she gave me had me turn around and go play with Tricky.

Shonda did not like anyone—except Sienna—in her kitchen. I had to talk her into letting me make dinner. In the end, I did not make dinner and we didn't eat lasagna soup. Shonda made grilled salmon with avocado salad, and for dessert, she served me a permanent ban for life.

After we ate and put the youngest members of the Merchant clan to bed, we stayed up telling Sunny's parents everything that's happened since I moved into the Fairfield.

That night, I lay in bed propped against the pillows, massaging Sunny's shoulders. The pornographic noises he was making made me glad his folks had their own apartment and weren't bunking in the next room.

"I'm glad she pulled a Genny and horned in," Sunny continued. "Even with a hole in her shoulder and a bum leg, she's a ten-man security team in one woman."

"Why don't I doubt that?"

"I'm glad I won't have to worry about your safety since I'm going back to work tomorrow."

"Back to work?" I repeated. "What does that mean? You've been going to work."

"I've been at the shelter working out the terms of our new arrangement with River. Now that Merchants are allowed in Rockchapel again, I'm going in with Ryker, Makai, and Athena."

"Why? Liam said one of his guys was hunting down Vito. The best retriever in the city—now that your father is retired."

Sunny tipped his head back to look at me. His hair tickled my stomach, tightening my skin. We just had sex and I was quickly gearing up to go again.

"Roman will find Vito. The guy is the best, no question. But Vito and Grant both fled to Rockchapel to escape us. If those dumbasses got that idea in their head, smarter criminals did too.

"Tracking down all our enemies in every borough is impossible. Hunting Rockchapel for the ones that went eerily quiet is doable."

"So, that's what you mean by returning to work. You're blindly tracking down potential Brotherhood members in Rockchapel. Because living till twenty-six is for losers."

Sunny chuckled. "I won't die, babe. There are a lot of people waiting to pay for hurting you. The universe won't allow me to go before getting revenge."

"There has to be another way," I argued. "You've been kept out of Rockchapel for years. You don't know where their scum likes to hide. The Merchants don't have the home-court advantage on this one."

"You're sexy when you use sports analogies."

"Sole."

"I'm just saying," he breezed. "Look, everything you said we've thought of. That's why I've been spending quality time with my uncle. He's mapped out all of Rockchapel for us. The different gangs, their turfs, and the neutral areas where people freelance undisturbed."

"If River knows all of this, isn't he and his crew better prepared to hunt the Brotherhood in that borough? I mean, it's dangerous for them too, but at least he has the advantage."

"River needs to continue doing exactly what he is doing," Sunny replied. "Helping those women get their lives back. I won't ask him to stop for a job I can do myself."

I deflated on the pillows. "No, of course, you're right. We all have our jobs to do. They're all important." I peppered kisses on his temple. "But does it have to be just the four of you?"

"If I roll in there with twenty people, the rats bolt for their holes. Trust me," he said. "In the old days, I'd fuck shit up by myself or with Ryker if I needed a designated driver. I'm only inviting so many people along because I'm responsible now." He gave me a serious, upside-down look. "I'm a step-dad."

I was stuck between rolling my eyes and kissing him, so I did both. "If not twenty guys, how about five? Bane should go with you."

"Bane has his own business to take care of."

"Training me?"

"No, I meant that literally. You know his crew manufactures and sells weapons. They're about to increase production tenfold." Sunny sat up and faced me. "We'll do whatever it takes to cut the head off the snake, but if we don't stomp the Brotherhood out soon.

"It's war."

Chapter Seven

A waterfall of silk slipped through my fingertips, filling me with visions of the outfits I'd make for Sunny. I didn't think anything matched the feeling of running around Brocade. Clearly I forgot my days in the War Room.

Fabrics of all types, colors, and styles surrounded me on all sides, lit up under heavy neon white lights. Why was the second-floor fabric storage called the War Room? Because when the season came and it was time for us to enter our clothes into competitions, it got straight-up ugly in here. One woman lost a tooth fighting over pearl chiffon. Girl took her out with an elbow to the face.

That morning, it was peaceful. Or mostly peaceful.

Snickering drew my attention to the corner for the third time. Two junior designers huddled up, making out they were looking at the tulle. I'd buy it if I hadn't caught them watching me out of the corner of my eye twice.

Another burst of giggles ground my teeth. "You two," I called. "Got something to say?"

"Yeah, actually. We do." The short, blonde one rounded on me, arms folded. "We heard Anastasia was blotted off the Johnson account and it was given to you because you're sleeping with Vance."

I returned to measuring my silk, losing interest in the conversation immediately. "Don't believe everything you hear."

Their footfalls drew closer. "Don't get me wrong, I almost respect you for it," continued Blondie. "Obviously you didn't know this because you're an outsider, but HR really cracks down on that sort of thing." She clicked her tongue. "Don't be surprised if you're out on your ass by tomorrow. You'll have ridden Vance's dick for nothing."

My teeth clenched. *So that's Lyla's play. Spread rumors that I'm sleeping with the boss so HR will kick me out.*

I wanted to believe human resources would do a fair investigation, then back me up when there was no proof. But they didn't do that the last time.

Raising my head, I gifted them a serene smile. "I am not sleeping with anyone but my very hot boyfriend and his brother." Their eyes bugged. "Yes, I seriously just told you that because I'm proud of my current sex life and I'm doing nothing I need to hide. I don't lie, sneak around, or play games, ladies. Not like the gossipy harpy that poured those vicious rumors in your ear.

"What I do is come to work and get my job done. A job I got because I'm the best." I leaned over the table, getting in their face. "Let me repeat that for you: I am the best.

"I'm also senior designer for CH's top account who clearly has some favor with Hollywell, or he wouldn't have given me the job." I winked. "I'm a good friend to have in this building. So, think about it. Do you want me as a friend or...?" I let the rest dangle unsaid in the air.

The two shared a look. Blondie faced me, beaming wide. "Welcome to Caddell House. We're so lucky to have you." She shook my hand. "We eat lunch on the roof. Sit with us, yeah?"

I just waved them off smiling. That worked on them. Let's see if it works on the other designers who got Lyla's poison dripped in their ears.

I cut out my silk and brought it up to my office. It wasn't empty.

"Seriously, if you keep lying in wait for me like this, I'm going to start carrying pepper spray."

Lyla laughed from her spot on my window seat. Jace sat across from her.

"See? I told you," she said to him. "We're old college buddies. We're always messing with each other."

The nonsense that came out of her mouth stunned me into silence. Adeline's trick did work.

"What are you two doing in here?" I asked when my voice came back. "Where's Genny?"

"Your *friend* ordered Rylee to give her a tour," Jace replied. "Who is she? Why is she here?"

I gave Lyla a pointed look. "After Miss Dawson makes her way out of the exit, I'd be happy to tell you. Bye, Lyla."

She laughed. "Exit? I'm not going anywhere, silly. I've got designs to show you. Been working on them all night."

"The only thing you have to show me is your back."

Howling, Lyla nudged Jace's shoulder. "See how we joke with each other? Kenzie cracks me up." She nailed that beaming smile on me. "But it's time to get serious. I've got ideas for Ava Johnson that you're going to love."

A thick, sludgy feeling flooded my veins. "Why would you have ideas for Ava Johnson?"

She closed the distance, smiling wider if it was possible. "Because Vance assigned me to the Johnson account. Surprise! We're working together."

I held very still. That's what you did in the presence of a venomous snake. "Why would Vance assign you to my account?"

"Well, when he found out you were allowing an intern to design the wardrobe for our top client, it was clear you needed more help. Naturally, I offered to share your workload, old friend."

"Who the hell told him Rylee was submitting designs?"

Jace raised his hand. "Me," he sang. "It was all for you, Kenzie. Just helping out."

Lips peeling back, my eyes narrowed to slits. Jace's shit-eating grin twitched. "Don't play games with me, Carter. You want to undermine me, then own your actions. Better yet, if you've got a problem with me giving an intern more responsibility, open your mouth and say so."

"I— I wasn't—" He backed up into the window seat and fell on his ass. People like him were used to their bitchiness going unchecked. He met his match in the new Kenzie. "I didn't mean—"

I dismissed him, fixing on Lyla. "You are not on my team. I've informed Hollywell of your fondness for creating a hostile work environment. I'm happy to remind him—in more detail."

The corner of her mouth tightened. "I'm so glad you brought that up. Vance mentioned something about that when I spoke to him. Thankfully we cleared up the confusion, and I have the chance to clear it with you." Lyla grasped my forearms. My body hairs stood on end. "Kenzie, everything that happened with framing and getting you fired, that wasn't me, it was all Damien. He *forced* me to help him because we've known each other since college and had a friendly rivalry.

"When I refused to h-help him," she said, lips trembling. "Damien threatened me. We were sleeping together at the time. I know it was stupid, but you remember how charming he could be."

Each word pierced deeper into my chest.

"Damien said if I didn't help him get rid of you, he'd take me down with him when Talia destroyed his career. It was the three of us, or it was just you." She tried to touch my cheek and I shot away. "I hate that I gave in to him, Kenzie. I was naïve and stupid and afraid of losing my big shot, but the real villain here is Damien... which is what I explained to Vance."

Her expression changed. "He opened Caddell House to all sorts of lawsuits and bad press. I mean, Damien Stone, co-director of Caddell House New York, seduced and knocked up a junior designer, forced the intern he was fucking to help destroy her credibility, and then abandoned her to live on the streets. CH's reputation will be in ruins. People will boycott our clothes until he's fired, and he damn well should be."

I stood rigid as she closed the distance again. Touched me—again.

"Damien deserves what's coming to him and more, but after talking with Vance, we agreed this problem is best handled in-house. Damien doesn't get to take all of us down with him." She clapped. "But the first step is repairing my relationship with you. When Jace said you were in over your head, I saw that as the perfect opportunity.

"I want to help, Kenzie. I am here to support you during your transition back into the fashion scene. After all, you weren't keeping up to date while living on the streets." She laughed, setting my teeth on edge. "The best part is you already told Vance that you'll work with me without drama, so you have no reason to tell HR we'll create a hostile work environment. I want to work with you. You want to work with me. Everyone is happy."

I glared down my nose at her, considering what would happen if I let my balled fists do what they were ready to do. "Let me see if I've got this right, you threatened to leak *my story* and *my trauma* all so you could leverage yourself into a better position. A position that'll keep you conveniently close to me and make your eventual sabotage that much easier."

She gasped. "That's not what I'm saying at all! Kenzie, how could you even think that?!" Lyla whirled on the silent Jace. "Are you listening to her? If anyone's creating a hostile work environment right now, it's not me."

"There's no hostility here." Brushing past her, I centered myself in a single breath, pushing my rage down.

"It's chess, Kenzie. You're not playing the game. You're playing the person. For some, a few threats will do. For others, a couple stacks of cash. Couple of the hard cores won't be put down for less than a beating so savage they want to crawl back into their mother's womb. But for the rest… Enemies like Snyder, Adams, and the leader of the Brotherhood, they'll never stop coming unless they're put down for good."

I smiled as Sunny's voice filled my mind. I smiled… and Lyla stopped.

"I want to thank you, Lyla, for making your opening move so quickly. Now that I know your strategy, it makes things much simpler."

"What?" Her face crumpled in a frown. "What the fuck are you talking about?"

I flapped a hand, claiming my seat. "Nothing. Don't mind me." I flicked to Jace. "Carter, would you mind getting Rylee and Zoe? Looks like we'll be changing the assignments around. As for you, Lyla, welcome aboard. I'm looking forward to working with you in ten minutes—which is when I expect to see these sketches you worked all night on." Color bled into Lyla's cheeks. "Based on what you got, I'll decide which Johnson will get your exclusive attention. Although, from what I remember, your tastes tend to run a bit flashy for Ava Johnson. If it doesn't work out, you'll handle the everydays for the staff."

"Excuse me? You're not putting my clothes on the housekeeper." Lyla didn't seem to notice Jace wasn't all the way out of the room. If she wanted him as witness to her angel act, the plan was falling apart. "What the hell do you know about Ava's taste? We've been designing for the family for years. Anastasia groomed me to become one of her personal designers. I'd say of the two people in this room, the one most qualified to design for the family and *do this job* is me."

"I know what Ava wants because I'm a close, personal friend of hers. The family requested that I design for their account. They love my work, Lyla, and refused everyone else."

Genny chose that moment to walk inside. "Ava Johnson" tossed a nod at Lyla, parked on my window seat, and started messing around on her phone.

"I believe they said something like either I design for them or they'll take their business to another fashion house." *My piece slides across the board.* "That's part of the reason I felt safe to come back. If my coworkers ever came for me again, trying to force me out of a job, this time the director will listen better when I say I'm innocent. Hollywell wouldn't want to go down in Caddell history as the director that lost an account generating thirty percent of our annual earnings."

My smile shone wider than hers. "This is a new era for us, Lyla. We're going to get along much better this time around."

Lyla said nothing. Face beet red, she slammed out of my office. I doubted she was off to get those sketches.

Genny smirked at me over her phone. "Nicely done, Blaine. You're learning how to play."

THAT AFTERNOON, SIENNA picked us up from work. She trashed Lyla in all the right places as I recounted my day with the newest member of my team.

"She's going to mess you up every chance she gets," Sienna said. "First step is putting a lock on that office door."

"I can change the locks, but I'd have to give a key to the janitor. Lyla's smart enough to break through that flimsy security." I sighed. "I doubt I'll prevent the next move. I just have to be ready for it."

"Don't stress, little Blaine," Genny spoke up from the back seat. She was stretched out and chill like she was being driven around by her chauffeurs. "If Dawson gets out of line, I'll handle her. What we're doing is too important for anyone to get in the way."

"What does handle her mean?" Sienna asked.

"Eh. Depends on how pissed off I am at the time."

That wasn't reassuring. It probably wasn't meant to be.

"Gen, do you mind if we drop you off?" Sienna asked. "I wanted to swing by the shelter today. See if they need any help over there."

"Do what you gotta do. Dad's taking me bike shopping, but hit me up if it turns out they do need something. Honestly, it should be me and the Cardinals looking after these women, but River rescued them. They trust him. I won't take over as long as he doesn't fuck things up."

"He won't," I said. "I know you guys have a rough history, but River will look out for them. He'll do right by those women."

"Will he? He never has before," Genny snapped. "River *Delaney* has spent the last three years on some petty fucking crusade against me. He's convinced countless women in Harlow that I'm dangerous. I'll turn them into criminals and ruin their lives. Because of that, women who would've had homes, protection, and an income are instead living dirty and hungry on the streets with him! So don't talk your fucking boyfriend up to me. You forget I've known him a lot longer than you."

I pressed my lips tight together, keeping in a sharp response. Arguing with Genny wouldn't serve a purpose. She was right that I didn't know the full history between them.

We didn't say much on the ride to the Fairfield. Stopping before the front doors, Genny smooched both our cheeks, flipped us both off, then went on inside. The most confusing goodbye in the history of human interaction.

"I like her," Sienna mused.

"I like her too... most days."

Sienna watched me out of the corner of her eyes. "What do you think about what she said?"

"What do you think?" I stalled.

"Well, River didn't exactly lie, did he? I'm sure Genny doesn't force those women into anything, but they are a violent, criminal motorcycle gang, and she's damn proud of that. If people choose living on the streets rather than mixing with that life, no one else but us could understand that better."

I tossed my head, smiling. "I swear you're the cricket on my shoulder, sharing your wisdom."

"Oooh, a cricket. That'll be great to put on the logo for when I open my bookstore."

"That going to be soon?"

"I hope so. Liam said we can look at properties whenever I'm ready."

My grin wiped away. "Liam said? What are you talking about?"

"My bookstore, sis. Remember, I want to sell resources for people to find the answers before I'm forced to tell them the outcome. Actually, Liam was saying we could expand on the idea. Create a center where people don't just read up on their issues, but address them too. We can have meditation sessions, yoga, and classes." Sienna was bouncing off the seat. "I could rent rooms to AA and other recovery groups. Isn't that a great idea, Kenzie?"

"Hold up. You left me way behind. When did you and Liam have this chat? I didn't know you were ready to look at... centers," I cried.

"I'm not," she said with a laugh. "I wasn't keeping it a surprise. Last night, Liam brought up the bookstore and asked if that was still my plan. It turns out Liam created a fund for young female entrepreneurs after Lizzie was born. He said if I'm serious, I should bring him a business plan and we can move forward right away. Amazing, right!

"This is what he does. Those clubs and restaurants he owns, they're not all fronts for his other business. He's an owner and investor, just like his dads are. One of them invested in Caddell House, and look where it is today. Liam says I could turn a profit within eight months."

I was pretty sure my sister said Liam's name more times in this conversation than she has since we met the guy. "How is it you make a new best friend whenever I turn my back?"

She laughed. "We're not doing anything behind your back, Kenzie. It's just... Liam pointed out that I had dreams before I met the Merchants. I shouldn't give up on them."

"You shouldn't." I squeezed her shoulder. "Sienna, a self-help center is a great idea. You're going to do so much good, little sister. I always knew you would make a difference."

Her throat bobbed. "Don't get me misty while I'm driving."

"Tell me more about it. Will it be in North Quay or Leighbridge?"

"Liam said..."

We went back and forth the whole way to the shelter, mapping the start of her business plan. It's when Sienna said she couldn't wait to build something she could leave to Laurel that I got misty.

Pulling up to the curb, I wiped my eyes, getting my smile back. I found River in the kitchen, cursing at a bubbling pot. Flour decorated his dreads and a long red streak that I hoped was tomato sauce slashed across his apron.

"Need help?"

"Oh, hey, Kenzie." He glanced down. "Your hug is coming later."

"What's going on in here?" I asked, moving to his side.

"We're swimming in donations right now. Got enough money to be a little irresponsible, so I said we should cook something fancy tonight—give the ladies a real treat. Too bad I forgot my crew hasn't been brushing up on their culinary skills while living rough."

"Say no more." I playfully hip-checked him to the side. "I've got it from here."

"You? Do you know how to make baked scallops, angel hair pasta in lemon-butter sauce, or tofu tikka masala?"

"Whoa, very fancy. No, I don't know how to make any of that, but I do know how to follow a recipe. This is the only kitchen I'm not banned from, so I'll take this opportunity."

River held up his hands. "I pass it on to you. Just tell me what to do, Chef."

I put River on chopping while I got rid of the mess on the stove. It was just the two of us to start, but that quickly changed.

"Remember when we were sleeping in the Woodmire Tunnel?" Marty said. "Kenzie was the worst blanket hog. Girl would roll five feet in her sleep, just to get her hands on and tear off mine."

"I did not," I cried, wheezing laughing. "You were the hog! You woke up next to me every day because you were coming for my blankets."

Twelve of us gathered around. Some helping out in the kitchen and the others hanging over the serving window. Our laughs rang through the shelter.

"What I remember is the day Sienna announced we had to find a new place to sleep," Nathan said. "Cops raided the tunnel two hours after we cleared out. I'm still twisting myself up trying to figure out how you knew."

Sienna got lemon-butter sauce on her temple, tapping her head. "It's my gift, Nathan. Twists me up sometimes too."

"Nah, I still don't believe it," said Mandy, a thirty-year-old veteran of the crew. "Make a real prediction, Blaine. Like that there will be a plane crash on October third. Or the Channel Seven cameraman will drop his pants and moon all of Cinco tomorrow. Come on, something that no one but a psychic could know in advance."

"Wish I could, Mandy, but my gift doesn't work like that. I get a sense of the future of people I interact with. I've never met our nudist weatherman, or a pilot that may one day crash."

Mandy scoffed. "Always got a reason."

"How about this?" A voice broke in. "Predict when we're going to get some damn food." A thin, stringy-haired brunette appeared behind Mandy, glowering at the lot of us. "Oh, I'm sorry. Am I interrupting the party? Dinner was supposed to start twenty minutes ago."

"That was my fault, Solana. I made a complete mess of it and Kenzie had to come in here and save me," River said. His smile was all charm. "Sienna's plating it up now. We'll be ready in five minutes."

She muttered something under her breath and wandered off.

A stray thought consumed my mind, asking me what would happen if Genny did decide to take these women under her wing. River represented compassion and safety. Genny was all fire, rage, and vengeance. I wonder which one they wanted more right now.

Sienna finished plating as promised. We carried it out, serving our residents to hums, oohs, ahhs, or silence. Afterward, I piled a plate with leftovers and made for the kitchen rear door.

"Where do you think you're going, Blaine?" River appeared out of nowhere and slipped my plate out of my hands. "I'll take that."

"What? I can't get any?"

"Not a bite," he said. "You and I are having dinner somewhere else."

I arched my brow. "Oh, we are, are we?"

"Yes, ma'am." Grinning, he backed toward the door. "Tell Sienna not to wait up. I'll meet you out front in five minutes."

Electricity hummed beneath my skin. Was this really happening? After all the flirting, arguments, lies, moments, and waiting, was River finally taking me out on a date?

I raced out of the kitchen. Sienna was eating in the back, seated with a group of women that weren't a part of the crew. I bent over her shoulder. "Si, I'm going out with River. You have instructions not to wait up."

She snorted. "It's about time. Give him instructions from me too: Don't buy Kenzie's demure act. She wants to ride you like a carousel horse. Tell him I said that."

"I will not."

Her laughter followed me out of the dining room. I turned to go outside, stopped, and bolted to the bathroom. An hour and a half standing over a steaming stove, I was not date-ready. A look at the red-faced, frizzy mess in the mirror confirmed it.

Moving fast, I finger-combed my hair, then twisted it into a bun. A tube of lip gloss rolled around in my purse. I swiped some on and checked myself out. I was still wearing my clothes from work—strappy wedges, red skirt-pants, and a top cut above my midriff.

Not bad.

Taking a deep breath, I squared my shoulders and walked out. River and I collided like Ping-Pong balls.

"Oops—"

"Sorry—"

"I didn't mean—"

"Are you okay?" Grasping my shoulders, River set me on my feet. His hands skated down my arms, stopping when they reached mine. "I think you'll like where we're going."

My pulse raced under his stroking fingers. It was guaranteed he felt it, giving my nervousness away. "Do I get a hint?"

"Not one."

"How far is it?"

"Pretty close." River draped my arm through his elbow, leading me out. "I'm lucky you chose tonight to drop in on me. If you came tomorrow night, our first date would be on the wharf."

He said it. Date. I thanked the steam for making my face red. River wouldn't tell the difference.

"Why the wharf?"

"We don't get the stars in Cinco, but we are gifted the most beautiful sunrises coming over the Leighbridge wharf. Because it's Leighbridge, they have churro and organic soda stands on the pier. We'd have filled up on treats while hanging our feet off the docks—the waves coming off the speedboats splashing our ankles."

"That sounds perfect." I bumped his shoulder. "So, that's the date to beat, Delaney. Better hope I love plan B, or you'll have to take me to the sunrise wharf to make it up to me."

His eyes shone under the streetlamps, drowning me as he kissed my fingertips. "I'll take you either way."

I made a strangled squeak in my throat. No wonder people kept rolling their eyes and telling us to fuck and get it over with. The heat coming off us hazed the air.

River led me down the shelter alley.

"Are we walking?"

"It would take us thirty minutes to walk." He swept out his hand. "This is much faster."

"Uhh, that's a bike," I drew out.

A red and gold bicycle leaned against the brick wall, openly defying the warnings to chain these guys up.

"Yep. We bought a bunch so we can get around. Hop on."

I laughed. "River, do you see what I'm wearing?"

"Hop on the handlebars."

"No!"

"Trust me." River held out a helmet. "You will arrive as safe and beautiful as you are standing in front of me now."

I bit the inside of my cheek. I said once that River was the most devious man I ever met, but not when he told me to trust him. He never let me down after saying those words.

"But still, this took me three weeks to make," I dropped. "You're not getting me on that bike."

"You sure about that?"

Squealing, I took off running. River was on me in a bound, scooping me off my feet. He carried me bridal-style to my metal chariot. Five minutes later, I was screaming down Trapp Street.

Breeze chilled my wet cheeks. "River, slow down!"

"What was that? Faster?"

I screeched, speeding past shouting Leighbridgers with my legs kicked out. I don't think I laughed so hard in my life.

"Hold on tight, Blaine!"

"What else am I going to do?!"

We whipped around a corner, shouting at the top of our lungs. Then I saw it.

Paper lanterns dangled from the trees, casting down rainbow light. The music reached in my chest and thumped in time with my heart—fun, happy, and tantalizing. We were a block away and the smells hit me. My empty stomach growled. My brain shouted for me to follow the line of people on the sidewalk, joining in on the party no one told me about.

"Oh my gosh, River. Tell me we're going there."

"It's not the wharf, but still a decent plan *B*, right?" Smugness laced his tone. We hadn't gone in yet and I already knew he nailed it.

River slowed down in front of a pharmacy and helped me off. I stood on my tiptoes while he chained up the bike, trying to see into the park.

"What is this?"

"It's the fiftieth annual Cinco City Caribbean Festival. Ever heard of it?"

"No," I said honestly. "Fifty years. Wow, how did I miss this?"

"They don't really advertise it. No flyers, no ads. Everyone who needs to know—knows." He curled around my hand. "And they bring the beautiful women."

That should not have made me blush like a fifteen-year-old, but my warm cheeks said it did all the same.

River led me straight past the line. The guard spotted us coming up. "Hey, River. Thought you weren't going to make it this year."

"You know I'd never miss it." They shook warmly. "Baldric, this is Mackenzie. Mackenzie, this is an old friend of mine. We've known each other since elementary school."

I shook his hand, too surprised to speak. A childhood friend. River refused for months to even name a single person he knew from his childhood. Now he was introducing me to one.

"It's so nice to meet you." Baldric was as tall as he was wide, and it was all muscle. A charming smile sat on his lips. Not a strand of hair sat on his head. He shaved it, but the bald look suited him well. "Slip me your number. I want to hear all the embarrassing young River stories you've got."

River deftly plucked my phone from my hand when I passed it over. "I'll take that. See you around, B."

Passing through the gates was like leaving Cinco City behind. The paper lanterns weren't just colorful projects. A closer look revealed they were decorated with the flag colors of the different Caribbean islands. Beneath them were stalls, booths, dining pavilions, and on the other side of the path, a dance floor.

Not only had I never been to this festival, but I'd never been in this park either. Moon Maiden Park had an ethereal name to go with the beautiful pale Greek goddess statues peeking through the trees. Weaving through the park were polished cobblestone paths, taking us past a sea of white rose bushes.

"This is amazing, River."

"I'm glad you like it." His hand settled on my hip, pulling me in close. I liked that too. "Don't think I'm a cheap date. The best part of the festival is that all the best Caribbean restaurants in Cinco set up food stalls, and give out free mini-plates of their most popular dishes. I thought if this was your first time trying island food, you might like to try it all."

"Dude, I'm going to rack up more countries than you do. And when I win, it's you who'll go speeding down Trapp Street on my handlebars. Buckle up, Delaney. You're going down."

He bobbed his head. "That is the sexiest thing you ever said to me. And you're on."

I giggled, completely ruining my sexy, badass vibe. That kicked off one of the best dates of my life.

River and I flitted from stall to stall, scarfing down the yummiest food, chatting with people who all knew him by name, and sending our jokes and laughs up to mingle with the joyous sounds of the carnival. It was the opposite of the peaceful, relaxed date on the wharf, but I loved it so much better.

We wandered past dancing couples, smiling at men and women as old as seventy shaking it all, and doing it well.

"We're sixteen countries up, Kenzie. Ready to admit defeat?"

"Nope." I rubbed my pleasantly full stomach. "Though, I may revisit a few countries. I need a plate of those conch fritters to go."

"Got enough room for Jamaica?" River pointed out a booth decorated in yellow, black, and green. "Because you're about to have the best ackee and saltfish you ever tasted."

"It'll be the first ackee and saltfish I ever tasted, so I won't have a comparison."

"That's the spirit."

I buried my face in his arm laughing. I also did it because he smelled like rain and I wanted any excuse to touch him.

"Evening, Sylvia. Two, please."

"Three," replied the stout, middle-aged woman. "You're a rake with hair, River. We need to fatten you up." She unsubtly jerked her head at me, loudly whispering, "Who's this young lady?"

River introduced us, earning me a hug to go with his. Sylvia served me up a colorful bowl of red, yellow, and green food. It was twice the size of the other plates, and one sniff told me I had to eat every bite. Maybe I would lose this challenge.

"Thank you," I called back as we continued on. I took one bite and moaned. "Oh, wow. I take back what I said. I don't need to compare to know this is the best."

"Tell me about it. I lived above her restaurant when I was a kid. She's been on a mission to plump me up since I was five. Best part is that meant a lot of free meals."

"Ugh, I'm so jealous. We lived next door to this terrible woman who didn't bother hiding her crush on my dad. She'd flirt with him right in front of our mom, and bring over these nasty shepherd pies all the time so she could invite herself to dinner and make eyes with my dad."

"Yikes. Remember the days when awful people tried to hide it?"

My smile faded. "Yes," I whispered, recalling my father's handsome, charming face. "I do."

"I wish I was your neighbor, Kenzie. I would've thrown rocks at your window, slipped inside in the middle of the night to whisper secrets under the covers, and make out. Your dad would've forbidden you from messing around with the dreaded-up Black boy next door, so at sixteen, we would've run away Bonnie and Clyde–style. Tearing up the streets of Cinco."

My smile came back hard, warming me up. "Not gonna lie, even if I had the picture-perfect childhood, that fantasy sounds so much better."

"My mom would've loved you."

"She would? Why?"

"You're strong, brave, funny. You do whatever you want no matter what people think."

Ducking my head, I said, "That's a recent personality change."

"No, Kenzie." River tipped my chin, squeezing my heart under his wicked grin. "That's you."

"You're so sweet to me, River," I whispered. "Makes me feel bad that my mom would not like you."

He started. "Oh, shit. Really? Why?"

"You just admitted you'd have snuck in through my window and had your way with my innocence. Could've picked a sweet and wholesome fantasy, but you're a bad boy, River. Moms are programmed to want you far away from their daughters."

"I'm a gentleman," he cried, sounding mortally wounded. "She's gonna fricking love me."

"You run a crew of people loosely affiliated with the law. Know what they call that? A criminal organization. Know what they call you? A crime boss. Oh, yeah," I teased. "She's going to looove that."

River turned his nose up. "I don't know what you're talking about. Crime? Since when is it a crime to take from the rich and give to the poor? They tell stories about people like me, Blaine. Write songs. Praise us as heroes.

"Besides, your mom may not like a bad boy, but"—he traced my lips, stopping my breath cold—"that's not stopping you."

"I know," I groaned. "This will not work in my favor when Laurel's older. I've given birth to the most beautiful, perfect person there ever will be. Men will naturally swarm her, and I'll be the biggest hypocrite when I warn her off the bad ones."

River chuckled. "I hope I'm around to see you lose that fight."

"I hope so too."

Our eyes fell on each other's lips longer than socially appropriate. The devil on my shoulder purred, urging me to lean in just a few inches.

"I still haven't gotten my picnic with the most perfect person in the world," River said softly. "What if our third date is for three?"

"Third?"

"You have to forgive me if I want you all to myself for another night. It's the bad boy in me."

Our flirting was raising the temperature throughout the park. The chemistry between us had always been off the charts, but if this kept up, there would be a bad boy in me before the night ended.

"The third date for three sounds perfect. Laurel will love you," I said. "I mean, she really will. She's going to grab hold of your hair and never let go."

"I can pull off a baby necklace."

We cracked up. River was funny. Why didn't I know he was funny, smart, sexy, and sweet? It was too easy to miss that while I was perpetually pissed at him.

"My mom would like you too, by the way. I hope one day you can meet her. I want Mom to see that I'm... happy."

"Am I the reason?"

A smile tugged at my lips. "Do you want me to say it?"

"Absolutely."

"You, River Delaney, irritate me like no one else can."

He inclined his head. "Not where I thought that was going."

"But," I pushed on, "you also make me laugh. When I'm with you, I'm safe. After Luca, I'd see snakes in every man I came across, then you came in and proved me wrong. I've always known you have my back, and that means more to me than anything. You make me crazy happy, Delaney, and you know it. Didn't even need to be—"

My bowl flew out of my hand. River snapped me to his chest, claiming my lips under the lanterns. The man was a bad boy. He sailed right past sweet and chaste, and kissed the crap out of me.

Before dozens of people, River bent me back, making me hook my leg around him instinctively. Our tongues battled in a fight for dominance that I lost quickly. River sent my head spinning—he sent the world spinning. I clung to him, moaning as we gave in to months of smoldering attraction and aggravation. It was now so obvious to me that we kept digging at each other because what we really wanted was to be on each other.

River was the guy who put me back together after Luca smashed me apart. He was the one who made me laugh when I believed I'd never smile again. He kept me safe. He protected me. And when I needed him, he dropped everything to save me.

It was always going to be River.

Always.

"THAT WAS INCREDIBLE."

River and I strolled through the city, clasped hands swinging between us. The bike trailed next to us instead of under us. Why ride back and let the night end?

"I have to come back with Sienna."

"Tonight's the last night of the festival," River said. "Next year, we'll all go."

It made me stupidly happy that he knew we'd still be together in a year. "I can't believe I never asked this   Oh, wait. I can believe it because you were as open to questions as a barbwire fence."

River tossed his head back guffawing. "Let's see if I changed. What do you want to ask?"

"Is your family from the Caribbean?"

"My mom's parents were. Jamaica," he said. "I've never been, but Mom made sure I knew my culture."

"That's great." I snuck a glance at him. "What was your mom like?"

The corner of his mouth curved up. "I wondered when we'd get to this."

"It doesn't have to be tonight if you're not comfortable." I held his arm to my chest, resting my head on his shoulder. "I dropped by for a visit and you gave me one of the best nights of my life. I don't want to ruin it by pushing you."

"Shit. You say things like that and I feel like the world's biggest asshole. How could I not be comfortable telling you everything? You're more understanding than I deserve."

"I... haven't been completely honest either," I confessed. "There are things in my past that I held back. If anyone can be understanding, it should be me."

We didn't speak for a spell.

"Mackenzie."

"Yes, River?"

"If I tell you this, will you just listen? Don't make excuses for them. Don't argue their side. Don't say maybe we can all kiss and make up now," he said, lightness draining from his tone. "Just listen."

I didn't have to ask who "them" was. "I promise."

He nodded, but didn't continue. Patiently, I waited him out. The first person who heard the story of what happened between my parents from my own lips was Bane Alexander, and that took about a decade. River could do this at his own pace too.

"My mom was thirty when she got involved with Oscar Redgrave." I held still, just listening. "Oscar was older than her—by a lot. The night she showed up to family dinner on his arm, they made their assumptions about Mom before she opened her mouth.

"Gold digger. Con woman. Liar. Or worse, another potential threat trying to get close to the Merchants. They shut her out immediately, Kenzie. Didn't try to get to know her, though they were sure they had her figured out."

I imagined the scene for myself. A young, pretty thirty-year-old on the arm of a geriatric man. How many assumptions would I make before she opened her mouth?

"They were together for about a year," River went on. "Adeline remembers her father as a saint, but he wasn't the easiest man to get along with. He was closed off to everyone but Adeline. Mom said days would go by without them having a single meaningful conversation. It was during a rough patch that she... made a mistake.

"She got involved with an ex. She was sad and lonely and it was a one-time thing. But she didn't know Adeline had people on her, watching her every move."

"Oh no," I breathed.

"Yeah, you can guess what happened. She went straight to Oscar with the *proof* my mother was everything Adeline said she was. Nothing but a scheming, cheating liar using one boyfriend for money while the ex supplies the sex. Adeline didn't even give my mom a chance to come clean on her own," he barked. "Of course, when Oscar heard she cheated, he dumped her on the spot.

"He was done with her. Changed his number and told the doorman not to bother him if she showed up. She got the hint and stayed away, until she had to come back nine months later with me."

"Oscar didn't know she was pregnant."

River tossed his head. "Mom didn't know either. Not until a few weeks after they broke up. She wasn't going to keep a son from him though. She went there so they could work things out and make a plan for me. The worst thing was that Oscar was open to it. He let her up and Mom told me they had a great talk. They worked out child support and visitation. Oscar even offered to buy her an apartment in the building so he'd be close. Be a real father to me."

"Why was that the worst thing?" I asked.

"Because they were on good terms. Everything was fine, until Adeline got involved." River tensed in my hold. "She pointed out the timing. Oscar could be the father, or it could be the other guy. My mom was latching on to the wealthier option, but she wouldn't get a thing until the paternity test proved I was his.

"Mom refused," River rasped. "The two got into a screaming match. Mom told Adeline exactly what she thought of her meddling, insults, and questioning her integrity. Adeline replied that her refusal said it all and she wasn't impressed by her crocodile tears. She either consented to the paternity test or got the fuck out.

"Mom got the fuck out."

"River, I'm so sorry," I said, and no more. I sensed him loosen the tiniest bit.

"It was terrible the way they treated her. It's always been us versus them with the Merchants. Enemy or family. There's no in-between." River tipped his head to the cloudless sky, eyes falling shut. We slowed to a stop on the pavement. "She was too proud, Kenzie. Too proud to let me take that stupid test and prove I was worthy of being in their family. And she was afraid that even if I did, I'd always be the outsider. The bastard son of the gold digger."

I flinched. It hurt to hear River described that way. I understood why his mom wouldn't let him live it.

"So, she moved us into that apartment above a Jamaican restaurant and we lived our lives. I was happy, Kenzie. Sure, I wondered about my father and sister, and asked why I couldn't see them. But I wasn't missing anything," River said, "until I lost her."

I knew this was coming and my eyes teared up all the same.

"I was fourteen," River said flatly. "My grandparents were gone by then. Mom didn't have any brothers or sisters. I was headed to foster care until Adeline claimed custody of me."

"Adeline did?"

"Yep. It turned out she was keeping an eye on me. Oscar was gone by then, so there really was no one else to take me in. Without my mom to stop her, she could finally find out if she was welcoming a brother, or a charity case. The test proved what my mom said all along: I am River Redgrave."

"So that's how you wound up in the Fairfield. I can't imagine how hard it was for you."

"Impossible is the word," he gritted. "Mom told me the whole fucking story of how Adeline drove her away. Then all of a sudden, after fourteen years of nothing, she swooped into my life playing Saint Adeline, the patron of long-lost brothers.

"It was all pancake breakfasts, expensive private schools, new clothes, new room, new life. On the day they finalized the adoption, she had the fucking nerve to say how happy she was that we could finally be a family. She and her husbands never said they expected me to be grateful, but their kids did all the time.

"They couldn't understand why I wasn't falling over myself to kiss her feet. We fought every time I reminded them she was full of shit. It was really bad between me and Sunny," River confessed. "He'd come at me swinging, and I fought back. One day, we got into it at school. He threw me through a display case. I kicked him down the stairs."

"Holy shit," I cried, clapping a hand over my mouth. *Listen, Kenzie. Just listen.*

"It took five security guards to break us up and we both ended up in the hospital with a lot of broken shit." Opening his eyes, River met mine. "That's when Adeline decided something had to change. She'd started saying crap about the *Fairfield not being the best environment for me* and maybe *we needed space while we worked on our communication in therapy.*

"The subtext: she was kicking me out to live in some apartment with Fuller until I convinced a therapist I was ready to play nice with her kids," he said. "She was doing exactly what my mom knew she would. When shit got tough, the first one to go would be me.

"I didn't give them the chance. The second I was released from the hospital, I packed up my stuff and moved out. I've lived on the streets ever since."

"How old were you?" I whispered.

The word forced out of him. "Seventeen."

"Oh, River." Wetness flooded my lids, blurring the man I was finally beginning to understand.

The whole thing was exactly what River said: impossible. There were two sides to this tragedy and I could see it from both. A young, beautiful woman in a relationship with my wealthy, elderly father. That woman cheats on him and then gives birth nine months later. Would I have done any differently than Adeline? Wouldn't I demand a paternity test and then find it suspicious when she refused?

But then there was River's mom. Assumptions and judgments were made about her from the minute she walked through the door. Whether her intentions were true or not, there was one thing that couldn't be denied, pride and mistrust robbed River of his right to know his father. A father who wanted to raise him, and died without getting the chance.

That made me so fucking sad I sobbed. Burying my face in River's shirt, I squeezed him tight, crying for the little boy who lost so much before he knew it.

"So what do you think, Kenzie?" A warm hand settled on the back of my head. "It's okay. I want to know. Was I wrong for hating them? Should I have understood Adeline's point of view?"

"There is... one thing I want to know."

River stiffened. I don't think he realized he was bracing himself, waiting for me to tell him what the Merchants have for most of his life.

"What was your mom's name?"

River's face changed, transforming in front of my eyes from the hard, resourceful leader to that young boy—fourteen years old, and the one person who'd always been there for him... gone.

"Liliana," he croaked, eyes bright. "Her name was Liliana."

Cupping his cheeks, I brought him down to me, resting his forehead on mine. "I wish we had been neighbors, River. Together, we would've run away."

SUNNY

His head snapped around, spraying blood across my shoes. Rocking on my heels, I tipped my head toward the club entrance, brows furrowing.

"Damn, this song is good. Who's the artist?"

"Boss," Ryker said tightly, straining against his charge. "Should we get back to what we're doing?"

"Hmm? Oh, yeah." I nodded at Makai. "Hit him again."

"No, no, no—!"

Makai buried his fist in Yusuf's gut. He doubled over, saved from hitting the floor by Ryker and Athena locked under his arms.

"Sunny, p-please." He pleaded with me through two rapidly swelling eyes. "I'm paid up, I swear! Seventy percent cut every month. I haven't skimmed."

"Yes, your deposits have been prompt." I kicked over an empty Chinese food container pacing the alley. "Found out your brother has been taking care of that and the family restaurant while you moved out to Rockchapel. An odd thing to do," I mused. "You lived two streets over from the restaurant. Now you're a forty-five-minute bus ride away. Got me wondering if you moved out of Merchant territory for more than the shit commute?"

Yusuf's bleeding lips peeled back from his teeth. He was not a handsome man even before Makai fucked up his face. His nose was too big. His mouth too small. His eyes too beady. Hold up a photo of a sewer rat next to him and you couldn't tell the difference. And yes, that's a completely objective observation. The fact that in the single day that we've started looking, we found seven people that packed up and secretly moved to Rockchapel like Grant, was not making me set-a-building-on-fire-to-watch-it-burn livid.

Yusuf was getting his ass kicked because I was angry with him. Not with myself for letting this go down under my own nose.

"Didn't know I needed your permission to move, wifey. Want to know before I wipe my ass too?"

Makai punched him dead in the mouth. Yusuf spat out a tooth.

I shook my head, sighing. "Read the vibe, man. This isn't the time to backpedal from groveling to disrespect."

"I haven't done anything!"

"You moved without letting wifey know," I said. "Didn't I make it clear the day I took over your counterfeiting operation? I own you, Yusuf. I am the deity you pray to. It is my mercy you seek. Did you really think I wouldn't find out about you and the Brotherhood?"

I latched on his face for the barest hint of recognition at the name.

"What?" he cried, screwing up that ugly-ass face. "What the hell are you talking about? Who's that?"

I crouched before him, putting my face in his. "Think long and hard before you lie to me again, Yusuf. You still have a chance to receive my mercy. You can limp out of this alley, or die in it. Lie one more time and I choose for you."

"I—"

My gaze chilled twenty degrees. "One. More. Time."

Whatever he'd been about to say died on his tongue. Yusuf looked me right in the eyes, and laughed.

"Alright, Sunny, let's start telling the truth. Your time is over," he whispered, eyes brightening. "The Merchants have ruled for four decades, lording over us as kings."

I smacked him upside the head. "Kings and queens, jackass. We're an equal opportunity organization."

Rigidly, he turned back to me, rage twisting his mangled features. "Oh, Sole Bellisario. The funny one. The handsome one. The unhinged psycho."

"Sweet, but I'm taken. Let's go back to my time being over. That sounded eerily similar to Snyder's final words. Is that the Brotherhood's official pledge?"

Yusuf laughed again, earning a backhand from Ryker. "Sunny didn't say you'd limp out of here with your tongue. Tell us what you fucking know."

"So much more than you," Yusuf spat. "Look at you! One of the great, untouchable Bellisarios reduced to kneeling in a dirty alley, bargaining for information on an enemy. You want to know about the Brotherhood? They've already won."

"Who is they?" I asked with a calmness I didn't feel. "How did they recruit you? Where is their base?"

Grinning, Yusuf shrugged. "I have no idea."

"You don't want to get cute with me." I slipped a knife from my holster, spinning the blade over my knuckles. That small act sent stabbing needles up my back. "I should be screwing my girl over the bathtub rim right now, but as you pointed out, I'm stuck in this filthy alley with you. Ask yourself how long I'll let you test my patience."

"I'm not being cute," Yusuf replied evenly. "I really don't know who is in the Brotherhood or where their base is. Whispers have been going around for years, talking about a gang that was strongest enough to do it—destroy the Merchants.

"I didn't believe it at first, but then things started going wrong for you guys. Or did you think no one knew about your hijacked trucks and raided warehouses?" He smirked. "That's when I knew the Brotherhood was the real deal. Those whispers said to come to Rockchapel. Make myself known and the brothers will find me. They'll test my faith, and then I'll be welcomed in."

My lips curled. He claimed he wasn't one of them, but the more he spoke, the more I sensed Snyder speaking through that fanatic mouth.

"That's it? Just move here and they'll find you?"

It seemed like I was speaking to him, though I didn't need his answer. The Brotherhood must be watching the criminals under our control as closely as they're watching us. If one that's worth a damn makes a sudden move to Rockchapel, that's a sign they're ready for life free of Merchant control. All of this goes down without them actually having to recruit or reveal themselves too soon. The people they want come right to them.

This Liam clone is starting to piss me off.

"Thank you, Yusuf," I said, getting to my feet. "You've been a big help."

"You're gonna die, Sunny."

"Hardly a revelation. We're all gonna do that." I rolled my shoulders, cracking my neck from side to side. The pain was blinding—more reason I should be in a hot bath with my favorite girl.

"We're not all going to die knowing our empire is crumbling to its knees and there's nothing we can do to stop it." Yusuf grinned that disturbing, bloody smile. "It's over for you, Sunny. You might as well—"

My hand flashed, sinking my blade in his neck. Yusuf gasped, eyes bugging. I slid back a step as Athena and Ryker let his body hit the asphalt.

"Man, that dude can go on," I lofted. "Blah, blah, blah all the damn day."

"He might've blah blahed his way into saying something important," Ryker said. "Or he could've been important. If he was waiting around for someone to make contact, we should've let him go and watched him."

I shook my head, walking off toward the back of the alley. "No one in the Brotherhood would've made contact with him. Yusuf told us enough. They wait for the enemies they can use to move to Rockchapel. That guy wasn't valuable to anyone."

"He was one of the best counterfeiters in the city," Athena argued.

"You know who doesn't need fake money?" I said. "People who've got plenty of the real stuff. Whoever's behind the Brotherhood is loaded. Those were Bane-grade weapons they were aiming at our heads. Would've cost thousands."

"Okay," Makai drew out. "But Grant was a loan shark. All he had to offer was money too. What made him valuable?"

"He didn't just have money. Grant had dozens of desperate people on his hook. An offer to wipe out their debt could get them to do anything he asked. That's power, Makai. Power is always valuable."

Ryker bobbed his head to my speech. "You're right, Sunny. We can use that to narrow down the list of targets. Dinah Sands is one of the seven that up and moved to Rockchapel. She's offered her fixer services to some of the richest families in Leighbridge. The dirt she's hoarding is highly valuable."

"Now we're on the same wavelength, brother." The word popped out of my mouth and I grimaced. I don't think I'll call anyone brother for a long time.

We rounded the back of the building, continuing to the end of the street, far from the crime scene. Coming out onto the busy sidewalk, I paused.

Bodies brushed past me. Some made eye contact. Others didn't spare me a glance. Turning my head up, I fell on the apartment windows, giving a glimpse into the lives of a dozen random people talking, eating, or watching television.

"This is a first."

"What is, boss?" Makai asked.

"It's the first I stood on a street in my city... and felt like I was in enemy territory."

MACKENZIE

"I love the lines on this one, Zoe. It's perfect."

"Thanks, Kenzie. I'll pull the fabric right now."

Mint soap invaded my nose, preceding the hair tickling my cheek. "Ooh, perfect is such a strong word. I mean, what do we think about that neckline? I doubt the girl's a nun. And a dress? I've met Ava Johnson, and I don't think she's the wind-blowing-up-her-crotch type."

I spun in my desk chair, giving the meddlesome Merchant a look. Despite me reminding her—twice—that we shouldn't waste time in the design stage because they're not putting the trackers in drawings, Genny could not resist chiming in on her future wardrobe.

Five days passed since my date with River. I wished there was something to report in that time. Well, I could report that my relationships with Sunny, Liam, River, and Bane had never been better, and I felt like I was getting closer to them every day. Even Bane who insisted my plan to make him fall in love with me would not work. We've ended training for the last week with crazy hot shower sex.

The only thing that wasn't seeing much progress is our plan to find the rat in Caddell House. Everything was stalled until the sketches moved into the creation phase. Then I had to figure out how to be everywhere at once, watching every employee, and catch our culprit in the act.

No pressure.

"It's not a dress," Zoe said. "It's an overskirt. See?" She flipped the page. "Take it off and it's a casual, but sexy outfit. Put it on and you're gala-ready."

Genny's brows popped. "Damn, girl. Impressive. Get started on that immediately."

Zoe spun. "Yes, ma— Oh, wait." She turned to me, suddenly remembering who she worked for. "Can I?"

"Yes," I replied. "I want it done by the end of the week."

"It'll be ready in five days."

Genny and I shared a look.

"Even better." I checked the time. "Where's Jace? He said he had three new summer suits for David Johnson that are ready to be approved."

Zoe just shrugged and left.

"You'd know where he is if you'd let me put trackers on their asses," Genny said. She walked, not hobbled to her window seat. Hendrix removed the boot the day before. "Do I need to tell you that we have nine days left to find the bastard?"

"You do not." Crossing the room, I lifted her feet and sat next to her. "We're good, Gen. We're actually ahead of schedule. Two of my junior designers have designed for you guys for years, so they already know what you like. I've been approving their designs as fast as they're sketching them. As for my third junior designer, Lyla has to show me up in every way, so she's already pulled fabric for Bane."

Genny scoffed. "I still can't believe she snitched to Vance about you assigning her our staff. That bitch is truly shameless."

"Ugh. She said if anyone's making the housekeeper's mom jeans, it's going to be Intern Rylee. Vance is torn between keeping Sunny happy and keeping Caddell House out of the headlines. He was popping Xanax while asking me if we'd work together without a problem. In the end, I gave her Bane to shut her up. The man only dresses up when he deigns to leave the woods, so whatever profile she's trying to raise by dressing him, it's not going to work."

"Do you think she's the one bugging us?"

I started at the question. "Lyla? What? No."

Gen tipped her head. "Why? She's cruel, devious, and manipulative. Her games ruined your life and she laughed in your face when she saw how badly. If the Brotherhood promised her wealth or fame to betray some people she doesn't even know, why wouldn't she hop on the chance?"

"For one, Lyla has wealth. Her dad is the owner of an import/export company. Her favorite pastime in college was reminding me she had a seven-figure trust fund, and I have a family tree of felons."

"Rich people never have enough money, Feisty."

"True, but unless the Brotherhood promised to make her creative director of Caddell House, I don't see what they'd have to offer her. She's got money, status, and a career. The only thing left for her is to climb the ladder, and she can do that by doing exactly what she's doing now: undermining me and making a play for my job."

"Huh. Can't say you don't know your enemy."

"I do know her," I confessed. "But I don't know who's running the Brotherhood. Maybe they are powerful enough to catapult her to the top of the fashion industry."

Genny flashed me another rare serious look. "We can't rule anyone out. And we can't wait another five days for these stitch bitches to pump out clothes. That leaves a four-day window for the guy we're looking for to make a move. He, or she, sits on their ass those four days, we've got nothing."

"I thought of that. I assigned myself Sunny's wardrobe," I said. "I've been making clothes for him for weeks. Liam, Bane, and you too. It was going to be a gift, but—"

"—but you've got the rest of your life to shower me in gifts," Genny finished. "Bring them in tomorrow. Stuff them in the Closet but put the word out that they ship in three days. The surviving trackers are giving the Brotherhood nothing. They'll be desperate to get one on Sunny."

I held out my hands. "Exactly what I was going to say."

Genny smacked my thigh. "How fucking lucky are we that Sunny brought you home? This is why the Merchants will never die. Fate is ours."

"*I* brought Sunny home," I corrected. "I also brought Shonda's basil chicken sandwiches for lunch. Let's go up to the roof. I'm starved."

Genny and I grabbed our things and went upstairs. She let out a low whistle.

"If this is what it's like living the nine-to-five life, I'm thinking all the people I made fun of were secretly laughing at me."

"This is not the norm." I gazed around the rooftop garden. Tables butted up against the roses, petunias, and lavender, gifting the lunchers air perfumed with flowers over the rusty city smell. On our left, two guys worked the café stand. And on our right was the best view of Cinco for miles. "This is the nine-to-five life everyone dreams of. Minus the pressure, constant competition, and backstabbing."

"Quit while you're ahead, Feisty. I'm already jealous."

Genny claimed a table farthest from everyone, tucked within the white rose bushes. I joined her and she claimed one of my sandwiches too.

"Did you ever want something different?" I pulled out two bags of baked chips and a couple of water bottles. Genny had been stealing my lunch for five days. I wised up. "When you were little and your mom was telling you she'd support any dream you had. Did something other than"—I gestured to the tatted biker chick before me—"cross your mind?"

Humming, she tipped her chair back on two legs. "Good question. I guess like every kid I had a different dream each week. One day I wanted to be a singer. The next week Liam brought home a dog and I wanted to be a vet, but I was never serious about any of them. Trying to picture myself in another kind of life just didn't... fit."

I gazed down at my lunch. "Bane said the same thing, and he's willing to give up so much for it. Adeline said it was different for her and your fathers. Their paths were picked for them. You guys chose, but in a way, you still can't have everything. Wealth, respect, power, family, safety. Does that ever bother you?"

"We have those things," Genny said. "All except the last one—which no one really has. Look, I wanted the life my parents have and I do. I've got no regrets."

"So, you're not worried this life will be too dangerous for your kids?"

"Not at all," Genny said, kicking her boots up on the table. "I can't have kids." She patted her stomach. "Got two busted ovaries. They're just in there for decoration."

I froze chewing my bite. "Oh my gosh, Gen. I had no idea. I shouldn't have assumed— I'm sorry."

She waved that away. "Don't be. Do you know how much unprotected sex I have? I used to shit my pants every other month, buying up pregnancy tests, till a doc said I was good to go."

"Is that what they said?"

She barked a laugh. "I'm paraphrasing. Besides, can you imagine my pregnant ass riding my hog? I decided a long time ago if I wanted a baby, I'd just steal one."

"What do you mean steal one?!"

"Relax," she breezed. "I won't steal yours."

My eyes bugged. "Did that have to be said? Genevieve, no babies will be stolen! Legal adoption exists."

"Feisty, don't be ridiculous. Do you know how long my rap sheet is? Only the most corrupt adoption agency would give me a kid."

I tossed my head, mind spinning, crashing, and exploding. "This isn't a real conversation that we're having. This is a joke. You're joking."

"Hey, you brought it up."

"As an opening to discuss my lingering fears about choosing this life," I cried. "I wanted you to say you have no regrets, so I'd stop worrying about making my daughter's life more difficult. You were supposed to reassure me!"

Genny barked a laugh. "How'd that work out for ya?"

I seriously considered dumping both water bottles over her head. If anything, I knew I had to stick with the Merchants for life. If only to return the eventual kidnapped child to their real family.

"What do you want?" Genny barked.

I twisted around, landing on a sight more unwelcome than an approaching eighty-foot tidal wave.

Lyla dared to wave at me as she led Madison, Naomi, Skylar, and Brielle to our table. "Hello, ladies. I thought we'd join you."

"You thought wrong," Genny replied.

Lyla laughed. "See, girls? Isn't she funny? This is Kenzie's only friend, Genevieve. Genevieve, this is Madison, Skylar, Brielle, and Naomi."

This woman never missed an opportunity to insult me.

"Beat it," my only friend said. "You can take the door or the ledge. Come any closer and I decide for you."

Lyla's grin twitched—crushed by real alarm. Genny did not view our undercover job as reason to hide her violent and homicidal tendencies.

"Gen, it's okay," I spoke up. "Join us. It'll be great to catch up."

Her eyes narrowed. The past few days I've refused to acknowledge Lyla's taunts or take the openings to attack her. Despite what I told her about CH losing the Johnson account if I leave, I knew in that pit of hatred she nursed for me, Lyla was still looking for a way to get rid of me. I would be sweetness and pie until I figured it out.

"Don't mind if we do."

Five perfumed, beautiful, fashionable clones stole the remaining seats. They popped the lids off their dressing-free salads on cue.

"Are you really eating that, Kenzie?" Naomi asked. She was the opposite of Lyla with the short blonde hair, tiny mouth, and button nose, but she looked no less perfect. "Potato chips."

She said the name the same way people say battery acid.

"Kenzie is fine to eat whatever she wants," Skylar piped up. "Having a kid already wrecked her body. Doesn't matter what she eats now." She beamed at me. "I'm so jealous."

Gen moved fast and I snatched her arm under the table, stopping her before they saw the knife.

"I don't have to ask if you came over here to destroy my pleasant lunch with constant digs. I know that's exactly why you're here. But why don't we do something different for a change?" I asked. "How about we stop being every *Devil Wears Prada* stereotype and try to get along?"

Five scoffs hit my ears.

"You're so sensitive," Skylar said. "No one is digging at you. We're just talking."

The gaslighting begins.

"Tell us more about yourself, Genevieve," Brielle cut in. "How'd you get a job here?"

"Bribery and intimidation."

They laughed like she was joking. She wasn't.

"That's an interesting outfit you've got on." Lyla nibbled on a lettuce leaf. "Very nineteen-eighties hooker."

"Shit. I was going for nineteen-nineties hooker. Think Julia Roberts in *Pretty Woman*."

Damn, now that she said it, her cutout shirt, ripped shorts, and red leather jacket did kind of remind me of Julia when she was rocking the blonde wig at the beginning of the movie.

I ducked my head smiling as the lines around Lyla's eyes tightened. Genny was the wrong woman to go for. The day before, I witnessed her tackle her own father, Sinjin, for the remote. He flipped her on her ass, but the fact remains, she gives zero fucks.

"It's cute," Madison said. "Ow!" The brunette cherub-faced vixen glared at Lyla, reaching under the table to rub her leg.

"I can see why you and Mackenzie are such good friends," Lyla continued. "Her style always ran eclectic too."

"Ahh," I crooned. "That's the nicest thing you've ever said to me."

She ignored me. "Still, it's not very clear what you're doing here. Vance assured me you're not assigned to the Johnson account— Actually, he was shocked to hear about you in the first place. HR has no record of hiring you. It's all very strange."

Genny tore a bite off her sandwich, blinking lazily. "If you've got a question, ask it."

"I thought I did. Let me repeat it: What are you doing here?"

"I'm Kenzie's bodyguard."

The five of them flicked from her to me, then back to her in perfect sync.

"Excuse me?" Lyla cried.

"Oh, I thought you heard me. Let me repeat myself: I'm Kenzie's bodyguard."

Lyla rolled her eyes. "You need a bodyguard, Kenzie? Ugh. Were you that afraid I'd create a *hostile work environment*?"

The harpies laughed it up.

"No," I said flatly. "After you destroyed my career and I ended up on the streets. A crazy dangerous pimp set his sights on me and didn't like it when I said no. In the end, he abducted me and my daughter. It's because of the bodyguard you're laughing at that we were rescued."

"Damn right," Genny chimed in.

"Forgive me if I feel safer when she's close by."

Once again, I got identical wide-eyed shock.

"Did that really happen?" Skylar asked under her breath.

"It really did."

"Of course it didn't," Lyla snapped. "Fuck's sake, Kenzie. You never stop fishing for sympathy. Nonstop with the 'poor me, Mommy shot Daddy and ruined my life. Feel sorry for me and hand me everything.' When that doesn't work, you trot out the fake sob stories."

I pushed back from the table. "That's my cue. Enjoy your lunch, ladies. Gen, you coming?"

"Nah, I'm gonna hang back. Get to know the lovely Lyla a little better." They gave each other twin predatory smiles.

I got out of there before the chum hit the water. Bypassing the elevator, I made for the stairs, hoping I'd calm down before I hit the bottom floor.

There truly was no other monster on this planet like Lyla Dawson. If she went up against Luca, the woman would've just unhinged her jaw and swallowed him whole.

Calls me a liar, throws the worst day of my life in my face, then has the balls to say I use that tragedy to get things handed to me. What history book was she reading?! In the history of Kenzie and Lyla, that never fucking happened!

I practically vibrated down the stairs. I reached my level and kept going. There were still twenty minutes on my lunch break. A walk around would do me good, because Lyla would not be around.

Hitting the final step, I pushed on the first-floor exit, stepping out in the back of the building.

"—too much," a voice said. "Just get me more. Fine. Two days."

Is that...?

I stuck my head around the corner, and nearly collided with Jace. He jumped back, clutching his chest.

"Kenzie? What are you doing here?"

"What are *you* doing here?" I flicked over his shoulder. We were in a short, empty hallway. Behind him was an alarmed emergency door. "Who were you talking to?"

He plucked his phone out of his pocket. "My boyfriend. Why are you here?" he repeated. "Were you looking for me?"

"Yes, actually. You said you had designs to show me."

"Oh, that." He sidestepped me, walking off. "Next time just text me."

"Will do." I cast one more look, then followed behind him.

LIAM

That night, Kenzie set down the plates with no small amount of flourish.

"Oooh," Elizabeth said. "Looks yummy."

"Thank you very much. It's mushroom shrimp risotto." She passed over mine. "It's one of the three recipes I know how to make, and yes, if you don't finish it, you'll break my heart."

I chuckled. "I will clean my plate."

Kenzie passed me Laurel's bowl of shredded chicken, mushy peas, and sweet potato. The baby kicked in the high chair beside me, bouncing as her food made an incoming. I'd taken to feeding Laurel so Kenzie could focus on the avalanche of questions Lizzie pelted her with nightly. It's wild how easily we fell into this routine. The four of us—family.

"Kenzie, can you teach me how to sew?"

"I've already ordered you a sewing machine, Tricky Tricks. I'm going to teach you everything I know."

"Yay!"

"Tricky Tricks?" I gritted. "Do you do this to hurt me?"

Kenzie giggled. "I'm sorry, Liam. I know it bothers you, but when I was little, I wanted everyone to call me Jasmine because she was my favorite Disney princess. Eventually I grew out of it. Sometimes you just have to wait it out."

"Ah, so will Tooty Booty be Laurel's name till she grows out of it?"

Kenzie's grin vanished quick. "No, and as soon as I can take your sister, I'm kicking her butt for that one. One little baby fart, and now Genny won't quit with that nickname."

Laurel didn't seem to mind, happily munching on her potatoes.

"Did you know about her plan to resort to kidnapping when she's ready to have kids?"

"I did," I replied, grinning. "Her first plan was for me to have more and she'd take her pick. She forgets I've known her her whole life. Our oldest sisters felt the same way, so that left plan *B*."

"How is this a real plan that's happening?"

"Whatever happens, Uncle Liam looks out for all his nieces and nephews. Don't I, Laurel?" I tickled her nose. "Don't I have your back?" Laurel squealed, gleefully waving her arms. "Wow. She loves everyone, doesn't she?"

"Not everyone," Kenzie said, smiling at the two of us. "Laurel has a great sense of character. Hated Luca on sight, but loved you right away."

"That is the highest compliment I'll ever be paid." I shook the baby's tiny fist. "Thank you, Laurel."

"But you shouldn't call yourself her uncle." Something in Kenzie's voice drew my gaze. The smile on her lips shifted to something softer—private.

"No?" I asked softly. "What will Laurel call me?"

"It's a title you've heard before."

I dropped to her lips, pants tightening as she licked them. It's taken herculean strength to hold myself back since I blindfolded and bent her over the couch— No, since I met the woman.

Nothing had changed. Mackenzie was still too young for me. Our lives couldn't be more different for all that she was committed to becoming a Merchant. I shouldn't want her as much as I do, and she didn't give a crap.

What chance did I have of resisting her when she was practically my daughter's best friend? When she curled up under my arm when we watched those far-fetched Pixar movies? Or when she texted me filthy things in the middle of the night, so I'd wake up to a hard-on and then picture doing all the things she described to get rid of it?

Answer: I stood no chance at all.

"There's something I should tell you," I began.

Kenzie leaned back. "What?"

"It's over between me and Hendrix. It was just a bit of fun to begin with but... now it's over."

"That is something I should know." Kenzie's hand found mine under the table. "Does this mean you'll be having fun with me now?"

"There are two children at this table." That only made her laugh. "What it means is I won't sabotage this? I'm open to seeing where it goes."

She stroked the inside of my palm, tightening my pants further. Such a simple act had such an embarrassingly strong effect on me.

"I'm open to that too."

My phone buzzed, stealing my attention. "One moment." A glance at the screen read *Roman*. "Excuse me."

I handed Kenzie Laurel's food, and was up and out of my seat in a breath. "Roman, do you have him?"

"Hello, boss." There was a smacking noise on the other end—his gum. "I'm looking at our boy right now. I found him."

"Where?"

"Hotel in Rockchapel. Nice one," Roman said. "Decent security. Cameras on every exit."

"Can you get him out of there?"

"Won't need to. The chef received a fat wad of cash to suspend room service due to a kitchen emergency. Vito left the hotel twenty minutes ago and is at a restaurant right now, ordering two tables from me."

"Whatever I pay you, it is not enough."

"It's my pleasure to serve."

Again, from anyone else that would be sarcastic. But Roman was more than satisfied being paid an obscene amount to do what he did best—find what's hidden. The challenge kept him from spending too long in his overstuffed head.

"Bring him to Astoria." I cast a look over my shoulder. "I'll be there in an hour. Don't start questioning him until I get there."

"Yes, boss."

We hung up. In that single tap of my finger, I made a decision.

"Mackenzie."

"Yes?"

"We'll have to speed up dinner and put the girls to bed early. You and I have plans tonight."

"We do?"

I tipped her chin, stroking those perfect soft lips. "Tonight, I take over your lessons. You experience firsthand what it is to be a Merchant."

MACKENZIE

Liam was quieter than usual on the drive, and that was saying something. To be fair, I stopped asking questions after *where are we going*? I thought he'd fill in the details on his own, and ten minutes later I was still waiting.

"What is Astoria?" I finally asked. "You mentioned that place before."

"Astoria is my club in downtown Leighbridge."

I waited for more—none came. "I see I have to be more direct," I said, earning a laugh. "Why are we going to a club in downtown Leighbridge? What does this have to do with my lessons?"

"Vito Bernardi has been located."

I shot up in my seat.

"He's being brought to Astoria as we speak. You're going to question him."

My lips parted but nothing came out. The man gives me a direct answer, and that's what he has to say?

"I'm going to question him," I croaked. "Why me? I spoke to him twice, made a lifelong enemy out of him, and then he helped with my abduction to set a trap for you. Why would he talk to me?"

"He's got no reason to." Liam's tone was calm. "You have to make him."

"Make him? How exactly do I do that?"

"Creative thinking."

I stiffened, my delicious meal settling uncomfortably in my stomach. "Liam, do you expect me to torture this man?"

"Are you incapable of doing so?"

"I've been training with Bane for a week! What makes you think I'm ready to do something like this?"

"You were ready before you started training with Bane. I know about the man you kneecapped."

I froze. "How do you know about that?"

"That night in New York, I stayed behind to clean up. I questioned the men who survived. Among them was one of the men who took you. In an embarrassing display, he cried, pleaded, and went on that he should've left you in Cinco after you shot his partner."

Slowly, I sank back into my seat, a strange roaring filling my ears.

"When I invited you to question my valet and you refused, I thought you didn't have the stomach for this life. As such, you didn't have the stomach to share a life with me. Now I know you'll do anything to protect what's yours, and that's the first lesson, Kenzie. Protect what's yours at all costs."

My throat bobbed. "Liam, my daughter had been taken by a drugged-up mistress of the most dangerous man I knew. There was no question that monster would hurt my baby, and I couldn't let that happen. I found that strength within myself because my daughter needed me. Just like my mom found the strength to protect me.

"That doesn't apply in this situation," I said. "Laurel isn't in danger. This isn't self-defense. And Vito didn't lay a hand on me. Do I want to see him caught and thrown in jail? Yes. Will I torture him to find out what he knows…?" I just shook my head. "Liam, I honestly don't get why you think I could do this. I want to learn to protect myself, not numb my soul to the point it withers away and dies."

"You don't have to do a single thing you don't want to do, Mackenzie. I'd never force you," he said, "but I'll always be honest with you. The day will come again that someone knows something that will save our family, and neither threats nor bribes will get it out of them. That day might come sooner than you think as you're hunting down the Brotherhood's accomplice in Caddell.

"You'll have to make a choice to let them walk away with information that could save us or innocent people, or do what it takes to get it out of them." Liam met my eyes though he was driving. "So here's the choice, Mackenzie, you stay out of the fight, learn enough to defend yourself, and only get your hands dirty when forced.

"Or you can accept that we're fighting a war with the most capable enemy we've ever faced. They've chosen violence, bombings, murder, and aren't above hurting children."

My lips pressed into a thin line.

"You can accept, Kenzie, that we need to know everything Vito knows about the Brotherhood, so we can stop them. And you must accept that asking nicely will not work."

I didn't like this. Somehow Liam being bluntly honest with me was worse than his silence.

"Make your choice," he said. "I'll respect whatever you decide."

I was quiet for a long time. "Do you really believe this is the only way?"

"Vito does not hide how much he hates our family. He won't willingly help us, and any information he did volunteer—"

"We can't trust," I said softly. "He wants the Merchants destroyed. Any-thing that seems like helping us would have to be a lie."

"Yes."

Gazing out the window, I tried to picture myself hurting that young, bro-ken man twisted by tragedy. "That day is coming soon," I repeated. "Why do you say that like it's inevitable, Liam? Why must I accept torture as my new reality?"

"Because there's always another Vito. Another Adams. Another Snyder. In the fifteen years that I've been doing this, that's the one thing that's re-mained true. You can't wait to react in self-defense. You have to strike first and strike hard."

That was so close to what Bane said, I flinched. "This has been your life since you were twenty? That's the life you chose, Liam? Why?" I heard the judgment in my tone but couldn't stop it.

He didn't reply for so long, I thought he wouldn't answer. "My father's job was collecting information on everyone and everything. I thought he was amazing. My father—the man who knows everything.

"I was third eldest. My older sisters both chose college, dating, parties, and normal lives. I knew what that looked like, Mackenzie. I knew it could be mine too."

Something in his voice cooled my rage. "What happened? Why did you go a different way?"

"One day I was in my junior year at Cinco U. I got a message from a blocked number. I enrolled in school under a different name, but somehow the person on the other end found out who I was. They told me if I didn't leave a hundred thousand dollars in cash under the bleachers on the football field, they'd detonate a bomb they hid somewhere on campus."

"What?" I cried. "Liam, is that true?"

"Every word," he forced out. "He sent me a picture of the device so I'd know he was serious."

"Oh my goodness, what did you do?"

"I had no choice. They told me if they saw one cop on campus, they'd set it off and people would die. No amount of money was worth that, so I paid. That night, he set off the bomb."

"He what? But— But I don't understand. I went to Cinco U, I never heard of a bomb going off there."

"The bomb didn't go off there. It went off at a bus station. Four people died."

I slumped against the leather, horror filling me. The CincoTran bombing. That I did hear about. "They never caught the guy who did it," I whispered. "Why did he lie and say it was on campus?"

"Because he was on campus." Liam slowed to a stop. I glanced around, shocked to see the neon sign flashing *Astoria*. "I figured out it was a test. He was watching the campus and me to make sure those cops never showed up. His plan was to drain me of every cent I had. The ransom demands were never going to stop. So, he had to know I was scared enough at what he'd do that I wouldn't tell anyone, and then he detonated the bomb, so I'd never doubt he was serious. He killed four people, Mackenzie, just to prove he could."

"I feel sick," I said, swallowing hard. "Liam, that's so evil."

"When I got another text demanding money and another photo of a bomb, I knew I had to find him. End it once and for all. The little I had to go on turned out to be enough. With how certain they were that I didn't alert the cops and the fact they found out who I was, I figured they were in administration. I tracked the texts back to the provost."

"The provost? They make six figures a year. Why the fuck would that lunatic kill innocent people for money?"

"He didn't do it for money," Liam confessed. "His mother was a name in the ledger. It was revealed she was a client of a monster who auctioned children for sex. When the truth came out, their whole family was ruined."

My stomach heaved. I truly was going to be sick.

"Her son, Provost Samuel Dickerson, was forced to change his name to escape the shame on their family. But then a picture of me ended up on the school website, celebrating my team's win. Dickerson couldn't help but notice that I looked oddly similar to Adeline Redgrave."

"Of course you do," I said, eyes squeezing shut.

"He did some digging into my records, discovered a few things didn't add up, and put it all together. It was his dream come true. The son of the woman who ruined his life was sleeping two buildings away. He bragged about all of this when I burst into his office. Dickerson laughed in my face, bragging that it was already too late. He set off the bomb the minute he saw me enter the building on the security cameras. Once the timer hit zero, more people died."

It suddenly became clear to me why Liam was telling me this story. "You had to torture him."

"Hatred twisted his soul, Kenzie. I shouted that it was over. There was nothing to gain but two life sentences instead of three. I pleaded with him, and he just laughed. My family made him into this. Their deaths were on our heads.

"Time was running out. I was alone, scared, and by that time, the most pain I caused someone was tackling them on the football field. It was blind panic that made me pick up the bookend and hit him over the head. But when he just kept fucking laughing... I realized I couldn't stop.

"I tied him to the chair, and I kept hitting, and hitting, until he told me where that bomb was. The bomb squad found it in the public library, ten feet from children's story time."

I slowly bobbed my head. "That's when you accepted the ends justify the means."

"No," Liam said, tipping my chin to face him. "It was a year after that when one of Genny's best friends was gang-raped by the soccer team seniors that I accepted it. They terrified that poor girl into silence but Genny knew it was them. A week before, Nicole published an article that revealed half of them were on steroids. The principal disbanded the team and they all lost their scholarships.

"You know my sister. Fifteen years old, but she was set to plow her way through seven eighteen- and nineteen-year-old guys twice her size. Either she would beat a confession out of them, get caught, and be expelled at fifteen. Or I could get that girl justice. I questioned each of them, but they all swore they were innocent even with scratches on their faces.

"The guys stomped on her hands to stop her from typing another word. I only had to stomp on two to loosen their lips."

Wetness dampened my lids. "Then it was over. The end of your normal life."

"Then I realized the cost of my normal life. For years, my parents made the hard choices—doing things they weren't proud of to make a better city. As many people hated my mother for revealing the ledger's secrets and bringing countless rapists, murderers, and traffickers to justice. She ended that bloody war for the book and broke its power over Cinco."

Liam stroked my cheek—his touch impossibly gentle. "I did terrible things, but today Nicole is living happily with her boyfriend and those children were saved. I realized that even on my worst day, I can do good for this city and my family. I made my peace with that decision then, and I'm at peace with it now. You have to decide if you can be too."

I pressed my lips to his thumb. "Will you think less of me if I can't?"

"No, Mackenzie. Never." He kissed me—soft, perfect, and over too quickly. "But I will tell you: this time you won't be alone."

I considered everything he said truly and honestly. The average person didn't have to make the hard choices he did, but that's what Liam was trying to tell me. He wasn't an average person. Liam was the son of a Merchant. Just by spinning in their orbit, he was targeted by a violent, vengeful man. Isn't that exactly what happened to me? Didn't I react out of pain and fear because the monster before me could not be held above my innocent baby?

Liam said he would always be honest with me, and that's what he was doing then. The time would come— The time had already come that a bad person knew information that would save the people I loved. What was I going to do about it?

"I can't decide right now." It was me that said it, but I didn't recognize my voice. "Will you let me see him first? Talk to him?"

"Of course." Liam came around and opened my door.

My heart thumped faster than the bass as he escorted me to a back door. My palm was sweaty in his palm, which both made me want to let go and hold him tighter.

There was no question Vito Bernardi was a bad man. If he's been with the Brotherhood the whole time, he knew they were behind the bombing of Genny's warehouse, killing three of her people. He not only knew, he told Genny he jacked off fantasizing about their deaths.

What if he knows about the Brotherhood's next plot to attack the Merchants? What if he knows who the leader is? This war could end tonight, if I can summon the woman who put a gun to a man's head.

We entered a dim, carpet-covered hallway. I don't know what I was expecting of Astoria, but I should've known anything connected to Liam would be classed up in the extreme.

I inhaled freesia-scented air, marveling that the place smelled so good with so many sweaty bodies grinding on the other side of the hall's double doors. I could tell the main club was through there from the pulsating strobe lights peeking under the doorjamb. Scrawled in fancy lettering on the carpet was *Astoria* in a repeating pattern. The door Liam led me to had the name etched on the knob.

Pushing it open, he gestured for me to go in first. I walked inside and saw... nothing.

There was nothing in here except two couches, a pool table, and a wet bar. Beside the wet bar was the door I assumed led to where we wanted to go.

"This way," Liam said.

We opened on a set of stairs, leading down into a basement. Stepping off the final step, I walked into the scene I was anticipating.

Three tall, imposing men gathered in a dim, windowless room. The place had nothing to say for itself other than cinder block walls and a single locked cabinet. Between the men, handcuffed to a chair and grinning like an insufferable shit, was Vito.

"Oh, what's this?" he crowed. "If it isn't Sunny's wife. Got away from Luca's men, did ya? That's good news. You wouldn't have liked what their clients were going to do to that pus—"

One of Liam's men punched Vito in the mouth without a flicker of expression. "You will not disrespect Miss Blaine."

I started at a complete stranger knowing who I was. It shouldn't have surprised me. I probably came up at some point when all the Merchants took off to New York to rescue me.

Liam released my hand. "Miss Blaine will take over questioning from here." There was a lone chair against the opposite wall. Liam set it in front of Vito. "Leave us."

His men didn't question him, filing upstairs. My mouth went dry at the faint click of the lock.

"Mackenzie." Liam motioned for me to sit. Lifting my chin, I did so, coming eye level with that smirk. Liam moved behind Vito, and waited.

"Vito." I was proud of my voice for not shaking.

"Mommy Mackenzie. How's that kid of yours?" Something must've flashed across my face because his smile widened. "Just wondering. Sunny was so desperate to find you both. It'd be a shame if after shooting me through the leg and nearly killing me, it was all for nothing."

"She's just fine," I said lightly. "Thank you for asking."

Other than the bleeding mouth, there wasn't a scratch on Vito. He was the same oily, handsome leech I underestimated that night outside the bar. Does he underestimate me? Is that why he's smiling and making conversation like we're here to shoot the shit?

"I'm sure you know why you're here," I began.

"Oh yes. You're hoping I'll give up information on the Brotherhood and what they're planning." Leaning over, he dropped to a whisper. "I won't, by the way. Doesn't matter what you say or do. Even if you flash me those tits. You won't get a word out of me." He sat up straight. "So give up now. Or show me those babies and try to change my mind. We'll both see if it works."

I waited patiently for him to shut up. "I'm not here to ask you for information on the Brotherhood, Vito. What's the point? You don't know anything."

His grin twitched. "What?"

"Sunny shared a theory with me," I said, crossing my legs. "The Brotherhood needs an army of people who hate the Merchants and want them gone, but their soldiers are no use unless they bring something to the table. Grant was a loan shark with valuable connections in the community. Snyder was a ruthless assassin. Luca had horror hideouts all over the city, connections in New York and Eastern Europe, plus he could get his hands on a jet.

"Compared to all these people, what do you have, Vito?" The words were falling out of my mouth so easily. "Spare a half a minute to think about it, and I realized you have nothing. No money, no gang, no jets, no stash houses. You have nothing to offer the Brotherhood besides a willingness to risk yourself for the cause. A guy like that you give a gun and put on the front lines. But you don't tell him anything important." I shook my head, my grin growing where his faded. "You don't know a damn thing, Vito. I'd be shocked if you even know the name of the person in charge."

Something flickered behind his eyes, too fast for me to decipher. "I see what you're doing." The joking tone vanished. "But it's not going to work."

I tipped my head. "What am I doing?"

"You're trying to piss me off. Manipulate me into proving I know something by running my mouth." He leaned back. "What else you got?"

Liam raised a brow over Vito's head as if he was asking the same question.

"I wasn't trying to trick you into anything. On principle, we won't believe any information you voluntarily give up." I shrugged. "That means even if you gave me the names of every brother and details on their next strike, you'd still be in for a long night to make sure your story doesn't change under questioning."

"I'm not afraid of you, bitch. Or you, Liam Hunt! You're both pathetic. If the situations were reversed right now, I'd have smashed in that pretty mouth before you opened it."

I went on like he hadn't spoken. "But even though I'm certain this is a waste of time, we have to be sure. I can't leave this room until you've either given me everything, or convinced me you know nothing."

Liam moved to the cabinet. He opened it up to a sight less dramatic than I was expecting. It appeared to be a maintenance man's closet. There were hammers, pliers, wrenches, a saw, and blades. It quickly occurred to me what Liam expected me to do with them.

It occurred to Vito too. "Fuck you! You can do your fucking worst, you won't break me!"

"I would prefer not to do my worst," I said honestly. "Vito, you don't know much—"

"I know everything! I know they're coming for you." Spittle dotted my cheek. "You think you won something because you found me? They'll know you took me. It's only a matter of time before they bust through those doors. Neither one of you is leaving this room alive."

I waited him out. "As I was saying, you don't know much, but must know something. Where did you meet to make your plans? Or did you do everything over the phone?" I turned to Liam. "Give me a pair of shears, please." He placed them on my palm without question. "Give me an address or number we can confirm, and this doesn't have to go further.

"Where do you meet?"

Vito scoffed. "Get the fuck out of my face."

"How do you communicate with the other brothers?"

"Bitch, if you don't stop wasting my time. I'm not telling you shit."

I lifted the shears. Vito tensed the barest fraction. I caught him quickly clenching the armrest. He wasn't as cool as he pretended.

No one would be when you're about to take shears to them.

"One last chance," I said. "Where do you meet?"

His glare said it all.

Rising up, I dropped the tool on my seat. Vito narrowed in confusion as I pulled my phone out of my pocket and held it up to his face. I cleared my throat, and began.

"Hello, my name is Vito Bernardi. I'm the son of Tomas and Elena Bernardi. I live at 487 Roscoe Court in Harlow. I am a part of a criminal organization known as the Brotherhood. We are responsible for four murders that you know of. Many more that you don't. The La Belle's car bombing was us. The Harlow warehouse bombings were us. The Harlow bar bombing was me.

"Do not think us cruel. Those deaths were necessary to advance our cause. The Brotherhood is an organization of like-minded individuals who seek to free Cinco City from tyrant rule and restore its natural balance. Many don't understand our vision. They don't see the yoke around their necks, chaining them to a corrupt government. Under the Brotherhood you will be free and respected. So committed are we to truth and transparency, I am not hiding my face.

"The government of Cinco has forty-eight hours to donate half a million dollars to the Rockchapel mission. If you do not comply, a bomb will go off somewhere in the city. Mayor Gunderson, you can either improve the lives of Cinconites, or carry our deaths to your grave.

"A government that cares for you won't need to decide. In forty-eight hours, you'll know the truth of how they feel."

With that, I ended the recording and sat down. Vito gaped at me like I was a lunatic.

"What the fuck was that?"

"That, Vito, is the video I'm going to send to the police, the news stations, bloggers, and anyone else I can think of." Color drained from his face.

"The Brotherhood is not only going to become famous, but when that bomb goes off, you and your brothers will become the targets of a citywide manhunt.

"The cops will pick apart your life—combing through your records for forever. All the shady messages, the odd locations you've visited, and the new friends you've made will be put under a microscope."

"You can't do that!"

I plowed on. "The Brotherhood has gotten away with so much because they've hidden behind secrecy. How long will that last when everyone knows their name? How quickly will they cut ties with you when you're denounced as nothing more than a lunatic bomber?"

Vito twisted around, slicing to Liam as if he thought he would help him. "You wouldn't do it. You're not going to bomb anyone!"

My hand blurred.

"Ahhh!" Glistening red liquid decorating my new shears.

Calmly, I tore off a piece of his shirt and pressed it to the small cut on his cheek. "They'll find this by the bombsite and match it to the police record we both know your skeezy ass has. Just so there's no doubt that you, and your organization, are behind this."

"You're not fooling me, bitch!" he barked. "I don't believe you. You're not going to do it!"

I shrugged, turning away. "I guess you'll find out in forty-eight hours."

"Wait, stop. I said stop." My boot hit the bottom step. "You don't know what you're doing. They'll kill me!"

"Hmm." Turning, I leaned against the railing. "I'd guess they'd have to. There'd be a massive target on your back, and since you *know so much* about the Brotherhood and their plans, they can't risk you seeing the inside of an interrogation room."

Vito's glare could've melted the skin off my face.

"Unless," I drew out. "You tell me everything you know. Who is in charge? How many of you are there? Where do you meet? And what are you planning next? I'll take all those answers in whatever order you choose."

Vito rocked in his seat, head twisting this way and that. Sweat dampened his forehead, dripping into eyes that were blinking too fast. He was feeling the shackles on him more than ever.

Giving him my back, I headed up the stairs.

"Fuck's sake, will you wait?" he bellowed. "I lied—okay. I don't know anything! Luca vouched for me to get me into the gang, but he was the only one I had contact with."

I took a few steps down the stairs.

"He said he'd text me when we had a job. The night at the shipping yard was the first he did. We were going to kill every Merchant cockroach that wandered into our trap." He spat in Liam's direction. "He knows how that turned out."

"The shipping yard attack was the first time you met a brother other than Luca?" I said.

"That's right."

Humming, I pushed out my lips. "And are you feeding me that bullshit because you know Luca's dead and will never be able to confirm your story?"

"No," he gritted, lips peeling back from his teeth. "I'm telling you the truth. I don't know the answer to any of those questions. I'm at the bottom of the organization. Only the inner circle knows who's at the top. Only they meet. The rest of us just receive instructions through text."

I came all the way down. "This is unfortunate. You may very well be telling me the truth, but like I said before, we have to assume any information you voluntarily give up are lies—"

"It's the truth!"

"—so I'll be stepping out," I continued. "I'm going to edit the video, put on one of those creepy, deep voices, and then I'm going to send it out. Don't worry." I beamed. "You'll get the final look before we hit send together."

"Argh!" Vito leaped out of his seat, running at me. His arms wrenched behind his back and he flipped off his feet, crashing against the chair legs. I didn't notice they were bolted down until then. Apparently neither did he.

"Anyway, after the video goes live, you'll have forty-eight hours to rethink what you know. Before that bomb goes off, you're just another weirdo looking for attention. Some people may even call you a hero if the mayor really makes that donation," I said. "If I have to set that bomb off, you'll have one last opportunity to spill what you know about the Brotherhood... before we release you on the streets to take your chances. Maybe the cops will get to you first. Maybe the Brotherhood will. It'll be fun to find out."

"You won't do it," he shouted from the floor, straining to right himself. "You won't kill innocent people just to get me to talk. I can smell the coward on you, bitch."

I breathed deep. "And I can smell the urine on you. There are so much more effective methods than torture." My glance flicked to an expressionless Liam. "The Brotherhood is all you have. Without them, you're the grandson of a ruined King that no one cares about anymore, living on the sidelines while the young, pretty, badass Merchant rules on the remains of your kingdom.

"I'm going to take the Brotherhood away from you," I said, voice hard. "Whether or not you lose your freedom, then your life, is up to you."

"Hey— Come back here! I said come back!"

I clomped up the stairs, slamming out the door without a glance back. Liam's men gathered on the couches, raising brows at me as I picked up the pace and bolted into the hall. I wasn't expecting them to be there waiting.

My heart beat so loud it drowned out the club music. Who the heck was that down there? All those words came out of my mouth, but I didn't recognize the woman saying them. I made a man bleed. I threatened to ruin his life and get him killed.

And all of that was better than breaking his fingers or taking a hammer to him. Vito would not appreciate it, but I was saving him from a worse fate. I was saving myself too.

I rushed out the back door, falling on Liam's car. A couple tugs reminded me I didn't have the keys. Spinning around, Liam's and my eyes connected across the parking lot.

"I couldn't do it," I blurted. "It's not the same, Liam. They had my baby. When I shot that man, I was a mother protecting her child. That's not what I am now. That's not what this is!"

Liam slowly closed the distance.

"I'm this close to finding the mole in Caddell House. What if we torture Vito, and then in a week, I find out who's putting in the trackers and they tell us everything? I would've done this horrible thing for no reason."

He drew closer, expression giving nothing away.

"Vito is not our only hope," I said. "We still have options, and while we do, no one will be tortured. You promise me that, Liam. Promise me—"

Pressing me against the car, Liam cupped my neck, crashing his lips on mine. My eyes popped—mouth frozen as my brain sluggishly connected what was happening to reality. I was responding before it got there.

I wrapped my legs around his waist, giving over to the kiss. We battled in a fury of moans, grinding, and roaming hands. The next thing I knew, the car beeped and I was falling.

My back bounced off the cushioned seat. Liam was on me before I knew which way was up.

"This is not"—he tore my shirt clean off my body—"how I thought this conversation would go."

Liam dropped burning kisses along my collarbone. "You're an incredibly frustrating woman."

"Yep, still confused." He popped my front-open bra with his teeth, pulling a squeak out of me.

"You're constantly surprising me. Making me second-guess everything I know to be true."

"You sound very angry about that." The miniskirt I spent a week making joined my top in tatters on the floor.

"You have no idea how hard I fought to convince myself I didn't want you. Then to keep myself away from you. Then to go slow with you, build something real now that a breakup would hurt more than just us."

He was saying so many dizzying things while removing his clothes. Good fortune had gifted me a vision of Liam Hunt half-naked. I knew about the chiseled pecs, dusting of hair on his chest, defined *V*, and the above-average bulge barely hidden in his briefs. His power shouldn't affect me so strongly, and still my mouth went dry as he sprung free. I was not so dizzy and confused to realize what was coming next.

"I'm fucking tired of holding myself back, Mackenzie. You're unpredictable—never doing what's expected of you. Why should I?"

Only my tights remained. I struggled to save them, but it was too late. Liam tore a hole clean through the middle.

"You still sound kind of mad at me. Just to be clear, is this rage or admiration that I refused to torture Vito?"

Liam buried his head between my legs. I choked on my spit, head banging on the armrest. Now was not the time to ask him questions.

The first time Liam ate me out, he was a vortex of pent-up sexual frustration, and he wasn't interested in going easy on me. Not much had changed.

He slipped between my folds, teasing the treasure trove he found in there. Eyes crossing, my back arched off the seat till the top of my head replaced it.

"Holy shit." I ran fingers through his silky strands, drawing him closer to me. "If tonight was a test, I'm really glad I passed." Liam sucked on the bundle of nerves between my legs and I jerked, falling half off the seat. I was accepting quickly this would neither be sweet, gentle, nor slow.

Scrambling free, a deep, primal growl ripped from his chest. I shivered all the way down my spine.

"It's my turn," I said, pushing him back. "You've already made my body your playground, Hunt. Now I get to explore you."

"Until I lose patience." Liam plundered my mouth with the taste of me on his tongue. "Have your fun."

I intended to. Pushing him down, I splayed my fingers on his chest, slowly rolling them over the bumps and ridges of his perfect body. I closed over his length—humming at how right he was in my hands. I must've had a strong effect on him. A few hours ago he said he was willing to take it slow and see where we went. Now he was twitching in my fist.

Precum beaded on his tip. I licked it clean, trapping his gaze as I swallowed him to the hilt.

"Turn around."

I obeyed, swinging my body around to rest my knees on either side of his head. I moaned deep in my throat as he pushed three fingers inside of me. It was a bold man that skipped from two straight to three. I had a stray thought that all someone had to do was stumble behind the club, and get the up close show to him stretching me like a wanton slut.

The thought vanished the moment he hit that spot. "Yes, baby. Right there."

"Who told you to stop?"

I purred under his thumb rolling over my nub. "You're so ridiculously sexy when you take charge."

"I'm thirty-five years old, Mackenzie. I'm not one of these boys fumbling to take your bra off."

"Probably didn't have to rip it though." Liam smacked my left butt cheek. "Ah," I squealed, giggling.

"I told you not to stop."

I fantasized about what this hot single dad would do to me if he got me alone again. The reality was so much better than my fevered dreams.

Liam filled me to the brim—warm and pulsating against my tongue. I delighted in the different grunts and sounds I could get from him with the slightest change in pressure or movement. I was completely under Liam's spell. It wasn't until then that I knew he was under mine.

Liam tensed beneath me. I drew back with a "pop," jacking him faster.

"Mackenzie," he grunted. "Wait—"

Liam exploded on my face, chin, and neck. Hanging my head between our bodies, I winked as I tasted him on my lips.

"Come here."

Grasping my hips, he brought me down on his face. I grasped the back and passenger seat, barely holding myself up. Liam plundered my hole like there was gold.

"Uhh, yes." I rocked back and forth on his face, riding his tongue like a cowgirl. "Don't let me suffocate you. It would really suck if you died before we finished this."

His chuckle reverberated through my core, tightening my lower belly. What really sucked is that I didn't jump him the minute I met him. It pissed me off thinking that we wasted a single second of time we could've spent together. No wonder Liam was angry when he tossed me in the car.

The pressure built in my core, rising with the temperature. Sweat beaded my skin, dampening the single piece of clothing he allowed me. I was so close—

The car spun.

Blinking, I found myself staring at the back of the driver's seat, my cheek pressed into the leather. The sound of crinkling hit my ear. I held still—not so much as breathing in case the spell broke and Liam remembered all the silly reasons we couldn't be together.

He pushed in—slow at first and then picked up the pace.

"Liam, wait," I gasped. "I want to see you."

A swat landed on my right cheek. "Ask nicely."

"You have developed a taste for torture, asshole."

That got me another swat. I contracted so tightly around him, we both moaned. Fucking hell, I didn't think I could be this turned on in my life, then the Savage Princes proved me wrong one after the other.

"Please, Liam. Let me ride your cock until you pop like a piñata. Again."

"Much better."

It was an impressive feat, all the twisting, lifting, and sliding required for us to change position without breaking our connection.

Liam leaned against the door, his fingers digging into my waist. I didn't for a second believe this new position put me in charge, and he proved that by lifting me up and smashing my G-spot up into my throat with one hard thrust.

I screamed, losing all control as he bounced on the seat, drilling me till my brain turned to mush and all I could do was beg, plead, and moan for him not to stop. He squeezed my breast, tweaking my nipple between calloused fingers.

I came so hard I pitched forward and bumped my head against the window, leaving my mark in the fog. Liam followed a breath after me—his muscles clenching into tight, rippling cords running down his arms and chest.

I flopped on top of him, so deeply satisfied, I nearly forgot there was a man in the club basement waiting for me to destroy his life. Nearly.

"How long can we stay here before I have to make good on my threat?"

Liam tucked me between him and the seat, lazily stroking my hip. "Quite a while."

Smiling, I rested my head on his chest. "Works for me. So, to be clear, was it my refusal to torture him that turned you on? Because that's a very specific kink."

His laugh shook his chest and me. "It has nothing to do with him and everything to do with you, Mackenzie Blaine. You keep surprising me."

"But you do think it'll work?" I squeezed my eyes shut. "Oh, Liam. I want to stay in this moment with you forever, but what you said really did get through to me. Vito could have information that saves our family and ends this war before it begins. It's vital we make him tell us, but that has to be by outsmarting him. Not by torturing him." I rose up to meet his gaze. "I don't know if my plan is the way though. I confess I was making it up as I went along."

"Yes, I assumed you were borrowing parts of my history when you claimed you'd detonate a bomb in the city." He raised a brow. "That's not really part of the plan, is it?"

"No!"

He chuckled. "Kenzie, what you did in there took insight, cleverness, and quick thinking. You took the little you knew about him to conclude the most important thing Vito has is the Brotherhood. His parents are gone. The Kings are gone. All he has is his revenge. I don't have to tell you what it means to take it away from him. You saw his reaction for yourself.

"I do believe in your plan, but the key with intimidation is that you have to follow through with your threats. If you have no intention of going through with this, how will you convince him otherwise?"

"You're saying a lot of yous when you should be saying we." I kissed his cheek. "I'm your girlfriend now. It's all we from here on."

"Ah," he said gravely. "So that was your plan."

Giggling, I tried to tickle him and that backfired wonderfully. Liam flipped me over and screwed me against the doorframe.

It took a couple orgasms, arguing back and forth, his technical expertise, and a creepy voice-over app to finish part one of the intimidation and my first lesson with Liam.

Liam kept a spare change of clothes in the car. We fixed ourselves up and returned to Vito, catching him in the middle of yanking on his restraints. He drilled a hole through my head and poured his hate as I sat down.

"You'll see I'm a woman of my word, Vito." I played the video for him, giving him the first look at Channel Nine's trending news story. "I'm attaching it to this email that's already addressed to every news outlet in Cinco. Tomorrow when we're watching the coverage and the whole world is asking who is the Brotherhood? I hope for your sake that you have an answer for me."

"Stop!"

I hit send.

Chapter Eight

G*enny*

"Huh." I circled the mannequin, lifting and poking this or that. "You're actually pretty good at this."

"What's with the surprise, Hunt?" Kenzie knelt before the other mannequin, fussing with an imaginary problem. "I wear my own creations every day. You know I'm good."

"Eh," I replied, flopping back on my window seat. "You popped out a kid two seconds ago and still your body is banging. You'd think you'd flaunt it, but no."

"I lost the baby weight because I was starving on the streets," she cried.

"How does that negate my other point?"

I didn't have to see Feisty's face to know she was rolling her eyes. "Laurel knows where her lunch is. She's tried to get at it more than once by yanking on my top. There's a little cleavage, and then there's all of it."

I barked a laugh. "Oh, damn. Tooty Booty is even more feisty than you."

"I will kick your ass if you call her that again."

Yep, it was official. Mackenzie Blaine is my new favorite person.

"What's the point of this?" I asked. "These clothes don't need final touches. They need to be sent down to the Closet and prepped for shipment. If we're lucky, the lurking two-faced bitch will take their chance."

"They do need final touches actually." Kenzie crossed to the mini-fridge, got an ice pack, and passed it to me. One absentminded shoulder rub and she was ready with the mothering. Between her, my mom moving into the Fairfield, and this fancy-ass den of luxury that was called a fashion house, I was softening like a plum in the sun.

I needed to get back to Harlow where the beers are cold, the rides were sleek, and the bar fights were bloody.

"Because they're being sold through Caddell House with their label on it, Vance wants final approval. As soon as he gives these all a pass, they're going straight into the Closet," she said. "Have you checked it out yet? I told you there are lots of hiding spots that we can use to catch this guy, just like he may be using them to pull this off."

"I stuck my head in but I haven't gotten a real look around yet," I confessed. "A white-haired sea witch was guarding the place. I believe her name is Ursula. She said she didn't recognize me and gave zero shits if I was your bodyguard. I wasn't getting near the clothes."

"Her name is Maggie."

"Pretty sure it's Ursula."

Kenzie laughed. "They're serious about security here. I've asked Vance to give you an employee badge and he looked at me like I slipped into another language. I get the feeling he doesn't want you leaving this room. Can you figure out a way in? I'd do it, Gen, but you pointed out that I can't blow off my job and hide in a closet all day without looking suspicious."

"I'll get in. Even the strongest of sea witches are harpooned in the end."

"Do I have to tell you not to kill her?"

I hummed. "It is helpful to know that's off the table."

Lyla blew into the room carrying a pad and pen. "Kenzie, what are you doing? I need you to approve these designs."

This woman's disrespect for Kenzie was so blatant, it made no sense to me that Talia didn't believe her when she said Lyla framed her. Either Talia didn't know a fucking thing about her employees—and her fiancé—or she did know and jumped on a convenient chance to rid herself of a young, pretty, pregnant rival.

Both theories made me want to punch her teeth in. Of course she'd have to get in line after Lyla and Damien.

"What's this?" Lyla asked, eyeing the mannequins. "Who did these?"

"These are the newest additions to Anthony Johnson's wardrobe. Just awaiting Vance's seal of approval."

Lyla scoffed. "I'd be shocked if you got it. Anthony's always been the more adventurous of the Johnsons. He likes bold statements and unique designs, but he's not trying to look like a freak. He'll hate these," she announced. "They're too loud and cartoonish."

Kenzie didn't look up from her hem. "That's funny because Anthony already said he loved them. He likes that my work is fun and playful, but still appropriate for the boardroom. Now if you're done giving your unwanted opinion, leave the pad on my desk and go. Your boss is busy."

It was me that saw it—attention fixed on her standing over Kenzie. Her knuckles turned white around the pen. Eyes flashing, she raised it the barest inch, angled to plunge it into Kenzie's neck.

"Hey!"

Jerking, the pen and sketchpad went flying. Lyla gaped at me eyes huge, knowing that we both knew what she was about to do. Without a word, she spun and slammed out the room.

"What was that about?"

Frowning, I climbed off the seat, staring at that pen. "Kenzie, are you sure you don't know why Lyla hates you?"

"What? No. I mean, I guess it's because I did better than her in school. She was always trying to show me up."

"Did she say that was why?"

"No, and I've asked. She'd laugh in my face when I said it was because she was jealous of me. But if there's another reason, she hasn't come clean."

"There's another reason," I said before she finished the sentence. "That girl was two seconds away from jamming a pen in your spinal cord."

"What?!" Kenzie whirled around, gaping at the door. "Are you sure?"

"I'm sure. That was real hatred in her eyes, Kenz Benz. I've got a feeling it's about more than you beating her at everything." I reached out, helping Kenzie to her feet. "Lyla is still a junior designer, right? That means there is over thirty people above her and they have been for the months you've been gone. Why hasn't Dawson gone after them with the same single-minded insanity?"

"I... I don't know."

I flashed her a serious look. "Whatever she's got against you is personal. Big-time. Don't be alone with her and I mean it. I said I'd look out for you. I'm not about to tell my brothers you were killed because we underestimated that perfumed clone." I stuck my head in the hallway, checking if it was clear. "Keep working. I'm going to get into the Closet this time. And see if I can get the scope on Lyla."

"I'll be here."

I'd give Mackenzie credit. She said she wasn't afraid of Lyla Dawson, and she didn't sound it. She went back to work, actually picking up Dawson's pad and flipping through the designs. Fair enough, the woman had many opportunities to kill her and didn't take them, but I saw that look in her eyes.

Back then, Lyla and Mackenzie were on equal footing. Now the balance of power had shifted and Dawson was running out of options to take the woman she clearly hated down. I was not about to let her enact her revenge fantasy on my new friend.

Slipping out into the hall, I dashed a quick text to Sunny.

Me: What do you have on Lyla Dawson?

The reply buzzed me seconds away from stepping inside the elevator.

Sunny: Why? Is she the one planting the trackers?

Me: You got me back awfully fast. Are you in Rockchapel working or kicking back in your office with your feet up while Ryker and Makai do the actual work?

Sunny: Fuck you

My sweet baby bro's standard response to me.

Sunny: I always respond quick when Angel's involved. That woman hates her. I'm a cold bastard, but not even I would do the shit she did.

So Sunny knew too. Lyla Dawson may not be the Merchants' enemy, but she was Blaine's.

Who was I kidding? If she's an enemy of Mackenzie, she's our enemy too.

Me: Since you know this, I assume you've got her entire backstory. What's her deal? Do you know why she set her sights on MB?

The elevator dinged on my floor. I stepped out but didn't go anywhere, waiting for his reply.

Sunny: I'll send you everything I've got. These are the highlights: Raised by a single mom who married rich when she was twelve. Wanted to be a designer all her life. Got busted for driving drunk when she was seventeen and Stepdaddy made it go away. Dawson and Angel did not grow up on the same street, live in the same borough, or go to the same school until college. Whatever happened between them started there.

I absorbed this—disappointed. If these were the highlights, then the full profile on Dawson didn't say anything interesting.

Me: That's it? Did you check her accounts? Texts? SM? You gotta have more than that.

Sunny: Her security is impressive. She's got the bank account to pay for real protection, and she does. Plus, she's a scheming traitor. She knows firsthand what happens when you don't watch your back.

Me: You telling me we don't have the bank account to break her protection?

Sunny: We do but not quickly or I'd have done it already. Damien Stone and Courtney Hicks were as easy as breaking into an unlocked house. Dawson's more a vault. Ryker says he's still working on it.

Me: Tell him to work faster.

Sunny: Is she a threat to Angel? If you've got a feeling she's about to try something, kill her. Don't fuck around waiting for Ryker.

I grinned. No, Sunny was my favorite person. Violence first—the guy just gets me.

Me: Like I would. Don't worry about shit over here. Feisty is in good hands.

Sunny: Did Bane finally replace you as bodyguard?

Me: Fuck you

With that goodbye, I stuffed my phone in my pocket and marched into Hollywell's office. His shouting receptionist didn't slow my stride. Honestly, if she's not willing to tackle me, why does she even have a job?

"Hollywell."

"What the—?" He dropped the phone scrabbling to hang it up. "Who are you? You can't just—"

"I need to get around the building without getting held up by a writhing sack of tentacles in a tight dress. Give me one of those employee passes everyone keeps going on about."

He gaped at me. "I beg your pardon? If you're Miss Blaine's guard, you're to go nowhere without her. Now leave my office."

I bored over his desk, pressing the man's back against his seat. Some people asked how it is I—a slim, blonde beauty with a model's face and a porn star's ass—so easily intimidated men twice my size. Simple, it's in the eyes.

One look in my eyes and they see the pain awaiting them if they continue on the unwise path they're on.

I got my tenth-grade English teacher to change my *C* to an *A* with that look. Well, I was also holding a knife at the time, but it's still all the look.

"We haven't been introduced because I have better things to do than chat with soft-bottom dudes polishing the throne they somehow still manage to own in a female-dominated industry."

"What? I—"

"I'm Genevieve Hunt. I believe you know me as Ava Johnson," I breezed. "The rest of the world knows me as the golden child and favorite of the Merchant family. Now, do you take my photo here, or do I do that in the HR office?"

Plastering a smile on his face, he straightened and said, "They'll take care of everything in the HR office, Miss Hunt. I'll call down myself and tell them to expect you."

"Excellent, my good man," I mocked, putting on a high-brow accent. "Cheerio."

Skipping out, I blew past the security guards and slipped into the elevator while the receptionist screamed I was right behind them.

After my new pass was in hand, I began a proper, thorough tour of Caddell House—clocking every exit, noting the few security cameras, and getting a sense of where everyone was.

Dawson snagged herself the junior designer title. While she didn't have her own office on a separate floor like Kenzie, junior designers had their own shared area to work away from the interns. While the interns' workspace...

I ducked inside, taking in the racks upon racks of clothes against the wall, cutting through the walkway, or forming couture walls around hunched-over stitch bitches and their sewing machines.

It was interesting that they didn't call this place the Closet. It certainly looked like mine—a disorganized hot mess.

Two rows of workstations claimed free space on the floor. I watched one guy take a suit off the rack. It shared the hanger with a little velvet pouch. He emptied the pouch's contents, dumping the buttons on the table. One after the other, he got to work sewing them on.

The finishing touches. The grunt work. Could the guy we're looking for be putting the trackers in the clasps beforehand and then leaving it to an intern to sew on?

If you're type *A* and a victim of sabotage, you do it all yourself like Kenzie. Otherwise, you pass this kind of thing on to the free labor. So that's the question: Do I believe the genius that's gotten away with this scam for months did so by sticking their trackers in a pouch and passing it off to inexperienced hands?

What if they found one of the trackers and asked what it was? What if they didn't sew it on right and the damn thing fell off? What if Intern Bob spilled his coffee on it? Would a person that's been so smart leave this to chance?

No.

Even as the questions passed through my mind, I knew the answer. Kenzie and I floated a lot of theories back and forth, but just watching her fuss and hover over a suit she'd never wear, it became obvious. These weren't just clothes to her, they were her art. An artist doesn't pass off the final touches.

And this guy wasn't either. The trackers in the buttons were his masterpiece. The grand trick that makes the audience faint right out of their seats. *I bet he gets a hard-on every time he sews one on, laughing at the stupid Merchants handing the Brotherhood their deaths.*

No, the rat was definitely doing his own work, but was he doing it in here?

I studied the interns, making them all uncomfortable. It couldn't be one of these grunts—working in this exposed space with a dozen other people and more coming in and out every day.

Again, no. It's not an intern.

"Good work, everyone." I thumped some random guy on the back on my way out. I think he said thanks.

This is why I needed to be here. First week on the job and I've eliminated a dozen suspects.

My next stop was the junior designers' room. I made eye contact with Lyla coming through the door. She locked on me from her spot by the window and looked away just as fast, cheeks reddening. She hadn't meant for me to see her lose control. She's still trying to play like she's the angel.

That just means she'll make it look like an accident. I know that look. I am the living embodiment of that look. Kenzie's got a target on her back for as long as Lyla breathes.

I forced myself to look away, taking a slow scan of the room. The promotion from intern to junior was reflected in this room. It was as big as the intern space, but for fewer people. Each junior designer had a workstation and a desk—both with desk dividers that gave them a little privacy.

Was it risky to mess around with trackers in here? Yes, but it wasn't impossible. Position this or that just right, and no one sees what your hands are doing unless they're on top of you.

They could definitely be one of the junior designers. I narrowed on Lyla. *And it could definitely be you.*

I gave Dawson a reprieve and made for the Closet. I didn't need to check out the senior designers' offices to know they had plenty of privacy to get up to all kinds of shit. The rat could be one of them, the only issue was we never had just a single designer working for our account.

There were too many of us ordering new clothes up to once a week. One designer wasn't creating for all of us, but *all* of us had trackers in our clothes. They were dipping in on their fellow coworkers' handiwork, and Kenzie swore the easiest way to do that was to tamper with them while they were in the Closet.

When the clothes were done, fitted, and ready to go. That's when they all let them out of their sight.

I approached the doors fast. She shot out from the coffee nook.

"Hey, you. I told you that you can't go in—"

"Back, witch!" I flashed my badge in her face. "You're gonna have to steal another girl's voice, Ursula. Not me, not today."

She sputtered, "I beg your pardon? Who do you think you're—?" The doors closed in her face mid-sentence. Finally, I was in the motherfucking Closet.

"This is what all the fuss is about?"

The place wasn't a closet, it was a department store. The racks were laid out like library stacks that twisted, curved, and turned—inviting you to dip down a maze-like passage surrounded by clothes. Taking up the middle of the room were accessories display cases—belts, gloves, and hats. The closet seemed to go on for miles, providing more than enough cover and quiet for someone to work in here.

I turned to go.

"—going to do?"

Twisting around, I soundlessly crept past a case of ugly hats.

"...don't have a choice..."

That voice. I neared the eighth rack from the door. *I know that voice.*

I turned the corner, taking in the endless sea of couture. The voices got louder, leading me around the bend.

"...should stop... too risky."

Stopping, I shoved my hands through the fabric and shoved them apart.

"Ahh!" Zoe screeched, shooting back and tripping over her feet. Jace didn't handle it any more gracefully. He tipped over, collapsing under a pile of fallen garment bags.

"What the hell are you doing?!" the pile bellowed.

"What am I doing?" I said lightly. "I came down here to find out how easy it is to help myself to a dress, and then put it back without anyone knowing. What are you two doing hiding in the clothes?"

"We weren't hiding," Zoe snapped. "We were talking. This is the only spot in the building you can get any privacy."

Figured that out for myself, Zoe.

"Don't let me stop you." I continued on, tossing over my shoulder, "See ya."

I made it as far as the ugly hats when my phone went off. I fished it out. My grin twisted reading the screen.

Web Alert: Brotherhood

"What the hell?" I set up an alert for any mention of the title brotherhood in all of cyberspace. This was the first time I got a hit.

Ducking into my own curtain of clothes, I opened the link.

My eyes narrowed, then widened. My jaw clenched, then parted. My brows snapped together, then rose higher.

All the emotions crossed my face as Vito Bernardi filled my screen, promising Cinco he would blow up a random location unless—

"Half a million dollars to a charity?" I cried. "The only people you give a shit about is yourself and your reflection."

This was some kind of trick. A game. And I would find this bastard before he got to the end.

MACKENZIE

"It's not quite there."

I took a deep breath and let it out slow. Anger wouldn't help the situation. "Mr. Hollywell, you know I've got a direct line to the client," I said slowly. "He loves these designs as is. They don't require changes."

"If he loves the rough draft, he'll love the polished version even more."

I bit hard on my lip, penning in the response that flew to my tongue at "rough draft." I knew exactly what was happening. Hollywell was exploiting his modicum of power over me as an outlet for the frustrations he couldn't take out on Sunny. I knew why. Didn't mean I had to fucking like it.

"You're suggesting I give Sunny something other than what he wants?"

Vance's back muscles tensed. "Not at all," he said, trying for innocent. "What I'm doing is reminding you that these designs will wear the Caddell label. While Sunny's preferences are priority, everything that leaves this building must be on brand. This is not quite there."

He was having a lot of fun repeating that phrase while he circled my mannequins, frowning harder at each one.

Technically, I still had time on Genny's deadline, but I did promise her to speed things up. Hollywell didn't know or care about my promises.

"Can you be more specific with your notes?" I asked. "Which ones aren't on brand?"

"Oh, dear." He sighed mournfully. "Well, all of them, to be frank. These two are unsalvageable." Vance pointed to two blue patterned suits. I chose the color for how deliciously they brought out the blue specks in Sunny's silver eyes. "This one might work if we raise the cuffs. Write this down, Miss Blaine. We've got a lot of—"

The door flew open. "You, out."

"Excuse me? I—"

Genny propelled the man out the door and slammed it in his face. I stood there in bug-eyed shock, half reaching for my sketchpad.

"Gen, what's that about?"

"Look at this." Towing me to the window seat, she shoved her phone in my face. The news anchor prattled on for a bit, then a video came on the screen. "Vito resurfaces and does this? What the fuck is he trying to do?"

"Ah, yes," I drew out. "There's something I have to tell you…"

Ten minutes later, I was about to be hurled through the door.

"What did you say?" she hissed. "You and Liam found Vito, and you fucking kept that from me!?"

"We found him last night. It was all so quick."

"Not an excuse!"

"But there is one," I cried, throwing my hands up. "Liam didn't tell anyone else because he wanted me to be the one to torture him."

Surprise broke through her rage. "Wait, what?"

"He was giving me the cold, hard truth about what it is to choose this life. Honestly, I think it was a test. The point was that it just be the two of us. You, Bane, or Sunny couldn't step in and help me. I had to do it… or prove I couldn't." I blew out a breath, slumping against the window. "Spoiler alert: I couldn't do it.

"I came up with this video and bomb thing as another way to get him to open up. After that, I asked Liam not to say anything before there was something to tell. If I'm not going to torture him, *no one else will either*."

Rage returned fast. "The fuck I won't! Why the hell am I scaring people out of closets when the person with the answers is kicking back in Astoria? He is in Astoria, isn't he?" My face twitched. "I knew it. Liam is so predictable."

"Gen, please." I grabbed her arm as she shot up. "A news channel ran the story. More will too. My plan is working. Just let it play out."

"Kenzie, sweetums." She popped a kiss on my forehead. "Liam obviously threw you in the deep end before you were ready. I'll be kicking his ass for that promptly. But in the meantime, real shit is going down and real people are dying. Vito knew about my warehouse fire all along, and I know he's got more information in that dense skull. I'm not sitting around because you can't stomach doing what needs to be done."

Gunshots rang in my ears. "I can stomach what needs to be done," I exploded. "But this doesn't need to be done! Vito will tell me everything he knows, I promise you. Give me two days."

"No."

"Genny!"

She tore free from my grip. "We all have our jobs to do. Yours is playing with silk and lace while you pretend to be a badass. Mine is stepping in when you can't handle it." Genny pulled a face. "Ugh. That sounded all right in my head, but now that I hear it out loud, I sound like the *B* team. Let me fix that.

"My job is to rule this city, handing down sentences to stupid little boys who think they can defy me. Your job is to pretend you have the balls to do the same." Genny popped another kiss on my quivering cheek. "Later, Feisty. Stay out of locked rooms with Lyla Dawson."

Just like that, Genny was gone in a cloud of mint soap and stolen perfume samples.

GENNY

I jabbed the intercom button, cursing my brother to make my ears bleed. The fact we shared a mother and father unlike my other siblings, didn't mean anything. He was no more my brother. They were no less my siblings.

But since the father we shared is the one and only Killian Hunt. It's ingrained in our DNA to see the full measure of people—their greatest strengths and most embarrassing weaknesses. Add to that our mother being Adeline Redgrave, we were born with the taste of not using our powers for good. Put that together and throw in a penis, you get the most irritating fucking guy who ever messed with you just because he could.

"Hello, Gen." Liam's droll voice spread through the elevator. "Something I can do for you, baby sister?"

"Reminding me we're blood won't stop me kicking your ass. Let me in!"

"I'd never make that mistake," he said, chuckling. The doors slid open on the end of his sentence.

I slammed into his apartment, finding him reclined in his armchair with a glass of scotch.

"You—"

"Not in front of my kid," he sliced in.

The mist cleared. Staring at me from behind her princess playhouse was the first and only person who made me regret I couldn't have kids. Yeah, I had other nieces and nephews, but they were boring as hell. My Tricky was a Merchant through and through.

"Tricky, Grandma has gone a whole morning without showering you in gifts," I said. "You should go downstairs and fix that. Tell her you want a Princess Tiana Double Deluxe Castle, or you'll hold your breath till you pass out."

"Okay!" Elizabeth took off running.

"Don't tell her that!" Liam called. She was already out the door. "Must you, Gen?"

"Yes, I must. How could you keep from me that you found Vito? And asking Kenzie to torture him? What the hell is that about?"

He leaned forward in his seat. "I know you, Bane, and Sunny. Sunny puts a positive spin on everything. A week in the terminal ward and he'll have all the patients singing and skipping. You love our life and what we do, so you're not the one to give Kenzie the reality. And as for Bane, he won't lie to her, but he's got no intention of letting her use any of the skills he's teaching her. He's always sacrificed to make everyone's life easier. When the time comes, he'll sacrifice so she never has to stain those soft hands.

"I brought her to Vito because Kenzie needs to know what this life really is," he barked. "Right now, up front, and before she gives up the life she wanted before she met any of us. But when I put her in that room, expecting her to choose option *A* or option *B*, Mackenzie Blaine whips out option *C*. She asked me to let her do this her way, and I keep my word."

I blew a raspberry. "Save the code-of-honor act for someone who didn't watch you sneak out every night in Dad's favorite car—until you crashed it."

"I was sixteen," he gritted.

"You were a devious little shit then and you're still one now. Don't get mad," I said with a shrug. "It's what I love about you. That's how I know we're related."

"You always had a gift for making your insults sound like compliments."

"You're taking me to Vito. Now."

He sighed, rising from his seat. "Did you get a chance to hear Kenzie's plan before you ran out on her?"

"I heard enough. It's not going to work."

"It hasn't had a chance to work." Liam nodded at the television. "They're playing that video on every station. By tonight, everyone in Cinco will know the name Brotherhood. Whoever's running this has already cut ties with Vito. When the bomb goes off, he'll likely have Vito killed and displayed in hopes that heads off the FBI from creating a task force devoted to ending the Brotherhood."

I put up a hand. "Wait, hold on. When the bomb goes off? What the hell are you talking about?"

"Ah," he said, amusement twisting his lips. "So you didn't give her a chance to tell you the whole plan."

"Cork it and explain, Liam."

"How can I explain if I'm... corking it?"

See what I said about being a premium brand of irritating? "What bomb?" I gritted.

Liam explained the plan in full.

"Hmm. I admit it's clever. Kenzie's got the Hunt gift for picking people apart too."

"This is why I'm content to leave her to it."

I snorted. "Who asked you? You're not in charge."

"Excuse me?" The vein in Liam's jaw started ticcing. "You just said it's a clever plan."

"It is clever, but it's a waste of time we don't have. Do I need to remind you that you guys pulled me out of the wreckage of my new place two seconds ago? Do you also need the reminder that days before, they trapped and tried to blow your heads off? The Brotherhood isn't hiding anymore. They're actively hunting us down, and now our parents are here, so they can take us all out together.

"You shouldn't have put this on Kenzie, and you shouldn't have said shit about torture. I will squeeze out every drop of information he has on the Brotherhood. Either get me past the suits yourself, or I grab a couple of my girls and we storm the club."

Liam gave me a long look. "Granted, Gen, we weren't raised on society's morals. Sinjin frequently told us that if we saw something we wanted, we should just take it. But one thing he didn't teach us to do and fuck sure never did himself was torture a man because he could. Because it was convenient."

I stiffened ramrod straight.

"I know the danger we're in. I don't need a reminder," he snapped. "But I also know the terrible things I've done so you, my brothers, my sisters, and my parents don't have to. I wanted another way back then and now there is one. Kenzie is asking for two days. Why can't you give that to her?"

"Fuck you." My tone was a low, dangerous hiss. "I don't take pleasure in this, Liam. Nothing about this is fucking convenient!"

"Then why can't you wait?"

I shoved away, fists balling. "Because—"

"Because what?"

"Just because!" I shouted. "There's no time to wait."

"Why, Gen? Tell me why!"

"Because I know who was killed in the explosion!"

Liam reeled, anger blowing clean out of him. "What? What are you talking about?"

"Ugh!" I flung his glass of scotch across the room. It didn't make me feel better. "Damn you. Why can't you ever just do what you're told without asking questions?"

"Because I'm a Hunt." Liam pushed me down onto the couch. "Why would you say you know who died?"

Sighing, I flopped in a boneless heap. This was the second time Liam ever witnessed this—me giving in. "Because I did," I said flatly. "That night, I walked into my bedroom and there was a man sitting on my bed. I'd never seen him before."

Liam twitched for a weapon he didn't have. "What did he do to you?"

"He didn't do anything. That wasn't what he was there for," I said. "He told me his name was Isiah and he was with the Brotherhood. Just like that, Liam. Dropped the information like a pickup line in the club. He said he had a proposition for me and I could hear him out, or I could think about how easily the Brotherhood found me. The next time, they'll get the drive-by right."

"What was the proposition?"

"The guy banged on about the Brotherhood having the strongest presence in Harlow. The place is loaded with misogynist pigs chafing under the rule of a woman. Many jumped at the recruitment offer. Some of them I'd never suspect. A good amount of them I've never met."

Liam bobbed his head slowly. "You didn't recognize the men who shot at you. Sunny didn't know Snyder before the bastard threw him off a bridge."

"I know it wasn't an empty threat," I said. "Neither was I shocked they've gotten the bulk of their brothers from Harlow. I've always been about protecting the women in that borough. Never hid it, won't apologize for it."

"But what did he want from you, Genny?"

"He said the Brotherhood wanted to make a deal with me," I burst out. "He said me and my little girls' club are *cute*. Sunny's basically the youngest kingpin in Cinco City. You run the largest money-laundering operation on the East Coast. Bane's amassing millions through his arsenal, but me—" My lips curled. "Apparently, all I do is mess around in my bar with a bunch of women. My *goals* and *aspirations* did not harm the city or oppose the Brotherhood's plans. If I was willing to form an alliance with them, there didn't have to be another assassination attempt."

Disbelief shattered my brother's constant mask of perfect. "The Brotherhood actually thought you would turn against your own family? I thought the man behind this was intelligent."

"That was my thought, Liam. The guy's a clown and he sent his circus-trained buffoon to get killed on my floral carpet," I said. "That's when Isiah finished his speech. If I gave control of Harlow over to the Brotherhood, I could still run the Cardinals while making peace with the death of my entire family. Or I sided with the Merchants and every woman in Harlow who wears red will be slaughtered."

I swallowed through a tightening throat. "Not every Cardinal, Liam. Every woman. It'd be open season."

"It would not be because we'd never let that happen." He grasped my shoulder. "So you turned him down and he set off the bomb? While he was still inside?"

"No, that's the thing. It was all strange," I admitted. "The Brotherhood couldn't seriously think I'd turn against my own family. Somehow I was both a non-threat to them *and* a psychopathic monster? What the fuck kind of sense did that make?

"But then if that offer wasn't serious, why was Isiah droning on instead of killing me?"

"He was a stall."

I snapped my fingers, pointing at him. I said a lot of things about my brothers, but I never said they were stupid. "Every single attempt to kill us has failed. Even with their weapons, trackers, and assassins. Isiah was sent to *keep me in that building* when it blew up. Trouble is, I don't think he knew he was just bait.

"He really sounded like he believed the bullshit he was saying. I mean, the guy said my gang was a little girls' club with a straight face. If he knew the scale of my operation in Harlow, he wouldn't have bothered pissing me off right out the gate with that bullshit."

"But you got out of there. You made it down to the basement."

"I did," I said, wishing I drank that scotch instead of using it to decorate the wall. "Once I realized something was off, I knocked his ass out and beat it out of there. I was running through the bar when I heard tires peel out fast. I could only think of one reason someone was speeding away as quickly as possible.

"Bomb," we said at the same time.

I sighed. "So, I dove into the basement, and you know the rest."

"I don't know the rest." Liam claimed the spot by my side. "Why didn't you tell us this?"

"At first because it didn't matter. That offer wasn't real. The Brotherhood wanted me in a coffin right alongside the rest of you," I said. "But the more I thought about it, the more it bugged me. His threats were specific. The Brotherhood knows what I'm dealing with in Harlow. Worse—they know the right pressure points.

"If they have even half of my enemies on their side, they don't need a deal with me. With my death, they can make things very difficult for the women in my borough. Only a Merchant can run Harlow, so I haven't trained any of my girls to take over for me. With me gone, the Cardinals have no leader. They're vulnerable to attack from all those misogynist pigs— What am I saying? We've already been attacked. They blew up that warehouse with three of my people inside.

"By now the Brotherhood knows I'm not dead. It's only a matter of time before they make good on those threats and tear down our empires. If they've got the biggest presence in Harlow, why wouldn't they start with me?"

"I still don't understand why you didn't tell us."

"Do you tell me about every little issue in your borough? Does Sunny or Bane? I can handle my own business." I shoved up, shaking him off. "These people are willing to blow up their own 'brother' to take us out. We need to end this as soon as possible, and you know that, Liam. This isn't about making Kenzie happy, or about me being so impatient I'll take pliers to a man's fingernails without a thought. I don't want to torture Vito, but I will if it saves Harlow and the Cardinals."

I could see on his face, my logic was getting through. Grinding his teeth, Liam flicked to his phone resting on the coffee table. I wondered if he was thinking about Kenzie.

"Say... I give you an hour with him—"

"You *will* give me all the hours with him I need."

Liam held up a hand, silencing me. "Say I give you time with him. Do you really believe there's anything you can do to get him to talk? Vito Bernardi holds a particular hatred for you. Gen, I wouldn't trust anything he told you even under the harshest methods."

His words went in my ear and out the other. I'd get Vito to talk because I had to. End of story.

"Let me worry about that." I grabbed Liam's keys off the hook. "Let's go."

"We're leaving now? Are we stopping to talk to Bane and Sunny on the way?" he asked, tone dry. "You did just berate me for keeping secrets."

"From me," I finished. "Never keep secrets from me. You can tell those assholes what you want. From the car. On the way to Astoria. Now."

I slammed out the door, chuckling at whatever Liam muttered under his breath, though I didn't hear it.

The ride to Astoria was fast, because I broke the speed limit the whole way. The gift of a Hunt is seeing the measure of a man in an instant. Well, I had the measure of the Brotherhood. They used their own people as pawns.

Relied on every underhanded tactic that existed. And saw innocent people as collateral.

I gave Kenzie two weeks because getting rid of those trackers gave us a reprieve. We had a window to relax while the Brotherhood scrambled to find another method of taking us out. But two weeks was still an arbitrary number. They could have a new strategy in a month or a day.

All I had was the nagging feeling those bastards knew too much about my weaknesses. Sooner rather than later, they'd use that leverage to their advantage.

I squealed into Liam's parking space, killing the engine. "Is someone else here?" I asked.

"Blake and Henry."

Liam let us inside. The aforementioned Blake and Henry stood on either side of the door leading to the underground storage room. They were two silent sentinels.

It was creepy.

"Boss," Blake said, inclining his head. "She's down there waiting for you."

"She? Who's down there?"

"Miss Blaine," Henry said.

"Kenzie?" Liam rushed the door. "You left her down there alone!"

"She ordered us to give her privacy," Blake called after us.

We thundered down the stairs—my annoyance and respect for her growing with each step. Kenzie knew this place was my first stop, so she beat us here to keep me from putting a hand on the slug. The woman has her priorities out of whack, but she doesn't let anyone run over her. My kind of girl.

We tripped off the last step, startling Kenzie. She whirled away from Vito, lips parting and nothing coming out.

"Shit, Kenzie," I cried. "I know you didn't want me to torture the guy, but this is vindictive."

"It's not what you think!"

"Really?"

I took in Vito's huge, unstaring eyes. They leered at me for the last time as rivers of red gushed from his neck—coating the shears sticking out of his jugular. The same blood covered Kenzie's hands, top, and cheek.

"It looks like you killed Vito."

KENZIE

"I didn't kill him," I half screamed. My heart pounded so loud in my ear, I couldn't hear them or myself. I couldn't think! "It wasn't me."

Liam slowly approached. "You're the only one here, Mackenzie."

"Don't talk to me like I'm having a nervous breakdown. I didn't kill him because he killed himself," I cried. "He grabbed the shears and plunged them in his neck. I couldn't stop him."

Liam grabbed my flailing hands. Blood and all, he held them to his chest—pouring his calm into me. Or that's what it felt like as I felt his steady, pounding heart beneath my palms.

"He did this to himself?" Genny repeated. I saw her feel for his pulse. "Why would he do that? And what were you doing here in the first place?"

"What were you?! I said I wasn't going to let you torture him and I meant it. If I had to be here to stop you, then so be it." Something occurred to me. "Hold on. Why are you here, Liam?" I broke away from him. "You brought Genny here after promising you'd let me handle this myself?"

"Mackenzie—"

Genny shoved between us. "Can we get some perspective here? Vito is *dead*. Who the fuck cares what I was or wasn't going to do? None of that matters now. Just tell us what happened, Kenzie."

I glared at her. It mattered quite a bit, but Genevieve was right. The dead body in the room took priority.

Sidestepping her, I inched in front of Vito—picturing the scene with nightmarish clarity. "I guess it was my fault," I whispered, eyes stinging. "I came here to show him the news reports. I thought if he saw for himself that the Brotherhood was done with him now, he'd have no reason to continue protecting their secrets.

"Vito lost his mind. He shouted that I didn't know what I'd done. I ruined everything, and Brother Abraham would never forgive him. He kept saying that over and over. *Brother Abraham will kill me.*"

"Who is Brother Abraham?" Genny turned me to face her. "Who is he, Kenzie?"

I shook myself. "I don't know. I couldn't get anything out of him after that. I'm telling you, it's like seeing his name on the eight o'clock news broke him."

"How did he get the shears?" Liam asked.

I looked away, trembling. "I took them out of the cabinet. He wasn't listening to me, so I tried to get him to focus. I got the shears and reminded him that I had his blood. As bad as it was now, it would only get worse if he and the Brotherhood moved on from blackmail to terrorism. It didn't have to go that far if he told me everything.

"Next thing I know, he lunges at me. His arm broke free and Vito grabbed the shears. I thought—" My eyes fluttered shut. "I thought he was going to kill me, but Vito didn't even try. He stuck the shears in his neck without hesitation.

"I don't know who this Brother Abraham is. But he scared Vito a lot more than you or me."

Silence filled the desolate room. I didn't open my eyes—as if hoping I could wish myself away.

"Mackenzie." Hands grasped my forearm, pulling me in. "You did nothing wrong," Liam said softly. "I'm sorry we forced you to come here. You tried to save this man, and instead, your life was put in danger and you witnessed something horrible."

"Don't apologize, Liam. You tried to warn me. Sometimes I'll have to choose between pushing people past their limits, or going without information that could save lives. Today... I found out exactly what that means."

"Let's get out of here."

I looked up as Liam guided me to the stairs, but he wasn't looking at me. A silent communication passed between the Hunts.

"What? What?" I demanded when they didn't answer me. "Why are you looking at each other like that?"

Genny shrugged off her jacket and laid it over the body. It surprised me to see her show such reverence for the body of her enemy.

Or maybe she can't stand to look into those wide, accusing eyes for another moment.

"This is not good, Kenzie," Genny said. "Vito was the first brother we got our hands on. The first we could question. That's why Liam never *should've left this up to you.*" She said it to me, but it was meant for him. "Even so, you got us something."

"What did I get?"

"I've known Vito a long time. The only person he loves more than himself is his reflection. He'd never kill himself unless he was convinced a long, painful death was coming his way. Brother Abraham couldn't get him that piss-his-pants terrified if he was just another minion. Vito gave you the name of someone high up in the organization. Maybe even the leader himself."

"But it's still not enough," I said as Liam helped me up the stairs. It was mostly him because I stopped feeling my legs partway through the conversation. "It's just a first name, and a common one too."

"It's a start," Liam promised. "It's a name we can put out on the streets. I'll take care of everything from here, Mackenzie." Warm lips brushed my temple. "Just relax. You're safe."

Liam repeated that as he scooped me up, carrying me the rest of the way to the car.

I thought I accepted death and danger as the reality of my new life. But the look in Vito's eyes as he plunged the shears in his own throat proved one thing. Whoever was coming for him—coming for us—we were not ready for him.

We were not nearly knowledgeable enough, scared enough, or prepared enough for the monster hunting us down.

GENNY

I spent the better part of the night harassing Liam, filling in Sunny and Bane, and giving orders to my Cardinals. We had a name. That was more than we had twelve hours ago.

"I need another explanation for why you didn't tell either of us you found Vito, because the one you gave doesn't make any sense," Sunny said.

The five of us gathered in Sunny's living room, poring over every file Liam kept on every enemy the Merchants made over the decades. We were up to twelve Abrahams and counting. Damn, we've been busy.

The fifth member of the party munched on a fistful of my hair and babbled in Bane's direction. Laurel woke up a little while earlier. We all agreed it was best to let Kenzie sleep.

"I've given you every variety of explanation," Liam replied. "Mackenzie needed to understand what she's signing up for. Unfortunately, I believe she understands that now."

"Vito wasn't the one for your test," Bane said. He angrily paced the carpet. "You want to teach her a lesson on torture, you could've sent her out to hunt down the remaining guys in Adams's organization. Beating the crap out of a rapist is therapy. But Vito we needed."

"It's done," Liam barked. "We're moving on."

"We'll move on when you agree you and Kenzie won't go rogue again," Sunny said. "We're taking down the Brotherhood together. We make all decisions—together."

"Like we decided to kill Yusuf together?"

Sunny brushed that away. "Two different situations. Yusuf wasn't important. Vito was. Agree, Liam."

"Agree," Bane added.

"Agree," I said.

His clenched jaw was the only sign of his tension. Sweeping over us, I could tell behind those placid eyes he regretted nothing. Liam was the first to get a taste of the Merchant life, and even though our parents promised choosing this life would be his choice, one mad provost and a bomb decided for him.

Afterward, he stepped up in the gang and protected us, so Bane, Sunny, and I could truly have a choice. When we all decided the criminal life was more our speed, Liam took on the uglier parts of the jobs so we wouldn't have to. Though we didn't ask him to, and even though sometimes we still had to get our hands bloody.

With Kenzie, he acted as the protector again. Showing her the truth of this life so whatever happened, she knew the choice she was making.

It was all so... condescending.

What the hell is it with dads, boyfriends, and older brothers appointing themselves the leader before anyone takes the fucking vote?

Kenzie's dealt with kidnapping, attempted rape, losing her child, and a darkness in her past that Sienna finally shared—telling me of the day she heard a gunshot and ran to find her mother standing over her father's body.

Our childhood was roses and pancakes compared to Kenzie's. She didn't need to be tested. She learned that people do terrible things for a just reason long before she met any of us. Now she was beating herself up over losing our first lead when my hero brother shouldn't have put her in that room.

"Agree, asshole," I snapped. "Can't play the older, wise one when you're letting Kenzie's pussy twist your judgment."

All my brothers looked uncomfortable at that.

"I agree," Liam said simply. "I will not ask your permission, but I will share all information and everyone I pick up in connection with the Brotherhood." Liam cut a look in my direction. "As I expect you all to do with me."

I flipped him off. The guy turned that around on me fast.

"Are we missing something else?" Bane demanded.

Heaving a sigh, I spilled the truth about the body in my burned-out apartment.

"Blew up their own guy just to keep you in one place," Sunny said. "Wow. That's cold."

"Well, they can't pull that trick a second time now that we know about the trackers," I said. "Back to Brother Abraham. Could any of them be the guy?"

Liam pulled up the photos, arranging them across his laptop screen. I didn't recognize any of their faces but I noted they were all middle-aged or older. By that point, you should either be running the gang or retired from it. A fifty-year-old that's still an errand boy is just pathetic.

"They're all either retired from the life or in jail," Liam said, confirming the thought right out of my head. "It could be one of them, or it could be none. Brother Abraham sounds almost biblical. Like a priest who chooses a new name for the new life he's begun. Abraham might be an alias."

"But this is something," Sunny insisted.

Liam inclined his head. "It's something. I'll get the word out on this name—promising a high price for information on the guy. It's more important than ever now that we find the person behind the trackers. We need to move against this guy the second we have a location, and we can't do that if we're still wearing our trackers to keep the Brotherhood from getting suspicious."

"We know they're not." Laurel grabbed my nose and smothered me—a future assassin in the making. "None of the Caddell employees have mysteriously requested sick leave since Kenzie and I moved there. He or she is there. They're lying low, but they're not running. The Brotherhood won't abandon this plan easily."

"Sunny," Bane spoke up. "Any progress in Rockchapel?"

"Depends on what you call progress. We started with a list of people that could be with the Brotherhood. Now I've got a list of people I'm sure are with the Brotherhood." He got up and bustled around the kitchen, making Laurel a bottle. "They've got money, connections, and skills that are worth something to a gang trying to take down the most powerful family in the city. Add that to the fact we can't find a trace of them..."

"At least we know they're recruiting out of Rockchapel and the types they're looking for," Bane replied. "We can use that."

"Ryker had the same thought, but everything we're coming up with is too risky."

"What are you coming up with?" I asked.

"A spy. A mole. We get to our enemies before they do, and offer a high price if they dangle themselves out in Rockchapel and let the Brotherhood pick them up. Once they're in, they can get the full scope of the operation. Make sure we take all the bastards out in one strike."

"You're right," I deadpanned. "That's a stupid plan."

"We're running low on good ones, big sis. I can hardly send Makai out there. No one would buy that he's betraying me. It would have to be someone the Brotherhood wouldn't suspect, but anyone like that we couldn't trust worth a damn."

"Then we go after the ones they already got," Bane said. "Give me half your list. I'll put my guys on it."

"What's going on?"

Our heads snapped around. Kenzie stood in the hall entrance—hair messy and pajamas covered in bunnies. She came straight for me and took Laurel out of my hands. "What's going on?" she asked again.

"We're making a plan with the little information we've got, Angel." Sunny handed her the bottle, then tugged them both down on his lap. "We're circling, Kenzie. The Brotherhood doesn't know it, but we're closing in."

"Hopefully I'll have something to contribute soon," she said. "I'll get Vance's alterations done today. Because of the holdup, they won't be ready for Wednesday's shipment, but they'll be ready to go on Friday. The rat will have until Friday to sew their extras in. When they go for it, I'll be ready."

"Are you certain you want to do this?" Liam asked—the condescending ass once again.

"I am doing it, Liam. I'll be fine." Kenzie got up. "I'm going to try to get Laurel back down. She is *not* supposed to be in your strategy sessions. But I am. Tell me everything when I get back."

I watched her walk off, feeling a tad more respect for her. Vito's violent and sudden death shocked her, but it didn't break her. Makenzie knew what she had to do, and she was ready to get it done.

By Friday, I thought. *I'm sick to death of waiting around.*

FOUR HOURS LATER, KENZIE and I rolled into Caddell House with cups of coffee and zero patience. Or maybe that was just me.

"Why are you wasting your time altering everything?" I stabbed the button for the elevator. "I'll explain to Vance that the designs are perfect as is. Problem solved."

"I'd rather earn his respect than beat it out of him. Vance has proven he won't reject a good design out of spite. I gave him the chance to do that when he hired me. No, if I tweak the outfits, he'll approve them and we can move on." Considering where we were standing, Kenzie didn't say more. "Oh, and I forgive you, by the way."

I pulled a face. "Forgive me? For what?"

"For acting like a flaming asshole yesterday." I barked a laugh. "I get the pressure you're under, and all the people you're trying to protect, but you don't do that by taking it out on me. I consider us friends, Gen, but if you treat me like that again. I'll change my mind."

I eyed her up and down, lips twisted with humor. No one dared speak to me like that. Even Sunny put his fists up and braced himself when he told me to go fuck myself.

"I don't apologize, and I won't now. But I will admit yesterday wasn't about you." The elevator dinged, inviting us in. "You are a badass, Kenzie. I haven't known Laurel long and I'm already willing to kill everyone and anyone who hurts her. You survived months separated from her—refusing to give in to the instinct to kill that woman and take her—all to keep your kid safe. I've never been that selfless.

"I brag every day about doing and taking whatever I want, but I still envy people like you. It wasn't weakness that stopped you killing Charlie. It took unimaginable strength to put Laurel's needs above your own even while it destroyed you. We all hope to find half that amount of courage to protect the people depending on us." My Cardinals floated through my mind. "Because there's no forgiveness if we fail."

"Goodness," Kenzie breathed, eyes bright. "I'll take that over an apology any day."

"Oh no," I said, head shaking. "Your girl crush is deepening. Sorry, Kenzie. I was into you before but now that you're hooking up with my brothers, it can't happen for us. I don't share."

"Annnnd you're back."

My laughter followed her to the office. Kenzie set her stuff down on the desk, picked up her pad, and headed back out. "I'm going to grab some stuff from the War Room, then I'm getting more coffee. Want some?"

"You don't even have to ask. Get me the largest cup of espresso they sell."

Kenzie left and I parked it on my seat, getting comfortable.

Crinkle.

Frowning, I shifted, wiggling my back.

Crinkle, crinkle.

I reached behind me, slipping my hand under the pillow. My fingertips brushed paper.

Dear Genevieve Hunt,

We know you and your family are responsible for the disappearance of our brother, Vito Bernardi. We can only assume you bear similar responsibility for the fake video currently trending in the media.

Our cause is fair and just. We seek to free Cinco City from the rule of tyrants and restore freedom to its people. We will not have that purpose mocked by you or anyone.

As punishment for your crimes against the Brotherhood, the Cardinal motorcycle gang has been disbanded. Do not be alarmed. We have not executed them since their only crime was being coerced into the service of your corrupt family.

We believe in the innate freedom of all people in this city to choose their path, so provided the Merchants recognize the Brotherhood as the true and only governing organization of Cinco City and the underground, as well as committing no further crimes against this organization, these women will be released and allowed to return to civilian life.

If you disobey this and any future orders from the Brotherhood, drastic measures will be taken.

You will show your acceptance of these terms by publicly denouncing the fake video and admitting the Merchants created it to scare and lie to the people.

Signed,

The Brotherhood

I was out the door before the final word was read. Skidding out onto the street, I flagged the first cab I saw and shouted, "Barbarella's. Harlow. Now!"

We sped the whole way there—helped along by my promising to gut and let him bleed out in the trunk if he'd dared to stop for a traffic light. Still, it was ages until we squealed to a stop before my bar.

Their bikes lined up on both sides of the entrance, announcing who this place belonged to long before a fool tried to walk inside.

They're all here. That letter was bullshit. Planted to scare me. They didn't—

I ground to a halt, falling very, very still.

Barbarella's was a wreck. Tables overturned. Beer glasses shattered pieces on the wood. Broken pool cues. Smashed photographs. But nowhere in sight was a single Cardinal.

Silence pressed on my eardrums—taunting me, laughing at me. I knew there was something off. I had the worst feeling that my girls were in danger, and what did I do? Moved into the Fairfield and left them alone.

"No," I whispered. "Bugsy? Candace? Stella?"

No response traveled back.

"No!" Snatching a chair, I tossed it across the room. It was only the first object to get my wrath.

The cab driver stuck his head inside and quickly left, thinking better of asking for payment.

MACKENZIE

I checked off the items from my War Room shopping list, then headed up to the roof. Jace passed me coming down, glued to his phone.

"Jace, how are the suits for David coming?"

"Huh? What?" He blinked at me like I was a stranger. "Oh! The suits. They're great. I cut the fabric yesterday. Should have something for you next week."

I squinted at him. "Are you okay? You look pale."

"Just what every man wants to hear."

"I'm serious." I stepped into his path, stopping his escape. "You've been off the last couple of days. Are you feeling well?"

Jace's eyes flashed. "You don't know me. How would you know when I'm off or on? I said I'm fine, Mackenzie." He made a show of moving around me. "Now if you don't mind, some of us have work to do."

I let him go, though I watched him until he stepped off the stairs and disappeared around a corner. Jace was correct in saying I barely knew him, but what I did know was shifty-ass men and how much they loved deflecting. Whether Jace was still mad at me for calling him out, or there was something else going on with this guy, he was climbing higher and higher on my list.

"Morning, Dale."

"Morning, Kenzie." Dale, the coffee kiosk owner, started brewing my order on sight. He was round, bearded, and always smelled like coffee. "Can I get you a butterscotch muffin to go with this? On the house."

"Are you trying to make me fall in love with you? Because my boyfriends will hunt us down when we run away together."

He threw his head back, laughing a huge belly-shaking laugh. Dale was here back in the old days—pre-Damien's betrayal. No matter what kind of day I was having, Dale always had a smile and a muffin for me. Which said a lot about what I was going through. The man saw that I needed it.

"A large espresso too, please," I said. "So how have you been?"

We chatted about the little things while I nibbled on my muffin. He told me about his son's recital. I told him Laurel could throw her peas twelve feet.

"Impressive, but can she fling mashed carrots on the dog's head three mornings in a row? I think Rex was hanging around for it by the end."

I laughed. "That's a scary good plan. She dumps the carrots and Rex makes them disappear. Laurel is already outsmarting me. She does her hungry cry to get me to take her out of the crib, then she kicks back while her mom-sized carrier whisks her somewhere interesting."

"Bring her by sometime," he said. Dale popped the lid on my coffees and placed them in a small carrier. "I'd love to meet her."

"You know, I think I will. Laurel loves gardens. This place is her dream."

We said goodbye and I turned to go. The carrier slipped from my grip, exploding scalding hot coffee on my aquamarine boots.

He didn't react to the spill. Damien didn't take his widening eyes off me at all. "It's true," he hissed. "That fool hired you back."

I opened my mouth, but nothing came out. It was like no time had passed. The man who praised my talent, tickled me when no one was looking, fathered my child, shouted that he wanted nothing to do with me, and ruined my life... stood there looking the same as the last day I saw him.

The most expensive patterned suit from Caddell Spring Line clung to his frame. Wrinkles framed the green eyes he gave our daughter, but they made him look distinguished rather than old. And the curl at the corner of his mouth, sneering me down like he did that day he stood behind Talia like a fucking coward. That was the same too.

"What are you doing here?" I spat.

"Excuse me? What are you—?" Damien flicked over my shoulder to Dale. "Come with me. Now." He wasn't asking. Damien grabbed my arm and tugged me after him, speeding down the stairs.

"Hey! Let me go. I said get your hands off me, Damien."

He pulled off around the corner. I broke free of his hold, seized his arm, and wrenched it behind his back.

"Argh," he cried, forced to his knees.

"I said let me go." My hiss tickled his ear. "You don't get to push me around anymore, Damien."

I shoved him away, putting distance between us as he scrambled to his feet. We glared at each other across the divide.

"What are you doing here? How did you get Vance to give you a job?"

"How else? I impressed him with my talent."

"Bullshit. He knows you're a liar and a fraud. He wouldn't do this unless you forced or blackmailed him."

I scoffed. "No, Damien. He knows *you're* the liar and the fraud. Hollywell hired me because I shouldn't have been fired in the first place."

He advanced on me. "What the fuck have you been saying?"

"Back up!" The scream startled him, halting Damien in his tracks. He didn't need someone running over here to see what I was yelling about. "This is a foreign concept to you, but I haven't told him anything but the truth. If you don't like the light that casts on you, maybe you shouldn't destroy people's lives so your clueless fiancée doesn't dump you."

"Keep your voice down."

"Fuck off." I stormed off. "Fly back to New York, Damien. Talia and your three mistresses are waiting for you."

He shot in front of me, pulling me up short. "You're going to go downstairs, recant whatever bullshit you've told Vance, and then quit. If you do so, I will write you a check for a quarter of a million dollars."

"Oh? Are you giving me all that money for back child support?"

Damien went rigid. "I don't have a child."

The rejection stung. After all this time, it crushed me hearing him reject our beautiful little girl.

"You're pathetic, Damien. I don't want or need your money. I have no idea what you thought you were going to accomplish by coming here, but you can't get rid of me so easily this time. I'm staying," I said clearly. "And until you're ready to step up and be a father to your daughter, you and I have nothing to talk about. Stay away from me."

"Mackenzie— Don't walk away from me! Mackenzie!"

I marched off, leaving any lingering shred of feelings I had for him behind. Sunny said it perfectly. That man wasn't my daughter's father. Her real father wouldn't give her up for all the money in the world. He'd do anything to protect her, keep her safe, make her smile. My baby girl has three fathers and a family who loves her. We'd be perfectly fine if we never heard the name Damien Stone again.

"Mackenzie, you leave me no choice. You're fired."

I tripped, snagging my stained hem and tearing a hole in it. "Excuse me?"

"You heard me. I may have transferred to the New York house, but I'm still your boss. We will not have a fraud and a thief stain our name. You're fired," he growled. "Clean out your desk."

Stiffly, I turned on my heels—glare setting him on fire. "You can't fire me. If you could, your first move wouldn't be bribery. A fact I'll be happy to share with HR when this inappropriate and threatening conversation comes up."

"The only threats are yours. I bet you pulled the same crap to force Vance's hand. Maybe I can't fire you today, Mackenzie, but I promise you, your days at Caddell House are numbered. I suggest you start updating your résumé. Don't put us down as a reference." Damien brushed past me.

"Laurel," I called, throat tight. "Our baby's name is Laurel. She's sweet and beautiful and perfect. If anyone is an angel, it is Laurel Jennifer Blaine."

Damien paused on the steps, his back to me.

"I just thought you'd want to know... that she is nothing like you."

Cursing, he took off without a backward glance.

I stood there for a long time, gazing at the blank walls. I knew this could happen. My working here was going to get back to him sooner or later, and of course he wouldn't be happy about it. Even so, I wasn't prepared for all those nasty emotions to roar up in me, choking out the calm, in-control person I thought I was becoming.

One fight with my ex, and I was back to being that lost, angry girl who had everything ripped away from her.

Not everything, a voice whispered. *I had Laurel and Sienna. You had River and the crew. Now I have Sunny, Liam, Bane, and a family. It's that sad little man I should feel sorry for. His life is so empty, all the money and affairs in the world can't fill it.*

Steeling myself, I went downstairs, shoving Damien out of my mind. I pushed into my office.

"Sorry, Gen, the coffee didn't work out. You won't believe... who's here..." I trailed off at the empty room.

Letting out a deep breath, I knelt before my mannequin and got to work.

SIENNA WAVED TO ME from the driver's seat. I would've hopped in on the passenger's side, but it was occupied.

"Sienna. River." I climbed inside and kissed them both on the cheek. "What's up? Do we have plans?"

"First, where is Genny?" Sienna asked.

"I don't know. She took off this morning and hasn't answered my calls or texts. Genny does her own thing, so I figure she'll pop up when she wants to."

"Okay." Sienna set off, looking very comfortable behind the wheel of Liam's Rolls-Royce.

River twisted around, snagged my collar, and drew me in for a real kiss. My face heated as he swiped the bottom of my lip, then nibbled it for entrance. Even the way he kissed had to be unlike anyone I've ever been with. Something told me a life with River would always be full of surprises.

"Sienna said she was going to pick you up, so I tagged along."

"Fine with me," I purred.

"River, tell her the rest," Sienna said.

I pulled back. "The rest of what?"

"You know I've been helping out at the shelter," Sienna continued. "I can't sit around doing nothing when everyone is working so hard to stop the Brotherhood and help the people they've hurt. I've mostly been helping River track down those stolen kids."

My eyes popped. "You have? Sienna, why didn't you say? That's dangerous."

"No more dangerous than working alongside a Brotherhood member. Look, my visions haven't been helpful to the Merchants, but they have been helpful to the women in the shelter. For those who've let me do readings for them, I got a strong sense their children are close by. Adams didn't ship them to another country like he tried to do to you."

I swallowed my skepticism. Now wasn't the time to do anything but support my sister. Actually, it would never be any other time. "The kids are still in the city. What does that mean?"

"It's not just the kids I told you about," River said. "Turns out, the women were holding back because they didn't know or trust me at first. Doesn't help that the Rat King isn't spoken of fondly in the streets. But when Sienna came in—rich, kind, and not in my crew—they figured maybe I was who she said I was."

Rich? *Of course. Driving around in the guys' car, they figured she was outside the crew and therefore didn't have a reason to repeat their lies—if they were telling any.*

"What did they tell you, Si?"

"Digger didn't stop at dating single moms and taking their kids. After he forced them into the hell houses, he *bred* them, Kenzie. Those monsters raped them and then when they got pregnant, Luca had shiny, plump newborns to sell. Babies don't kick, scream, or cry for their moms when handed to their new parents," she spat.

"Oh my gosh," I cried, stomach heaving. "That's what he did to them? That's... what he was going to do to me and Laurel. Sell my daughter, force me to have more kids, and then sell them too."

And then I did throw up. Pitching myself across the seat, I emptied my stomach on Liam's spotless floor.

It took a while to calm me down. Sienna pulled over the car and they both climbed in back with me. Sienna held my hand while I rested on River's shoulder—his fingers gently stroking my temple.

"I'm sorry."

"Kenzie, why are you apologizing?" Sienna asked.

I sniffed. "Because I'm making it about me when it's about the women who had to live through this." Pushing myself up, I swiped a hand across my eyes. "But that's why you didn't tell me earlier."

"I wasn't going to tell you Digger was even more of a depraved monster unless I had something good to tell you too," Sienna said. "We think we might've found Marie's son, Jake. If we're right, we're that much closer to finding the other kids."

"Wait, back up." They had my full attention. I shoved all thoughts of that monster deep down and burned them. I was closing the door on Luca Adams for good. He didn't get to spend his afterlife making me feel horrible too. "How did you find Jake?"

Sienna motioned to River, smiling. "He had the force of the underground network out on this one. Every homeless person in every borough in every corner of the city—all of them watching, listening, and looking for a boy that looked like Jake."

"Wasn't easy," River said. "A homeless man or woman staking out a middle school—people tend to take issue with that. They kept chasing my guys off, but I just sent them back until finally, a little boy that looked exactly like how Marie described came running out of Weston Parker Middle."

"Was it really him? Did you bring him back to Marie?"

River and Sienna shared a look. "It's not that simple."

"What do you mean it's not that simple? Marie is his mother."

River stroked my cheek. "We know, Kenzie, and he will be reunited with his mom. I'll do whatever it takes, but what we're saying is, it wasn't until we got the whole truth, and then found Wesley, that we understood the full scale of Luca's operation."

"He wasn't just taking children and doing who knows what to them," Sienna added. "That's the only part of this that's good news. From what it looks like, Luca was privately adopting them out."

"How do you know this?" I asked.

"That day, Jake left Weston Parker and got into a car with a dark-haired, middle-aged woman," River said. "Sammie followed them to a townhouse in Leighbridge. Swanky place with a tire swing on the oak tree and a backyard jungle gym. We looked her up and found out she's Angelina Forbis of Forbis Luxury. Her family sells yachts all up and down the coast."

"She adopted Jake," I said slowly. "The child that was kidnapped and sold by a sociopath."

Sienna nodded. "There's no other explanation. I mean, she enrolled him in school and drives around with him in broad daylight. She wouldn't do that if she thought she was walking around with twenty-five to life."

"Come on. How could Luca fake a legitimate adoption agency? Especially after she got her hands on Jake and he begged to see his mother. That woman had to know she was filling her need for a child with another mother's misery."

"Of course, we can't say for sure how much Mrs. Forbis and her husband knew, but they're wealthy, Kenzie," River said. "They haven't dyed his hair to change his appearance. They haven't tried to leave the city, even though his face could end up on a milk carton any day. They could hop on one of their many yachts and sail off with their stolen child, but they're not trying to hide. Somehow, Luca made his operation seem legitimate enough that this couple was fooled."

I tossed my head. "Why does any of that matter? You found Jake. We need to get him back to Marie."

"How do you think that's going to go?" Sienna asked softly. "If he made things look real, then he had papers that looked real too. The Forbises would've signed things, sent in documents, gotten a birth certificate. While Marie has none of that. Luca destroyed any documents that prove she's Jake's mother.

"If Marie busts in there and tries to take him, she could end up arrested. Sure, a DNA test would prove she's his mother, but it doesn't prove anything else. Meanwhile, they're rich and connected while she's homeless and broke. Who wins in that situation, Kenzie?"

I looked away, jaw clenched tight. This situation was sickeningly familiar. "I'm really hoping you're moving on to the part of the conversation where you tell me the foolproof plan to get him back."

"We do have a plan," River said. "If these are good people, they won't keep a child from his mother. We're going to talk to them, Kenzie. Tell them what's happened and what was done to these women. Like I said, if these are good people, they'll tell us how Luca approached them and faked a real adoption. We can use that information to track down the other kids."

"And if they're not good people? What does Marie think about all this?"

"Of course we asked her," Sienna said. "We told her the minute we knew he was Jake. Marie is coming with us to speak to Mr. and Mrs. Forbis. If they refuse to do the right thing, then she's calling the police and we won't get in her way. But you only have to meet Marie and hear her story to know keeping her apart from Jake for another minute is wrong."

I relaxed slightly. "Okay. As long as she agrees. But do you really think the Forbises can tell you enough to help you find the other kids? How many children are we talking about anyway?"

"Twenty-three."

I choked, eyes bugging. "Luca kidnapped and sold twenty-three kids!"

"Yes," River said gravely. "Most of them were newborns when they were taken away. Their mothers can't tell us what they look like now, so standing outside preschools and daycares isn't going to work. The Forbises are all we got."

"Okay, okay," I breathed. "Then, I want to help. I'll go with you to speak to the Forbises instead of Sienna."

"Um, real nice, sis—booting me out of the way." Sienna laughed to take the sting out of it.

"It's not like that," I said. "This could be dangerous. Just because they haven't locked Jake in a basement, doesn't mean they don't know the *adoption* was illegal. Plus, who knows how they'll react to a couple of strangers coming in and saying they have to give up Jake? It could get ugly."

Sienna patted her biceps. "Bane's a good teacher. If a fifty-year-old woman and her fifty-six-year-old husband come for me, I can take them down. Seriously, Kenzie, I can do this. My visions are positive. Hopeful. I see Marie happy—something she hasn't been for a very long time." She dropped her head on my shoulder. "I can do something good, Kenzie. Trust me."

"I do," I whispered. "I know you can do this, Sienna. Both of you. You'll bring Jake and those children home." Twisting, I captured River's lips and kissed him soundly. "Thank you."

"No, thank you," he said, brows popped. "What was that for?"

"That was for sending your people out day after day, even when they were chased off. That's for not giving up, River. I can't believe I ever thought you only did things when there was something in it for you. I finally understand how many people you're taking care of. Sometimes you have to make hard choices to... protect your family." Visions of him floated through my mind—seventeen and alone. "You don't abandon the people who rely on you."

He smiled, pressing a kiss to the tip of my nose. "I'm still the duplicitous bastard who pissed you off on a daily basis, but yes, I do always have a good reason. Hope that lets me get away with stuff in the future."

I poked his side. "And what kind of stuff are you trying to get away with?"

"Well, I'm definitely going to lie to you and say we're doing something boring when I'm really surprising you with an incredible date. I'm going to steal all kinds of shit—your time, your attention, your love. And I'm going to kill," he said. "Kill anyone who hurts you. Destroy anything that makes you unhappy. So as long as you can live with that, I'm your crime boss for life."

I broke the seat belt jumping him.

"Okay, time to go," Sienna rushed. "I'll be in that bakery over there while— And you don't care."

She got out quickly. Good thing because our make-out session got dirty real fast. It wasn't until a uniformed officer banged on the window, shouting at us to move on, that I tugged on my bra and pulled my underwear back up.

Eventually, Sienna and I made it home—her giving me knowing looks all the way up the elevator. Inside Sunny's—our—apartment, I found my silver-eyed devil pacing our bedroom with Laurel bouncing in the baby carrier. I smiled at the perfect picture they made.

"I love how much you love her."

He looked up from the paper in his hand. "Hey, Angel." Sunny dropped a kiss on her curls. "Laurel doesn't give me much choice. Today, she took my pen and lobbed it across the room. Perfect technique. Released at the right angle. Babe, we're looking at a knife-throwing prodigy here."

I laughed. "Too bad she'll never develop the skill."

Sighing, he stage-whispered to Laurel, "Don't worry, I'll work on her."

"You won't believe what happened today. Damien is in Cinco." Sunny's smile wiped away. "He showed up at Caddell House and promised he'd get me fired if it's the last thing he does."

The sheet crinkled in his fist. A glance down told me what was holding back his reaction.

I took Laurel and put her on the carpet with her toys. I didn't want him holding back. Exploding was exactly the right reaction to my son-of-a-bitch ex blowing back into my life just to threaten me.

"How did he know you were back?" Sunny gritted.

"Anyone could have told him. Top of my list is Lyla. If she pulls something, Vance isn't likely to buy the innocent act, but with Damien here, she can put it all on him again. But she won't have to," I said, voice quavering. "He flat-out said he's happy to take me out all on his own."

"He's not going to touch you." Sunny gripped my waist, pulling me in close. "Because I'm going to kill him."

"Sunny," I said, smile tugging at my lips. "You have to stop threatening to kill my ex. It's getting harder to know when you're kidding."

"I'm not kidding."

I pecked his mouth. "I don't want him dead. But I do want the world to know the truth about him. I can clear my name once and for all, and Damien will know what it's like to lose his reputation and the only job he ever loved. Who knows, maybe he'll come out on the other side of this a better person."

Sole bobbed his head. "We could do all of that *or* I could break into wherever he's staying, hang him from the fan, and make it look like suicide."

Chuckling, I picked up my baby and carried her to the door. "Run the water, baby. Laurel will have some Auntie time while we have a bath."

"Completely serious on this fan thing, Angel. Just blink once for yes."

My laugh floated through the hallway. It was crazy how much I loved that ridiculous man, so much that I finally understood what I had with Damien was like comparing a diamond to horseshit. What Sunny and I had was real, honest, passionate, and a little chaotic. I felt like I was falling without a parachute whenever I looked at him.

Damien and I were never like that. Sure, the sex was good, but that's all it was. We didn't have conversations long into the night—sharing the things we couldn't talk about with anyone else. He didn't let me see him at his best and worst, knowing he could because I'd love him through everything.

I never really knew Damien Stone, but when I was through with him, the whole world will.

LIAM

Kenzie and Laurel arrived to dinner right on time. The two were dressed in matching outfits—pink and blue dresses with laurels along the hem. Kenzie pulled Elizabeth's identical dress out of her bag and my kid was out of commission for a full thirty minutes. First, she had to change, then I was required to take a billion pictures of her, her and Laurel, the three of them, and then I was allowed in the pictures after I found a blue suit in the same color. It took all of that time for me to finally tell Kenzie that we weren't having dinner together.

"We're not?" Her face fell. "Why?"

"We're not having dinner together with the four of us." I brought her fingers to my lips. "But we are having dinner just the two of us."

"Oh?" she said, smile returning. "What did you have in mind?"

"It occurs to me that our relationship has progressed in many ways, but I've yet to take you on a real date. So, Fuller is waiting downstairs with dinner, toys, and a movie. She'll put the girls to bed, and you and I will have the whole night together."

"You had me at just the two of us."

Together, we carried the girls downstairs to Sunny's place. Of course Bethany had her own apartment, but she liked that to just be her space—which we respected. She made us her whole life since the day Mom introduced us to our new nanny. Least we could do was keep our mouths shut about the handsome, older gentlemen that frequently picked her up outside the Fairfield, and not ask when she developed a taste for the heavy metal we occasionally heard blasting from her place.

"There are my girls." Fuller picked both Laurel and Elizabeth up, carrying them off to the table. "Bye, Liam, Mackenzie. Have a great time."

"Are you sure you're okay with this?" Kenzie asked as I gently tugged her out the door. "We can do it another night. Or wait and let me see if Sienna can babysit with you."

"Mackenzie, I wrangled the Redgrave children while Liam was trying to break out of the house, Bane was destroying everything in sight, Genevieve was pulling my hair, and Sole was spitting up in it. If I can handle that, these angels are no problem. Now, you two have a good time and don't come back before noon tomorrow morning."

"Yes, ma'am," I said.

"We won't be gone that long," Kenzie protested.

"Yes, we will." I was over the threshold and getting her there inch by inch.

"Okay, if you're sure. Bye, Lizzie. Bye, Laurel. Mama loves you."

"Da!"

I chuckled at that girl's stubbornness. Kenzie was "Da" and would be until she decided otherwise.

Finally, we were out in the hall and the door swung shut. Kenzie turned her nose up at my amused expression. "Don't give me that look. I can both want to go out and stay with my baby at the same time."

I put my hands up in surrender. "You don't have to tell me. For three months, I put considerable effort into how I could work out a situation where Lizzie could come to work with me."

Kenzie slipped her arms around mine, melting against me. "So, where are you taking me, Hunt?"

"I've got something special in mind. Romantic and private. I hope you don't expect to be back before noon because I've got you booked."

"I'm sure you can persuade me to keep the date going."

We flirted all the way downstairs and on the ride. It was wild how easy it was with Kenzie. I dated many women before she came along and there was always a barrier between us. For some, it was because I couldn't tell them the full truth of what I do.

Owning nightclubs explained why I was out at all hours of the night, but it didn't explain the calls I sent to voicemail because they couldn't be a witness to what I'd say. It didn't explain why I lived in a fortress or was cagey with details about my family. Dating Hendrix was supposed to be freedom from all that. She didn't want anything serious. Knew exactly what the Merchants did. She was my age and a single parent too.

Then Mackenzie Blaine stumbled out of a cab with my unconscious brother.

Mom used to say that love doesn't tick off boxes on a checklist. You'll find the person who is perfect for you, but not in any of the ways you planned or tried to control. Naturally, I spent years trying to prove her wrong.

"You did a terrible thing to me when you sent that damn text and blew the first hole through my resolve."

Kenzie blinked. "Terrible?"

"Oh, yes." I shifted lanes, heading for the final turn. "You forced me to admit my mother was right."

"I get the feeling Adeline is rarely anything but." She peered out the window. "Why are we in this part of the city? Oooh, is there some cool, underground pop-up restaurant out here? One night only, the chef cooks an incredible menu for their exclusive guests."

"Ah, you've been talking to Bane."

"The guy wasn't kidding when he said he knew where to get the best of everything in the city. How does a twenty-nine-year-old hermit manage to hit every legal and illegal eatery in the fourth-largest city in the country?"

"By cheating. He's borrowing the majority of his recommendations from our mother, I guarantee it. Let me guess," I said, "Bane issued you a challenge for naming all the bests."

"Wow. How did you know?"

"It's what he does. Issues a challenge when he has an ace up his sleeve." I gave her a look. "Ask my family and they'll tell you I was the problem child, but that's only because I didn't care about getting caught. I had nothing on Bane, and neither did anyone else. No evidence."

She laughed—the sound light and beautiful like that first rush of morning air when you stepped onto your balcony. It made you feel alive.

Rounding the final turn, we arrived at our true destination.

"An airplane hangar? Oooh, is this where we're eating?" She kissed my cheek. "Private and romantic. It's perfect."

Laughing, I went around and offered her my hand. "Mackenzie Blaine, when you're with me, you have to think bigger."

"Wait, we're not— Are we flying somewhere?"

I winked.

"But we can't," she cried.

"I assure you we can."

"But what about Laurel and Elizabeth? We can't just take off and leave them."

"We are coming back," I said, trying and failing to hide my amusement. I once again towed her in the right direction.

"But what if something happens and Fuller needs us to come back?"

"Nothing is going to happen. Fuller knows where the fire extinguishers are."

Kenzie promptly spun around and marched toward the car. I was on her in a blink, scooping her up and carrying her laughing through our family's hangar, into the waiting jet.

"Don't worry." I claimed my seat, remembering that day we sat in the same ones on the way from New York. "For the last few weeks, we've poured all our attention into the Brotherhood. Our days aren't promised, Mackenzie, and I won't waste another one that I could spend with you."

She ducked her head, burying a private, enigmatic grin in her shoulder. "I feel the same way."

Mackenzie said that, but she didn't give permission for the plane to take off until she talked to Fuller and was assured they'd be fine. I didn't fault her. Anyone paying attention noticed she had more separation anxiety than Laurel these days. This was a big step for her—letting go and trusting Laurel would be safe while they were apart. I was honored she was willing to take that step with me.

"Can I guess where we're going?" We kicked back, sipping glasses of champagne and apple cider. "We'll be back by noon tomorrow, so we can't be headed to Paris or somewhere like that."

"Say the word and we could be."

She winked. "One day, I will. But for tonight, I want to experience the first date you have planned for us. Speaking of which, you said I had to think big, so it's guaranteed to be somewhere I've never been before. Off the Cinco coast is the Isle of Maribel. Most of the isle is luxury hotels, diving vacations, and beach houses." She smirked, pleased as ever with herself. "That's where we're going."

"Just to be clear for the future, there's no point trying to surprise you, is there?"

"None."

"Come here." I held out my hand, drawing her onto my lap. "See that collection of lights in the distance? That's where I intend to feed you the most delicious meal prepared by human hands and then make love to you on the beach until the sun comes up. Not too bad for a first date—if I may compliment myself."

She kissed me slow and sweet. "Not too bad at all."

In no time at all we were touching down on the isle. A private car idled on standby, whisking us through the palm-shaded streets. It was ten minutes too long to get to my place. Just mine. Years ago, I bought this beach house to get away with Lizzie, and some days, just to get away.

"Wow, Liam. It's beautiful."

Three stories of floor-to-ceiling windows let you watch the sunrise and sunset from every room in the house. A hot tub waited for us in the back, overlooking the crashing waves. A firepit in the sand to keep us warm through multiple sessions of beach sex. This house wasn't just beautiful. It was about to become one of my favorite places in the world.

"Dinner is waiting for us inside," I said. "All we have to do is heat it up. Tonight it's just me and you—alone."

"You can stop selling it," she said, racing off. "You're already going to get laid."

I chased her around the house and up the back wooden steps. Mackenzie squealed as we fell on the lawn chair, our lips connected before we hit the cushion.

Someone I could have fun with wasn't on my checklist either. It's a good thing I threw the thing out.

Eventually, we made it inside. Kenzie spun on the living room carpet, taking it all in at once. "We have to come back soon with the girls. They'll have so much fun playing together on the beach."

"We can come back any time you want—all four of us or just you. This place is just as much your home as the Fairfield." The smile she gave me made me consider skipping dinner and moving right to dessert.

"What are we having?" she asked while I heated up the oven.

"It's a favorite on the isle. Lobster tails with lemon cream sauce, mango rice, and pomegranate salad. It sounds like too many flavors competing, but all together, they're the finest symphony of food I've tasted."

"Sounds perfect." Mackenzie was beautiful in her pink and blue dress, padding barefoot over the rug. Her halter straps caressed her smooth, tanned throat—drawing my eye to the hollow of her collarbone where I was dying to find that spot that had her moaning in the back of my car. I also smacked her firm, plump ass while I had her bent over in my car. I was dying to do that again too.

Kenzie helped me get dinner ready and take it out to the candlelit table waiting for us on the balcony. One bite and the food got the moan I was hunting for.

"Incredible. Who made this? Maybe they're the one who's getting laid tonight."

My brows climbed my forehead over the rim of my wineglass. "Oh, I see. You want me to spank you too."

She sent me a look that tightened my pants. "A lady doesn't ask for one, she earns it."

It was entirely possible I would have to marry this woman. Now I understood why my dads chose to love Mom equally. When you're obsessed with a woman and killing your rivals isn't an option, it's the conclusion you come to. If Kenzie wanted another man who wasn't a Merchant, I felt no twinge of conscience saying that man would disappear and never be found.

"What are you thinking about, Hunt?"

"Killing any non-Merchant man who touches you."

A smile curled her lips. "Hmm. This is what I get for dating a man who is always honest with me. What if I ask what's your most embarrassing childhood story?"

"I'd tell you it's the time we went to Cinco Theme Park and I begged my parents to let me go on the Typhoon Twister, even though they kept saying I couldn't handle it. Long story short, I threw up mid-ride and splattered everyone in a five-cart radius."

"Oh no," she squealed, clapping her hands over her mouth. "You didn't."

"Sadly, I did. As soon as the ride stopped, Baris lifted me up and took off running. I swear there was a roving hit squad of vomit-covered tourists hunting me through the park."

Mackenzie laughed so hard, she wheezed—tears running down her face. Before that day, the only people who knew that story were me, Baris, and my victims. Yet, I didn't think twice about telling Kenzie.

I can tell her everything—good, bad, and embarrassing. That wasn't on my checklist before either.

"I'm sorry I'm laughing," she said. "I'm actually jealous. I wish I had fun, crazy stories from my childhood."

"You and Sienna were angels?" My tone said I didn't believe it, for which I got a swat on the arm.

"We tried to be when we were home. Mom always seemed tired or stressed, and we wanted to make things easier for her. The only times we goofed around were when Dad took us out for movies, treats, and water parks. Now that I see my childhood for what it was..." She trailed off, not needing to say more. "Can I ask you something?"

"Anything."

"Would you change anything if you could? Like have you ever wished your parents were a couple of law-abiding citizens? Or that you grew up in the suburbs and lived the high school television show life?"

"No one has lived a high school television show life."

"Ugh, you're telling me," she cried. "They're like soap operas with the super gorgeous. In my high school, the guys all had faces like a foot and not nearly as many kids were sleeping with their teachers, doing drugs in the bathroom, or selling test papers as they want us to believe."

"This is really going to shock you. I went to an exclusive private school for the uber rich, and it was the most boring place that ever stole four years of my life. Nothing like— What was it my six-year-old tried to convince me she was old enough to watch? Oh yeah, *Gossip Girl.*"

"What?" she gasped. "You guys didn't all sit around congratulating yourself on being young, rich, and pretty, in between trading partners?"

I shook my head gravely. "I hope this doesn't change your opinion of me."

We cracked up. "No," I said when I sobered. "Strange as it is, I don't wish things were different. Not in any real way. I wish Elizabeth's mother didn't leave, but I don't regret that we're not together. And I don't regret the hell she put me through, because in the end, she gave me Elizabeth.

"When I was young, I hated watching my parents walk out the door and wondering if it would be the last time I saw them. With age and wisdom, I understand that's why I acted out. If they were home dealing with my latest disaster, they weren't out on the streets. But despite all of that, I don't wish we were another boring suburban family.

"It's a rare parent that truly accepts everything about their kid—good and bad. They never rode me, expecting me to be perfect, and then got disappointed when I wasn't. When I was sixteen, my dad, Killian, had to go on a business trip overseas. He was gone for three weeks and missed my final football game of the season. So I snuck out in his favorite car and totaled it."

"What did he do?"

"Sent the jet to pick me up and fly me out to Greece. I acted the surly shit the whole way—bracing myself for the lecture." My eyes glazed remembering it then. "But when I got there, Dad picked me up, drove us out to the beach, and while we were sitting there on the sand, he apologized. Said he'd never miss something that was important to me again, and that was a promise he was making to my face. Know what? He kept that promise.

"I think if we were a 'normal' family, they wouldn't have been there for us the way they were. They knew every day could be their last, so they made the most of the time we had together. You don't do that when you think a long life is promised to you. You take advantage. Let too much time pass between talking. Skip this or that event because it's just the one time and there'll be other games."

I laced our fingers together. "I know you still have lingering doubts about if this is the best life for Laurel. I can't answer that for you, but I can tell you, she just got a family that would burn the city down if she said the pretty colors would make her smile. I can say from experience, that's worth a lot."

"I hope my sweet baby girl never makes such a request," she teased, "but that is worth a lot, Liam. It's worth everything."

We enjoyed our meal—talking and laughing over the candlelight. After dinner, we kicked off our shoes and walked barefoot on the sand, letting the chilly water wash over our ankles.

That night and well into the morning, I made love to her on the sand—moving inside her warm, wet pussy like a starving man devouring a buffet. I told myself it'd be sweeter, slower, and gentler, but—

"Fucking hell, yes, baby. Right there." Mackenzie's nails pierced my back, pinpricking dots of pain through my pleasure. It anchored me to earth—on this beach where only the two of us exist. "Fill me with that fat cock, Liam."

My control snapped. This is why gentle and slow kept flinging themselves out the window. The mouth on this woman was just begging to be fucked—literally.

She milked me of every last drop, raked my back, dotted my chest and neck in possessive marks, and then laid my head between her breasts, running her hands through my hair as we drifted off to sleep.

Yes, Mackenzie Blaine did a terrible thing to me.

She made me fall in love with her.

Chapter Nine

Mackenzie

Liam and I made out like teenagers the whole way up to my apartment. We stumbled out, making it as far as the door and lingered just short of the knob—stretching our perfect night just a bit longer.

"I was thinking..." I began, running my hands over a body that was now all mine. "Laurel and I live with Sunny, and I love that. But I'd love to live with you too."

"Are you asking to move in after one date, Miss Blaine?" Liam nipped my nose. "You move fast."

Giggling, I nipped him back. "There's no rush. When the time comes, we can set up a nursery for Laurel, I'll split my nights in your bed, and in the mornings, the four of us will wake up and have breakfast together. Like a family."

"That would be—"

"Kenzie!" We jerked, snapping around as Genny stormed out of the elevator. "Where the hell have you been? You called out sick today. Let me guess." She eyed her brother up and down. "You caught a bad case of the D."

Liam straightened. "Good morning to you, Gen. I'm going to check on the girls and send Fuller off for a well-deserved break."

I murmured *thank you*, even though I should've said the opposite for leaving me alone with his irate sister.

"Did I not fully explain how serious it is that we find that fucking Brotherhood puppet as fast as possible?!"

I inched back a step, blown away by her anger. This wasn't always-on-pissed-and-loving-it Genny. Her face was red, blue eyes blazing, and dark bags riding beneath them.

"You were supposed to finish those stupid alterations so we could get those clothes in the Closet and be done with this already? Now is not the time for you to *call out sick*!"

"Gen," I said calmly. "I called in for the morning and told Vance I was going to the doctor, but would be back in the afternoon around two. At that time, we'd meet in my office for him to give the *completed* designs their final inspection. If you'd take it all the way down and give me five minutes, I'll be ready to go."

She folded her arms, eyes narrowing. "If the clothes are done, where did you put them? They're not in your office. If they were, I would've skipped this foolishness and shoved them in the Closet myself."

I frowned. "They're not in my office? They should be. Maybe Rylee, Jace, or Zoe took them off to use the mannequins. There are never enough of those to go around."

"Whatever. Chop-chop, Blaine. We've got business to take care of."

Even though she popped my good mood like a blimp, I swallowed my retort and went in to change and kiss my daughter goodbye. Genny explained the pressure she was under to solve this quickly and get back to Harlow. She took her duty to protect the women of Harlow seriously. Just like River did whatever was necessary to protect the homeless men and women of Cinco.

I didn't know what it was like to have that many people relying on me, but I did know there was nothing worse than letting your family down.

Genny and I sped fast—but not fast enough—to Caddell House. I studied her out of the corner of my eyes as we passed through the lobby.

"Gen, is everything okay? You've got a strange energy around you." Years of living with my sister put phrases like that in my head, but it was the right phrase for the anger coming off her in waves. "Did something happen?"

"Nothing happened, Mackenzie. I'm just tired of waiting around while this guy laughs behind our backs. I feel useless, and that's a new one for me."

I squeezed her fingers. "We're doing something about that today. Once they're in the Closet, they'll make their move. This is their money-printing machine. We know this plan will work, Gen. We're ready."

She didn't reply.

We headed upstairs where I confirmed Sunny's new wardrobe and the mannequins they were hanging on were gone.

"I'll find the team and see where they put them."

"Let's go," she said.

"Why don't you stay? Relax. I'll bring you back a coffee after I've got them and Hollywell."

Genny blew past me. "Are you still standing there?" she called over her shoulder. "Let's find these clothes, Blaine."

Sighing, I gave up and went after her. We went down a floor to the junior designers' room. Jace bent over his workstation, fussing with ever-finicky silk.

"Jace," I said. "Have you seen the clothes that were in my office?"

"Hmmm." He didn't look up from his work. "Oh, yeah. I think the intern said something about borrowing the mannequins."

That sent us off and down another floor. Genny burst into the intern space, me following at a more sedate pace, and called out for Rylee. Eleven owlish faces looked back at us, but none of them were hers.

"You've got to be kidding me," Genevieve snapped. "Is everyone out sick?"

"Gen, look. The mannequins are over there by her station." I crossed the room, taking the chance to see her creations in thread and cotton. I could tell by the colors that the outfits I was looking at were meant for Shonda. "She's probably just late coming back from lunch."

Rylee chose that moment to walk in with coffee and the remains of her muffin. Seemed Dale had other favorites he never told me about.

She beamed. "Hey, Mackenzie."

"Hey, Rylee. We're looking for—"

"Where are the clothes that were on these mannequins?" Genny sliced in.

"Oh. They looked like they were done and I needed the mannequins. Zoe said she'd move them to the Closet with the pieces she just finished."

This information sent us back up the stairs. Zoe was in there waiting for us on the second trip. She leaned against the windowsill, chatting with Madison.

"Zoe, did you put the clothes that were in my office into the Closet?" I asked.

"Yes." She flicked between me and Genny. "Was I not supposed to? I finished two outfits last night. Mr. Hollywell told me nothing gets approved for the Johnsons unless he gives the okay. I asked him to take a look, and he said to bring what you made for Anthony Johnson, so he could approve them at one time."

My teeth gritted. I gave Hollywell too much credit too soon. This guy was going to micromanage and push in on my authority whenever it suited him.

"Thank you, Zoe. Where in the Closet did you put them?"

"Row D-Three. The shipping rack," she said. "I took care of labeling, prepping, and putting them in garment bags."

"Thanks again," I replied. "I—"

"Row D-Three?" Lyla stepped out from behind her desk, mouth turned down. "That's funny. I was just down there with Brielle, hanging up some more clothes that are going out on Friday, and there was nothing else on the rack."

Genny advanced on her. "What are you saying?"

She shrugged, eyes huge. "I'm saying I don't know where the Johnsons' clothes are, but they're not in the Closet." Lyla gasped. "Oh no. You don't think someone stole them, do you?"

"We had a problem with that a couple months ago," Skylar spoke up. "Dresses were stolen from the Closet. You don't think—"

"The clothes weren't stolen," I said, though I narrowed on Lyla. "I'm sure they are down there. Lyla just mistook the rack she was looking at."

"Hmm, nope. D-Three—just like Zoe said."

I didn't bother responding to her. Gen and I hurried to the Closet and raced through the maze-like fashion paradise to the shipping rack. The only garment bags hanging on the metal rod were Brielle's creations.

"I'm going to kill her," Genny hissed, whirling around.

"Wait, Gen. You can believe if Lyla did this, she'll have all her friends backing up that she only went in the Closet with Brielle and didn't lay a finger on them while they were down here. We don't have to go off on her," I said. "Just finding them stuffed in her desk or trunk is enough to get her fired. Lyla's finally gone too far in trying to embarrass me."

"Good. Then, you take her desk and I'll take the car."

Genny took off in one direction and I went the other, finding myself back in the junior designers' room. My skin prickled walking past Lyla's grin. "Zoe. Jace, come with me."

"Excuse me. Where are you going?" Lyla trailed us out the door. "If this is about the Johnsons, then I should be included. We're all on the same team."

I ignored her. "The clothes are missing from the Closet."

"What?" Zoe cried. "They can't be. I put them down there an hour ago."

"They're not in there now. Let's hope they were misplaced and we find them soon. If they were stolen..." My gaze drifted to Lyla. "I feel bad for that person, because they will be found and fired."

"Damn fucking right they will," Zoe growled. "I pulled two all-nighters to finish those outfits. Vance said my overskirt outfit was fit for the catalog. Once people saw it on Ava Johnson, orders would go through the roof."

"Grab security and search," I said. "They're serious about this kind of thing, so they'll let you look *everywhere*."

Lyla just smiled at me. "Right away, boss."

Zoe and Jace raced off with Lyla strolling casually behind. When they turned the corner, I spun around and marched straight up to her desk. Her crew fussed and shouted at me. Brielle even grabbed my arm. I shook her off, ready to smack her if she tried again.

In the end, I didn't need violence because there was nothing hiding in Lyla's desk other than a bag of gummy bears.

She's too smart to leave incriminating evidence where it can be pinned on her. Lyla would hide it somewhere else... where it would get someone else in trouble.

I raced upstairs, bursting into my office. It was genius. I insisted the clothes were stolen, got security looking for them, made a whole big fuss, and then when they were found stuffed under my window seat cushion, it looked like I tried to divert suspicion off myself, so no one suspected I was the thief.

She's trying to get me out by branding me a thief. Why not? It worked the first time.

I tore my office apart looking for an overskirt, patterned tie, fitted pants—anything. They were not there.

Do I keep looking or do I stay here to make sure Lyla doesn't double back?

"Ugh!" I hated these stupid games. Lyla had me paranoid and thinking plots were around every corner. "If you didn't put them here, where are they?"

Maybe they're in the Closet on some random rack. Lyla "finds" them later and pretends to be the hero.

That was as good an idea as any. Just to be safe, I put my phone on record and hid it under some papers on my desk. If anyone came in here while I was gone, I'd know.

Beating it down to the Closet, I searched the racks up and down. I made it as far as Row G when a voice pulled me out.

"Mackenzie? Mackenzie, are you in here?"

"Zoe?"

She hung off the doorknob, bun askew and a smudge of dirt on her cheek. "You're not going to believe this." Zoe was near tears. "Come and see."

"Zoe, what's wrong?"

She ran off, leaving me to follow. I tripped in my heels trying to keep up with her speed walk to the stairwell. We hurried down and came out on the first floor.

"It's horrible, Mackenzie. I don't know why someone would do this."

"Zoe, wait. Wait—!"

Zoe shoved on the alarmed emergency exit door. It swung out without a sound, banging off the opposite wall.

"Over here."

My surprise at the busted alarm faded quick, replaced by a dull, sludgy emotion eroding my veins.

"The alarm's been busted for months." Zoe sniffled. "I came down here because I thought if someone did steal the clothes, this was a good place to hide them until they left for the day. I didn't expect to find... this."

I approached the dumpster—a strange, emptying calm falling over me. My clothes and Zoe's littered among the garbage bags. There was no point in fishing them out. They were all shredded to pieces.

"Why would anyone do this?"

"I don't know," I said honestly. "There isn't any sense in this, Zoe. It's just cruel."

"I guess we just have to start over." She said that though tears stained her cheeks. "Fuck. It would've just been mine if I didn't put your stuff for Anthony in the Closet."

"None of this is your fault." I stared at the ruined overskirt, picturing Lyla's smile. "We'll let security find and fire the person who did this. For now, we'll do our work. When it's time to ship, I'll put it in the box myself."

"Okay." She hugged me, staining my shoulder with tears.

I understood why she was upset. What she was showing on the outside was how I felt inside. We poured every ounce of our talent, time, and creativity into this work. To have it destroyed in the one place where it should be safe—surrounded by designers—was a violation.

Lyla didn't do this to get me fired or play some trick. She just did it to hurt me.

Zoe and I trudged inside. I found Genny in my office, tearing the place up like she had the same thought about Lyla.

"Gen, you can stop. We found the clothes."

"Where are they?" she asked, looking around me like I had them behind my back. "You said you found them."

"I did find them. In the trash." I shook my head. "They're ruined, Genny. Unsalvageable as Hollywell would say. We have to start over."

Genevieve stood very still. "What do you mean start over?"

"Everything we had ready was destroyed. Jace just started on Liam's, so they definitely won't be ready by Friday. Rylee's close to done, but because she's an intern, I suspect Hollywell is going to be extra picky with her even if I say the clothes are ready."

"Lyla did this," Genny hissed.

"Almost certainly. And we'll never prove it." I took a deep breath and let it out slow. "Okay. I'll pull all-nighters and get an outfit ready for Monday, so it goes out Wednesday—"

"What's the fucking point of that?" Her harshness shook me. "We can't leave anything in the Closet if your psycho nemesis is just going to rip it up. She's fucked up the plan, Kenzie! After this, they'll post security down there and the rat's not going to try!"

"Whoa, Gen. The Closet was just our theory for how they're getting their hands on clothes made by other designers. If it's Jace, he can still tamper with Liam's. Same for Zoe. We still have a chance—"

Genny threw my desk chair. "How are you not getting this?! We don't have a chance. We don't have time! We did it your way and now"—Genny shoved past me out the door—"we're doing this my way."

"Genny? No! Don't—"

She punched the fire alarm. Ear-piercing rings chimed through the building, bringing the senior designers grumbling out of their offices.

"We're getting this done," she snapped. "Now."

I didn't know what that meant, but she wasn't up for explaining. Genny pushed through the people heading downstairs, getting too far ahead of me too fast.

The building emptied out into the lobby. I spotted Lyla coming down the other staircase with Brielle, Madison, Skylar, Naomi, and Zoe. Lyla had her arm around Zoe—a sympathetic look on her face as she murmured to her.

The fucking nerve on that one. Damn Caddell House for refusing to put more security cameras! The higher-ups were so paranoid about leaks, they didn't even trust the minimum-wage security guards they had watching the tapes. To be fair, eight years ago one of those minimum-wage security guards got paid an obscene amount by one of our rivals to do just that.

Clearing the way for another rival to fuck with me to her heart's content. I snorted. *What am I thinking? The dried-up husk in her chest cavity wasn't a—*

"That's far enough." Genny rang out through the lobby. "Stop! There is no fire. I brought you all down here for a chat."

Heart thumping through my rib cage, I strained to see over the heads.

Genny stood between the crowd and the revolving doors. "Sit down!"

"Excuse me?" someone said. "Who the hell are you? Get out of the way."

"I said sit. I won't ask again."

I shoved through bodies, moving as fast as I could.

"Listen, little girl." I winced. That was the wrong thing to say to Genevieve Hunt. "Move aside or I'll move you."

The crowd surged forward, pushing in on Genny.

Bang! Bang!

"Ahhh!"

Screams shattered my eardrums—my own scream among them. The crowd surged again, and came straight at me.

"Don't move! All of you, sit the fuck down!"

There was a time when I didn't understand what made this beautiful, petite blonde so frightening that she ruled one of Cinco's toughest boroughs. I would never wonder about that again.

Screaming, pushing, shoving, cursing, crying, and above it all, Genny bellowing for order and silence. Finally the designers and weaponless guards crouched on the floor—hands shaking above their heads. All of them except me.

I ran at Genny gasping, and it wasn't from being winded. "What the fuck are you doing?!" My voice hit decibels I didn't know about. "Are you insane?!"

"Sit down, Blaine!" She spun the gun on me. "Seriously," Genny whispered under her breath. "Sit and keep your cover. They can't think you're in on this with me."

It took a full five seconds for the words to penetrate. Genny wasn't out of control. Her plan was to scare a confession out of the rat. When this was all over, she couldn't step inside this building again, but I could as long as they think I'm another hostage.

Slowly, I backed away—hands raised. I crouched next to Zoe who immediately latched on to me, quietly sobbing into my shoulder. This was not her day.

"Now," Genny began. "That's much b— Dawson, take another fucking step and you'll find out just how much I hate you."

Lyla smacked the tile so hard, the sound reverberated through the lobby.

"What do you want?"

"Why are you doing this?"

"We don't have money."

"Shut up," Genny barked, silencing a dozen sniffling pleas. "And I'll tell you exactly why I'm doing this. You see, one of you here knows exactly who I am. You thought you could fuck with me, my family, and my gang, and get away with it. But we know, bitch.

"We know about the little presents you've been leaving in our clothes, so that trick isn't going to work for you or your organization anymore."

I scanned faces through my lashes. All shocked, angry, scared, or surprised. All what I'd expect to see if they were working with the Brotherhood, or if they were currently being threatened with a gun.

"I know all of you now." Genny paced the length of the welcome mat, her muzzle sweeping the huddled crowd. "I know your names, your faces, and your addresses. No one leaves this building until the rat shows himself. If you do, you'll be shown mercy. I'll only kill you instead of your entire family and everyone you've ever met."

I choked over Zoe's sob. *Barely an incentive, Genny!*

"Show yourself!"

Vance rose up. "Miss Hunt, I assure you, none—"

"Ah, so it was you, Hollywell. You fucked with our clothes and turned us into walking targets."

"I—I—I did no such thing!"

"Then, sit the fuck down. The next word out of someone's mouth I'll take as a confession. So whoever speaks better be the rat, and you better do it by the time I count to ten. Because if I have to find you," she gritted, "I swear on the gangsters who came before me, your death will be excruciating."

Sobs broke the silence, but no one moved. No one spoke.

"One.

"Two.

"Three."

My head swung back and forth. *Come on. We know you're in this room. Stand up, you coward.*

"Four.

"Five.

"Six."

"I don't want to die," Zoe cried. "Where's the fire department? Where's the police?"

"You're not going to die," I whispered. "Everything's going to be okay."

Stand up!

"Eight.

"Nine."

I landed on him just as he turned his head toward the back hallway. I knew what he was going to do before he did.

"Ten."

Jace bolted—shoving aside and leaping over people, tearing for the busted emergency exit.

"Hey! Stop!"

Genny ran and so did Zoe. The weepy, clingy woman tackled Genny, roaring like a jungle animal. The two went down hard, and then everyone was on top of Genevieve. Attacking, jumping, and trampling her to get out the door.

"Go!" I heard clear over the noise.

Genny wanted me to run after Jace. Stop the bastard before we lost another Brotherhood thug for good.

I turned my back and rushed the pile on Genny. We could still catch up to Jace and stop him, but not if one of us was killed by an angry mob.

"Stop!" I screamed. "She's not a threat anymore! Calm down! You'll kill—"

An elbow came flying at my face. Pain ricocheted in my skull and I fell, sinking into darkness.

SIENNA

"No. No!" Angelina Forbis shot off the armchair. She spun toward the front door like she wanted to shove us out of it and pretend none of this happened. "What you're saying isn't true. Nathan is our son."

"His name is Jake," Marie cried. "He's my son. My baby!"

I silently took her hand, sending waves of comfort into her. Marie's stress was valid and understandable, but I've seen her future. Jake and Marie would be reunited. There's no other way I'd let this end.

"You can't just come in here and make these wild claims," shouted Maurice Forbis. "We adopted him through an agency. We did everything right. We're not kidnappers!"

"We're not saying you are," River said. "You heard Marie's story. It's the same as dozens of women who came to our shelter after the monsters holding them captive fled and left them to die to escape the cops."

That was the version we agreed on. We could hardly tell the couple that Marie was captured after River and members of the Merchant gang busted in and slaughtered those sex-trafficking rapists. It would also explain why the Forbises couldn't look any of this up on the news.

"She was tricked and imprisoned by the lowest form of human cockroach that scuttles on this earth," River gritted. "Her son was given away to put more money in the pockets of that man. Jake wasn't the first kid. He was one of twenty-three."

Swaying, Angelina sat down hard. Her husband rushed to her side, resting her head on his lap. They were both so pale they could blend into their white carpet and disappear.

We sat in the living room of a lovely Leighbridge townhouse. They had a massive television, fancy game systems, expensive toys all over the carpet, and framed photos on the wall of the Forbises, Jake, and a young girl who doesn't appear older than ten in any of the pictures.

By being in their house and shaking their hands, a vision of their tragedy gripped me. Their daughter died young, and now they would lose the little boy they loved.

Hatred was an emotion I wanted nothing to do with. It clouded my energy and affected my gift. How could I be clear enough to see someone else's issues if I was drowning in a red mist of my own?

No, I did not let myself give in to hate... except when I thought the name Luca Cunt-Sucking Adams.

Marie and the Forbises both lost so much. The pain they were going through right now was all because of him and his psychopathic greed.

"Twenty-three children?" Maurice rasped. "How is that possible? How are twenty-three children kidnapped and given away without anyone knowing?"

"Easily," Marie said, "when their mothers are chained to a wall."

Angelina flinched. "Please, stop. I can't— This isn't happening. Maybe children were taken from their mothers, but Nathan wasn't one of them. We went through a legitimate adoption agency. They were recommended to us," she cried. "We went through all the proper channels. Got all the right documentation. We didn't just pick him up from some warehouse on the wharf! He's our son!"

"I have proof too," Marie cried. She thrust out her arm, ripping up her sleeve. "The blood in my veins. He is Jake Willard and I will take as many DNA tests as you ask. They will all say the same thing."

"So what if they do?" Angelina raised her chin. She tried and failed to sound imperious. "That doesn't mean anything. Just because you're *Nathan's* biological mother. It doesn't mean your story is true. Maybe the state had to take him from you, and now you think you can con us into getting him back."

"How dare—?!"

"Please," River cut in. "I know this is hard to believe, but we didn't come here to upset you. We came to tell you the truth. Marie lost her home, her family, her friends, her freedom, and her son. You're a mother, Mrs. Forbis. I think that you"—River flicked to those photographs—"understand the pain of losing a child.

"Can you really look into another mother's eyes and tell her to give up? To walk away from her son after she thought he was lost forever? I can tell that you're not cruel people. You'd never ask Marie to live another second with that pain."

Angelina tried to hold our gaze, her eyes welling. Bursting into tears, she ran from the room.

I thought Mr. Forbis would go after her, but he didn't move. I wasn't certain if he was breathing.

"What about our pain?" he croaked. "What about what you're asking us to do? You're strangers who came into our home to tell us our life is a lie."

"We didn't invade your lives with a lie," I said. "Luca Adams did that. You're a victim of him just like Jake, Marie, and all those women and children."

He shook his head and a tear flew off his nose. "We don't know a Luca. No one by that name had anything to do with Nathan's adoption. Why can't you see that you have the wrong family?"

"I know my son," Marie cried, motioning to a photograph. "He is Jake."

Mr. Forbis didn't seem to have heard her.

"Just because Adams was smart enough not to let anyone see his face, doesn't mean he isn't behind this," I said. "Can you tell us more about the adoption agency? How did he make it look real?"

"It is real," Maurice insisted. "It's called Sunflower Adoption Agency. It's a real office with a waiting room, a receptionist, and a kind, young woman who helped us adopt Nathan. Nothing about it was suspicious."

"Sunshine Adoption Agency," River repeated. "Do you have a card or a number?"

"Yes! Yes, I do." Maurice rushed to the end table and riffled through the drawer. He came away with a white and yellow business card that he thrust in River's face. "Do you see? Our son was not kidnapped."

River looked to me. "Sienna?"

I already had my phone out and dialing. "*We're sorry. The number you have reached has been disconnected. Please hang up and—*"

"The number is disconnected."

"No, that can't be," Maurice said. "You dialed it wrong."

We sat silently while Maurice called the Sunshine Agency again. And again. And again.

On the fifth try and fail, he collapsed on the chair—bloodless lips shaking.

"What about the young woman who placed Jake with you?" River gently pushed. "She can clear this all up for us. If she has the connections to Child Protective Services and willing birth mothers that she should have, they'll vouch for her."

Maurice raised his head. Hope returned to his eyes, and it smashed my heart to pieces. I had to remember River wasn't doing this because he wanted to. He was trying to return a child to his mother. It killed me two loving people would be hurt in the process.

Digger did this. I only hope there's fire in the spiritual plane that got dumped with his soul.

"Of course. Katherine— No, Kathleen," Maurice said. "Kathleen was amazing. We loved her and so did Nathan. She even kept in touch for a few months after the adoption was finalized to make sure he was settling in okay. Does that sound like a kidnapper to you?"

Yep. It sounds like a smart one that got away with selling twenty-three kids.

"Look. I'll show you." Maurice got up and left the room.

Marie deflated. She held so tight to my hand, she cut off the blood to my fingers. "This is hopeless. They were never going to let Jake go without a fight. We have to call the police."

"It might come to that," River said. "We—"

"See here." Maurice returned holding a frame. "Kathleen was a friend to us and a godsend to many children—including our son. Does that look like the face of a child-trafficking monster?"

Maurice showed us the picture. I took one look and my slack fingers slipped out of Marie's hand.

"Oh, no..." The words stole off my tongue.

"Sienna?" River asked. "What's wrong?"

Staring back at us were Mr. Forbis, Mrs. Forbis, little Jake, and the beaming woman hugging his shoulders.

"I know exactly who that woman is," I rasped. "And her name is not Kathleen."

MACKENZIE

I was moving. A steady *thump, thump, thump* assaulted my ears, forcing me from a peaceful, dreamless sleep.

Groaning, I peeled an eyelid open. Sunlight rained like knives in my eyes.

"About time you woke up."

"Genny?" I pushed myself up, looking around. We were in a car— Actually, we were in a cab. Familiar surroundings told me we were in Waterford. That was the end of the list of things that made sense.

Genevieve plowed through traffic. Her face was a mass of bruises and scratches. "Graphic, right? Who knew you stitch bitches packed such a punch?"

"Gen, I can't— You— What were you—?" I threw up my hands, giving up.

"Eloquent. A taste of the smooth talker that got all my brothers to fall for you."

"Fuck you."

She laughed. "Relax, Kenzie. We're off to catch a rat."

"You mean like you did today when you held innocent people at gunpoint!"

"I did what I had to do," she breezed. "And it worked. Jace Carter ran out of there so fast; he left his shape in the wall like the Kool-Aid man. I warned them that I knew where they lived. Carter lives at 487B Blueview Apartments in Waterford. We're dropping by for a visit."

"What if he's not there?"

"He can't hide in my city, Mackenzie. We'll find him."

I swallowed the urge to point out that the Brotherhood had been successfully hiding in her city for months, maybe years. No reason to rub that in.

"This is really, really bad, Genny. There'll be a warrant out for your arrest. And I'm riding shotgun like I'm your accomplice!"

"You've got to relax. Actually, don't." Genny hit the brakes. "We're here. Save that freak-out for Carter." She fished her gun out of the glove box.

"Leave that here!"

Genny popped her gum. *When did she have time to get that?!*

"Make me." With that she climbed out, making for the steps of the Blueview building. I sat there for a full minute wondering if Sunny, Liam, and Bane would miss her that much. They had two other sisters. That was more than enough.

You have to go upstairs. If only to make sure Jace doesn't tell his story under torture. That thought forced me out of the car.

Genny wasn't in the lobby. I rode the elevator up alone and stuck my head out on the fourth floor. The last door on the end hung ajar.

I walked in on the scene I was expecting.

"Ah, Feisty. Nice of you to join us."

His place was actually quite nice. Leather sofas, gorgeous paintings, huge entertainment center. Beside me was a kitchen decked out with more high-end gear than Shonda's domain. That was the bad news. It didn't add up that he bought all these things on his salary.

Genny knelt over a sobbing Jace. When he saw me, he tried to shout. It was a little hard to do with her gun in his mouth—the worse news.

"Close the door, will you? We'll need our privacy."

I scrambled to close it. "Let him up," I hissed. "At least give him a chance to explain."

"That's exactly what I'm going to let you do. I'll let you explain, Carter, why you sewed trackers into my clothes? Explain how you hooked up with the Brotherhood? What imaginary wrongs deluded you into hating the Merchants so much, you helped your brothers blow me up!"

"Hmmph!"

Genny pressed the muzzle between his eyes. "Speak!"

"Blow up? What are you talking about?!" he shrieked. "Holden Shultz pays me to be the middleman between his dealer. His parents are crazy strict. He's already been busted for possession once. They said if they catch him using, they'll empty his trust fund and cut him off. They've gone so far as to have him followed." Jace spoke so fast, I was barely keeping up. "His dealer drops off the coke and I put it in his clothes before they're shipped out.

"Zoe caught on to me and made me ask for more. Word got around. And somehow I ended up using the Closet to supply half the building and our clients with d-drugs." Tears and snot soaked his face. "I'm sorry. I'm so sorry. I needed the money. I wasn't trying to hurt anyone, I swear."

"Shut up," Genny snapped. "Tell me about the Brotherhood. When did they approach you? Who's in charge?"

"The Brother-what?"

"That's it." Genny cocked her gun.

"No!"

"Wait! Gen, let me talk to him." I dropped to my knees beside them. "Jace, someone's been hiding more than drugs inside Caddell outfits. Right now, that person looks like you. Convince us that you're not hiding trackers inside the clothes for the Johnsons."

His eyes popped. "Trackers? I don't know anything about that!"

"Hmm. I'm not convinced." Genny got in close, making his eyes cross. "Maybe I should count to ten."

"No, no, no, wait! I don't know what you're talking about. What trackers? I never put anything like that in their clothes. Why would I?"

"Why would you put drugs in people's clothes?" I shot back.

Jace bucked. "That's different! They paid me to."

A thought crossed my mind. "How about this, Jace? We record a little video saying the Brotherhood is not a hoax. They're real and they approached you to put trackers in the clothes of Caddell clients, so they could stalk, harass, and even kill them. You refused them. You wouldn't have anything to do with it, and now you're warning everyone in Cinco to prepare for this new threat.

"If you say all of that on camera and let me post it to the media, you'll never see her again." Genny beamed at him. "We'll leave you alone. Most importantly, we'll keep your secret. If anyone finds out about the drugs, it won't be from us."

Jace shook his head hard. Relief brought even more tears to his eyes. "Yes, okay. Whatever you want. Let's do it."

"Are you sure?"

"Yes," he cried. "Turn on your phone. If that's all I have to do, I'll do it."

Silently, Genny climbed off and moved to the corner where she stayed while I recorded Jace's speech. He smiled at us when he was done.

"Is that it? Are we done?"

"That's it, Jace," I replied. "I'm genuinely sorry for what you've gone through today. But word of advice: I have a feeling security is about to triple at Caddell House. You need an exit strategy out of your side business."

Genny and I left him a thankful puddle on the living room floor. We didn't say anything to each other in the elevator or on the ride to the Fairfield. There was nothing to say.

Vito stabbed himself in the neck when a video connecting him to the Brotherhood hit the news. A fate worse than death awaited him for exposing the organization. So why wasn't Jace afraid of the same fate?

Answer: He didn't have a flipping clue about the Brotherhood.

We caught a shady designer slipping stuff into clothes, but it was the wrong one. And the right one... got away.

"There's still a chance, Gen. The real rat knew you were talking to them. I bet they'll run. Whoever doesn't show up for work is our guy."

"There isn't a chance." A dull emptiness leeched into her tone. "A lot of people aren't going to show up for work, Kenzie. A gun-toting maniac scared the piss out of them. They're not stepping into that building until the guards have machine guns and there's a security camera up everyone's ass. My only leverage got away. They got away," she whispered.

"You're not giving up, are you? That's not the Genny I love and loathe in equal measure." I thought that would get me a chuckle. She didn't twitch a facial muscle. "We're not out yet. We'll come up with another plan. Just trust me."

Silence came from her end of the car.

Genny parked the likely stolen cab in front of the Fairfield and climbed out. I trailed behind her, determined to get her to open up and talk to me. Something was wrong, I could feel it.

Headlights lit us up. We twisted as squealing tires cut above the city sounds.

"Genevieve! Mackenzie!" Thatcher shouted. "Inside now!"

The car jumped the curb, barreling right at us. My brain screamed for me to run, but it was too late.

The car swerved around and something hurled at our feet. The driver raced off—clipping the cab coming off the curb.

I looked down at what they threw, and screamed.

"Bugsy? Bugsy, no!" Genny fell on the body, brushing away hair that was sticky with blood. "Fuuuccckkk!" she screamed, clutching her second-in-command to her chest, and doing something I'd never seen her do.

Cry.

Chapter Ten

Late that night, Sunny held me in bed and I held Laurel. The baby was fast asleep in my arms—the envy of everyone in the building. She was the only one who'd have sweet dreams that night.

"How'd they even get to her?" Sunny's voice sounded far away. "Did they find a way to get trackers into their clothes? Maybe they have for all our gangs. I didn't go around sprinkling Caddell on people like candy, but we're all wearing something. The Brotherhood could've found another way."

I slowly shook my head. "You had Ryker, Makai, and the guys check after we found out their little trick. They found nothing."

"They could've used a different trick. There are lots of places to put trackers," he said, kissing a line down my throat.

It both soothed and saddened me. Genny didn't have anyone to comfort her like this. After Bugsy's body was taken away, she went up to her apartment and slammed the door in our faces.

"Bugsy was one of the toughest women around. If they can get to her..." Sunny trailed off, but I filled the rest in for myself.

If the Brotherhood could get to her, no one in their gangs was safe. The war had finally gone beyond the family.

"To dump her like trash at our feet..." Tears prickled behind my eyes. "The kind of hate these men must have in their hearts, I don't understand it. What could Adeline or Sinjin or Killian or any of your parents have done to someone that they'd create an organization of monsters?"

"Revenge makes monsters of all of us, Angel. It's one of my favorite things about it. The things we'll do to the men who killed Bugsy... The human language doesn't have a word for what we'll become when we're through with him."

It was a testament to how much I'd changed that I never agreed with anything more.

"Kenzie?" Sienna whisper-shouted through the door. "Kenzie, are you awake?"

I handed Laurel to Sunny and jumped up. "Sienna," I scolded, throwing my arms around her. "Do you have any idea how worried I was? You weren't answering your phone. Did you hear what happened?"

She nodded gravely. "Thatcher told me on the way in. It's awful, Kenzie. I feel even worse now for not texting you, but I didn't want to until I was sure."

"Sure about what?"

"It turns out that cockroach Luca didn't show his face to the adoptive parents—not a surprise since you know how much they hate sunlight." Sienna's expression said if Luca was alive and she got to him first, she'd earn that title the human language didn't have a word for. Of course she'd have to get in line after me. "Everything we thought was right. Luca set up an office, website, fake recommendations, and hired a pretty young puppet to lure families in. The Forbises said they handed over a total of fifty thousand dollars to adopt Jake. Fifty thousand times twenty-three."

"It's over a million dollars. That's why he targeted me. When I showed up in his building pregnant, he took one look at my belly and saw a check for fifty thousand dollars."

"And this is the woman who would have split the money with him." Sienna fished out her phone. "Look familiar?"

I fell to the floor, taking Sienna's phone with me. No matter how many times I squinted, enlarged, or studied her face, it remained the same.

"You get what this means, don't you?"

"Yes," I breathed. "I know exactly what this means. We need to talk to Genny. Right now."

THAT WAS EASIER SAID than done.

I sat in the elevator for half the morning, buzzing for Genny to let me in. She didn't even bother to come on the intercom and tell me to go away. Nothing but radio silence.

I stopped at one point to eat, feed Laurel, and shower. Then I was back in that elevator, buzzing, buzzing, and buzzing Genny. At three o'clock in the afternoon, my growling stomach forced me down to my apartment for Shonda's chicken wraps.

"I've been calling her," Sienna said from the floor. She was on the carpet playing with Laurel. She was extra clingy after seeing firsthand the future Luca had picked out for her. "Over and over, but it just goes to voicemail."

"She's grieving. Any other day, I'd leave her in peace, but—"

"I know, Kenzie. Keep trying," she said, grabbing her phone. "I'll call for reinforcements."

After lunch, I prepared for another several hours standing in an elevator. I had my finger on the button for all of a second when the doors dinged open. My surprise cleared up at the sight of the figure standing in Genny's doorway.

Adeline.

"Sienna explained that it was important. Go on in, Kenzie."

"Fuck off!" Genny shouted. Adeline just motioned for me to step inside.

I did—biting back a hiss at the wreckage. Genny destroyed... everything. The pillows, the pictures, the television, the furniture, and the couch she and her father, Killian, were on.

Hair wild, knuckles bruised—she curled up, her head on his lap. Gen looked right through me as I knelt in front of her.

"Genny," I began. "Our time in Caddell House was a complete bust. Vance called this morning and fired me. No one with a connection to the *Johnsons* is allowed anywhere near Caddell House. Your account is closed and there's a warrant out for the arrest of the Blonde Bandit. That's what Zoe dubbed you. She's quite proud of herself for taking you down.

"After all that—losing my dream job, adding another line on your rap sheet, and getting beat up by *stitch bitches*—we didn't even get the right guy. Jace is somewhere toasting his lucky break right about now."

"Is there a point to this?" Killian snapped. "Now is not the time, Miss Blaine."

I held my ground, even though this man intimidated me more than a little bit. Liam wasn't deemed cold because he was. They called him that because he inherited this man's eyes.

"Now is the time," I replied. "Because Genny needs to know that despite how royally we screwed this up, none of that matters. We've got the rat."

Her gaze focused, narrowing on me. "What are you talking about?"

"We've got her, Gen. I know who's been working for the Brotherhood. More importantly, I know where she is. How about we pick her up and ask a few questions about the men she's gotten into bed with?"

Genny pushed herself up. "What's everybody standing around here for?" she asked, voice even. "Let's go."

GENNY AND I SAT IN the stolen cab, watching her apartment building. I was surprised, angry, and disgusted when I saw her in that picture. As we sat in that car, I felt none of those emotions. Honestly, I felt nothing at all. My feelings were wrung out and splattered along the road from the Fairfield to her building. I just wanted this done with.

"We need to get inside," Genny announced for the fourth time. "Waiting around hoping she comes out is idiotic."

"Sunny once told me that you don't follow an assassin to their house. They're the only one in the room who knows where all the weapons are hidden. What we know about this woman right now is that we don't know a damn thing about her. She got in bed with a rapist, sex trafficker, and child abductor. Underestimating her is a mistake," I said, also for the fourth time. "Let her come to us."

"She's got five minutes."

Genny was in her war gear. I was calling it that because ripped jeans, fishnet stockings, fishnet top, and a red bra were what she changed into after peeling herself off the couch.

"Gen, you bribed the doorman to tell you she comes out every morning to walk her dog in the park. Dogs have to do their business every day—rain or shine. She's coming."

"Four minutes."

I sat up straight. "Don't need four minutes. There she is now."

Genny was out the door before I finished.

Wild Springs Apartments was in one of the swankier parts of Leigh-bridge. The building stretched to the sky, carrying luxury apartments and penthouses to the top floor. Beside it was Wild Springs Park—a patch of green nestled among a concrete paradise. Walking trails, biking trails, a water fountain, a playground overrun with laughing kids—it had everything. We trailed her into the perfect spot with so many people going about their fun, they wouldn't notice one random woman disappear off the trail.

She rounded a hedge, setting down one of the walking trails. A little toy fox terrier trotted beside her.

"Not too close," Genny said. "You need to be close enough to see them, but not so close that they can turn around and clock your face."

"Thanks for the tip. Now here's yours: don't shove your gun down her throat. Just knock her unconscious and we'll take her to Astoria. Afterward, we'll tell the guys the truth."

"Surprised you agreed to keep this from them in the first place."

My voice hardened. "This is between me and the bitch that would've sold my baby. The more I think about this, the scarily clear my past becomes. I don't need anyone trying to protect me from this. And for better or worse, Genny, you'd never stand between a woman and her target."

"I like you more and more every day, Blaine. Please, feel free to kick the bitch's teeth in. I'll hold her hair."

The path lined with hedges and trees—gifting the parkgoers with a green and flowered maze. She and the dog disappeared around a hedge and we let her, keeping well back as she headed for a small tunnel bridge.

"As soon as she steps inside the bridge, we run," Genny ordered. "I'll go around and catch her in the front. You come in from the back. No one will see us take her."

I glanced down at my hands. *Perfectly still.*

"Got it."

She got closer... closer... closer. We sprang into action the moment she stepped into the tunnel.

Genny sprinted across the lawn and up the hill, disappearing around the other side of the bridge. I left my usual boots, skirts, and handmade labels at home, opting instead for jeans, a simple shirt that concealed the zip ties, and rubber soles absorbing the strikes carrying me down the path into the tunnel.

Genny and I burst inside at nearly the same time and came face to face—
—with each other.

The tunnel was empty.

"What the fuck!" Genny bellowed. "What the hell happened?"

"That's my question."

I whirled around, shock snapping a band around my throat as Madison James appeared behind me, her yappy little puppy tucked under her arm.

"Why are you following me, Mackenzie?" She flicked over her shoulder at Genny. "And you. Shouldn't you be in the back of a prison van?"

"That's my question," Genevieve mocked.

"Excuse me?"

I slid back a few steps, putting some distance between us. I was standing in front of one of the most devious, sociopathic monsters ever spat out of a womb. I didn't know what she would do, but I wouldn't be in striking distance when she did it.

"We know, Madison," I said. "We know everything."

She cocked a brow. "Everything about what exactly?"

"Don't you fucking stand there acting innocent!" Rapid footsteps echoed in the tunnel. "When I'm done with you—"

I shot in front of Genny, glaring into her eyes. "Don't stand in the way," I said simply.

A thousand emotions warred on her face. There was no question Madison did horrible things that hurt her family, but she started with mine first.

"Fine." Genny gestured for me to go ahead.

I turned on Madison. The amusedly confused mask on her face was getting better by the second.

"Here's how it's going to go," I began. "I'm going to tell you what I know. You'll deny being a psychotic, evil bitch. Then I'll show you our proof. After that, you get to explain just how you got to be this way. Prep that sympathy defense for the jury."

She laughed. "Oh my gosh, Kenzie. You're just as crazy and desperate for attention as Lyla said. I do not have time for this, but whatever." She shrugged. "I'm kinda interested in how I'm a *psychotic, evil bitch* and what proof you have of that besides the voices in your head?"

My lips stretched to match her smile. "You used to work with a man named Luca Adams, also known as Digger. He supplied you with kidnapped children, and you put them up for *adoption* through a fake agency called the Sunshine Adoption."

"Hmm, no," she said, scratching her puppy behind the ear. "Never heard of the place."

I went on like she hadn't spoken. "Luca was able to supply you with children and babies, because he owned a string of cheap housing with his pick of women and single mothers to prey on. He tricked or forced them into prostitution, then handed their kids to you.

"I don't know how you hooked up with Luca. He was handsome and charming, so maybe he seduced you like all the others. But instead of putting you through hell, he realized you were soulmates. You were both dead inside.

"With your sweet act, pretty face, and clean background check greeting couples at the door, you had no problem making over a million dollars off of those poor women and their misery."

Madison just looked at me like this was boring and she was waiting for me to skip to the end.

"The Brotherhood didn't approach Luca." I leveled between her eyes. "They approached you. The Brotherhood recruits enemies of the Merchants who can be useful to them. You were in the building where their clothes were packed up and shipped. That put you in the perfect position to slip a little something inside. Tell me, did you come up with the idea for the trackers, or does a brother get the credit?"

"I really have no idea what you're talking about. But can you hurry this up? Poppy needs to make."

"I guess it doesn't matter who thought of it. You did your duty for the cause by tampering with all the clothes going out to the Johnsons. As for Luca, you made the case to the Brotherhood that another psychopath would be good for the organization. Who knows, maybe they liked how easily he made women... disappear."

Madison put her dog down, letting him run off to sniff the grass. "You're spinning a scary story, Kenzie, but it has nothing to do with me."

"It has everything to do with you, Madison," I forced through gritted teeth. "See, you were always different. Back when we started the internship and you became a part of Lyla's bitch crew, you didn't always blindly follow along with what she said and did. You weren't a nice person, but every now and then you openly contradicted her—earning yourself a glare or a kick under the table.

"I used to think 'she's an asshole, but at least she's an asshole that thinks for herself.' I thought the same thing the day Lyla got me fired and you approached me as I was leaving." I flashed back to that day. Me carrying a box of my things and about to shove them into a cab when Madison's call made me stop. "You said I was done in fashion. No one in our world would hire me, and even if I deserve what I get, my kid doesn't. You dropped a business card for Allison Raines on my things, told me she helps women in trouble, and said to call the number.

"Allison was a sweet old voice on the other end of the phone that helped me get the job at the diner. And when I lost that job and my apartment, I called her again, and she sent me to Luca's apartment building. Allison was you, wasn't it?" I rasped. "It's not a coincidence that you gave a pregnant woman a card that led her right into the hands of that monster. You knew he would take me, and hand Laurel right to you."

"Nope," Madison popped, rolling her eyes. "I was just trying to help you. This is what I get for feeling sorry for you."

I grinned mirthlessly. "That's good, Madison. We're already through parts one and two. Now it's time for me to show you proof." I fished out my phone. "You say you know nothing about the Sunshine Adoption Agency. You had nothing to do with Luca Adams and the children he kidnapped. And you're just an innocent designer that knows nothing about double lives and fake identities."

I shoved the cellphone in her face. "Then tell me what the hell you're doing in that photo, *Kathleen*—smiling away as you congratulate the Forbises on their adoption of this kidnapped boy, Jake Willard." The lines around her eyes tightened. I'd never seen a smile wipe away faster.

"The Forbises are pissed, by the way. They're heartbroken that they were made complicit in kidnapping, and now they're going to lose the boy they love. My sister said by the time they left, the Forbises were on the phone with their three-hundred-dollar-an-hour attorneys and the FBI. The investigation has already started into the mysteriously vanished Sunshine Agency and the woman who ran it."

"What?" Madison screeched. "What did you do?!"

"Whoops," Genny sang. "Guess we dropped the innocent act."

"I am innocent," Madison cried. "That's not what you think. I didn't—"

"Save it," I snapped. "You met with the Forbises every weekend for three months. You don't think they remember who took fifty thousand dollars from them and then gave them the answer to their prayers? They could pick you out of a lineup with fifty of your evil clones! Admit it! You and Luca were working together! You set me up!"

Madison's gaze darted around, looking for an escape. "Okay, I did, but—"

I punched her dead in the face. Madison dropped like a stone, laid flat out on her back. "You evil piece of shit." My voice shook. "You picked me out and offered me and my daughter up to Luca, knowing exactly what hell he'd put us through. What went wrong with you, Madison? How did you become... this?"

She pushed herself up, clutching her bleeding nose. The fury in her eyes burned me where I stood. "Fuck you! Why should I give a shit about trash like you? You're the spawn of some crazy murdering psycho who shot your daddy over tea and cookies. When you faked those designs and conned your way into the Phenomenal Five, it was obvious you didn't fall far from the criminal tree."

"Ah. Here we are," I said. "Part four. Before you continue explaining why you're justified, you should know I didn't fake or steal anything. I was set up by Damien and your buddy, Lyla."

"Oh, please," she scoffed. "No one buys that crap. If you've never done a thing wrong, why are you shacked up with her family! Another band of crazy murdering psychos! No, Kenzie. I saw you for exactly what you are. There was no saving you, but there was still a chance for your kid. Whatever Luca did to you was his business, but I knew he would give me your kid, and I'd place her with a proper family. I would've been doing that kid a favor."

I bristled. The urge to punch her again welled in me so strong, I cut my palm clenching my fists. "Who gave you the right to decide? No one asked you to be my baby's fairy godmother."

"Someone had to be," she shouted. "Someone had to look out for those kids and give them a better life. You weren't going to do it, and the Merchants sure as fuck weren't either."

Genny stepped forward. "What does my family have to do with any of this?"

"You have everything to do with it! My mother got involved with the Merchants. She was like you, Kenzie. A fake. A fraud! She used to run scams and cheat people out of their money. And of course, any criminal that operates in the Cinco city limits pays a tax to the Merchants." She spat the name like it tasted foul on her tongue.

"When she was my age, she quit the life, changed her name, and met my father, Richard James. Our life was good," she cried. Her whole body shook. "We lived in a penthouse in Leighbridge, and had two other homes overseas. I went to the best schools. My best friends were the sons and daughters of models and movie stars.

"Too bad dear old Mom missed the thrill. She started up again, but this time didn't tell the Merchant overlords that she was back in business. Eventually, they found out and you know exactly what they did, don't you?" Madison didn't give me a chance to answer. "They ordered her to cut them in or they'd shut her down. Mom refused and the Merchants gave her up to the police! While she was fucking being arraigned, they hacked her secret accounts and drained them."

I asked, though I could guess, "What happened to you?"

She lifted her shoulders, eyes dull. "Dad paid to get her off, but after the charges were dropped, he was done with her. He invoked a clause in their prenup that left her with nothing... except me. Just like that, I went from penthouses and private schools, to living in a Rockchapel dump. Unfortunately for Mom, she wasn't running any scams after her face ended up on the news. She had no choice but to take a string of dead-end jobs just to make rent. In the end, she fell into depression and killed herself." She jabbed a bloody finger at me. "Your precious Merchants did that to us. They destroyed my life for nothing!"

Madison stood up, lifting her chin high. "When Luca suggested we partner up, he told me about the kind of women that came through his buildings. Alone, on drugs, drunk, with more baby daddies than they can count, and just as twisted up with the Merchants as all the criminals in this city. The Sunshine Agency was his idea, but it was a good one.

"I've lived these kids' lives. I know the hell of crime and poverty. The families I placed them with were the opposite in every way. These parents are wealthy, responsible, stable. They're giving those children everything they could ever want and more. If those mothers really gave a shit about them, they'd give me an award. I did what they couldn't do—give their kids a decent life."

One moment I was six feet away from her. In the next breath, I tackled her to the ground. "How dare you!" My hands were around her throat, throttling her as burning corrosive hate shattered my self-control. "We weren't trash to be thrown away because of money! Because of our pasts! The lives we'd give our children were not less because we couldn't send them to fucking private schools or summer in St. Tropez! How dare you decide I wasn't worthy to love and raise my daughter! How dare you! You crazy, evil bitch," I screamed into her reddening, bulging face.

At that moment, I hated her more than Damien. More than Lyla. More than my father. She handed me the card that destroyed my life and put my daughter in the path of a beast like Luca Adams, and she didn't have the decency to be sorry. I could *kill her*!

And Genny just stood there as I knew she would, letting me deal with the demon who haunted my life from the shadows in my own way.

But not this way. Sense broke through the fog. *Madison has more to answer for now. She has information that will help the men I love. And who knows, maybe after she and I make a video, she'll stab herself in the neck.*

It was an ugly, vicious thought, but I had nothing less for the woman who plotted to sell my child while she was still in my womb.

"Madison." I released her throat and flipped her on her stomach. She sucked in deep lungfuls of air, hacking and choking. "It's too bad you didn't take a hint from your mother about what happens when you piss off the Merchants. Good thing for you, they'll give you a chance to make it up by telling us everything you know about the Brotherhood."

"Never!"

I wrangled her hands behind her back. Genny was there before I said anything, helping me secure her in the zip ties.

"You can't do this," she bleated. "I'm not going with you!"

"You are and so is little Poppy." I hauled her up. "Laurel is going to be so excited when she meets her new puppy."

"I'd die before I betray the Brotherhood." She thrashed like a wild animal in my grip. Genny had to help me keep a hold on her. "Their cause is just. It's right! The Merchants have bred criminals in this city like rats, so they could appoint themselves the judge, jury, and executioner. They don't care how many innocents are ruined to keep their power."

Madison flung her head back. I jerked to the side, nearly catching her skull on my nose. This *sister* was not going down easily.

"They're loyal to nothing and no one," she shrieked. "You Merchants are the crazy, evil bitches. Your precious Cardinals will curse your name, Genevieve Hunt, when one is slaughtered for every day you hold me captive!"

Genny dropped her arm in shock. "What did you say?"

"You heard me. If I disappear, my brothers and sisters will know it was the Merchants. You got a taste of what happens when you defy us. What was that bitch's name? Oh yeah, Bugsy."

I strained to hold on to her. "Genny? Gen, what's wrong? Help me."

"She can't help you. Oh, did *Genny* not tell you that we cleared her bar of the trash? The Cardinals are all enjoying new accommodations with the Brotherhood, and they're not comfortable."

"What?" I whispered, eyes widening. "That's not— You're lying!"

"She knows I'm not."

Genny stood still, her face melding into the tunnel's shadows.

"I'm your only hope," Madison said. "Let me go and surrender to the Brotherhood. If you serve us faithfully, your Cardinals will be released unharmed—"

"Stop listening to her! Genny, grab her arm and help me get her to the car."

Madison shouted over me. "Or you can prove everything I know about you people is true! So much for protecting the women of Harlow. It's the Merchants over everyone else."

"Kenzie," Genevieve rasped. "Let her go."

"You can't be serious." I held even tighter, dragging her back away from Genny. "She doesn't just want to get away with helping the Brotherhood throw Sunny off a bridge and put a bomb in Liam and Tricky's car. She wants you to give yourself up to those bastards. They'll kill you!"

"Of course we'll kill you." Madison's amusement was back. "But only after we've used you to kill the rest of your family. With the Merchants all dead, there's no reason to kill your gangs. The Cardinals will be freed, Hunt. The women you swore to protect. What's it going to be?"

Genny shook with every word. "I said let her go, Kenzie!"

"No! You're grieving and you're not thinking straight. They can't make you choose between your friends and your family. Evil psychopaths that would force such a choice aren't going to keep their word! They'll kill the Cardinals anyway." I moved us back again, chilling under Genny's dead gaze. "Trust me, Genny. We'll get her back and question her. She'll tell us where they're holding the Cardinals."

"No chance of that since I don't know where," Madison breezed. "I just know that we have them."

"Kenzie." Genny took a step. Then another. "It takes strength to put others' needs above your own even while it destroys you. We need that courage to protect the people depending on us." Her speech that day fell from her lips, leadening my bones. "Because there's no forgiveness if we fail."

"Please don't do this. They're your family."

She flinched. "They are my family. The Merchants are the toughest sons of bitches in this whole damn country. I could give the Brotherhood every secret they have and it'll never be enough to take my bros down. They will win this fight, and I'll be back in my borough with my girls—using her brothers and sisters as target practice.

"Let her go, Kenzie. I won't ask again."

I tightened around Madison's wrist, refusing to let go. Genny seized my shoulder and threw me. I hit the ground hard—chest stunned as air fled me.

Madison's smile swirled in my vision, taunting me over the sound of the zip ties snapping.

"Good," she purred, standing my hairs on end. "Now just one more thing.

"Kill her."

"What?" Genny shot away. "No!"

"I said kill her! I won't have this bitch running her mouth about me."

"Hey, dumbass." I pushed up on shaky knees. "My sister. And my boyfriend. And the Forbises. And their lawyers know all about you. Even if you kill me, the truth is out."

Madison flushed a nasty purple. "Kill her!" She snatched up her dog's leash and shoved it at her. "Strangle her. Do it now, or those biker bimbos—"

Genny flashed. She snapped the leash around Madison's bruised throat and knocked their foreheads getting in her face. "You don't give me orders, bitch. If anyone dies here today, it'll be you, so *don't tempt me*."

She shoved Madison away, and turned on me. "But still, I can't have you following us. You'll tell my brothers where I am, and they'll bust in with some cowboy shit before I can get my girls out of this." Genny advanced on me. "I'm sorry, Kenzie."

"No, Gen, wait— No!"

The last thing I saw was her fist flying at my face.

Chapter Eleven

Poppy, my busted nose, and I trudged out of the elevator. The door flew open as I reached for the knob.

"Yes, Thatcher. She's here."

"Sun—"

He grabbed me around the waist, carrying me inside to the waiting horde. Thatcher's alert went out to the whole building.

"Oh my gosh."

"Kenzie, are you okay?"

"Who did this to you?" Liam demanded.

"When I get my fucking hands on them," Sunny barked over Lizzie's giggling. "I'll kill them!"

Bane shoved through them both. "What happened?"

"Uh, well." My voice was barely above a croak. "Good news first: We have a dog now." I tried for a smile and didn't get one back. "She's actually quite friendly, which is good because I didn't feel right leaving her at a shelter. Plus, she deserves much better than her current owner—"

"Forget about the animal!" Sunny took Poppy and promptly handed her to Elizabeth. The little girl ran off squealing happily. Good. I didn't want her to hear the bad news. "Who did this?"

I flicked over their heads, landing on Sienna. She raised her brows—questioning. Meeting her gaze, I smiled.

"It worked," I said, grinning though it hurt something fierce. "The plan worked."

"What plan?" Fuller asked.

"I should start from the beginning." I moved around them and eased myself onto the couch. I'd be sore all over in the morning. "Sienna discovered who was putting the trackers in your clothes."

"Wait. What?" Sunny dropped next to me. "Why am I just now hearing this?"

"Because Genny was grieving and beating herself up. I wanted her to be the first to know it wasn't all a waste. It turned out to be Madison James. She..." I told them the entire story from the day she handed me that card, to the Forbises and the discovery of the Sunshine Adoption Agency.

"After I told Genny all of this, she finally told me the truth," I continued. "The Brotherhood stormed Barbarella's and abducted the Cardinals. Bugsy— I mean, Laura's death and the horrible way we found out about it was punishment for not obeying their first order to denounce Vito's video."

"Holy shit," Bane breathed, rubbing his head. "How did we miss this? Why didn't she tell us?"

"Because your violent, frustrating, wonderful sister does everything to protect the people she cares about. She couldn't accept that she failed. And I couldn't either. So, Genny, Sienna, and I came up with a plan—"

"There are many people missing from that list," Liam said, voice hard. "Three to be exact."

I shook my head. "Too many things could've gone wrong. We agreed not to tell you beforehand in case you behaved like—these are Genny's words—condescending jackasses."

Liam, Bane, and Sunny geared up to say something about that until Fuller broke in. "I don't quite understand. What did you two do? And what happened to your face?"

"Genevieve Hunt happened to my face." Sienna passed me some tissues. "We had to confront Madison. After the disgusting and horrible way they punished her for disobeying them, I knew Madison would use the Cardinals to bargain for freedom. I also guessed that if she was clever as she proved she was, she'd realize their little tracking plan was over.

"There's no way they'd sneak something like that on you guys again, so the Brotherhood needed a new money-printing machine. What better way to control you than by doing exactly what they're doing to Genny? Holding someone you love hostage."

Liam held up a hand, his jaw clenching. "Hold on. Are you telling us that Genny is being held captive by the Brotherhood right now? The same people who shot, bombed, and threw her friend's mangled body at her feet!"

Goodness, when you say it like that. "Yes. That was the plan."

They were up so fast they blew me back against the couch.

"Fuller, watch Elizabeth, please," Liam said. "Don't let her get too attached to that dog, because we're finding her owner and my sister. Now."

"Wait—"

"Where did you last see her?" Bane asked. "How long ago?"

"If you just listen—"

Grasping my chin, Sunny smooched me. "I love you, baby, but this was a terrible plan."

"I'm seeing where the condescending part comes in," I snapped. "If you all would just listen for a second, you'd realize neither of us is so stupid that we'd let her skip into the Brotherhood's lair without assurance she could get out!"

The three of them stopped in their tracks.

"What does that mean?" Liam said.

I flicked to Sunny. "You said something very accurate the other night. There are lots of places to put a tracker."

"You're kidding," Bane said. "Genny's wearing a tracker?"

"And now we get to the part where you take back everything you said and tell your girlfriend she's a genius. I figured if the Brotherhood's happy to track us, we'd give it back just as hard. Madison's going to take her back to the boss to show off their new prize." I held up my phone. "GPS says they're still driving in circles around Rockchapel. Once Madison thinks they lost any tail, we'll know exactly where the Brotherhood is holding up."

Liam claimed my phone, squinting at the screen. "What if they find the tracker? They're going to search her—twice. Then a third time."

"We thought of that. They'll dump her phone for sure. They might even take her shoes and make her change clothes, but there's one thing no one thinks to take from a woman."

"Which is?" Sunny asked.

Sienna tossed her arm around me. "Tampons." She beamed. "My idea."

"Ah," the brothers said, all looking vaguely uncomfortable. But neither one said we were wrong.

"So." Folding my arms, I stared them down. "I'll hear it now."

"Kenzie 'Candy Nipples' Blaine," Sunny said, grinning that grin. "You're a genius."

"You deserve more praise than I can express," Liam spoke up. "The car stopped moving, and this location is very familiar to me.

"We know where the Brotherhood is."

GENNY

"Move." A hard shove propelled me forward.

I gritted my teeth, swallowing the urge to bloody my knuckles on Madison's face. She was only getting so bold because we were finally in the Brotherhood's hideout.

My gaze swept over the long hall of nothing. Madison was smart enough to stick me in the trunk for the drive. She let me out in a parking garage, then prodded me into the hallway we were walking down.

A lone figure stood at the end, waiting silently beside the only door in the hall. I studied him but couldn't place his face among my long list of enemies. Dark hair, tall, average build, average height. I bet his mother couldn't place him among all the mediocre gang fodder.

"Stop there."

I took another step just to be cheeky, smirking at him all the way.

"Arms up."

"There's no hiding anything in this outfit," I breezed. "That's kind of the point."

"Shut up!" Madison ordered. It was hard to believe a short while ago, she was playing Lyla's simpering minion. Of course I never suspected her of being the rat. I didn't look twice at Madison James.

The guard patted me down a little too thoroughly. He snapped back when he hit my back pocket. "What is that? Take it out slowly."

"Relax," I said, rolling my eyes. "It can't hurt you."

I pulled out the tampon—my face effortlessly neutral. The stupid idiot grabbed and squinted at it like he didn't know what he was looking at.

"You can confiscate the oh so dangerous tampon if you want, but between you and me, it's about that time when I need it."

He grimaced. "Whatever."

I was still the kind of woman who didn't share, but I seriously considered making an exception for Mackenzie Blaine when the fool put my tampon/tracker back in my hands.

"You will be allowed inside," he began. "The rules are as follows: no vulgar language, no disrespect, do not speak before you're addressed, do not sit unless invited to do so, do not make threats, do not speak positively of the tyrant organization known as the Merchants. Do you understand these rules?"

"Do I look like a preschooler? Go give someone else a fucking comprehension test and let me in the damn room."

A hard blow struck my back, dropping me to one knee. I slowly twisted, burning her with a look that made her step back. "When I get out of here, you're first."

"You're never getting out of here."

"You," I hissed. "Are. First."

Madison pressed trembling lips together. Good. She was learning.

A knock sounded from the other side of the door.

"You may enter now," said the guard. "Remember the rules, Merchant scum."

And you're second, I thought as he swung the door open.

I inched inside the front room. There was nothing else for me to call the space. Concrete gave way to hardwood floors topped with a small area rug, leather couches, an ottoman, and a coffee table. An entrance peeked from the other side of the furniture. I made my way to it.

"Good evening, Genevieve Hunt."

Whipping around, I fell on a person reclined on an armchair in the corner behind the door, tucked inside the shadows.

"I'm honored you could join us."

"Who are you?"

He stood, revealing inch by inch another face I didn't know—though a pleasant one if you went for the sexy silver fox thing. Silver salted his not-so-pepper mustache and beard. The same gray streaks swirled through his locks, granting him a look both distinguished and fake. You could almost believe he dyed it to achieve that whirlwind of ebony and silver.

Light brown eyes tracked my retreat as mine tracked his approach. He wasn't getting close to me until I was packing more than a tampon.

"We're very happy to have you with us, Miss Hunt. Though you may not see it now, you're going to help us free the chains around Cinco City and lead it to greatness."

"That sounds great, Mister..." I trailed off pointedly.

He smiled like I amused him. "But of course, where are my manners?" The man bowed to me of all things. "I go by many names, but there's only one that suits me within these halls.

"Call me Brother Abraham."

I hope you enjoyed the latest story in the world of Sunny, Kenzie, Liam, Bane, Genny, and Cinco City. The next book in the series, *King of Cruelty*, is coming soon!

To be the first to know when it releases, and to get a taste of teasers and excerpts on the way, join this fantastic group of readers such as yourself: Ruby's Knights and Diamonds[1]

Or you can keep up with all the news by joining my Ruby Vincent mailing list: https://www.subscribepage.com/rubyvincentpage

---

1. https://bit.ly/3bNuCOq

About The Author

Ruby Vincent is a lover of all things dark, twisty, romantic, and fun. She was born in the sun and now spends her life chasing it all over the world in between writing characters who find their own version of coming out of the darkness.
Ruby writes books of all kinds: contemporary reverse harem and M/F. Coming soon to Kindles everywhere is her spin on paranormal romance and fantasy.